Praise for
the novels of the Nine Kingdoms

A Tapestry of Spells

"Charming, romantic, and verging on the wistfully sweet, Kurland's paranormal serves as a strong start to a new series . . . Kurland deftly mixes innocent romance with adventure in a tale that will leave readers eager for the next installment."
—*Publishers Weekly*

"Ruith and Sarah captured my interest from the very first page . . . Lynn Kurland's time travel series might occupy a favored place on my shelves, but I think she truly shines in the Nine Kingdom books. I am beside myself with anticipation of the next book—it's going to be a long and agonizing wait."
—*Night Owl Romance*

"Lynn Kurland takes her audience back to the Nine Kingdoms with a strong opening act. Fans will feel the author magically transported them to her realm."
—*Midwest Book Review*

"Once again [Kurland] uses her gift for place and character to weave an adventurous tale that will have readers breathlessly awaiting the next chapter. Good stuff indeed!"
—*Romantic Times*

Princess of the Sword

"Packed with enchantment, adventure, terrifying battles, and a love so strong that no wizard or mage can affect it . . . Beautifully written, with an intricately detailed society born of Ms. Kurland's remarkable imagination, this is an extraordinary tale for fantasy readers as well as those who just want to read a good love story."
—*Romance Reviews Today*

"Over the course of this splendid trilogy, Kurland has provided an action-packed fantasy as well as a beautiful love story between characters who respect each other's talents."
—*Romantic Times*

"An excellent f   . . Readers will
relish Ms. Kurl   *Go Round Reviews*

The Mage's Daughter

Star of the Morning

Lynn Kurland

SPELLWEAVER

BERKLEY SENSATION, NEW YORK

THE BERKLEY PUBLISHING GROUP
Published by the Penguin Group
Penguin Group (USA) Inc.
375 Hudson Street, New York, New York 10014, USA
Penguin Group (Canada), 90 Eglinton Avenue East, Suite 700, Toronto, Ontario M4P 2Y3, Canada
(a division of Pearson Penguin Canada Inc.)
Penguin Books Ltd., 80 Strand, London WC2R 0RL, England
Penguin Group Ireland, 25 St. Stephen's Green, Dublin 2, Ireland (a division of Penguin Books Ltd.)
Penguin Group (Australia), 250 Camberwell Road, Camberwell, Victoria 3124, Australia
(a division of Pearson Australia Group Pty. Ltd.)
Penguin Books India Pvt. Ltd., 11 Community Centre, Panchsheel Park, New Delhi—110 017, India
Penguin Group (NZ), 67 Apollo Drive, Rosedale, North Shore 0632, New Zealand
(a division of Pearson New Zealand Ltd.)
Penguin Books (South Africa) (Pty.) Ltd., 24 Sturdee Avenue, Rosebank, Johannesburg 2196,
South Africa

Penguin Books Ltd., Registered Offices: 80 Strand, London WC2R 0RL, England

This book is an original publication of The Berkley Publishing Group.

This is a work of fiction. Names, characters, places, and incidents either are the product of the author's imagination or are used fictitiously, and any resemblance to actual persons, living or dead, business establishments, events, or locales is entirely coincidental. The publisher does not have any control over and does not assume any responsibility for author or third-party websites or their content.

PRINTING HISTORY
Berkley Sensation trade paperback edition / January 2011

Library of Congress Cataloging-in-Publication Data

Kurland, Lynn.
  Spellweaver / Lynn Kurland.—Berkley Sensation trade pbk. ed.
      p. cm.
  ISBN 978-0-425-23863-9
  1. Magic—Fiction.   I. Title.
  PS3561.U645S64   2011
  813'.54—dc22

                                            2010038743

PRINTED IN THE UNITED STATES OF AMERICA

10 9 8 7 6 5 4 3 2 1

One

The magic was a mighty wave that rose with terrifying swiftness toward the sky, hovered there for an eternal moment, then crashed down again to earth, washing over everything in its path.

The lad who had been standing at the edge of a glade watched with horror as the wave rushed toward him. He started forward to save his mother from being washed away only to remember that he had another task laid to his charge. He took hold of his younger sister's hand only to feel her fingers slip through his grasp despite his efforts to hold onto her. He shouted for her, but his calls were lost in the roaring of the evil as it engulfed him, sending him tumbling along with it. He groped blindly for his sister in that uncontrollable wave—

Only to realize he wasn't a lad of ten winters, but a man of a score-and-ten, and it wasn't his younger sister Mhorghain he was so desperately seeking.

It was Sarah of Doìre.

And it wasn't a wave of evil from a well he was running from, it was a terrible storm washing down the hill from the castle that had collapsed in on itself, the castle at Ceangail where his sire had lived for centuries, endlessly honing spells that never should have been created . . .

R uith woke with a gasp.

He forced himself to remain motionless and breathe shallowly, simply because it was his habit. When one had to rely on more pedestrian means of protecting himself than magic, one learned early on to not give an attacker any more advantage than necessary.

It took him longer than it might have otherwise simply because he was still fighting against the memories that flooded back in a rush that was unpleasantly similar to the wave of spell that had overcome him in his dream, and, it would seem, in his waking life. He kept his eyes closed and felt for Sarah's hand—

Only to realize that he couldn't move.

But that could have been because he was sitting with his hands tied tightly around the tree behind him. He opened his eyes a slit, then fully when he found that no one was watching him. His companions were none but a trio of rough-looking lads who stood twenty paces away, arguing not over the best way to put him to death, but the quality of his weapons and how they might reasonably poach the same without harm to themselves. He prayed their discussion might go on for quite some time so he might determine where he was and why he seemed to be the only one within earshot who wasn't talking about his knives. He took another slow, careful breath, then looked around himself.

There was no one else there.

Sarah.

He suppressed the urge to panic. Anything could have happened to her. She could have been lying where he couldn't see her, or been slain, or carried off beyond his reach. There were any number of mages infesting not only the keep up the way, but now no doubt the woods surrounding the keep, mages who would have taken her and . . .

He wrenched his thoughts back from that unhelpful place. He

couldn't rescue her if he were dead, so the most sensible thing to do was get himself free and make certain he remained alive. Sensible sounded so much more reasonable than frankly terrified at the thought of what could have befallen her, which he was.

He quickly assessed his own situation. His knives were both still down his boots and two others were still strapped to his back—not that he could have reached either set at the moment, but he would remedy that as quickly as possible. He also still had his magic, safely buried inside himself in an impenetrable well capped with illusion and distraction that he knew from recent experience was impervious to all assault. Lastly, and perhaps most fortuitously, the lads in front of him weren't paying him any heed.

He kept those lads in his sights as he focused on his hands, working the rope binding them against the bark of the tree and finding the knots poorly tied indeed. If he had been in the market for potential guardsmen, he would have invited them to tie a knot or two so he might examine their work before entrusting them with anything more complicated than securing a bedroll to a saddle—

The rope gave way without warning. He froze, partly because he didn't want to reveal what he'd just managed to accomplish and partly because the pain of blood rushing back into his hands was so intense, it almost rendered him senseless. He closed his eyes and concentrated on breathing evenly until his hands stopped throbbing enough that he could think clearly again. And once he could, he turned his mind quickly to how best to escape.

Fortunately, luck was with him. The lads were so involved in their conversation, they weren't paying him any heed. Then again, they hadn't paid heed to the mage standing just outside the circle of their torchlight either.

Damn it anyway.

It was Amitán of Ceangail who stood there, watching silently. Ruith held out no hope that his bastard brother hadn't seen him. He was only surprised Amitán hadn't already plunged a knife into his chest.

Then again, that might have been because it would have been

deflected by a spell of protection Ruith suddenly realized he was covered by. It was, he had to admit, a rather elegant thing, fashioned from Olc—if such grace were possible from that vile, unwholesome magic. He was so surprised to find it there; he could only stare at it in silence for several moments. Given that he certainly hadn't provided the like for himself, he had to wonder who had. Obviously someone wanted him alive and unharmed.

He wasn't sure he dared speculate on who that might be.

He supposed he could at least eliminate from the list his half brother, who stepped close to the spell, had a look at it, then swore at him in a furious whisper.

"Don't think that will save your sorry self," Amitán hissed. "Once I have what I want from you, I'll kill you in spite of that rot. And once you're dead, I'll find that pretty little wench of yours and have what I want from her as well."

"But she has no power," Ruith said, because it was true. Sarah had no magic, and the sooner he convinced everyone within earshot of that, the safer she would be.

"You fool," Amitán said scornfully, "she sees spells. Did you think we hadn't noticed?"

Ruith didn't have a chance to respond before Amitán strode out into the light cast by the fire. Aye, he'd very much hoped his bastard brothers hadn't noticed what Sarah could do. But if they had and if they thought they could force her to use that gift to further their own ends . . .

Nay, he wouldn't let that happen to her. He rubbed his thighs as surreptitiously as possible to bring the feeling back to his legs and watched his guardsmen spin around to face Amitán, their hands on their swords.

"Oy, what do ye want?" the largest of the three demanded, with an admirable amount of fierceness.

"Tidings," Amitán said shortly, jerking his head in Ruith's direction. "Who captured that one?"

"Can't say," the first said stubbornly.

"Can't, or won't?" Amitán asked in a low, dangerous tone.

The second stepped up to stand shoulder to shoulder with the first. "I don't see as that matters, friend, do you?"

"It matters, *friend*, because I want the answer. And if you have two wits to rub together, you'll give it to me before I reward your refusal in a way you will find very unpleasant indeed."

The lads stood firm, but Ruith imagined they were beginning to regret having taken on the task of guarding him to begin with. He couldn't blame them. He had his own very vivid memories of encounters with his elder half brothers. They were, to a man, unpleasant and without mercy. He supposed he could concede that they were justified in their hatred of him and his siblings given that he was certain they had looked upon them as usurpers, but he'd suffered enough as a child thanks to their abuse not to feel compelled to extend any undue understanding their way now.

"There was a woman with him earlier," Amitán pressed on relentlessly. "Where is she?"

The third elbowed his way to the front of the group. "Sold her to traders, did His Lordsh—"

Ruith watched as his companions jerked him backward and shouted him into silence. He wasn't sure if it was because Sarah's fate had been revealed or if the man had been on the verge of unwittingly revealing who had hired them.

If Amitán didn't pry the entire tale from them, he certainly would.

He continued to rub his hands against his legs as he listened closely to Amitán and the men carrying on their discussion in increasingly belligerent tones. He quickly looked around him for a convenient escape route, then noticed something he hadn't before.

The spell he was covered with was sporting a great rent in itself, as if someone had sliced through it. He would have assumed it was Amitán to do the like, but if he'd managed it, he would have continued on by making a great rent in Ruith's chest. Perhaps someone had been trying to rescue him and been interrupted in the act—

But the rent had been made by another spell of Olc, Olc mixed with something he couldn't quite see.

That was odd.

He would have examined that a bit more closely, but he was distracted by Amitán beginning to lose what little patience he possessed.

"I don't care about the traders from Malairt!" he shouted, "I want to know who hired *you* and why he wanted you to guard that *thing* over there."

The third of the group, the bravest by far, told Amitán in the most detailed of terms just what he could do with his questions.

That man crumpled to the ground quite suddenly, either dead or senseless. That seemed to bring the other two to a spirit of cooperation they hadn't enjoyed before.

"I don't know who the man was," the second blurted out. "In truth. He just gave us orders to keep watch until he returned. Said that lad over there was a lord's brat who needed tending."

"What did this beneficent lord look like?" Amitán demanded.

"I couldn't look at him," the first answered promptly. "He was all darkness."

"But that could have been anyone!" Amitán thundered.

Ruith had to agree. Given the nature of every bloody soul inhabiting the keep up the way and the surrounding environs, the description could have applied to anyone within a thirty-league radius.

But why would darkness have wanted to keep him whole? He ran quickly through a list of black mages and dismissed them all as he watched the escalation of hostilities in front of him. Amitán was demanding that the guardsmen bring Ruith to him; the remaining two were refusing just as adamantly. It said something about the man who had hired them that they were terrified enough of him to choose facing down the angry mage in front of them presently to facing his wrath later.

Amitán cursed them, then turned and flung a spell at Ruith.

Ruith shifted away from the mysterious rent in the spell of protection, more than willing to use something not of his own making to save his own sweet neck. Amitán's spell was absorbed easily, then it gathered itself into something quite different and hurtled back toward him. It slammed into him with the force of a score of fists, then encompassed him from head to toe.

Amitán began to scream.

Ruith wasted no time in making his escape. He shoved apart the spell, dove through it, then rolled up to his feet, drawing his knives as he did so. The pain of that almost sent him to his knees. He looked at his palms in surprise only to find them covered with blisters.

What in the hell was *in* that spell?

He would have given that more thought, but he was too distracted by watching the spectacle of Amitán clawing at his face, trying to remove what had attached itself to him. Ruith winced as Amitán staggered about the glade, making altogether inhuman sounds of agony before he dropped to his knees.

Ruith turned away from the spectacle. He took a firmer grip on his knives, ignoring the pain of his ruined skin, and walked over to the remaining guardsmen who were gaping at him as if he'd been the cause of Amitán's suffering.

"Where did the traders go with the woman?" he asked shortly.

They lifted their hands, then, as one, pointed to the south.

"Fair enough," Ruith said, trying to sound calmer than he felt. "If I were you, I would hurry away and hide somewhere you think you won't be found. Because that"—he tilted his head toward Amitán—"will be the least of what's coming."

The men looked at each other, then turned and bolted.

Ruith would have followed them in like manner, but there was at least one answer he needed to make his journey less perilous. He resheathed his knives, then turned to his bastard brother, who was now lying on the ground, panting.

"Who survived the fall of the keep?" he asked.

"I wouldn't tell you . . . if my life . . . depended on it," Amitán gasped.

Ruith cursed him. Though that list of what had now been loosed into the world would have been useful—perhaps even critical—he didn't have the time to wait until Amitán was in enough distress to unburden himself.

"Help . . . me," Amitán wheezed.

Ruith actually considered it, even though the little stinging things Amitán had tossed at him whilst he'd been captive in Ceangail's great hall were still quite fresh in his mind. Unfortunately, he possessed nothing—or, rather, nothing he would use—to counter what had taken his half brother in its painful embrace.

"I think you'll need a mage for what ails you."

Amitán looked at him with naked hatred on his face. "I'll find you . . . and kill you."

"I imagine you'll try," Ruith agreed.

Amitán struggled against the spell that seemed to be wrapping itself ever more tightly around him. Ruith wasn't above seeing a black mage come to his own bad end, but he wasn't one to enjoy overmuch the watching of that journey there. He started to walk away, then paused. He turned back to Amitán.

"There appears to be one end of the spell near your left boot," he conceded. "I think if you could reach it, you might be able to unravel the whole thing."

Amitán wasted a goodly amount of energy condemning Ruith to a score of different deaths, each more painful than the last, before he apparently decided he would be better off saving his breath. Ruith left him to it.

He left the camp in a southerly direction, following the tracks of a handful of horses. He hadn't gone twenty paces before what had struck him as odd before presented itself as slightly more than odd.

Someone had made a rent in that spell of protection. He was willing to bet his knives that the maker of the spell and the maker of the rent were not the same mage simply because it made no sense to weave a spell then slice it in half. But if that was the case, who had cut through that spell, and why?

He leaned down absently to adjust one of the knives stuck down the side of his boots and found the answer.

The pages from his father's book of spells that he had rolled up and stuck down his boots were gone.

He turned immediately and strode back to the camp. It cost him precious time, but he forced himself to methodically look through everything his guardsmen had left behind. He ignored the continuing shrieks of his bastard brother as he rifled through packs and searched all about the tree where he'd been bound. The spells were gone. He started to curse, then felt the hair on the back of his neck stand up.

Someone was watching him from the shadows.

He straightened his knives, furiously considering the facts he was now faced with. Sarah was captured and carried off to points unknown, he was being stalked by an unnamed mage—either the maker of the spell of protection or the mage who'd broken through it to take the spells Ruith had been carrying—and his magic was buried, which left him unable to address either problem easily. But if he released his magic and someone took it, he would be unquestionably powerless, which would leave Sarah alone, unprotected, unable to fight what he was quite sure would be hunting her.

Then again, perhaps the fact that he was still breathing said something about who was following him. Apparently he was worth more to that mage alive than dead, which led him to wonder if perhaps his unexpected benefactor intended to follow him and take his magic at a later time.

That left him with only one choice. He would find Sarah, then remain as attractive a prize as possible until he could get both himself and Sarah somewhere safe. He didn't dare hope the mage standing motionless under the trees behind where he'd been captive would simply give up and go home.

He left Amitán trying to bring his foot up toward his face where he could presumably take hold of the end of the spell with his teeth and pull, then walked off toward the south, looking for tracks. There were two sets: one made by horsemen and the other made by a single soul.

That single set of tracks would eventually lead him all the way back to his own house where he could shut his door on things he didn't care to look at anymore. It was the road he had taken as a lad of ten winters when he'd been seeking refuge from the storm. But he was no longer a lad of ten winters, and he had taken on a quest willingly, knowing that it would lead him into a darkness he knew all too well.

Only now that quest included a woman who had relied on him for protection and been repaid with harm.

He turned away from a path he wouldn't have seriously considered and started quickly down the other because the truth was, the quest was no longer just about finding Sarah's ridiculous brother and stopping him from trying to make magic far beyond his capabilities. He had himself loosed things in Ceangail's keep that would need to be contained, he had lost spells that could wreak untold damage on the world, and he had failed to hold on to a woman whose only error in judgement had been desiring to do good.

And to trust him.

He would give her no reason to regret that trust in the future. Once she was found, he would seek out the closest safe haven for them both where they could hide until she was rested and he had unraveled a mystery or two. Perhaps by then he would have had the time to consider just who might have protected him with magic whose main purpose was to destroy.

He wasn't sure he would care for the answer.

But have it he would, then he would leave Sarah safely behind and follow the trail of his father's spells himself. There was naught but darkness in front of him and darkness following, and he would be damned if she would have any more of it.

He pushed aside his absolute dread that he would find her too late and concentrated on the tracks before him.

He could do nothing else.

Two

S arah of Doìre was finished with mages.

She had, she would readily admit, entertained that thought more than once over the course of her life. Being the daughter of the witchwoman Seleg had given her ample opportunity to watch magic and its practitioners at close range. Her brother Daniel, whose ultimate goal was to destroy the world with his self-proclaimed mighty magic, had laid yet more twigs upon the fire of her aversion.

But the last score of hours had turned aversion into full-blown loathing.

She leaned her pounding head back against the tree she'd been propped up against and tried to think clearly. It was possible that her ill feelings toward those of a more magical inclination might have been exacerbated by her recent journey made with her own poor self cast over a horse's withers where her head had apparently bounced quite enthusiastically against its shoulder. She hadn't blamed her very unmagical captors for setting her rather ungently against a tree, nor had she faulted them for tying her wrists and ankles together. How else could they have kept her where she was meant to stay? But there were others she could most certainly blame for the events leading up to her sitting where she was, freezing, and blame them she would.

Better that than the alternative of giving in to the fear that threatened to steal her breath. She wasn't sure how much longer she could bear the darkness, and the things that lurked in the darkness—

She let out her breath slowly and tried to think about something else, *anything* else. Unfortunately, there was little else on which to fix her thoughts, given that the twisting path that had led her to where she was at present had begun with darkness.

There she'd been, innocently planning to shake Doìre's dust off the hem of her cloak, when she'd become embroiled in a bit of do-gooding she'd thought she could manage. It was only as she'd stood in the great hall of the keep at Ceangail that she'd learned how unyielding and merciless the world of magic could be, how awful mages with terrible spells could become, and just how far out of her depth she was.

If that had been all, she supposed she would have been justified in her loathing of all things magical, but there had been more. The final blow had been discovering that a man she had unbent enough to actually have a few fond feelings for had not been a simple swordsman as he'd led her to believe, but instead Ruithneadh of Ceangail, youngest son of one of the most vile black mages in the history of the Nine Kingdoms.

She didn't trust easily, but there had been moments over the past month where she had actually looked at Ruith and felt herself lower her sword, as it were. It had been poorly done. She would tell him that just as soon as she could get close enough to him to do so. The traders wouldn't have been foolish enough to tie him next to her, which meant he was most likely tied to some other sturdy tree.

She opened her eyes a slit. The traders were standing there in the middle of the glade, warming their hands against a fire and speaking in a language she didn't understand. They didn't have blades in their hands, which meant they had obviously secured Ruith as well if they were that at ease. She looked around her as unobtrusively as possible, fully expecting to see Ruith trussed up securely across the glade.

But he wasn't.

She forced herself to breathe evenly in spite of her rising panic. There was no reason to assume anything untoward had happened to him. Just because she couldn't see him didn't mean he was dead. He might have been picketed with the horses, or deemed to be too heavy a burden and left behind. There were a myriad of things that could have befallen him.

Things he could easily have countered.

That thought was a brisk slap. The truth was, he had lied to her, led her to places she never would have gone even in her nightmares . . . and he had continued to lie to her and take her to horrible places until they'd wound up in the worst place of all where he'd only admitted who he was because he hadn't had a choice. What made all of it so galling was that at any time, he could have stopped it. He, the son of an elven princess and a mage full of untold power, could have saved her grief, fear, and danger if he'd simply been willing to use his magic.

Which he hadn't been.

She turned away from any concern she might have felt for him. He would save himself, if saving could be done, but he would do nothing for her. That much was obvious, given where she found herself. All she could do was get herself free, then take herself somewhere safe. She would then lock the door and hide in obscurity where she would no longer have to fear the dark or peer into shadows and worry they were full of things they shouldn't have been—

Things such as the mage standing suddenly in the clearing in front of her.

He was one of Ruith's bastard brothers from Ceangail. The last time she'd seen him, he'd been part of a circle that surrounded her and Ruith, a circle of men connected by spells that had dripped with evil. He hadn't said anything in the keep, but she had noted his black, soulless eyes, eyes that had looked at Ruith mercilessly. He was simply watching the traders as he had Ruith, as if they were insects he would allow to scuttle about for a few minutes more before he crushed them carelessly under his boot.

She wasn't sure how long he'd been standing there, watching. Apparently her escorts hadn't noticed him before either, but they noticed him presently. They whirled around suddenly with their swords drawn.

Sarah would have told them not to bother, but she thought her strength might be better spent seeing if she couldn't get her hands free before she became the center of attention.

The first of the four traders threw himself suddenly forward. Ruith's half brother didn't move, but the man stopped suddenly and dropped to the ground, as lifeless as his sword. The mage then turned and looked at her. Sarah felt her mouth go dry.

Damnation. Too late for escape.

He lifted his finger and her bonds fell away. "You won't be needing those any longer," he said in a soft voice that was all the more unpleasant for its lack of malice.

Sarah was pulled to her feet, but not by any hands she could see. It was only as she was standing there, swaying with dizziness, that she realized how badly her right forearm pained her. She looked down at the black streaks that trailed over her flesh, black mingled with red that burned like hellfire. She didn't want to think about where she'd come by that wound, so she instead looked up. Ruith's half brother was still watching her.

"I will take care of you later," he said.

She imagined he would. And she imagined she would be able to do about it what she was always able to do about magic and its vile practitioners, which was exactly nothing. She was tempted to turn and bolt, but she had the feeling that would end badly for her. All she could do was hope that something unexpected would happen and the vile man in front of her might be distracted by other things long enough for her to slip away.

Then again, the fact that he had left her unbound said all she perhaps needed to know about his fear of that happening.

She watched him herd the remaining three traders into a little group and ask them politely if they'd seen anyone else who might have needed transport south, anyone of a male persuasion, perhaps even a companion of the woman over by the tree who they'd carried so carefully south.

"Nay," the leader blurted out, sounding very near to tears. "No one—"

"Nay, there was a man," another of the trio interrupted. "But we were told to leave 'im be."

"Describe him," the mage invited. "If you please."

"Tall, dark-haired, well built," the trader said, looking happy to speak about something that had nothing to do with him. "A brace o' knives strapped to his back." He shrugged. "'E was assuredly dead when last I looked."

Sarah's knees buckled, but she didn't fall. That was perhaps because someone was holding her up. She turned her head, half expecting to find Ruith standing there, but she was sorely mistaken. Another of Ruith's bastard brothers stood there, one she'd encountered more than once. He was still sporting the very puffy lip Ruith had given him, and Sarah wasn't entirely sure his nose wasn't broken thanks to the same encounter. There were things in his hair, muck from a less-than-clean floor that he was enjoying thanks to a hearty shove by Ruith as they'd escaped the keep. Táir, she thought his name might have been. He seemed less interested in her, though, than he was in his brother. He shoved her out of his way and walked into the firelight.

"What are you doing here?" Táir demanded.

His brother looked at him as if he'd lost his wits. "Looking for Ruithneadh. What else would I be doing?"

"Waiting behind like a woman until I've taken what's mine," Táir snarled. "Perhaps, Mosach, you forget your place."

"And perhaps you forget to think," the brother named Mosach

said with a snort. "If you wanted Ruithneadh's power, you should have taken it earlier whilst Díolain was distracted with that whoreson who brought the bloody hall down around our ears. Not that you could have taken anything but his pocket handkerchief with your patched-together incarnation of Father's spell—"

"Then I'll have your power instead," Táir said hotly. "And hers."

Sarah realized he was pointing at her. She wanted to quickly reassure him that she had nothing he could possibly want, but she couldn't find breath to speak.

"She has no power," Mosach said.

Sarah nodded, no doubt more enthusiastically than she should have.

"Are you daft?" Táir demanded. "She *sees*."

Mosach started to speak, then shut his mouth abruptly. "How do you know?"

"Because *I* have two good eyes and use them now and again!"

Mosach looked at her with renewed interest. Sarah started to give voice to the strangled noises of denial she could feel bubbling up in her throat, but before she could, a kerfuffle of sorts distracted the brothers. The traders, those cold-eyed, heartless lads, had apparently decided that they were more interested in their lives than a bit of gold.

A pity they made so much noise when they fled.

Sarah didn't dare turn and flee as well—having just seen what that would earn her, which was instant death—but she wasn't above easing a single step backward so she was standing next to the tree. The bark was rough under her fingers, a solid reminder that there were things in the world that were still as she would have expected to find them. It was a rather comforting contrast to the battle of spells that had begun in front of her.

Ruith's brothers, robbed of their sport with the traders, had turned on each other instead. Mosach was apparently every bit Táir's equal in whatever unwholesome magical studies they'd engaged in over the years, and both of them seemed to have fury to spare.

She would have moved, but every now and again, one of the

brothers would cast a look her way, a look that said they were perfectly aware of where she was. She had no doubt they would hunt her down if necessary.

Or perhaps not. As the minutes dragged on, their curses and spells became less frequent and a calm descended over the glade. There came a point where they were simply standing there in the flickering firelight, glaring at each other, completely immobile. The spells they had cast were wrapped around each other, as if they had been bobbins in the hands of a master weaver of things no one could see.

Only she could see the spells.

She held her breath, then slowly and very carefully took a step backward.

Then another.

The brothers didn't seem to notice—not, perhaps, that they could have done anything about it *had* they noticed. She eased back into the darkness in absolute silence, grateful for all the practice she'd had at it over the years.

Once she was certain she could no longer be seen, she turned and strode away swiftly. Or she would have, if she hadn't walked into horses she hadn't realized were collected together so closely behind her, contentedly crunching on the underbrush.

She closed her eyes briefly in gratitude. Surely no one would begrudge her a means of escape given that the beasts' masters wouldn't be needing them anymore. She started to select a pair of them, then realized she would only be needing one.

Because Ruith was dead.

But he couldn't be. She had seen him the day before. She had *rescued* him the day before, felt his arms go around her, heard his heart beating—

She took a deep breath and shoved aside thoughts that didn't serve her. If she didn't hurry, she would share his fate. If nothing else, she might manage to meet someone someday who could avenge him. She couldn't do that if she were dead.

She tethered the fastest-looking horse of the group to a handy tree, then turned to the others. She stripped off their gear, finding a happy cache of gold she was quite certain one of the lads had been hiding from the others, then sent the beasts off away from the fire. She found a heavy food bag hung on a nearby tree and put it without compunction into one of her newly acquired saddlebags.

She took the reins in hand, then found herself simply standing still again, staring off unseeing into the darkness. She could scarce believe what she'd heard, but Ruith's brothers would have had no reason to lie. And the truth was, he had been facing lads who had been positively salivating at the thought of watching him draw his last.

She shook her head, shaking aside thoughts that she couldn't yet face. She swung up into the saddle and turned her horse south, then paused. Perhaps she couldn't rush off as easily as she thought. She'd had companions on her journey, companions who were presumably waiting for her in Slighe. But how could she possibly take care of a farm boy, two wounded mages, and an alemaster named Franciscus who she had recently realized was quite a bit more than a mere brewer of very fine apple-flavored ale? She had no magic and no skills past weaving a bit of wool into something useful. She couldn't even look into the shadows with any sort of courage at all—

She shivered. If Franciscus was a mage, which she had no doubt he was, and if he had survived the collapse of Ceangail, which she could only hope he had, he would no doubt go and collect the rest of her company and keep them safe.

Leaving her free to disappear, which she should do without hesitation. She considered what locales she could bring to mind immediately thanks to all the time she'd spent studying the geography of the Nine Kingdoms on the off chance she had the opportunity to escape to one of them.

She couldn't go north, because it was the way she'd come from and was host to far too many unpleasant mages. West led her back to Shettlestoune where there wasn't enough rain yet too much of her past. East was nothing but ruffians, endless plains of grasses that boasted few if any towns of any size, and the schools of wizardry.

South didn't sound very welcoming either, but it might do for a couple of years until she could earn enough money and wrap enough anonymity around herself to be able to move a bit more freely and go where she wanted to.

She silently wished her companions good fortune, promised herself enough time to grieve for Ruith when she was settled, then turned her mount south and gave him his head. She saw nothing, heard no swearing, didn't find herself immediately felled by magic.

Perhaps things would improve sooner than she dared hope.

Two days later, she had to face the fact that, despite her tentative hopes, things weren't improving as quickly as she had wanted them to. That was mostly because she was obviously a worse judge of horses than she'd thought herself. She'd taken to calling her mount *Plodding Clod*—which he perhaps resented—because he'd had absolutely no interest in her terrible haste. Keeping him in a canter had been almost impossible. His trot had been a horrible thing that not even her decent riding skills could compensate for. She couldn't help but think she would have made better time and been less weary if she'd used her own two feet.

She looked up at the darkening sky and decided she'd had enough for the day. She was only a few hours into her ride across the plains of Ailean, which was something of a two-edged sword. She had left forests and hills behind, which made it more difficult for anyone to follow her unseen, but being out in the open left her less unseen herself. There was a line of trees in front of her that shimmered with something that spoke quite strongly of illusion. It was a pleasant illusion though, so she felt somewhat safe in making for the spot.

She told her horse to stop, but he, being who he was, completely ignored her. She finally wrestled him to a halt, then dismounted.

He reared. The moment his feet touched the ground, he ripped the reins from her hand and bolted, displaying a gallop she could have certainly used long before then.

She stood there and gaped as he carried off not only her pilfered gold but her borrowed sword and all her food. His hoofbeats faded so quickly into the distance that she imagined she wouldn't manage to catch him without considerable effort, if at all.

She turned and looked around her, half expecting to see something horrible leap out at her from the trees. There was nothing save that strange glamour that was woven into the last of the winter grasses at her feet and hanging like a curtain from the bare winter branches of the trees before her. There were spots in the grass that were burned, as if someone had recently made a great bonfire there. She could only hope they hadn't chosen to remain behind to see who might come along and admire their work.

Well, there was nothing to be done but seek shelter for the night, then regroup on the morrow. She had started off her journey with only a handful of coins, her meager store of courage, and her skirt pulled over her head to be used as a cloak. At least now she had a decent cloak to keep her warm and a pair of elegant and useful knives stuck down the sides of her boots. Things could have been much worse.

She took a deep, calming breath, then walked through the trees, trying to ignore how quickly twilight had fallen and how much darker it was in the trees than it had been out in the open. She pulled her cloak more tightly around her and walked silently to the stream she could see glimmering in front of her. She knelt down at the water's edge, then had a long drink whilst there was still enough light to manage it. She sat back on her heels and rested her hands on her knees. Perhaps she would find a bit of peace after all.

Or so she thought until she heard the crack of a twig behind her.

She suppressed the urge to shriek. Truly, she was finished with the dark and magic and things she couldn't possibly fight any longer. She managed a deep, quiet breath, then pulled the knife from her boot with a badly trembling hand. She took it by the tip, took her courage in hand, then rose, turned, and flung the blade at the hooded figure standing ten paces away in a single, fluid motion.

Curses filled the air.

Sarah closed her eyes, because she was fairly sure the curser wouldn't see her at it. Apparently, Ruith's bastard brothers were as poor at judging his condition as she was at judging horses, for Ruith was most certainly not dead.

He was also not rushing forward to proclaim his joy at seeing her alive. He merely turned without comment to fetch her knife that she could see quivering in the tree behind him. He pulled it free, then walked back toward her and handed it to her wordlessly before he squatted down and had his own drink. Judging by the time he spent at the task, it had been a while since he'd managed it.

Sarah stood there, unsure if she should stab him whilst he was otherwise occupied or let out the shuddering breath she was still holding.

He was alive. She was slightly surprised to find out how relieved she was by that fact.

She was still trying to master her rampaging emotions—and recover from the fright he'd given her—when he finally splashed water on his face, dragged his hands through his hair, then rose and turned to look at her. His face was so deep in shadows, she couldn't see his expression. He wasn't bursting into tears or pulling her into a joyful embrace. He wasn't doing anything save standing there with his arms folded over his chest.

"I thought you were dead," she managed weakly. "How did you—"

"I don't suppose you brought any food," he interrupted coldly.

She blinked in surprise at his tone. "Well, actually, nay—"

"I imagined not, but never mind," he said, taking hold of her good arm. "I don't have enough myself for even a pair of days. You'll see to earning meals if we're fortunate enough to find farms along our road."

She found herself stumbling alongside him as he pulled her away from the river. She was dumbfounded—nay, appalled—not only by the unfriendliness of his tone but the roughness of his grip. It was as if none of their previous journey had taken place. Instead of Ruith, she was now facing that gruff, intimidating mage she'd first met as she'd been desperate enough to brave his front door to beg for aid.

"What is wrong with you?" she managed, trying to pull her arm away.

"Be silent," he said harshly.

"I don't understand—"

"Of course you don't," he said curtly. "No matter. I'll explain it to you in simple terms as we go, that you might. Now, come along, wench, and don't argue with me."

She would have pulled away and plowed her fist into his face, but she wasn't a brawling sort of gel. That and since it was too dark to see him properly, she feared she might miss.

"Need aid with your slurs along with your spells?" he taunted, the sneer plain in his voice.

"I . . . I . . ." She groped for something useful to say, but couldn't find anything. She continued with him only because he didn't give her any choice. She was so surprised at what he'd said—and how he'd said it—that she didn't think to stop walking until they were free of the trees and out in the open. The moon gave no light, but that was because it was obscured by a healthy collection of rain clouds.

Sarah slipped as she tried to jerk away from Ruith. She found her feet and whirled on him, fully intending to give him back as good as he'd given—

Only she felt the hair on the back of her neck stand up.

There was something in the trees behind them. Or some*one*, rather.

Ruith pulled her along with him. "Don't dawdle," he said sharply.

Her desire to stab him was quite suddenly and fully eclipsed by an intense desire to flee. She would have, but Ruith seemed determined to keep her beside him. She imagined that was so she could shovel a bit of manure at their next stop so he could have something to eat.

She began to wonder if she'd strayed into a waking nightmare. She was only hours into a journey across an endless plain with no gold, no food, and no means of protecting herself. She was being followed by something whose menace she could feel from where she stood—or stumbled, rather. And then, as if that wasn't enough, she

had been reunited with a man whose loss she had been fully prepared to mourn greatly only to find that he had become easily the
most arrogant, unfeeling, unpleasant lout—

"Hurry," he snapped.

She did, because he gave her no choice. She immediately discarded the thought of running away from him. If she did, the shadow
behind her might follow her, and then she would be dead. If Ruith
noticed anything, he was either too tight-lipped to say as much, or
he didn't care. She wasn't sure which it was, nor was she sure she
cared to know.

She just knew she didn't want any more of the things that made
up his life.

She trotted alongside him, numb from what he'd said to her and
too unsettled to even attempt to muster up enough energy to tell him
to take himself and his rude words and go to hell, and formulated a
plan with what few wits remained her. She would go with him until
they'd reached some sort of civilization. And then when it was safe,
she was going to walk away from mages and spells and elven princes
who looked like mercenaries and behaved with no manners at all.

She had the feeling her life might depend on it.

Three

Ruith walked up the slick cobblestone streets of Beinn òrain toward the schools of wizardry, trying to ignore the memories that assailed him. The last time he'd walked his current path, he'd been with his mother and a pair of his brothers as they'd prepared to breach those formidable walls for a visit to a particular master. The castle had been draped in heavy mist on that morning, just as it was now. He almost couldn't decide if he were dreaming or awake.

He supposed some of that came from weariness. He had either walked or run with Sarah for the entirety of the last four days—in the pouring rain, no less—stopping only to drink when necessary and eat from the rather meager bag of food he'd snatched from the camp of the dead Malairtian traders. He hadn't dared linger to look for more supplies at that particular camp.

He had, however, taken the time at that camp to wrap Mosach and Táir up in each other's spells a bit more securely, which he'd considered nothing more than just recompense for the lives of those slain traders. He hadn't cared to stay and exchange pleasantries with them. He'd simply looked for hoofprints leading away from camp and decided, with a fervent hope that he hadn't chosen amiss, to follow the single set of tracks. Finding Sarah alive and well had been a vast relief.

Or it would have been, if he hadn't realized as he'd caught up with her that he'd brought along more with him than not enough food to see them across the plains.

He'd immediately decided to adopt the attitude that he'd used to save Sarah's life in Ceangail. He'd forced himself to keep up the ruse of treating Sarah as his servant—or worse—simply because he hadn't wanted to give whomever had been following them any reason to think that she meant anything to him. He had regretted every harsh word that had come out of his mouth, knowing full well that each one wounded her.

Or at least he'd flattered himself that such might be the case, but given how quickly she'd descended into silence and ceased looking at him, perhaps he had overestimated his appeal.

He peered past his dripping hood to judge the distance between himself and the keep, sitting like an enormous bird of prey at the head of the street. Perhaps it was madness to think that he could even get past the gate guards. Even if he managed that, there was no guarantee he would gain the particular set of chambers he hoped for—or that the master who lived in those chambers would allow him entrance.

Unfortunately, at the moment he had no other choice. The idea of taking Sarah to Shettlestoune had been unthinkable, simply because there was no safety there. He would happily have taken her either to Lake Cladach or Tòrr Dòrainn, but he couldn't bring himself to sully either place with his father's bastards—assuming, perhaps poorly, that they were what hunted him.

That he wasn't sure galled him, but he had no one to blame but himself for not being able to identify his enemy. He had grown accustomed over the years to looking out for foes of a merely mortal nature. Keeping a weather eye out for mages hadn't been a skill he'd cultivated, though now he wondered why not.

He suppressed the urge to look over his shoulder to see if they were still being followed. He hadn't seen anyone since they'd reached the city, but again, he couldn't be sure. The only thing in his favor was that Beinn òrain was a busy port town and getting lost in a crowd was easily done. And now they were less than two hundred paces from the gates. Safety was within his grasp.

And once he'd reached the particular chamber he was aiming for inside those intimidating walls, he would set Sarah down in a chair before the fire, then fall to his knees and apologize profusely for his boorish behavior. He wasn't entirely certain that he would manage to blurt out an apology before she either buried a knife in his gut or simply turned and walked away from him. He could safely say he wouldn't have been surprised by either. It had been all he could do on the plains to make sure she stayed beside him—

Which she wasn't, at the moment.

He spun around, dragged his damp sleeve across his eyes to clear them, but saw nothing of her. He hadn't felt anyone with magic around him, but then again, he was hardly one to judge such a thing. He cursed fluently, then strode back the way he'd come. He ignored the pubs and inns. She had no more gold than he did, which was none, and whilst she might have been willing to work for a meal, he suspected she would have first sought nothing more than a place to hide. He passed two alleyways before he hit upon the right one. Sarah was there.

So were a handful of lads who had apparently found her worth a second look.

He strode forward, took the two lads closest to him, and cracked their heads together. They slumped to the cobblestones with remarkable grace, all things considered. Sarah struck the third in the nose, sending him stumbling backward. Ruith reached for the fourth only to have him cry out suddenly and bolt past him.

Never a good sign, that sort of thing.

Ruith felt the shadow sweep over him before he saw it, but

shadow it was and not one made by the heavy clouds hanging over-head. He reached for Sarah's hand and pulled her into a stumbling run over the slippery stone toward the alley's entrance, hoping to blend in with the shrieking thug who was clutching his nose and stumbling about. Sarah fought him briefly, then fell abruptly silent.

Ruith pulled Sarah under his cloak and backed her against the wall with more force than he meant to.

"Careful, damn you—" she gasped.

"Feign interest," he begged.

She glared at him before she wrapped her good arm around his neck and pulled his head down where she could whisper furiously in his ear. "If I thought I could stick you between the ribs and not swing for it, I would, you unfeeling, unpleasant . . . *impolite . . .*" She spluttered a bit, seemingly unable to lay her hand upon an insult vile enough to suit her. "I would call you a mannerless whoreson," she said finally and with a distinct chill to her voice, "but that would be an insult to your honorable dam, who I'm quite sure would be terribly ashamed of how you've behaved over the past several days."

He agreed, silently. He would have attempted a brief apology, but he didn't suppose Sarah was in the mood to hear it, and he didn't dare take his attention off what he feared was coming their way. Sarah's arm trembled so violently, he feared she would either truly do him a goodly bit of damage or collapse from weariness. He slipped his arm behind her back to hold her up, which displeased her every bit as much as he'd expected it might.

"If you think I'm going one step farther with you, *Your Highness*," she said in a voice that trembled as badly as the rest of her, "you are sorely mis—"

"Sshh," he whispered frantically, pulling her closer. He hazarded a glance to his left. A dragon had swept but a foot over the heads of the local civilians, sending most of them sprawling onto the cobble-stones. The dragon laughed before it disappeared and a man stood in its place.

Ruith turned back to Sarah and bent his head forward to hide hers. He heard footsteps coming toward the alley, then heard them pause. He held his breath, because there was nothing else to be done. The evil that flowed ahead of the man standing there was like a strong wind before the brunt of a storm. Ruith didn't consider himself particularly self-effacing, but he would readily admit he wasn't up to besting even the forefront of that storm.

Damn it anyway.

After several eternal moments, boots scuffed, then walked on, their heels clicking against the stone.

Ruith would have dropped to his knees if he'd had the strength to. Instead, he held himself upright by means of his hand against the wall. He kept Sarah close likely longer than he should have, but he supposed it might be the last time he would manage it so there was no sense in not having the memory to keep him warm in his old age.

"Who was that?" she managed.

"I have no idea," he said, though he supposed he could hazard a guess. Students at the schools of wizardry were under strict instructions not to torment the townspeople. The punishment for it was ejection from the school and damage to the reputation that anyone with a care for it wouldn't possibly want. Of the masters, Ruith could bring to mind only one who would terrify people simply because he could.

Droch of Saothair, the master of Olc.

Sarah shuddered again, once, then shoved him away from her. He looked down, then winced. Her pale green eyes were bloodshot, her hair uncombed and hanging in straggling curls over her shoulders, and her face grey with weariness. A pity that didn't detract at all from her beauty.

He wondered absently if he had lost his mind that he could be thinking about the fairness of her face when they were walking into a clutch of mages—one of whom, at least, would quite happily have seen him dead.

She glared at him. "I'm finished with this, Your—"

"Don't," he said, with more sharpness than he'd intended. He opened his mouth to apologize, but she shoved him out of the way and started toward the street before he could.

He caught up with her and stepped in front of her, blocking her way. "If you could just have another half hour's worth of patience," he began, "we could be inside—"

"Nay," she said, taking a step backward, then another. "I don't want to go any farther with you." She gestured toward the street with a hand that trembled badly. "I don't want any more of *that*."

He had never once doubted over the course of their acquaintance that Sarah of Doìre would manage whatever was necessary because she was just that kind of woman. A courageous, resilient, terribly responsible woman who would do what needed to be done simply because she found herself the only one who could do it. But for the first time since he'd known her, he thought she might have reached her limit.

He didn't attempt to move toward her, didn't attempt to reach out and brush any stray locks of damp hair back from her face. He merely clasped his hands behind his back and looked at her gravely.

"Would you continue on," he began slowly, "if I could promise you a safe place to sleep for a few days?"

She considered. "Will you be there?"

He maintained a neutral expression, though it cost him more than he'd thought it might. "Aye, and I can well understand why you wouldn't want any more of my company."

"I imagine you can," she said stiffly, "for which you should at least have the good grace to blush."

"I vow I will," he promised, "when we're safe."

She pursed her lips. It was obvious she didn't trust him, which he'd known would be the case. He wasn't above hoping, however, that at some point in the future she might be willing to bring to mind a few of the more pleasant moments of their journey.

Before he'd been fool enough to take her first to his father's well, then to the keep at Ceangail where no woman should ever have had to set foot.

"Very well," she said with a dark look, "I accept, because I have no choice. And also because I'm not through repaying you for what you've put me through over the past few fortnights *and* all the terrible things you've said to me."

He caught up to her quickly, before she walked out into the crowd that was still apparently recovering from almost being singed by a renegade dragon. He knew she didn't want to remain with him, but the truth was even though she wasn't safe next to him, she was even less safe away from him. He had also realized over that rather lengthy and anxious journey spent chasing her that he didn't particularly care for his life without her—something he hadn't expected that particular winter evening when he'd gathered his gear and locked the door of his mountain house behind him.

Odd, how things could change so quickly.

He paused as they stood on the edge of the street. "Would you be opposed to taking on an alias?"

She looked up at him quickly. "Why does that matter?"

"Because we won't make it past the guards up the way without one."

She shivered. "And just what sort of hell is His Royal Highness deigning to take me to?"

"One that leads to paradise," he promised. "And please stop calling me that."

"'Tis what you are."

"Not any longer, and there are other ways you could wound me that would hurt less."

She looked up at him seriously. "Do you think I want it to hurt less, Ruith?"

He suppressed a grimace. Nay, he imagined she didn't. He'd known at various points along their journey from Doìre that he would regret not having told her who he was, he just hadn't known how much. He pulled her borrowed hood up over her hair, did the same for himself, then nodded toward the castle.

"I'll invent a tale as we walk. We'll go quickly."

She didn't look happy about it, but she nodded. He walked up the way as if he'd been nothing more than a traveler seeking shelter. He felt the hair stand up on the back of his neck, but again, that was likely from imaginings brought on by weariness. All he had to do was put his head down, blend in, and walk past anyone whose notice he might not have wished to garner. He took Sarah's hand and drew it under his arm. Perhaps she felt uneasy as well, for she didn't fight him.

He hazarded a glance at the keep, then wished he hadn't. The walls were still sheer, rising a hundred feet into the air with a ruthless exuberance that defied anyone to scale them. The front gates were a forbidding barbican with two towers and a portcullis that was made of more than just steel. Ruith half wondered why the masters bothered with guards there. Surely the magic even he could sense was enough to keep any but the most foolhardy at bay.

Wizards. What an unruly, arrogant lot. Ruith remembered as he walked with Sarah up to those gates why he'd never wanted to waste time earning any rings of mastery. The thought of having to sit under the supposed tutelage and substantial scrutiny of most of the masters within would have been absolutely insupportable. And dangerous—for them. He hadn't had the patience for it at ten summers; he certainly didn't have the patience for it now.

But within those hallowed, if not stuffy, walls lay absolute safety, and he was willing to endure a bit of genuflecting to have it.

"Your plan?" Sarah asked.

He wasn't unaccustomed to inventing identities for himself on the spur of the moment, so he set about it as they walked slowly toward the barbican gate. "We're parents of some talented lad who was recommended by our local mage. The guards will have memorized all the wizards of note in the Nine Kingdoms, so we'll claim an acquaintance with Oban."

She nodded, then looked up at him reluctantly. "You didn't see Master Oban on your way south, did you?"

"I didn't," he said quietly, "nor any of the others, but I didn't look for them either." He was quite eager to discuss the apparently undisclosed identity of their local alemaker-turned-mage, but now wasn't the time. Perhaps he would use it as an excuse to keep her nearby for another day when the time came that she wanted to leave.

He nodded toward the keep. "Just so you know," he said slowly, "there are spells of ward set inside the gates, wards which alert the headmaster should anyone with magic enter and not announce his power beforehand. We'll present ourselves at the gates and look innocent. If our luck holds, we'll request a tour, then whilst on it run like the wind for a certain chamber."

"Why don't we just ask for directions to this certain chamber right from the start?" she asked, frowning.

"Because the man we're here to see doesn't have anything to do with novices and the headmaster won't believe he's asked to see us. He is, though, the only one with the power to fight what hunts us."

"And you can't?" she asked tartly.

"I can't," he admitted, though he found the admission a little less palatable than it should perhaps have been. "And here we are. I'll tell you the rest later."

"If we survive this descent into madness."

Now that he was at the gate, he found himself agreeing with her, though he supposed it was unwise to say as much. He stopped well in front of the foremost guardsman's outstretched sword.

"Oy, stay where you are," the man said firmly. "State your business, my good man, else you'll wish you had."

"I have business with the masters here," Ruith said, with as much deference as he could muster. "I would prefer to discuss it *inside* your gates, if you don't mind. The streets of Beinn òrain are a dodgy place, aren't they, and one must keep one's lady safe from harm."

The man either couldn't argue with that or didn't find them particularly dangerous-looking. He did, however, motion for a bit of aid in containing the potential threat as he escorted them under the barbican gate and into the courtyard.

Ruith felt rather than heard Sarah's breath begin to come in gasps. He put his hand over hers that rested on his arm and squeezed it reassuringly, though he couldn't say he was any more comfortable than she was. He had forgotten just how the spells pressed down on a body once inside the gates, how the very air was full of magic, how centuries of tales echoed faintly along the stones.

"Now to your business," their escort said, looking at them suspiciously.

"We're here because of our son," Ruith lied without hesitation. "We bear a message from Master Oban of Bruaih, who bid us come and speak with the masters here. We are simple folk with no magic, but our son . . ."

He paused. Was that a bell?

The guardsman frowned as well, then cocked an ear to listen.

Ruith was now certain he'd heard a faint ringing in the distance. It surprised him enough that he looked at Sarah before he could stop himself.

"Very well," another guardsman said, pushing past the first. He was accompanied by a handful of equally burly lads bearing both sharp blades and long arrows. "Which one of you is lying?"

Ruith patted himself, figuratively of course, to see if he might have left any untoward parts of himself exposed, but nay, his magic was all safely tucked where it should have been and covered by impenetrable layers of illusion and diversion. There was no lingering whiff of the spells that had been wrapped around him in Ceangail, and even the blisters on his hands where he'd touched that spell of protection fashioned of Olc were almost gone.

He looked at Sarah, but she was only glaring at him as if it were all his fault.

"Oh, Tom, 'tis you," the second guardsman said, nodding at someone behind Ruith. "Announce yourself next time, won't you?"

"Are you daft?" a lad squeaked. "And have me master find out I've been gone?"

"Bah, Droch is more bark than bite," the guardsman said dismissively, waving the lad on. "But I'd not like to have either from him, so you'd best hurry. He came through here not a quarter hour ago, looking less than pleased about something."

"He's still sour over that chess game he played with that mage a bit ago," Tom said, stopping in front of Ruith and shuddering. "Never seen him in such a temper. He's been out looking for new pieces, don't you know, to replace what was lost."

"I'd like not to be one of them," the guardsman said nervously. "Where've you been?"

"Oh, here and there," Tom said with a shrug. "Searching for the odd spell to keep tucked away for appeasing Droch when needful. It served me well this past fortnight, believe you me."

"You're daft to be within ten paces of him," the guard said, shooing Tom away without delay and looking rather more unsettled than he had the moment before.

Ruith had no idea what sort of chess Droch played, but he suspected it wasn't anything he would want to be involved in. He wondered who the fool was who'd found himself led into such a terrible situation. No one he knew, no doubt.

A single, delicate bell rang again.

Just once.

Ruith suppressed a wince at the sight of a man rushing across the courtyard from points unknown. He was adjusting his tall, pointy hat as he did so, which adjustment was hampered by his long, voluminous robes flapping in the breeze created by his haste.

Ceannard, the headmaster of the schools of wizardry and the possessor of the loosest tongue in the bloody place.

Ruith knew he shouldn't have expected anything else. The truth was, he'd all but asked for the headmaster, though he'd hoped someone of lesser stature might be sent. He looked over his shoulder to find his rear guarded by men he hadn't realized were there. He was flanked by equally enthusiastic lads with obviously well-used weapons.

He had two choices: bluster his way through what was in front of him, or release his magic, change himself into a dragon, and hope he could fly over the walls with Sarah before they were slain. The masters didn't care for those who tried to bluff their way inside their gates whilst possessing no magic. But to be caught inside those gates having lied about what magic ran through one's veins . . . well, that would be a dodgy bit of business indeed.

Especially given that the penalty for that sort of lying was death.

He held on to Sarah's hand to keep her from bolting and cast about quickly for a believable tale that would distract Ceannard long enough for him to prepare to escape. He watched as Master Ceannard was thirty paces away, then twenty, then—

And then, a miracle.

A man stepped out of nothing and caught Ceannard by the arm. Ruith closed his eyes briefly and thought he might have to sit down in truth this time. The second guardsman, the one with the sword he seemed inordinately fond of, walked over gingerly toward the two mages standing not ten paces away.

"Masters," he said, bowing without hesitation, "we have a couple here come with a recommendation from Master Oban of Bruaih—though I haven't seen the letter yet, of course—eager to see the inside of our magnificent walls. They've no magic themselves." He cast Ruith a suspicious look. "Or so they claim."

Ruith watched from the relative anonymity of his hood as Master Ceannard frowned first at the guardsman, then at the much younger-looking man standing to his left.

"Eh?" he said, taking off his hat and scratching his head. "No magic? But I heard the bell—"

"I believe it must have been a mistake," the blond man said with a faint smile. "There is no magic here in this humble couple."

Master Ceannard readjusted his robes stiffly. "I don't like these things which have been afoot of late, my lord Soilléir. Too much excitement. I don't know about you, but I could certainly do with a little rest."

"Then allow me to see to these two for you, my friend," Soilléir of Cothromaiche said gently. "I see nothing else in your afternoon but a well-deserved cup of tea by your fire. I believe we'll see a bit of snow before the day is out, don't you agree?"

Ruith hoped that would be the least of what they would have before the day was out. He didn't move as Ceannard shot him a frown, turned the same look on Sarah before he plopped his hat back down on his head and walked rather unsteadily back the way he'd come. Ruith wondered absently what had had the whole place in such an uproar, then decided he was better off not knowing. He had trouble enough of his own without borrowing any from others.

The guardsman looked at Soilléir nervously. "They say they're from Shettlestoune—"

"Which I daresay they are," Soilléir agreed.

"Don't suppose you'll be wanting a guard," the man asked doubtfully. "To help keep you safe from them, of course."

"I think I can manage them," Soilléir said dryly, "but I thank you for your efforts so far."

The guardsmen retreated, muttering to each other. Ruith supposed he shouldn't breathe easily until he and Sarah were sitting in front of Soilléir's fire, so he remained where he was, prepared to flee if necessary.

Soilléir walked over to them and stopped. He stared at Sarah searchingly for a moment or two, then turned the same look on Ruith. Then he tilted his head to one side.

"Have a son between you, do you?" he asked mildly.

"He could only dream it," Sarah muttered.

Soilléir smiled. "I imagine you have quite a tale for me. Why don't we repair to my solar and you can tell it to me, er . . ."

"Buck," Ruith said without hesitation. He looked at Sarah. "And this is—"

"No one of consequence," she said smoothly.

Soilléir only smiled as if something had amused him quite thoroughly, then stepped backward. "Come with me then, *Buck* and our lady who wishes to remain unnamed, and we'll see if we might find you something to eat and a place to lay your heads. You look weary, what I can see of you hiding in your hoods."

Ruith didn't bother to ask Soilléir if he had recognized him. There were no coincidences at Buidseachd, which meant Soilléir had come to meet him at the gates.

Or so he hoped. He was almost stumbling with weariness and began to fear that perhaps his judgement had become so clouded with it that he had judged amiss. If he had walked Sarah into danger instead of safety . . . well, it hardly bore thinking on. He knew what lay inside Buidseachd's gates; not all the passageways were pleasant ones. Even his mother might have paused whilst contemplating

standing against all the masters of the schools of wizardry, especially given that two of them were each more powerful than the seven
who proudly had their names inscribed on the front gates combined.

He shoved aside his unproductive thoughts. They would reach
Soilléir's solar without incident, then he would beg for a bed large
enough where he might pull Sarah down next to him and throw a
leg over her so she didn't escape before he could begin his apology.
Indeed, keeping her captive might be the only thing that allowed
him to spew it out.

Then he would turn his mind to the true reason he'd come to
Beinn òrain, something he'd scarce been able to look at on that
interminable journey across the plains of Ailean. Something that
felt a great deal like Fate. Again. Pushing him along a path he hadn't
wanted to take, a path that had seemingly been laid out under his
feet for a score of years, simply waiting for him to find it.

He could only hope to face that path without his soul shattering.

Four

❧

Sarah slipped her hands up her sleeves and walked alongside Ruith with as much energy as she could manage—which wasn't much. She didn't dare lose her way, though. If her first views of Buidseachd had left her with little liking for the hulking keep sitting atop its bluff, scowling down on the poor inhabitants of Beinn òrain, a closer acquaintance with it had only worsened her opinion. She'd seen the spells draped over the walls and falling to the bulwark like heavy drapes, though she would admit, reluctantly, that most of those spells hadn't been anything out of the ordinary. She hadn't wanted to look any closer on the off chance that she might see something she didn't like.

She put her shoulders back as best she could and marched on doggedly. She wouldn't know what other sorts of echoes of cast spells filled the place because she had no intention of being there long enough to find out. Her mother, surprisingly, would likely have agreed. Seleg hadn't done anything but disparage the university every chance she had, without giving any specifics as to why she might have disliked it so. Sarah had assumed that had been because Daniel had been so keen to attend it, which her mother had no doubt considered a slight to her own magical tutelage. For herself, Sarah could hardly face the irony of her situation. Her recently made vow to have nothing to do with mages was still fresh in her mind, yet now she found herself surrounded by no doubt the largest nest of them in all the Nine Kingdoms.

She turned a jaundiced eye on the blond man walking but a pace or two in front of them. He had, she could say with absolute certainty, simply stepped out of thin air and stopped that other agitated mage from asking all sorts of questions she'd been sure Ruith wouldn't want to answer. It wasn't possible that he was a master of anything but the most rudimentary of spells given that he didn't look any older than Ruith. Perhaps he was an apprentice, or an underling sent by someone to fetch Ruith, or had just happened to be in the right place at the right time.

She squinted upward, just to help herself feel as if she were still in the world and not lost in some terrible dream full of spells and mages and things she couldn't begin to understand. The sky was already dark with heavy clouds, but she found that the morning had grown even darker, as if a strange and unpleasant fog had suddenly sprung up.

She realized she had wandered away from Ruith and their guide only after she found herself standing at a convergence of passageways. She had lost all the light she'd had, lost Ruith, lost everything but an overwhelming desire to find a place to sit down and rest. There was a cool, not unpleasant breath of air coming from the passageway on her right. She turned toward it and started to walk only to have someone catch her and jerk her backward. She spun around, curses halfway out of her mouth, only to find Ruith standing there with the mage at his side. They were looking at her with no small bit of alarm.

"I'm tired," she said crossly, because it was all she could manage. She pulled her arm away from Ruith's hand. "I wasn't lost."

Apparently he didn't believe her. He took her again by the arm and the pain was so intense, she thought she just might faint.

She realized only as she woke that she had done just that. She watched a door be opened by a tall, frightening-looking man, then realized all that was alarming about him was the fact that his face was completely shadowed by a deep cowl. An odd thing to be wearing inside a chamber, but perhaps the chambers were very cold.

"Put me down," she said, attempting to crawl out of Ruith's arms. "Damn you, put me down."

He complied reluctantly, though Sarah wasn't sure what he thought she was going to do. She certainly wasn't going to go back out into that passageway without some sort of guide or perhaps a map. She was absolutely not going to attempt any sort of journey without at least an hour to sit and rest. With any luck, she would manage a meal as well.

She looked around her to see if she might find the latter. The solar was enormous, but what left her turning round and around again—and forcing Ruith to turn with her given that he wouldn't let go of her arm—was the light. The day outside was dark, she knew that, but somehow the windows that stretched from floor to ceiling captured what little light shone on that bleak morning without and drew it inside where it could happily tumble through the air.

Whatever else might be said about the man who inhabited the place where she stood, it had to be supposed that he didn't care for shadows.

Their rescuer followed them inside, sending dogs she hadn't noticed following them bounding into the chamber before him. They turned on her and sniffed her enthusiastically.

"Leave off," the man said with a half laugh. "I don't know why I keep the damned things."

"To torment your guests?" Ruith asked pointedly.

Sarah looked at the blond man, who only sent the dogs off to their places with a stern look, then turned a much lighter look on her.

"Welcome to Buidseachd," he said, making her a small bow. "I am Soilléir. And you are Sarah of Doìre, I believe."

She felt her mouth fall open. "How did you know?"

He smiled. "A good guess." He glanced at Ruith. "I don't suppose you and I need introductions, do we, Prince Ruithneadh?"

Sarah looked at Ruith quickly to see what his reaction would be to someone else—and possibly a servant, no less—calling him what he was. He only pursed his lips.

"I don't suppose we do and I don't suppose you need to break with the tradition of calling me *lad*, given that you've called me that the whole of my life."

"The first ten years of it, at least," Soilléir agreed. He turned to Sarah. "What will you have first, my dear? Food, sleep, or a bath?"

"All," she said, then realized Ruith had said the same thing at the same time.

Soilléir laughed and it was like the first bit of warm sun after an endlessly brutal winter. "Perhaps a bath first, then the rest to follow in short order." He nodded toward the back of the enormous solar. "There's a wee chamber back there to the left of the hearth, Sarah, complete with a hot fire and even hotter water. I fear I have no maidservant to attend you, but perhaps you might make do just the same."

Sarah wasn't particularly comfortable simply marching off into someone's private bathing chamber, especially since she wasn't entirely sure Soilléir wasn't just a servant, but if he was going to have the cheek to invite her to make free with his master's things, she wasn't going to argue. She managed to slur out her thanks, then walk unsteadily across the polished stone floor. She avoided going too near that frightening-looking man standing near the window, then continued on her way, weary beyond belief, almost too weary to be terrified.

She found the door to the chamber set back in an enormous alcove to the left of the equally large hearth that dominated one end of the room, then paused with her hand on the doorknob and looked over her shoulder.

Ruith and Soilléir were standing in the middle of the solar, talking quietly. They were of a height and similarly built. Soilléir with his golden hair was all light and clearness, though she could almost see under it all a core of steel, as if his secrets were not dark ones, but were nonetheless unyielding. He was, she had to assume, who Ruith had come to see, though she couldn't imagine why. She frowned, then looked at Ruith.

He was as she had always known him, sunlight behind a cloud. Now, she suspected that sunlight was more than what it appeared. It was his magic, an enormous, unlimited, unending source of power. The darkness that shadowed it had nothing to do with that magic, though she supposed he wouldn't have listened to that from her if she'd shouted it at him.

She yawned, then turned away. The truth was, she wasn't at all accustomed to seeing so much male beauty on endless display in front of her—Shettlestoune was not known for its handsome men, after all—and having to look at the two behind her was a bit much in her current state.

She let herself into the little chamber, then shut the door behind her. And there, as promised, was not only a hot fire in a modest-sized hearth, but an enormous copper tub filled with steaming water, buckets full of equally steaming water for rinsing, and a lovely selection of fine soaps for her use. There was also, set near the fire, a tray full of heavenly smelling, delicate-looking edibles that she had to force herself not to fall upon like the starving woman she was.

She took a deep breath, reminded herself she was a lady and not a tavern wench, then made herself at home. She would bathe, eat a bit, then hopefully feel slightly more herself so she could make her plans.

Which, she reminded herself sharply, would not include mages.

An hour had surely passed, perhaps longer, before she managed to pry herself from the bath that seemed to be perpetually warmed to just the right temperature—she supposed there was some use in knowing a mage, but a bath hardly made up for all their other flaws so she tried not to feel too grateful—and dress herself in something she found in a wardrobe full of things that seemed to be just the right size.

More magic at work, apparently.

It seemed a little ridiculous to put on nightclothes—painfully soft and luxurious—and swathe herself in a gorgeous brocade dressing gown—silk she guessed, not having ever touched the stuff before— during the daytime, but since her plan was to retire to a corner as quickly as possible and sleep away the hours until dawn, she supposed she might be forgiven for it. She was modestly dressed. They couldn't ask for anything more than that.

She took her knives with her, slipping them into one of the deep pockets of the dressing gown. They were nothing more than a false bit of security, but since they were all she had, she wasn't going to give them up.

She saw Ruith immediately, sitting in front of the fire, freshly scrubbed as well and dressed in clothing that was quite a bit simpler than hers was. She imagined that if he'd exited his bath to find lord's garb, he had put up a fuss.

She yawned before she could stop herself. Perhaps the rest of her life could wait for another day until she'd slept off the trauma that had led her to where she was at present.

Ruith rose the moment he saw her. "Feel better?" he asked, looking at her gravely.

She nodded, because she couldn't say anything without saying too much. She didn't want to forgive him, she didn't want to understand him, and she definitely didn't want to look at him and feel her heart softening toward him. She looked away to find one large pallet laid there before the fire, looking as fine as what she'd always imaged the princes of Neroche would have slept upon in their royal palace. She looked at Ruith.

"Where are you going to sleep?"

"Right there. With you."

Softening feelings for the man? She realized abruptly that she didn't have to wring her hands over the potential for those any longer.

"You most certainly are *not*," she said sharply.

"I don't want you escaping before I can have speech with you."

"You forget, Your Highness, that I've no interest in anything you have to say."

She said the words with vigor, but she found that she sounded less angry than shrill and that wasn't in her nature. Or at least it hadn't been before she'd embarked on a quest that had turned out to be far more difficult than she'd anticipated it might be.

"*One* bed will suffice," he said.

"Aye, because *you* will be sleeping on the floor," she retorted.

The hooded man standing against the wall made a muffled sound of . . . something. She didn't think it was polite to glare at him—nor did she have the courage given that he was easily as tall as Ruith was and much more intimidating—so she settled for glaring at Ruith. She was half tempted to march back into that luxurious bathing chamber, change into something suitable for travel, and leave, but she wasn't sure how she was going to get from her current locale to the gates without running afoul of spells she might not be able to see.

"Sarah."

She looked at Ruith coolly, but said nothing.

He clasped his hands behind his back. "I apologize for the things I said on the way here. I feared that if what followed us thought I held you in any esteem, you might be in danger."

"You could rather have used your magic, I think."

"That wasn't an option."

Then what good were you to me was almost out of her mouth, but she stopped the words just in time. It was something her mother would have said, having been the sort of witch to look at things, animals, and people with a jaundiced eye and judge them according to their usefulness to her.

The unpleasant truth was, Ruith had kept her as safe as could reasonably have been expected along their journey, never mind that he had said terrible things to her in Ceangail. Those were things she knew he had said in an effort to get her away from his bastard brothers so he could instead die at their hands. Apparently, he'd done the same thing again on the plains of Ailean.

She drew herself up and wrapped as much of her tattered pride around herself as she could manage. "Well," she said, reaching for all the haughteur she could muster, "the next time we're faced with death by a thousand spells, I would like you to simply keep your mouth shut instead of treating me like a servant."

"I will."

"And just because I don't have any magic doesn't mean I can't do some fairly important things," she said, though she couldn't bring a damned one of those things to mind at present. Hopefully Ruith wouldn't want any examples.

"I watched you before," he said very quietly, "and I agree. You have strung your loom with warp threads of courage and determination, then woven us all into a pattern that would have been the envy of any mage I know."

She scowled. "Prettily spoken, but I'm still not going any farther with you."

"I know."

"And I don't trust you."

"I haven't given you very many reasons to."

That was unfortunately not true either. He had been willing to sacrifice his life to save hers. That he'd taken her into a place where that had been necessary was a bit problematic, but to be fair, she hadn't given him much choice.

She managed to dredge up another scowl. "I imagine you'll want my apology now for not having been particularly forthright about my lack of magic."

He shook his head slowly. "There is nothing to apologize for."

"Since you likely knew from the beginning."

"I didn't, and it made no difference to me once I did, except to be profoundly tempted to bring spells to life under your hands—"

"Stop it," she said sharply. "Stop being kind to me."

He looked at her, then nodded slowly and went to sit back down in front of the fire.

She looked out the windows for a moment, then glanced up at the ceiling. The firelight flickered against it, revealing it to be covered with all sorts of lovely carvings of heroic scenes. She wondered, absently, if any of the masters of Buidseachd had been a part of those, or if Soilléir simply enjoyed contemplating someone else doing the deeds depicted there.

She took a deep breath, then looked at Ruith again.

He looked impossibly tired. He was also watching her with a very grave expression on his unnaturally beautiful face. She didn't want to feel comfortable around him—he was who he was, after all—but there was something so ordinary about the sight of him sitting there, she almost let her guard down.

Almost.

The truth was, it had hurt her far more than she wanted to admit to trust him and have him betray her—never mind that she was well aware of his reasons. And if she were to face a bit more truth, she would have to admit that what bothered her the most was not that he was a mage, it was that he was an elven prince. She was not his equal in any way.

Unfortunately, he didn't act much like an elven prince.

"Did you eat already?" she asked, because she had to say something.

He shook his head. "I waited for you. That, and I didn't want to be distracted by food and possibly have you escape without my noticing."

"You don't need to worry about that. When the time comes—and it will come, I assure you—I will go openly. I'm finished with all this business of mages and magic," she added, on the off chance he'd forgotten her plans.

"Hmmm," was all he said.

Sarah found his lack of interest in a fight profoundly unsatisfying. He did seem to be interested in food, though, which she agreed with. She refused his hand when he offered it, just on principle, but if he was determined to hold out her chair for her, or see her served first, or pour her wine as if she'd been a fine lady, who was she to argue? He was no doubt brushing up his manners for the endless line of princesses who would be eyeing him purposefully once word got out he was available.

"So," she said, once they'd finished their meal and the silence began to make her uncomfortable, "who is this Soilléir person and where is his master?"

Ruith smiled faintly. "*He* is the master here."

"Impossible," she said promptly. "He can't be any older than you are."

Ruith shrugged. "I would say he's been here several centuries, but my knowledge of the schools of wizardry perhaps isn't what it should be."

She felt her mouth fall open. "Centuries?"

"He's every day of two thousand, I daresay," Ruith said thoughtfully. He smiled. "Doesn't look it, though, does he?"

"Nay, he does not, though I'm increasingly alarmed at how poor a judge I am of these things." She felt her eyes narrow. "How old is Sgath? The same?"

"At least," Ruith agreed.

She pushed back from the table, then rose and began to pace, because she had to. She wanted to tell Ruith she didn't want to know any more, but she was afraid if she allowed too much silence, he might be tempted to fill it by asking her what she was thinking to leave her brother possibly alive out in the Nine Kingdoms to bring them all to ruin. Then he would likely point out his need for her to come with him and find the spells he had stuffed down his boots.

Which, she realized, she couldn't see.

She looked at him in surprise. "Where are the spells?"

He had to take a deep breath. "I lost them. Well," he amended, "not precisely that. They were taken from me after we were overcome and whilst I was senseless. I still have the cloth you so cleverly filched from Connail of Iomadh's chamber, but nothing else."

She sank down in a chair opposite him because it was the closest thing available to keep her from landing on the floor. "Who took them, do you think?"

"I have no idea. Whoever it was didn't take the trouble to slay me whilst he was about it, though he certainly could have. I was covered in an Olcian spell of protection by someone I can't name, then relieved of the pages by another mage who slit through the first spell with another spell of Olc—all whilst I was senseless." He shrugged. "An interesting mystery, I daresay."

That was understating it. She wasn't sure what, if anything, she could possibly say. Ruith's expression was inscrutable, though she knew that was a ruse. He had to have been greatly surprised to find himself alive but very upset over the loss of what they had so carefully collected.

It occurred to her abruptly that he'd had to decide between searching for the spells and searching for her.

She put her hands over her face for a moment or two, then took a deep breath and looked at him. "Thank you for coming after me."

"The choice was easily made, believe me." He looked at her gravely. "Sarah, I truly do regret what I said on the way here and at Ceangail. In the keep, I had no other way to take Díolain's attentions off you. On the plains, I feared our hunter might have been someone from Ceangail, so it seemed prudent to carry on with that charade."

She nodded, though that cost her quite a bit. It also took her quite a bit longer than she supposed it should have to manage a decent breath. She cast about quickly for something else to discuss before she had to think on the forgiveness she should no doubt offer after such a flowery bit of sentiment.

"Tell me of this place," she said, hoping she sounded more casual than pleading.

Ruith sat back and fussed absently with the spoon he'd used to stir honey into his tea. "The school has been here for a pair of millennia, perhaps longer. My grandmother, Eulasaid, was here at its founding, and she's at least that old. It was begun to formalize the training of mages, as you might imagine, though over the centuries it has perhaps evolved into less of an elite school for the finest of mages and more of an all-encompassing place where even a village lad might earn a ring or two to call his own."

"My brother wanted one," she admitted. "He wasn't disciplined enough to even attempt to gain entrance here, though."

"I understand it isn't easy," Ruith conceded.

"Did you never think about—" She shut her mouth before she went on with that question. Of course he wouldn't have thought about coming to the schools of wizardry. He had been too busy living in seclusion, no doubt trying to forget who he was. She stole a look at him, fully expecting him to be offended, but if he was, he didn't show it.

Damn him anyway. She would have felt better about insulting him if he'd actually given her a fight about something.

"Actually, in my youth, I considered it beneath me," he said with a shrug, apparently willing to answer the question she hadn't finished. "Now? I don't want any of it, but for different reasons. Others, though, want the seven rings of mastery very badly indeed. Very few lads manage all seven. I imagine Soilléir could name all those who have without having to scratch his head once."

"Is he one of the seven masters, then? I assume each ring has a master who gives it."

"It does," he agreed. "And whilst Soilléir could certainly offer the instruction that is associated with each ring, he doesn't. There are other mages here, mages not associated with the levels of mastery, who teach things that not everyone should know—or would want to know, for that matter."

Immediately, the memory of that dark-haired man came back to her. She looked at Ruith and swallowed with a bit of difficulty.

"Who was that?"

"Droch of Saothair," Ruith said very quietly, obviously knowing exactly of whom she was speaking. "He is master of the spells of Olc."

Sarah shivered in spite of herself. "Was that his passageway I . . ."

"Aye." He paused. "'Tis how he amuses himself, leading novices astray until they find themselves tangled so fully in his spells that they cannot free themselves without aid."

"And you would know?" she asked casually.

"I would know," he agreed. "'Twas a good thing my mother was so protective of us and always knew where we were. I was caught in his trap for only a moment or two before she swooped down and rescued me. Ironic, though, that I didn't recognize spells fashioned of my father's favorite magic."

She sat back and shook her head. "I don't understand how your father could use that when that wasn't his lineage. I thought you could only use what you had a bloodright to. My mother could only use Croxteth."

"Indeed," he said, sounding faintly surprised.

"We didn't discuss it often, as you might imagine, but she was rather proud of her roots."

He toyed with his spoon a bit longer. "Did she vex you because of, er—"

"Aye," she said shortly, "she did, but let's talk about you instead. Why did your father choose Olc? It isn't a pleasant magic, is it?"

He looked at her briefly, then set his spoon down. "'Tis a seductive magic," he conceded, "but the seduction doesn't come without a heavy price. It eats at the mage's soul, something he doesn't realize until it's too late."

Her brother had been dabbling in Olc. She suspected that was what had destroyed her mother's house.

Ruith rose and went to fetch a blanket. She thought to decline it, but she realized as he wrapped it around her that she was far colder than she should have been.

"Tell me something else," she said, wishing quite desperately for anything else to discuss. "What does Master Soilléir do here if he doesn't dole out rings? Obviously he's not involved in—" She had to take a deep breath. "Well, in that dark sort of business."

"He holds the spells of Caochladh," Ruith said, sitting back down in his chair and rubbing the fingers of his hands as if they pained him somehow. "Spells of essence changing. He rarely gives them out, and then only to lads who hold the seven rings of mastery. Actually, I'm not sure how many of those ring-holders have proven themselves to be trustworthy enough for his spells. I understand the process to win them is . . . arduous."

"Are those spells so powerful, then?" she asked doubtfully.

He looked at her seriously. "Powerful and terribly complicated. Of course, there are easier ways to effect a change, with a spell of reconstruction, perhaps, which would change something into something else for a fixed amount of time—usually not more than a day or two. Rock to water, air to fire, man to toad."

"Tempting."

"Isn't it, though?" he said dryly. He looked at his hands thoughtfully. "With the spells of essence changing, however, you change the substance in question permanently. Air to fire, rock to water, man to beast. And thus it remains until the mage changes it back again, though I understand that it is enormously difficult, even with great power, to have the restoration be complete. I suppose that is what keeps a mage from turning his valet into an end table on a whim."

"Does Master Soilléir ever use the spells himself?" she asked faintly.

"You could ask him," Ruith said. "I'm quite certain he keeps Droch in check with the threats of it. I wouldn't be surprised if he's had the occasional pointed conversation with other black mages of note from time to time."

"Would you want those spells, Ruith?" she asked, before she thought better of it.

He looked at her evenly. "Don't ask."

She wasn't sure why the question bothered him so. Perhaps he feared if he had those mighty spells, he might turn all his bastard brothers into mice and set a herd of starving cats upon them.

She nodded, consigning all conversation about spells and their wielders to hell where they should have been, then pushed back from the table. "I don't know about you, but I'm tired. I need my rest if I'm to be on my way tomorrow."

He nodded. "Of course. It has been a very long journey here."

She didn't fight him when he pulled out her chair for her, then escorted her over to the fire. He sat and looked at her.

"You can sleep in peace here," he said, nodding to his knives hanging on a hook near the hearth. "I'll keep watch for a bit."

She paused unwillingly. "But surely you're weary."

"Soilléir will want details of our adventures so far," he said with a faint smile. "When he returns from the bit of scouting I'm sure he's done, I'll satisfy him, then sleep as well."

"I hope you'll find the floor comfortable."

"I hope you won't step on me in the night on your way to the loo."

She scowled at him, because it made her happy to do so, then nodded briskly, because she could do nothing else. She didn't want to think about a mage who could turn her brother into a flea taking the time to make certain she and Ruith were safe. She didn't want to think about what lay outside walls she had feared would be worse than a prison. And she most definitely didn't want to think about a man who had put his blades where she could see them, that she might fall asleep without fear.

She lay down on a pallet that somehow managed to feel like what she'd always imagined a bed for a princess might, then closed her eyes, partly to block out the sight of Ruith sitting there, staring into the fire, and partly because she was past the point of exhaustion. She reminded herself that such luxury was only to be hers for a single night and then she would be on her way to places where magic was nothing more than rumor the locals spoke about in hushed tones down at the pub. She would be happy to leave them to it and leave mages, including grave and silent elven princes, behind.

Truly.

Five

❧

Ruith paced a bit back and forth in front of the windows of Soilléir's chamber, watching the twinkling lights of the city reflected in the river he could see in the distance. The scene looked innocent and peaceful, even for Beinn òrain, which wasn't precisely a city of innocents and peacemakers. It was odd, however, to look down over the same view he'd looked at a score of years ago yet now be who he was. He had assumed, the last time he'd looked at that view, that he would succeed with his brothers in helping his father along to hell, then live out the rest of his life in bliss, dividing his time with his mother and siblings between Seanagarra and Lake Cladach.

Odd how life didn't turn out how one expected it would in one's youth.

He turned away from the window and ran bodily into Soilléir's servant, who only backed away, apologizing by inclining his head slightly. Ruith smiled at him, then walked across the chamber to stand in front of the fire. It wasn't so he could stave off the sudden chill he felt, truly. It was so he could watch Sarah whilst she slept.

He stood with his hands clasped behind his back and looked down at her, lying a comfortable distance away from the fire with her glorious hair spread out behind her. It occurred to him that even if he were able to convince her to look on him with favor, there would come a time when the disparity in their ages would grieve them both beyond measure. His years stretched out before him as Soilléir's did, century after century with no end in sight, whereas Sarah would live out the tally of a mortal woman, then find herself waning before she passed through to that reputed place in the east where sorrow and death were no more.

Leaving him behind, alone—

He spun around when he heard the door across the chamber shut softly. Soilléir held up his hands as he walked silently across the floor.

"Friend, not foe," he said with a faint smile, coming to warm his hands against the roaring fire. "I saw nothing unusual, but I didn't go outside the city walls themselves. There might be things lurking there, but they will leave you in peace here for a bit, I'll warrant."

"One could hope," Ruith said grimly. He watched Sarah a bit longer, then looked at his host. "Well?"

Soilléir only looked at him innocently. "Well, what? You act as if you think I'm preparing to pepper you with questions."

"You forget, my lord, that I knew you quite well in a former lifetime and watched you grill my mother more than once."

"I never grilled your mother."

Ruith had to concede, grudgingly, that Soilléir's questioning of Sarait had always been very gentle, but it had been undeniably relentless. It had been motivated, no doubt, by love and concern. He didn't want to credit the man with such warm feelings for him, but since he had provided such a useful and convenient refuge, satisfying his curiosity perhaps wasn't out of the question.

He sighed deeply and suppressed the urge to pace a bit more. He wished with equal desperation for something to do with his hands.

"I don't suppose you have any decently kilned wood hiding in your chambers, do you?" he asked.

"Nay, short of pulling apart my favorite armoire made especially for me by King Uachdaran's third son—"

"How did you flatter him out of that?" Ruith asked in surprise.

"I imagine you would want to know," Soilléir said mildly, "having found flattery unequal to the task of winning you the spells you would have happily had out of His Majesty's solar." He lifted an eyebrow. "I don't suppose you did the unthinkable and actually *pilfered* them, did you?"

"I had help," Ruith said defensively. "Miach of Neroche was the one who opened the door."

"And you opened the glass case containing the book."

"That the blame might be spread about equally," Ruith agreed, smiling a little at the memory. "And aye, all because flattery didn't serve us."

Soilléir sat and looked up at Ruith. "I'll find you wood on the morrow. I'd rather have a bit of your tale tonight, if you're of a mind to give it. I'll leave the difficult questions for when you don't look as if you'll fall asleep in the middle of the answers."

Ruith had no doubt that Soilléir could see the entire journey written there on his soul, but perhaps there was something healing about the recounting of a tale that had been created with such difficulty.

"Very well," he said, sitting down with a sigh. "Where will you have me begin?"

"With why your lady isn't happy with you."

"She is not my lady," Ruith said, though he certainly wished it to be otherwise, "and she's irritated because I led her to believe I was a simple mage, then I didn't correct her when she incorrectly assumed I was nothing but a swordsman."

"When did she find out the truth?"

Ruith pursed his lips. "As we were standing in the great hall at Ceangail and Díolain was making a production of reminding us all of our familial connections."

"I would smile," Soilléir said, pained, "but I can imagine it was very difficult for her. And you might be surprised, Ruithneadh, just how many gels don't care for that sort of thing and the violence of their reactions once they realize they've been—how shall we say it?"

"Misled for their own good?"

"Lied to," Soilléir corrected with a smile. "How long was it before you knew she had no magic?"

"How did you know that?" Ruith asked in surprise, then he held up his hand. "Never mind. I know: you are who you are. I knew early on, though she is quite adept at hiding it. I imagine her lack made for a very difficult life with Seleg and that damned brother of hers."

"I suppose that's understating it a bit, but those are likely happenings she would rather leave in her past. Let's discuss your past instead. What were you doing all those years whilst our lovely Sarah was trying to stay out of Seleg's sights? I know about the well, of course, and I knew you'd gone south to regroup—"

"That is one way to put it," Ruith muttered.

"You were a lad of ten winters, Ruith, and not your father's equal—though that was simply a matter of age and experience, not raw power. You'll remember that not even your mother was able to stand against him in that glade, empowered as he was by the acquisition of your brothers' magic."

"Acquisition," Ruith echoed grimly. "Aye, I suppose you could call it that."

Soilléir shrugged. "What else is there to call it? 'Tis an awful business, and your father was a master at it. You could not have fought him at your tender age, and for all you knew, he was still hiding there in the woods, wounded but alive. You made the choice to retreat in order to fight another day."

Ruith dragged his hands through his still-damp hair. "You're trying to assuage my guilt."

"You know I'm not," Soilléir said without hesitation. "There are many, including me, who have been faced with that same sort of decision and live now with the consequences of our actions. You cannot go back and change what's done, but you can accept that you did what was needful at the time."

Ruith wasn't sure he cared to know what sort of choices Soilléir had made. He couldn't imagine they'd been easy ones.

"And in case you're wondering, I have left you your privacy all these years—not that I didn't think about you now and again and hope you were well."

"I appreciate that," Ruith managed.

Soilléir laughed a little. "I imagine you do. And I will admit that I hadn't given you much thought recently until you healed Seirceil of Coibhneas. You woke me out of a dead sleep with that little piece of magic, if you're curious."

"I wasn't," Ruith said sourly, "but I appreciate knowing as much. How far does your sight extend, anyway?"

"Not to the innards of your stewpot, if that eases you any." Soilléir poured more wine for them both, handed Ruith his cup, then settled back comfortably in his chair. "I've often wondered how it was you so easily found a place to land. Perhaps someone knew you were coming."

"I shudder to think who that might have been," Ruith said. "No one could have suspected I would travel south. I imagine it was just a matter of happy coincidence."

"Others might have a different opinion," Soilléir said with a smile, "but we'll leave that for now. What happened after you shut your door and no doubt slept for days?"

"I survived," Ruith said, then he stopped as something else occurred to him. "I don't suppose you have stretched your sight to looking for other things besides what I put in my stew, have you? Perhaps as far as determining if any of my siblings are still alive or not?"

"I might see," Soilléir said mildly, "but I don't divulge."

"Damn you."

Soilléir laughed softly. "Ah, Ruith, it is good to see you again."

Ruith only grunted. "I'm sure my lack of deference is refreshing.

And since you won't divulge, I will. Keir is alive, if Díolain is to be believed."

Soilléir didn't look particularly surprised. "Is he, indeed?"

"You're impossible."

"Discreet," Soilléir corrected with a smile. "And instead of your past, tell me of your journey east. I'm curious about the particulars of it and what you saw on your way here."

Ruith set the cup aside for future need and began with his encounter with Sarah at his front door. He related with no relish at all the events that led up to his realizing that his father's spells were still out in the world and that his task would be to find them. It took another cup of wine to get him through the journey to his father's well and their subsequent trek to Ceangail to look for more of his father's spells.

"We fled the keep," he continued, "but were overcome by magic from a source I didn't see. I woke to find myself alone and Sarah carried off by traders. I followed, gave her no choice but to come with me, and here we are in your very comfortably appointed solar, enjoying your very fine wine."

Soilléir looked at him assessingly. "You're leaving out details."

"Details I don't care to think on at present, actually."

"Such as who would cover you with a spell of protection fashioned of Olc," Soilléir agreed. "Any ideas?"

Ruith took a deep breath. "I was hoping you might have one or two."

"Well," Soilléir said with a bit of a laugh, "I think we can safely say it wasn't Droch. If he encountered you in a darkened alleyway, I imagine he would just as soon slay you as greet you pleasantly."

"After he attempted to take my power, you mean," Ruith said, wondering just how much Soilléir had seen that morning. "How is his little spell of Taking coming, anyway? What is it he calls it—Gifting?"

"Thankfully it isn't what it should be, in spite of his centuries of attempting to perfect it. I daresay he would give much to have Gair's spell of the same, though fortunately he hasn't found it yet. It isn't for a lack of trying, believe me."

Ruith paused. "I had half of the one my sire had written down in his book, if you're curious."

"Did you?" Soilléir asked in surprise. "How did you come upon it?"

"Sarah's brother found it in the bottom of a peddler's cart." He nodded her way. "Perhaps you can look at her arm when you have a moment. She touched the half page of my father's spell of Diminishing that her brother had left lying about." He paused. "Oddly enough, I touched something akin to it in a dream and my arm bears the same mark." He paused. "I can't see it, but she can."

Soilléir studied her for a moment or two, then moved to kneel down by the low cot on the floor. He took her hand that lay atop the blankets in his, then ran his fingers over it gently. He took a deep breath, sighed it out, then wove a simple spell of Camanaë over her skin. The words hung in the air, then dissipated, leaving behind the scent of clean, wholesome herbs that refreshed in a way that eased Ruith as well. The angry red disappeared from the lines that wrapped themselves around her arm like vines, but the black remained.

Soilléir frowned, then looked up at Ruith. "That's odd."

"Very," Ruith agreed.

Soilléir put his fingers on several of the lines and wove a more complicated spell. Ruith wasn't familiar with it—though he memorized it immediately, out of habit. He supposed it was a spell of Caochladh and was faintly surprised that Soilléir had used it aloud.

The lines faded, but they didn't disappear.

Soilléir sat back on his heels for a moment or two, then rose and resumed his seat in his chair. "That sprang up from your father's spell of Diminishing, did it?"

"Aye. Half of it, at any rate."

"That, my lad, is a mystery there. Simple healing will not work, nor will attempting to change the essence of what's left buried in her flesh." He frowned thoughtfully. "Let me see your arm."

Ruith pushed his sleeve up and held out his arm. He could see nothing, but when Soilléir traced trails on his skin, similar vine-like marks flashed silver. They remained for a moment or two, remained remarkably painful for just as long, then faded to nothing.

"Interesting." Soilléir sat back in his chair and stared into his fire for quite some time before he looked at Ruith. "Memorized that spell I used, did you?"

"You shouldn't have spoken it aloud," Ruith said placidly.

"I should have checked your pockets for poached rings of mastery on your way in before I blurted it out, I suppose."

Ruith pursed his lips. "I don't want them."

"Not even for a chance to have all my spells?"

"Not even for that, my lord."

Soilléir studied him for a moment or two in silence. "Could you earn them, do you think?"

Ruith shrugged, though now found that the question felt a bit more serious than it had when Sarah had asked it. "I've spent twenty winters in a place with a library that, for all its remote location, rivals what you have downstairs—"

"And you would know, given all the time you spent in the bowels of this keep, looking for obscure spells," Soilléir conceded.

"I would," Ruith agreed. "So, without being a braggart, I can say that I think I am familiar enough with lore and craft to satisfy the masters below."

"And your collection of memorized spells no doubt rivals Miach of Neroche's," Soilléir agreed.

"Since we appropriated many of the same things together, I suppose that might be true."

Soilléir studied him for several minutes in silence. "But you didn't come here for rings."

Ruith suppressed the urge to shift uncomfortably. Nay, he hadn't come there for rings, but the truth of it was, what he had come to Beinn òrain for was something he couldn't even begin to admit to himself.

Because if he did, it meant a change in his life that would leave him never being able to retreat to that safe, fairly comfortable, undeniably isolated house on the mountain where all he needed do to carry on was worry about what he would have for supper.

"I came here for safety," he said, when he realized he hadn't responded.

"You could have provided that for yourself."

Ruith opened his mouth to protest, but found he couldn't. He drew his hand over his eyes, then looked at Soilléir.

"I don't want to continue this conversation."

Soilléir only raised one pale eyebrow.

Ruith looked at him evenly. "It is, as I said, the only safe place I could bring to mind on short notice."

"Not all magic is evil, you know. Your legacy is more than your father's spells, which Sìle would tell you, were he here."

"Fadaire is smothered by Olc more often than not," Ruith said.

"If you believe that, Ruithneadh, then you do not give your mother's power its due. However, if you fear losing control of yourself and undoing the world with your mighty power, then I can understand your reticence." Soilléir smiled pleasantly. "You always were a hotheaded, impetuous boy."

"I have outgrown whatever you think you imagined in me," Ruith said with a snort. "And I was never hotheaded."

"Then what have you to fear?"

Ruith found himself standing in the midst of a trap he hadn't realized he was walking into. Obviously he had been out of the world too long. He didn't waste time answering, for there was no answer that satisfied. Soilléir only looked at him, but said nothing. Ruith didn't bother to wonder if he agreed or disagreed. With Soilléir, one just never knew.

"And you know, all this could have been Fate," Soilléir continued with a shrug, "shoving you in a direction you needed to take for reasons you have yet to discover, reasons we'll look at later." He dropped his booted foot to the floor and put his hands on his knees.

"I don't think your lady will want a midnight supper, but you might. Then you can toddle off to bed and curse yourself to sleep."

Ruith cursed him just the same, but it was without any true malice. He would admit, almost readily, that he had always rather liked Soilléir of Cothromaiche. If he were to be entirely truthful with himself, he would have to admit that more than once he had wished his mother had wed the man instead of Gair of Ceangail. He had come with his mother to Buidseachd several times and found Soilléir's chambers to be where he felt most comfortable. No pretentious trappings of nobility, though he knew Soilléir's lineage was a noble one. His forefathers, many of whom Ruith assumed were still alive, were content like Hearn of Angesand to simply tromp about in their boots, doing whatever it was those lads from Cothromaiche did. Weaving spells that truly would have undone the world if they'd gone awry, no doubt.

Yet Soilléir had chosen none of those things for himself. He could have walked down any street in any large city in the Nine Kingdoms and passed himself off as a youthful, not hideous-looking man of no especial distinction. Not even those with any powers of seeing would have recognized him as the keeper of the spells of Caochladh, had Soilléir not revealed himself as such.

But there was no reason Ruith couldn't glare at him a bit, just to make himself feel better.

"And perhaps you would indulge me in a game of chess after supper," Soilléir suggested, rubbing his hands in anticipation.

Ruith looked at him sharply. "What sort of chess?"

"With pieces fashioned from marble," Soilléir answered, looking at him with wide, innocent eyes. "Is there any other kind?"

They'd played chess often enough in the past, but the pieces had been ones fashioned out of their imagination, leading to glorious battles on a board that had continually expanded to suit their needs, often growing to cover a sizeable block of Soilléir's floor.

"Don't corner me, my lord," Ruith warned.

"I don't corner," Soilléir said cheerfully. "I nudge."

"Aye, like a battering ram."

Soilléir laughed and rose. "I'll go fetch supper, then we'll play. You should put another blanket over your lady, for she shivers." He paused. "Her dreams are unpleasant ones."

"Of me, no doubt."

"Actually, Ruith, I think you might be right."

Ruith cursed him, but had only a faint smile in return. Nay, he didn't care for the nudging, though he was no fool. He couldn't remain in Buidseachd forever, nor had he intended to. But what galled him the most was that he'd needed refuge in the first place.

He stood with his hand on Soilléir's mantel, looking down into the fire. There, in front of him, was the vision he'd had in the mountains of Shettlestoune, the vision of that river of Fadaire, laughing and singing as it tripped over rocks and rills and cascaded around his feet. As beautiful as that had been, the truth was, the bedrock of that river had been Olc and Lugham and half a dozen other dark magics his father had taken and blackened with his own twisted powers.

And Ruith wanted nothing to do with any of them.

And if that meant that his own powers would remain buried for the next several millennia, perhaps that was for the best. He would figure out, sooner rather than later, just how he intended to keep Sarah safe from what hunted them with just his steel.

He supposed that might take a while.

He fetched a blanket, draped it over Sarah, then stared down at her by the light of the fire for several minutes in silence. He looked about him, then sighed. It was surprisingly lovely to be in a place where he was known, where his past lay layered with pleasant memories, where he was known by someone who entertained the odd, kind thought about him.

And that was something he supposed Sarah had never enjoyed.

He wished, quite suddenly, that he could provide her with that.

"Ruith?"

He looked up and nodded at Soilléir, then reached down to brush Sarah's hair back from her face before he went to help Soilléir bring a table over in front of the fire for supper.

He would eat, satisfy Soilléir with a game of chess, then have a decent night's sleep for a change. And then on the morrow, he would decide how it was he was going to carry on with the rest of his life.

All he knew was that magic wouldn't be a part of it.

Six

Sarah smoothed her hands over the dress she'd chosen from a selection of things contained in that dressing room that seemed to have been provided for just her comfort. The gown was made of exquisite fabric, far too glorious for her humble self. She knew her possession of it was destined to last as long as her peace of mind.

Which she suspected wasn't all that long.

She paused with her hand on the door of that very luxurious bathing chamber, unsure what she should do. Her plan had been to wake, beg something with which to break her fast, then ask for an escort to the front gates where she would happily leave magic and all its practitioners behind.

But then she'd woken to find Ruith and Soilléir gone, which had left her unable to ask for anything given that her only companion had been that hulking shadow who seemed to ever hover constantly at the edge of the firelight. She wouldn't have asked him for a cup of water if she'd been perishing from thirst. She'd escaped to the little chamber off the main solar, then decided that whilst she was there, she might as well take the chance to bathe again. Afterward, she'd remained near the small fire in that chamber, swathed in a robe of glorious softness, drinking sweet tea and trying not to think of anything at all.

Unfortunately, she'd been assaulted more than once by memories of waking briefly during the night to find Ruith lying on the floor next to her, holding her hand as if he truly thought she might flee if he didn't keep her from it. Master Soilléir had been sitting in a chair in front of the fire, staring into it with a look of such deep contemplation that she had hardly dared breathe lest she disturb him.

Now, as she stood with her hand on the heavy wooden door and wondered why it was there had been no traveling clothes among what she'd found apparently made especially for her, she began to give thought to things she hadn't had the leisure to the night before—namely the kindness of mages.

If such a thing were possible.

Soilléir had given them not only a place to hide, but comforts he hadn't needed to, without having been asked. Ruith had left the anonymity of his mountains to aid her with her quest, grudgingly, but simply because she'd asked it of him. It wasn't as if he'd known she would be able to dream his father's spells and see their location in those dreams. And, worse still, even when he'd had those spells in his hands and had them taken from him, he'd chosen to look for her instead of going off to look for them.

But now those spells, along with however many others there might be, were out in the world. Along with her brother. And Ruith's half brothers. It made ignoring the fact that she might be of some use to Ruith suddenly less easily done than it had been the day before.

And since that was a thought she couldn't face at the moment, she wouldn't. She took a deep breath, then opened the door and walked out into Soilléir's chamber. She quickly sidled by his servant, who was standing in his usual place, his hands tucked up his sleeves and his face hidden by his hood, only to find that the chamber was no longer empty.

Ruith was sitting in front of the fire, making arrows. A bow stood there, propped up against the stone. More gifts from Soilléir, perhaps. Ruith looked up at her before she could back away and return to her hiding place.

"Good morning, Sarah," he said gravely.

She nodded quickly, then turned away before she had to look at him for any length of time. Perhaps if she put some effort into it, she could turn away from her quest with the same sort of ease. She could stay another day or two, sleep, eat, and then be on her way without any undue discomfort.

Surely.

She almost walked into the long table set near the windows before she realized what she was doing or that Soilléir was standing behind one of the chairs there. He pulled it out and inclined his head slightly.

"Breakfast, my dear?"

She was not at her best. That was the only reason she couldn't latch onto a decent excuse for why she wasn't hungry. She sat, because she couldn't think of a good reason not to, and accepted the plate that Soilléir prepared for her, because she apparently didn't have an independent thought in her head. She smiled uncomfortably, then set to her meal as single-mindedly as possible.

She was tempted, once she'd finished, to push her plate away and bolt, but again, there was the problem of not knowing exactly how she would get herself free of Buidseachd. She wasn't quite sure how to go about asking that, so she put off the necessity of it by sipping a very lovely tea for several minutes before she realized her doom was simply sitting across from her, waiting for her to finish procrastinating. She set the cup down, sighed, then looked at her host.

He was only watching her with a small smile.

"I appreciate the meal," she said politely.

"You're welcome, Sarah."

She shifted uncomfortably. Good manners perhaps demanded that she at least make a bit of polite conversation before she thanked the man for his hospitality and fled for safer locales. She wondered if mages made polite conversation, or if they could sense discomfort, or if she could simply think her thoughts very hard and hope Soilléir could read them without her having to say anything. She honestly didn't doubt the last was possible. Soilléir had a way of looking at her that made her feel as if he were looking *through* her. It was extremely unnerving.

"Who are you?" she managed.

"Just a man," Soilléir said dismissively.

"Liar," Ruith muttered.

Sarah pursed her lips and looked at Soilléir. "I suppose His Highness would recognize that sort of thing," she said, "given how many of them he's indulged in recently."

There, that made her feel a bit more herself. She was drawing battle lines in the sand. Ruith might have been kind to her recently and he had certainly dredged up a decent apology, but he had also lied to her endlessly and without remorse for far longer than he should have.

Soilléir laughed a little. "Good heavens, gel, but you are hard on him."

Sarah looked over her shoulder at Ruith, but he was only continuing to sharpen an arrow. She frowned, then realized there was not one, but two bows leaning against the rock. And the arrows he was currently working on weren't as long as the ones they'd left behind with an obliging farmer. Perhaps he intended to take someone else along on his quest, which should have left her feeling quite content.

But somehow it didn't.

"Who are you making those for?" she asked in surprise.

He looked up. "You. I promised you I would."

She closed her eyes and turned away, then opened them to find Soilléir watching her. She took a deep breath. "I'm considering forgiving him," she said, finally. "I'm not sure I'll ever trust him again, though."

"I wouldn't blame you if you didn't," Soilléir said with a grave smile, "though you know as well as I that he had good reason for what he did."

Sarah would have preferred to ignore that last bit, but she couldn't. She couldn't look at Ruith that she didn't think on the daggers he'd given her, the attempts he'd made to keep her safe, her quest that he'd taken on initially simply to aid her. She also owed him for the magnificent dress she wore thanks to the generosity of a man she never would have met without Ruith's having brought her to his solar.

And in Ruith's defense, he had tried to leave her behind during the more perilous parts of their quest, and he hadn't actually told her a flat-out lie. Then again, she'd never asked him if he happened to be related to the most evil black mage in the history of the Nine Kingdoms.

"Have you read many histories of the Nine Kingdoms, Sarah?" Soilléir asked mildly.

She dragged her attentions back to Soilléir. "I haven't, actually," she said. "Why do you ask?"

"Just making conversation," Soilléir said with a shrug. "Do you know many tales of black mages?"

"I don't," she said uncomfortably, "and I don't want to."

Soilléir smiled. "I imagine you don't, my dear."

She feared that he did. She was very afraid, now that she'd had five minutes of conversation with the man, that her entire life was laid before him, for him to look over. The nights she had spent in the barn of her own volition, the many more she had sought refuge there because she'd been barred from her mother's house. The overwhelming desire to belong somewhere, to have a home where she had a place that was her own—

"So, was Ruith's floor clean, or was it littered with manuscripts?"

She was grateful to be pulled from her thoughts before they overwhelmed her. "Clean enough, though I didn't have much time to look at it very closely before he shoved me out his front door."

"His mother would have been disappointed in him," Soilléir said, clucking his tongue. "I wooed his mother, you know."

Ruith threw an arrow. It whizzed past Soilléir's ear to stick quite firmly in the wood of the window frame behind him.

"Very well," Soilléir conceded, "I *wanted* to woo his mother. I was terribly fond of her, but once I realized she couldn't stand the sight of me—"

"Lying," Ruith said. "Again."

Soilléir smiled. "So, because I couldn't help myself, I sent Ruith his first gift, which was, if I may say so, a marvelously fashioned rattle that whispered *Soilléir is the one* each time he shook it. Sarait sent it back, I'm afraid."

Sarah smiled in spite of herself. "You didn't."

"Oh, I did," Soilléir assured her. "And she did send it back. But she also brought him along every time she came here, just to soothe my tender feelings. Well," he added slowly, "except once."

"Did she come over the walls?" Ruith asked.

"Aye, and it wasn't my solar she was interested in."

Sarah started to ask which chamber she *had* been interested in, but she suspected she could answer that question without aid. If Ruith's father had been as entangled with Olc as Ruith had hinted at, then perhaps the fair Sarait had been looking for things of that nature.

From that horrible mage, Droch.

"Why don't you tell me of yourself, Sarah," Soilléir said, leaning back and smiling, "and how it was you came to brave the trek up the side of the mountain to knock on Ruith's door."

Sarah was happy to think on something else besides Droch, which said much about her aversion to him if speaking of her brother's evil was preferable. "I needed aid," she began, "to stop my brother from nefarious deeds. I thought Ruith to be the ancient, curmudgeon of a mage who had lived in that house for centuries. His manners certainly denoted as much. At first, I should say. He followed me on my way to Bruaih and was good enough to share his bread with me, burned as it was."

"Then all those years perfecting your recipe weren't wasted, eh, Ruith?"

Another arrow whizzed by Soilléir and terminated in his window frame.

Sarah almost smiled. "I was grateful for it—and even more grateful that he didn't hold against me my knocking him upon his, ah—"

"Arse," Ruith supplied.

"Aye, that," Sarah agreed. "He ignored the indignity of it, thankfully, and continued to help me along a path I soon found I couldn't walk alone."

Soilléir studied her for a moment or two. "How did you find your first views of the land beyond Shettlestoune?" he asked.

Sarah thought it an odd question, but she answered him just the same. She continued to recount her journey, but he seemed to be most interested in what she had seen. And not just seen, but *seen*. Then again, he was a mage, and they were no doubt interested in all sorts of things she wouldn't have cared to examine too closely.

She did understand an invitation for chess, however, which she happily accepted, grateful beyond measure to concentrate on something that didn't involve spells or magic or things beyond her ken.

"Who taught you to play?" Soilléir asked as he held out a chair for her at the board.

"The alemaster, Franciscus," she said, "though now I believe he's less alemaster and more mage." She looked at Ruith, who was watching her in silence. "You didn't see him after the castle collapsed, did you?"

He shook his head. "I was in a tearing hurry to take up your trail. I suppose given how many of Gair's bastards escaped we can safely assume Franciscus escaped as well." He shrugged. "I thought to do a bit of looking for him amongst lists of notable mages I'm sure will be found in the library downstairs. Just to pass the time, of course."

"Why don't you pass that time quickly," Soilléir said wryly, "before you eat through my larder—nay, no more arrows my way, Ruith." He smiled at Sarah. "Tell me he's behaved better than this on your way here. His mother did try to instill manners in him, you know."

Sarah didn't dare look at Ruith. She would have happily trotted out all manner of terrible stories about him, but she couldn't. She considered for a few minutes, then looked at Soilléir seriously.

"He was a perfect gentleman," she said honestly. "He protected me, tried his best to leave me behind when there was danger ahead, then he lied to keep me safe when we were in the great hall of Ceangail."

"Was he polite about that last bit?" Soilléir asked, politely.

"Not at all."

Soilléir smiled. "Very sensible of him. And what did you think when you found out who he was?"

"I wanted to kill him."

"Yet you rescued him instead." Soilléir finished laying the pieces out on the board. "How did you do that, exactly? Given, as it were, your . . . ah . . ."

"Lack of magic?" she finished for him. She found, to her surprise, that admitting as much to Soilléir wasn't as painful as she might otherwise have thought it would be. She shrugged. "I could see the strands of the spells woven around him."

"Could you indeed?" he asked, sitting forward. "How did you break them?"

She reached down to pull one of her knives from her boot to realize she wasn't wearing boots, she was wearing soft shoes. "I slit them with a knife Ruith bought me," she said. "I'll fetch the pair of them."

She found them on the chest where she'd found clothes, then brought them back and handed them to Soilléir.

He froze.

She started to ask him what was amiss, but before she could find her tongue, he had taken the knives and was looking at them as if he noted nothing especial about them.

"Interesting," he said with absolutely no inflection to his voice.

"Can you make out the runes?" Ruith asked, looking up from his whittling.

Soilléir set them down next to the chessboard. "I think there

might be a book in the library below that would be useful in translating them. I'll see if I can't remember the title of it." He looked at
Sarah and smiled easily. "You say you slit the spell binding Ruith
with one of them?"

"Aye," she said, sinking down into her chair. "It was easily done,
once I realized it was wrapped around him like thread around a
spindle."

"Intriguing," Soilléir said. He gestured toward the board. "Your
move, Sarah, my dear."

Intriguing was what she'd just seen—or, rather, *not* seen—in
Soilléir's reaction. There had been something about the knives
that had given him pause. She couldn't imagine what that had
been, but what did she know of any of it? He was a mage, and mages
were prone to bouts of capriciousness, as her mother would have
said.

She turned her attention to the chessboard, happy to concentrate
on something besides talk of spells and knives and things she fully
intended to have nothing to do with as soon as possible.

"A spell is an interesting thing," Soilléir said, studying the board
thoughtfully.

"Is it?" she asked, trying to sound as uninterested as possible.
She was certainly indebted to him for his many kindnesses to her so
far, but that didn't mean she had to do anything past listen politely.
"Do you use them often?"

He moved a pawn to a more advantageous place. "Actually, I
don't. I prefer to simply watch events unfold and not tamper with
them. I've found that people generally make the decisions they're
going to make without any magical sort of help from me and that
things work out as they should."

She noted the trap he was laying for her on the board and moved
to counter it. "Even if those people are black mages?"

He shrugged slightly. "Am I to turn them all into toads? We then
wouldn't be able to sleep for the noise."

Ruith snorted, but said nothing.

"But they cause so much pain," she said.

He looked up at her. "They do, my dear, but if that is their choice, who am I to take it away from them? Not all suffering is needless and not all evil is final. If there were no evil, what would there be to fight against?"

"Nothing," Ruith said with a snort, "which would leave us all warming our toes quite comfortably against our fires."

Soilléir looked at Ruith with a smile. "I think I've had this same conversation quite recently with someone else, but I can't call to mind whom. I'll think on it and tell you later."

"Your memory is failing you quite regularly this afternoon," Ruith said dryly.

"'Tis all about timing, my lad," Soilléir said, "as your lady knows now that she's distracted me from the game and I am in peril. Sarah, tell me of your plans whilst I think on a way out of this trap you've laid."

"I had no plans for a specific place," she admitted. "It was initially enough just to be free of Shettlestoune. I can earn my way by weaving, so perhaps there is some remote village somewhere in need of my particular skills." She paused. "Somewhere where I can simply be . . . well, not involved in magic any longer." She wanted to give him an entire list of reasons she loathed magic and its practitioners, but that was a little difficult when she was sitting with a man who held so much power in his hand, yet seemed so ordinary.

And also considering who was sitting there in front of the fire, making arrows for her with his own two hands. Because he'd promised her he would.

"Remote?" Soilléir asked, moving his queen to a more advantageous position. "That sounds a little unpleasant, doesn't it?"

"I'm not afraid of being alone."

He looked up. "Why would you be?"

Because whilst she wasn't afraid of being alone, she was very afraid of the dark, and she feared the dark because she'd seen in it things that would have sent her mother pitching over in a dead faint. She had seen things she couldn't possibly hope to counter with harsh words and her hunting knife that she had lost somewhere between Ceangail and Buidseachd. She didn't dare hope that even her knives that lay next to the chessboard would keep her safe. So aye, she was very afraid of the dark.

But she wasn't going to admit as much.

"We all have things that frighten us, Sarah."

"Including you?" she asked in surprise. "Surely you could simply use your magic—" But nay, he'd said he wouldn't. She supposed, judging by just looking at him, that he could defend himself well enough with a blade if he had to. Against a mortal enemy.

But a mage?

He tipped his king over. "If a spell were necessary, I would use it. Judiciously."

"If you were fighting against, say, Gair?"

Soilléir met her eyes. "Aye."

She swallowed with difficulty. "And could you, if you wanted to, go off to some far distant place and be just a man? Or would your past follow you there?"

Soilléir looked at her gravely. "Those are terrible questions I'm not sure I can answer, though I can't blame you for asking them. I also don't blame you for wishing you could leave all this behind."

"I have no magic," she said. "Nothing anyone would want me for."

He only smiled. "I think you underestimate your gifts, my dear."

But she suspected she wasn't underestimating his. She cleared her throat. "Could you tell me if my brother's still alive?"

He leaned back and looked at her for a moment or two in silence. "Aye, I could."

"But he won't," Ruith put in.

Soilléir smiled briefly at Ruith. "I think it would be unwise to."

"Even if you could sort this whole sorry business for us?" she asked, pained.

"And what would that leave you to do, Sarah?"

"Go hide in an obscure little village in the middle of farmland and weave," she muttered.

"And how would that serve you in your life's journey?" he asked mildly.

"I wouldn't be dead," she said. "Or terrified."

"Everyone dies at some point," he said with a shrug. "More important is how you live."

"And I would like to live out my life in obscurity, if it's all the same to you," she said without hesitation. "This business of mages and magic and books of spells is far beyond my ken. I would much prefer a little house with space for a loom, a fire in the hearth, and rain outside."

"It sounds as if Chagailt might be the place for you," he mused.

Sarah had her opinions on where she would have preferred to live, but even the thought of it was so far beyond her reach, she couldn't bear to think about it.

"Though perhaps not yet, for you have realities to face," he continued relentlessly. "Daniel is still out in the world, no doubt looking for more of Gair's spells. Gair's bastard sons now know a legitimate heir is alive, also looking for those same spells. And you're being hunted by trolls and mages and things you cannot see."

"*I'm* not being hunted," Sarah said hastily. She pointed to Ruith. "*He* is."

"Which is why Mosach and Táir followed after you," Soilléir said. He looked at her, clear-eyed and unperturbed. "Or do I have that wrong, my dear?"

She sees, Táir had said. Sarah wished she could forget that. She put her shoulders back.

"An aberration."

"When dealing with mages, Sarah, 'tis always best to assume that if they've stirred themselves to move away from their fires and mugs of ale, they are not pursuing an aberration."

"They'll forget about me."

"A woman who can see spells?" Soilléir asked. "An interesting talent to have, if I might offer an opinion. Some might call it magic. I suspect there are at least two mages from Ceangail who share that opinion."

Sarah felt her mouth become appallingly dry. "Are you trying to frighten me into continuing on with a quest I don't want? Or merely attempting to talk me into helping Ruith when he could be helping himself?"

"I'm only making conversation," Soilléir said. "My friend leaning against the wall behind us has heard all my conversation, so I like to trot it out with guests as often as possible and spare his ears." He began to reset the chess pieces. "But perhaps you would care for something else to do besides listen to me. I think there's a loom languishing somewhere in the bowels of the keep. I'll have it fetched for you, if you like. I might even manage to find yarn."

"I would repay you," she managed, feeling very grateful. If she could even begin to weave something, repay him somehow for the yarn, then perhaps make a bit of profit to use to buy other wool. It was a very great gift indeed.

"I'll be satisfied simply with looking at what you make," he said with a smile. He finished with the chessboard, then rose. "I'll go see what I can find."

Sarah watched him go, then looked out the window for quite some time before she could bring herself to look at Ruith. He was leaning back in his chair, a half-finished arrow across his knees, simply watching her. She took a deep breath.

"I think Daniel's dead," she offered, hoping if she said it often enough, she would begin to believe it.

Ruith only looked at her steadily. "Perhaps."

"Are you," she began, then had to clear her throat. "Are you continuing on? Looking for Gair's spells, that is."

He hesitated only briefly before he nodded.

"You'll find them," she said quickly. "I'm sure of it. You certainly won't need any help in that endeavor."

He raised his eyebrows briefly, just once.

"I can't help you," she blurted out. "I have no magic."

"Neither do I."

"Of course you do," she said, happily latching onto irritation.

It drowned out quite nicely her feelings of guilt at running away from her quest. "You just won't use it."

"You're right," he said very quietly. "Which makes it rather useless."

She found herself on her feet, though she couldn't bring herself to pace. She could only stand there with her arms wrapped around herself. "I can't go any farther with you, Ruith. The thought of . . . well, I just can't."

He looked up at her solemnly. "I understand, Sarah."

She turned and walked away from him, because it was all she could do. She couldn't help him any longer. He wasn't just traipsing after Daniel of Doìre, a bumbling mangler of spells, he was following after bastards sired by Gair of Ceangail on heaven only knew whom. Those lads were powerful beyond belief. She was a simple village witch's magic-less daughter. She couldn't hope to stand against them, and she couldn't bear to even consider facing them when all that stood between her and a horrible death by a terrible magic was Ruith's sword—which he no longer had.

She paused in her pacing and watched him bent again over his work, patiently fashioning an arrow to fit the bow he'd obviously made for her. His dark hair gleamed in the firelight, and firelight caressed what she could see of his terribly beautiful face. His long-fingered hands were sure as they worked the wood, his very aura was one of competence and knowledge—as long as one was dealing with what to put into the stewpot or how to keep the fire going.

But dealing with mages?

She couldn't believe he intended to walk into darkness and allow himself to be killed, but the forces he was facing could not be bested with ordinary weapons. And as long as that was all he was going to allow himself, she wasn't going to be anywhere near the battle.

There was nothing wrong with wanting to be simply Sarah who carded wool and spun it into yarn before she wove it into cloth, was there? She didn't have to be Sarah who saw spells and dreamed pages from Gair's book. Obviously her time in Soilléir's solar and the uncomfortable discussions she'd had with him had been more deleterious to her peace of mind than she'd feared. In truth, there was no reason to feel guilty about turning her back on her quest or worrying that Ruith might not manage his task without her.

She wondered how many times she would have to tell herself that before she began to believe it.

Seven

✦

Ruith wandered down the aisle between shelves of books, trailing his finger along the spines of tomes that had been read countless times by countless students over the course of the university's existence. It made him feel useful to be in the bowels of the keep, looking for things that might aid him in his quest. He paused to study an interesting-looking book with a tooled leather spine. He pulled it from the shelf—the librarians really should make different decisions about what sorts of things they left in circulation—then thumbed through it, making a considerable effort to pay attention to what he was reading.

He'd been making considerable efforts to do several things over the past day. He'd worked very hard at pretending to be a simple fletcher, making arrows for both himself and Sarah that he could have sold in Istaur for enough to purchase six months' worth of supplies for hiding in his mountain house. Taking the time to be about that useful labor had also allowed Sarah what he hoped was a decent bit of rest.

She had spent the day before either in conversation with Soilléir or quietly reading in front of the fire things he'd been certain were of a completely unmagical nature. Soilléir might have nudged, but he did, damn him anyway, know when to retreat from the fray.

Ruith didn't imagine he would enjoy that same sort of restraint.

Which was one of the reasons he'd escaped to the bowels of Buidseachd before sunrise that morning—after another night spent on the floor, if anyone had been curious—and trusted that Sarah would be safe inside Soilléir's solar with its bastion of spells of defense to keep her thus.

Now, he was contentedly doing a good work in looking for . . . something. He was most definitely not hiding, nor allowing others to protect him where he should have been willing to protect himself, nor avoiding thinking about his plans for the future.

He was certainly not doing the last.

He sighed deeply and put the book back in its place. As much as he would have preferred to think otherwise, the truth was that whilst he'd been pretending to be what he wasn't, the world had turned and evil had multiplied.

The question was, what was he willing to do about it?

He would have happily turned his back . . . nay, that wasn't true. He wasn't sure when it had happened, but he found he couldn't turn his back happily on anything any longer. Not on Sarah, nor his past, nor his father's spells. The truth was, he had the power to do something to make up for what his father had done, to contain what his sire had loosed. To not use that power was now almost unthinkable.

He rubbed his hands over his face. He was tired, more tired than he should have been after a life of austerity and not sleeping to avoid his dreams. There were things that troubled him deeply, things he was positive wouldn't be dealt with easily. Or without magic.

Bad enough that his bastard brothers now knew he was alive. He might have believed they would stay and hover over Ceangail like vultures, waiting for Díolain to die, but he'd seen three of them outside the keep. He'd been unsurprised to see Amitán following him—he supposed he might have insulted the man once too often in his own youth for there to have been no revenge sought—but he'd been quite alarmed to find Táir and Mosach following Sarah.

She sees, you fool, Táir had snarled at him as he'd tied the ends of their spells together in an excellent example of a weaver's knot, proving yet again that his time in Shettlestoune had been well spent. *And we'll find her and use her for our own purposes.*

Ruith hadn't said as much to Sarah, but he'd spent more than enough time thinking on just what sorts of purposes they might have for her. He would have preferred to believe his half brothers had been reeling from the battle up at the keep and imagined things about her that couldn't possibly serve them, but he couldn't. She was just as much in their sights as he was, something that unsettled him greatly. For all he knew, they wanted her to find spells they couldn't see.

He was resigned to the fact that the rest of his tangle centered around his father's spells. The trolls he could leave for later. They were obviously made from the evil of his father's well and whilst he certainly would have preferred they cease to exist, he wasn't going to waste time chasing them. Not when his father's spells were out in the world, ready and willing to be used apparently by whomever found them first—which he had to concede would include that mage who had pilfered the trio of them from the depths of his boot.

It was puzzling, that spell of Olc that had protected him. It had been, as he had reluctantly noted before, imminently suitable and very powerful. He supposed wondering who had laid it over him so carefully would take up quite some time. Determining who had managed to slit through it and take Gair's spells was even less pleasant an activity. Who would have had the power? How had that soul known he had pages from his father's book stuffed down his boots?

More unsettling still, what did that mage intend to do with what he'd found?

He turned away from that unpleasant thought to face perhaps the worst one of all which was what in the hell he was going to do in those few moments after Sarah had walked out of his life. He could easily speculate on how miserable those moments might be. If he'd

had any inkling just how miserable, he never would have opened
the door to her that first evening. He most definitely wouldn't have
followed her out of Shettlestoune—

Unbidden, a vision of a garden, the garden of Gearrannan, suddenly presented itself to him, as if it had been simply waiting for him
to stop looking at other things long enough to notice it.

He had to take several slow, deep breaths before he could manage to face the thought of that place without flinching. And once
he had control of himself, he was able to step back and consider it
rationally. It was a lovely garden, true, but it wasn't a place he had
time to visit, or even wanted to visit—

He closed his eyes and bowed his head. Nay, the truth was, the
garden of Gearrannan wasn't a place he *dared* visit. There was a particular sort of magic there, a magic that assured the king of the elves
that no undesirables would make free with his sanctuary whilst he
wasn't there to inspect the visitors himself.

Ruith let out his breath slowly. That was understating it. There
were spells of ward woven into the very fabric of that garden
that would not simply repulse anyone undesirable who attempted
entrance.

They would slay him.

He had to simply stand there in the middle of a row of books and
breathe until he thought he could look at the thought he'd avoided
thinking on for almost a se'nnight, since he'd first considered Beinn
òrain as a place to flee. The desirability of Soilléir's chambers as
a place to hide had been uppermost in his mind, of course, but he
could no longer deny that he'd had another thought as well. A wee
trial, as it were, to see just what might become of the world if he
stopped being who he wasn't and became who he had been.

If he walked to the garden of Gearrannan and put his hand on
the gate, would it let him enter, or would it slay him as it would have
slain his father had he not had a very well-developed sense of self-
preservation and retreated from its gates whilst he was still able to?

Ruith wasn't exactly sure he wanted to find out.

He realized he was cursing—not quite under his breath—only to realize that he wasn't the only one listening to himself cursing not quite under his breath. He jumped a little when he saw Soilléir leaning back against the wall at the end of the row, his arms folded over his chest, his face expressionless.

Damn, caught.

Ruith reminded himself that he was a man of thirty winters, not a lad, and he was under no obligation to answer any of what he was certain would be not the polite inquiries he'd faced before, but terribly prying and uncomfortable questions about his motives, his ambitions, and his heart. He wouldn't answer them, not even out of courtesy. He continued on his way to the end of the shelves, stopped, then inclined his head.

"My lord."

Soilléir only continued to study him, as if he searched for something he'd hoped to find there. Good sense, perhaps. Ruith returned his look steadily. The man hadn't come to make certain he wouldn't perish from fatigue over reading too much or outright death from slices to his fingers from pages of books with minds of their own. If there was one thing that could be counted on in the world, it was that Soilléir of Cothromaiche didn't indulge in idle conversation or haphazard visits.

Soilléir nodded to his left. Ruith didn't want to but followed him as he walked away, because he had decent manners.

But as he followed, he cursed himself. Not because of the pointed questions he knew were coming his way—he had watched Soilléir pester his mother, after all—and not because they were questions that needed to be answered, but because he was uncomfortable in his own skin. The truth was, he wanted none of what was being thrust upon him, nothing to do with his bastard brothers and his father's arrogance and idiocy, not one more moment wasted in being brought up hard against the consequences of actions he hadn't made himself and therefore shouldn't be responsible for.

How much simpler it would have been to be in his house on the side of a forlorn mountain, baking his bread, enjoying his stews, and indulging in Master Franciscus's lovely apple-flavored ale.

Though perhaps a little bit less like a man's life than the life of a child.

He rubbed his hands over his face and wished he indulged in hard liquor. He was fairly certain that with enough time and effort, he could drink himself into oblivion and keep himself there for quite some time. If he had difficulty at the task, perhaps he could send word to Adhémar of Neroche for advice on how the like was most easily accomplished.

"He's an ass," Soilléir said mildly over his shoulder, "but not a drunkard."

"Stop that," Ruith said in annoyance.

Soilléir only smiled and opened the door to a chamber Ruith hadn't known existed. That was surprising because he'd certainly done his share of investigating during his visits to Buidseachd in his youth. His brothers Rùnach and Gille had been happy to investigate the bowels of the keep with him, having themselves been on a constant search for obscure, ancient texts that might have contained something to contain their father. Ruith could bring to mind more than one scolding his older brothers had had from their grandfather for inciting insurrections in the other grandchildren and great-grandchildren who had run wildly about Seanagarra when their parents hadn't been watching.

He sat down on a stool pulled up to a worktable and looked at the crumbling manuscripts stacked there in a scholarly sort of disarray along with a bookmaker's tools for the restorations of said crumbling texts. He glanced at Soilléir.

"Are you an archivist now?"

Soilléir shook his head with a faint smile. "'Tis my assistant—if that's what he could be called—who labors with these. I just come now and again to see what he's dug up."

Rùnach would have been teary-eyed with joy over what Ruith could see were more stacks of things to be pored over placed carefully on shelves against one wall. He sighed, then looked again at the keeper of dangerous spells.

"Well?"

Soilléir looked perfectly comfortable perched on the other stool. "I'm curious about a thing or two."

Ruith pursed his lips. "I imagine you are."

"'Tis what makes a good mage, Ruithneadh."

"And you are that, Master Soilléir."

Soilléir winced briefly, as if something about that reply grieved him somehow. Ruith couldn't begin to presume to guess what that might have been, so he settled for steeling himself against questions he wasn't going to enjoy.

"Why did you come here?" Soilléir asked, apparently having decided that making polite conversation before beginning the inquisition was unnecessary. "In truth?"

"I told you yesterday: for refuge."

"You could have found that at Seanagarra."

You were closer was halfway out of his mouth before he called it back, because it wasn't true. "I needed time to think in a place where Sarah would be protected."

"You have magic," Soilléir pointed out. "Why didn't you use it?"

"Do you need to ask me that again?" Ruith answered, more sharply than he'd intended. Damn that Soilléir. Was there not a time in his life he could dance about a hurt for a bit instead of stabbing it straight to the heart?

Soilléir wrapped his hands around one knee and leaned back a bit, assuming a pose that belonged to a man of a score, not a man of a score of centuries. "You know, Ruithneadh, vows made in one's youth are often rash."

Ruith had no patience for where he knew Soilléir was heading. "I believe we discussed this at length before."

"I thought it merited further scrutiny."

Ruith shifted to face him fully. "Then allow me to satisfy your curiosity fully, my lord. I don't use magic because I have rattling around in my wee head almost every last bloody spell that my father ever used. I imagine I could write down for you almost all the spells in his damned book and likely improve upon them because I've dreamed them every night of my bloody life, despite how I've managed to ignore that fact during the days."

Soilléir only continued to watch him, unblinking, pitiless, and in his own impossible way, demanding.

"Very well, here's more," Ruith said, taking a deep breath. "Almost a month ago, I stood in that accursed glade near Ceangail where my father slew my entire family, unleashed all my wondrous power, and killed three dozen trolls with Olc as easily if I'd been swatting flies. I suffered no ill effects save a weariness that rendered me senseless for several days, but the trolls, however, were very much worse for the wear, which says much about the unwieldiness of my power." He had to take another deep breath, because he found he was shaking. "I don't use that power, my lord, because I am so full of rage, a foolish, ten-year-old's rage, that I can scarce bear it."

"Ruith, that's understandable—"

"Would you give me the spells of Caochladh?" Ruith asked flatly. "Would you trust me with them?"

"All of them, Ruithneadh?" Soilléir asked mildly, "or just a few?"

"A pair of them," Ruith snarled, "damn you to hell. A pair of *my* choosing."

Soilléir studied him for several minutes in silence. "And if I were to allow you to make free with my collection of spells capable of truly undoing the world and all in it, which ones would you want?"

Ruith looked at him steadily. "Return and Alchemy."

There was a noise, followed by a curse. That might have been Soilléir tipping so far backward in surprise that he only saved himself from an undignified sprawl because he was, as Ruith had noted before, fairly spry for a man of his advanced years. Soilléir put his hand on the stool to steady himself and looked at Ruith in surprise. "Why Return?"

"So I could bring my father back to life."

Soilléir sat down. "To what end?"

"To take your very elegant spell of Alchemy," Ruith said shortly, "and turn him into a rock, after which I would walk back to his damned well, open it, then drop him inside to fall endlessly into the evil he loved so much."

"I think you've given this a bit of thought," Soilléir managed.

"I think you're right," Ruith said. He realized his hands were clenched into fists, so he forced himself to lay them flat on his thighs. "And since we are discussing this fascinating topic, let us say, my lord, that I were to take the afternoon, stroll into the council of the masters and show them exactly what they wanted to know to earn their paltry bits of gold and silver to wear on my fingers. Then let us continue down this path of madness that finds me trotting back into your solar to present myself to you as an aspirant. Would you give me your spells?"

Soilléir studied him in silence for a moment or two. "Could you convince me to give them to you?"

"Have you not already seen what lies at the bottom of my soul?" Ruith countered. "Can you not already divine where the point is that you could break me?"

Soilléir sat back down and looked at him gravely. "I know where that point is, Ruithneadh. The question is, do you?"

Ruith didn't fall off his own stool, but he came damned close. Nay, he didn't know where the breaking point of his own soul was, but he had the feeling he knew exactly where he could learn the location of that unhappy place. All he needed to do was walk through Buidseachd's front gates, follow that unseen path that would lead to his grandfather's garden, then attempt entrance into a place that would be a far better judge of his own capacity for evil than any mortal.

He looked at Soilléir, but couldn't muster up even a halfhearted glare. "You are a heartless bastard," he managed.

"I know."

"You were never this vicious to my mother."

"Your mother never wanted any of my spells."

"And if she'd asked for them?"

"Ruith, my friend, I would have given your mother anything she wanted," Soilléir said with a deep sigh. He studied his hands for a moment or two, then looked up. "Do you want them? In truth?"

"Don't ask," Ruith said, shaking his head sharply. "I've no stomach for joining the ranks of those you've shown where their souls will shatter. I can only imagine who is on that very short list."

Soilléir smiled. "I imagine you could name a pair of them."

"Yngerame of Wychweald," Ruith said without hesitation. "He couldn't resist complaining about you to my grandfather every chance he had. I remember one particular evening when he described in great detail just how heartless you could be."

"He just wanted to ingratiate himself with Sìle so he wouldn't have to spend the night in the stables, no doubt," Soilléir said dryly. "I don't imagine Desdhemar of Neroche was that unkind." He frowned. "Or her son, though I imagine you haven't had a chance to discuss the same with him."

Ruith felt his mouth fall open. "Adhémar?" he asked incredulously. "You gave your spells to *Adhémar*?"

"Nay, to Miach," Soilléir said with a smile, "but you would have realized that, had you thought about it long enough."

"Did he crawl out of your solar when you were finished with him?" Ruith asked sourly. "Or did you just toss him out into the passageway and hope for the best?"

"He walked, if not a little unsteadily," Soilléir said gravely. "But he was but a lad of ten-and-six when he'd passed all my tests. And he hasn't used any of my spells . . . yet."

"Which means Adhémar still sits on his throne, instead of lounging on a lily pad in the back garden," Ruith said with a snort. "Though how Miach bears him, I'll never know."

"Actually, Adhémar is now residing somewhere quite a bit less comfortable, but I won't bother you with the details since you're not terribly interested in the goings-on in the Nine Kingdoms."

Ruith blinked. "What are you talking about?"

"Are you referring to your disinterest in the realms of the world or Adhémar's fate?"

Ruith glared at him. "I never said I wasn't interested. At least in the former."

"Careful, Ruith," Soilléir said mildly. "You might find yourself getting involved in things that will require more than sitting in front of your fire and avoiding Fate's heavy hand."

Ruith found himself on his feet, pacing, without truly knowing how he'd come to be doing it. He turned to Soilléir and folded his arms across his chest. "What happened to Adhémar?"

Soilléir looked up at him. "He was riding the border with his lovely bride, Adaira of Penrhyn—"

"A perfect choice."

"Miach thought so too," Soilléir agreed. "Unfortunately, she might be regretting her choice now given that her husband was too stupid to take the sort of guard he needed and both of them now find themselves unwilling guests of Neroche's neighbor to the north."

"Lothar?" Ruith asked in astonishment.

"The very same."

"What an idiot," Ruith said without hesitation. "Adhémar, I mean."

"Agreed," Soilléir said. He looked up tranquilly. "Very foolish to take one's lady anywhere close to a nasty sort of mage when one has no magic to protect that lady." He paused. "Wouldn't you agree?"

Ruith started to agree, then realized just what Soilléir had said. He wished the words felt less like a kick in the gut. He wished he'd not been so stupid as to fail to continually remind himself that with Soilléir of Cothromaiche, conversation was rarely just words. He had to take a handful of decent breaths before he could speak with any success.

"Do you ever just talk for the pleasure of it?" he managed.

"Only to myself."

Ruith closed his eyes briefly. "I would say I loathed you, but I am not a silly serving wench."

Soilléir shrugged. "What else am I to do with you, Ruith? Slap your good sense back into you?"

"It wouldn't work."

"I didn't think it woul—"

Ruith realized that Soilléir had stopped bludgeoning him with things he didn't want to listen to only when he realized someone else was talking in a hoarse, ruined voice that made him flinch just listening to it. He turned around to find Soilléir's servant standing at the doorway.

"The young miss," he rasped. "I left her at her loom whilst I went to fetch her something to eat. When I returned—"

Ruith leapt forward only to run into Soilléir's outstretched arm. He cursed, but the words died on his lips when he realized Soilléir was looking for Sarah.

That Seeing magic was . . . well, it was damned spooky, that's what it was. He could see spells, of course, and he had been, in his youth, able to hear the sentient things in Tòrr Dòrainn—brooks that laughed as they bubbled and flowers that sang as they bloomed. He'd been able to remain unaffected by elvish glamour cast by his grandfather. He'd heard rumors that some kings could see what was passing in their realms, though most of those sorts of tales had come from Neroche. He had assumed, over the years, that Adhémar's sight had been limited to the quickest path to the ale kegs in every village pub cellar, but perhaps he'd been mistaken about that.

But Soilléir's craft of sight?

It was unsettling.

Soilléir swore suddenly. "She's walking toward Droch's garden."

Ruith pushed past him, but Soilléir caught him by the arm. "And just where do you think *you're* going?"

"I'm going to rescue her, of course," Ruith said.

Soilléir shot him a look. "With what magic, Ruith?"

"I don't need—"

"Don't be a fool," Soilléir said sharply. "Against Droch? You cannot aid her with good intentions."

Ruith supposed over the course of his life several things had stung him to the very quick. His father telling him he would never be his equal was one. Sarah telling him she couldn't bear to be within five paces of him was another. Soilléir telling him in not so many words that he hadn't the skill to fight the master of Olc, the master of the magic his father had taken and twisted in ways that Droch envied to the depths of his soul.

It was almost enough to make him reconsider his vow of magical celibacy, as it were.

"Go back to my solar and wait," Soilléir said shortly. "We'll be there presently."

Ruith dragged his hand through his hair and hesitated. He had never hesitated in his life and it galled him to the depths of his soul to do so now.

Nay, that wasn't what galled him. It was being sent back to the house like a woman whilst another man went off to rescue the woman he loved.

"You cannot aid her," Soilléir repeated.

Ruith would have cursed Soilléir, but it was difficult to condemn someone else for telling the truth. He couldn't fight against Droch's spells with a sword, and he couldn't fight off the spells of death he knew Droch would throw at him the very moment he realized whom he had within reach.

But he would be damned if he would go upstairs and wait like a woman.

Eight

❧

Sarah began to suspect she might have taken a wrong turn.

The journey to her current location had started out quite innocently, actually. She'd woken to find Ruith gone but a loom waiting for her in the corner of Soilléir's chamber. She'd happily spent part of the morning weaving, but found that whilst the warp threads had been innocuous enough, the yarn Master Soilléir had found for her to use was full of things she hadn't expected, tales she hadn't wanted to listen to gathered up with the roving, memories and magic she hadn't wanted to be a part of spun into the wool. Not that any of it had been unpleasant; it had just been too much to look at. She liked her yarn to be just yarn, in colors she had made herself without any magic attached. She definitely didn't like it to feel like a live thing under her hands.

She had remembered, as she'd sat at that loom, a particular fire she'd seen along their journey to follow Daniel. Seirceil of Coibhneas had made it, but as she'd sat there, she'd seen other things dancing along the wood. She realized now that it had most likely been Ruith to add those little touches. It had been elven magic, of that she was now certain.

It had been beautiful.

That memory had pushed her to her feet and left her hastily snatching up a cloak before she left Soilléir's chambers and went for a walk to clear her head. Not that being outside in the passageways was much of a help in that. The entire place was crawling with spells, though she'd realized that if she closed her eyes, it wasn't so obvious.

Of course that had presented the unforeseen hazard of almost running afoul of trouble.

She was almost on top of the men whispering furtively together before she had time to open her eyes and see them. She pulled back quickly and, as an afterthought, pretended to fuss with something in her shoe. No sense in giving an overzealous mage a reason to question why she was where she found herself.

"But my master wants a parley with *him*."

"No one parleys with *him* without a damned good reason," said the second man, making a sound of impatience. "Look, friend, I slipped you in the back door because we've done business before, but—"

"I have a spell."

Sarah felt something slither down her spine, which was remarkable given where she was and the quantity of spells she imagined were surrounding her. She also thought she might have recognized one of the voices. It was the man who had come in the gates behind her and Ruith that first day.

He was Droch's servant, Tom.

"What sort of spell?" Tom asked.

"Wouldn't you like to know," the other man said with a snort, "and I'm not telling. My master told me to just bring a corner of it, for proof."

"And did you?"

"Better than that. I tore the whole thing to pieces and brought a pair of scraps."

"And just where did you hide the rest?"

"I'm not sayin', but if things go south for me—if you know what I mean—I'll scatter the bloody thing about and make my exit before my master can catch me."

"Powerful is your master, is he?"

"Stupid, more's the like." The other man laughed. "But young and arrogant. From Shettlestoune, if you can believe it. Thinks he'll trade a spell for a ring, I daresay. Worse still, thinks Droch is the one who gives 'em out."

"Stupid, indeed."

Sarah could scarce believe her ears. From Shettlestoune? How many mages once possessing pages of spells could possibly come from Shettlestoune? It wasn't possible that Daniel had stolen the spells back from Ruith.

Was it?

There was a long pause. "Seems a shame to waste a decent spell on someone that stupid, don't it?" the first man mused.

"What are you suggesting?"

"A bit of pocket lining."

"Gold won't mean much to you if you're dead," Tom warned. "And Droch doesn't like to be played."

"I wasn't thinking of playing *him*."

There was again silence for a very long time, then a grunt of assent. Sarah listened to their footsteps recede and made a quick decision. Of course she still planned to go off to seek her own fortunes—most likely in the morning—but there was no reason she couldn't at least ferret out a bit of information that Ruith could possibly use to find his father's spells. He was going to need help, especially since she wasn't going to be there to dream their location for him.

She pulled her hood more closely around her face and walked around the corner as if she had every right to. She continued on, following the two men in front of her into a passageway that seemed to be quite a bit colder than the one she'd just left. She thought that observation might have been something simply conjured up by her frenzied mind, then she realized that not only was the passageway growing cold, it was growing dark as well. The men faded, then disappeared as if they'd never been there.

She had almost decided it was time to panic and turn around, when the passageway ended and she walked out into a garden.

It was like nothing she'd ever seen before and never could have imaged existed. She set aside thoughts of the men she'd been following—indeed she suddenly couldn't remember why she'd been following them—and was enveloped in a feeling of profound pleasure, a secret sort of pleasure, as if only she could have been clever enough to have found such a place. Haunting music filled the air, music that she was suddenly certain only she could hear, a song that wrapped itself around her like a luxurious cloak fit for a princess. She pulled it closer to her, then lifted her face up and found that the sky was obscured with something. That might have bothered her at another time, but since that spell seemed to be keeping most of the rain off her face, she wasn't going to complain. She turned her attentions instead to the long, lush space that stretched out in front of her.

There was a path beneath her feet, carpeted with soft moss that led toward a small flower garden so gloriously colored that it seemed a lush oasis in the middle of the desert where she was parched with thirst. There was a bench at the end of the path, a bench that sat under a tree that beckoned to her with dozens of branches that turned into delicate fingers.

She paused. She knew that was wrong, but somehow she couldn't bring herself to make anything of it. There was a cushion on the bench and a little table within easy reach, a table laden with luscious-looking fruits and a pitcher of something cool. She could tell it was cool because condensation had beaded up on the glass, dripping down to pool gently at the base, as if a well had overflowed and spilled its contents over its side.

That was wrong, too, that image. It reminded her of that cobalt bottle of potion in her mother's workroom that her brother had stolen from her and left sitting on his table next to a spell that had reached up and wrapped itself around her arm. Her arm burned with renewed vigor, which troubled her. Remembering the spell troubled her as well, because it made her think of black mages and wells of power and castles covered in spells . . .

She pulled herself away from those memories and concentrated on the garden in front of her, because it was a welcome relief from things that disturbed her.

A wide swath of marble lay between her and the bench, marble that glistened from the gentle rain that fell. She put her foot on it, walked a few paces, then had to stop. The scent coming from the flowers blooming by the bench was so overwhelming, she found herself almost turning away from it. Or she would have if she hadn't been so mesmerized by it.

In time as she managed to take another pair of steps across the marble pavers, the smell became less troubling than intoxicating. She took another deep breath, then another step forward.

She studied the flagstones beneath her feet, wondering why it was they were alternating blocks of grey and black, then realized she wasn't alone. She looked up to find a man now standing behind the bench, all strength and terrible beauty. He was smiling pleasantly, holding his hands open, as if he invited her to come enjoy the coolness of the contents of the pitcher on the delicate table, the shelter of the tree, and the comfort of a place to sit and be safe.

Safe.

The very thought of it was such a profound relief, she started to walk forward—

Only to find herself distracted by something she couldn't quite hear. It bothered her, that sound, interrupting the music and buzzing against her ear. She swatted it away in annoyance and tried to concentrate on what was in front of her. The buzzing didn't abate; it increased. It took several minutes, but she finally realized that it wasn't a fly or a bee troubling her, it was a voice coming from behind her.

Sarah.

She looked over her shoulder. Soilléir was standing there, quite a ways away, as it happened, surrounded by a rather ordinary light that

seemed dull when compared to the glorious sparkle of what she'd
been walking toward. She realized it was his voice she was hearing,
cutting across the music and fraying it at the edges. She wondered
why he'd followed her, then found herself growing increasingly
annoyed at him that he'd interrupted the first moment of true pleasure she'd had since Ruith had dragged her into a place she hadn't
wanted to go. She frowned at him, then turned away, back to what
was so much more appealing.

Sarah!

"Sarah, is it?" the dark-haired, exceptionally handsome man in
front of her said, still smiling. "What a lovely name. And how fortunate that you are here in time for luncheon."

Sarah couldn't have agreed more. She wasn't sure she'd eaten in
Soilléir's chamber. She'd been weaving, true, and trying to ignore
Soilléir's servant, who had simply stood in his accustomed place near
the window, swathed in robe and cowl, no doubt keeping watch over
her that she didn't poach any of his master's more valuable texts. If
he hadn't gone on his self-appointed mission to fetch her something
to eat, she never would have managed to escape Soilléir's chamber,
she was certain of that—

"Sarah!"

Sarah paused in mid-step and frowned a bit more. That wasn't
Soilléir. When Soilléir said her name, his voice washed across her
mind in a particularly magelike way. This new voice was nothing
more than some fool standing behind her and shouting.

She turned back over her shoulder to see a man standing next
to Soilléir, someone who wasn't covered in light, however garish.
She realized, with a start, that it was Ruith. He and Soilléir began
to argue, which somehow annoyed her more than their calling her
had. Their voices grated on her and made her feel very out of sorts.

Not like the man in front of her. The more she looked at him, the
more at peace she felt. Best of all, he didn't look like he would use a
spell unless the welcoming smile on his face could be called magic.
She happily turned her back on Ruith and Soilléir both, ignored Soilléir's repeated calling of her name, then took another step forward.

She paused, because it suddenly felt to her as if the world held its breath for something truly unprecedented. She couldn't believe that could be for her sake, so she took another step forward—

And the world rent in twain.

Or, more precisely, she did.

It was the most horrendous, terrifying, *unbearable* thing that had ever happened to her. If having Gair's spell attack her arm had been painful, this was agony. She dropped to her knees, feeling as if her body had been torn from her, leaving her kneeling there on the hard, wet marble in her soul alone.

And then she opened her eyes.

And she saw.

She wasn't standing in the middle of a garden; she was standing in the middle of death. The flowers should have been flowers, but they were actually thorns pretending to be flowers. The moss wasn't a soft carpet beneath her feet, it was the putrid leavings of spells that had been cast aside like refuse. The bench was a cage built to trap and hold those foolish enough to wander under a sky that wasn't overcast, it was full of dank, rotted spells of Olc. She could see them writhing and twisting in a wind of their own making, reaching out for her.

She looked at the master of Olc—and she now knew him for who he was—and didn't manage to even open her mouth to cry out before his spell slammed into her, stealing her breath. The only reason it didn't steal her life was because of what Soilléir had thrown over her the split second before Droch had cast his spell. As it was, Droch's spell sent her sprawling back along the marble. She crawled to her feet, then looked down in horror at what she was standing on.

It was a chessboard.

She knew without being told that Droch had intended her to be one of the pieces.

Soilléir stepped in front of her suddenly and faced Droch. Sarah would have warned him to be careful, but she supposed he knew that already. That, and she feared that if she opened her mouth, sounds would come out that would terrify them all.

She was pulled backward. She knew it was Ruith even though she had closed her eyes to the terrible battle going on in front of her. Unfortunately, that didn't seem to help, as she could see it just the same.

Droch and Soilléir were fighting with spells. Droch's were easily identified for what they were. Soilléir's, though, were not. They sounded familiar—or at least the language did—but she couldn't place it. Then again, her education was perhaps not what it should have been in order to find herself moving comfortably in such a high and lofty place as the schools of wizardry.

She realized she was babbling—in her own head, no less—but she found she couldn't stop. To say she was terrified was to completely understate the chill that enveloped her. To think how close she had come to walking willingly into not death but something far worse . . .

"Let's go," Ruith said hoarsely.

She couldn't move. Ruith must have realized that as well when he almost wrenched her arm from her shoulder.

"I can't get my feet free," she said, feeling terribly alarmed. Actually, *alarmed* didn't describe it. She was completely panicked. She looked at Ruith, who was now standing in front of her. "Help me—nay, you cannot. Soilléir must—"

He cursed, then looked about himself, presumably for something to use in getting her feet free of spells she could see had already wrapped themselves over her toes and were now beginning to crawl up to her ankles. She pulled one of her knives out of the back of the belt of her dress, bent, and slit the spells, leaving them waving frantically, just as the ones she'd cut in Ceangail had done.

The smell of them was so vile, she almost lost her breakfast right there in the midst of more spells that sprang up out of nothing and reached for her.

Ruith swung her up in his arms and carried her out of the garden.

"What of Soilléir?"

"He'll manage."

"Can't you help—" she began, then she shut her mouth. Of course he couldn't help. Well, he perhaps *could* have, but she knew he wouldn't.

Though after what she'd seen, she could understand why he was so adverse to magic in general and Olc in particular. She felt a rush of sympathy for his poor mother, having had to endure all those years in Ceangail with its halls slathered in vile spells. She wondered how often Sarait had been there, if she'd managed to shield herself and her children from the brunt of that horrible magic, if Gair had ever been anything but darkness.

She wondered what horrors Ruith had been subjected to, having spent even a part of his youth in that terrible place.

All of which reminded her that since she didn't want anything to do with magic and mages, she couldn't have anything to do with Ruith.

"I can walk," she said, trying to crawl out of his arms.

He let her down reluctantly, but put his arm around her shoulders. She would have told him she didn't need any help, but she wasn't entirely sure she could manage any sort of escape on her own. It was all she could do to resheath her knife.

She stumbled along a stone-floored corridor worn smooth by the passage of countless boots over the centuries, then finally had to close her eyes against the sight of the trails left behind by those feet, shadows she certainly hadn't been able to see earlier but now could for some reason.

Simple. Unmagical. Very far away from anything to do with mages. Aye, that was the life for her. She finally gathered enough strength from that thought to push away from Ruith—

Only to step forward, then fall flat on her face. She realized at that moment that she was so ill, she wasn't entirely certain she wouldn't sick up her breakfast on the first thing that moved in front of her eyes. She had never drunk anything stronger than Master Franciscus's mildest ale—and that sparingly—but she had once smelled something her mother had brewed which had made her almost as ill as she felt now, as if she couldn't scrub the smell or its terrible aftereffects out of her skull.

Ruith's hand was suddenly against her forehead, smoothing her hair back from her face.

"I can't move," she whispered.

"'Tis the spells."

"I'm going to be ill."

"Well, we're in front of Droch's door," Ruith said quietly. "It might be fitting."

She would have heaved herself to her feet and bolted, but she found she could only rest her cheek against the cold stone passageway floor and keep her eyes closed. Ruith continued to stroke her hair, as if he sought to comfort her.

And then suddenly, he was pulling her up and into his arms. "Hold on."

Sarah felt the world spin wildly, but she'd heard the shouting as well and had no desire to find herself sprawled in the passageway in front of Droch's door whilst Droch was trying to get inside his chamber to put his feet up in front of the fire and grumble about conquests unmade. She clapped her hand over her mouth and kept her gorge down where it belonged through sheer willpower alone.

Ruith stopped eventually and used his foot to bang on a door. The door opened, then a man gasped. Ruith pushed into a chamber, sending that someone stumbling backward. Sarah didn't protest as Ruith carried her a bit longer, then set her down in a chair. She leaned her head back against the wood and kept her eyes closed, trying not to tremble.

She failed miserably. She shook so hard, her teeth chattered. She wasn't sure what had been worse, being so beguiled by Olc that she had come within a heartbeat of casting herself into its depths or finding herself suddenly aware of just what she had thought so beautiful.

She wondered if Gair had ever been in that place, or if he had realized all along what he was doing, chasing after the illusion that was Olc.

She opened her eyes and looked at Ruith, who was sitting on a low stool in front of her, watching her closely. The worry in his eyes was difficult to look at. Worry, and something else, actually.

Shame.

She would have told him that wasn't necessary, but she found she couldn't speak. And that was because she was suddenly seeing things she had never seen before in her life, things she'd never dreamed existed.

The man sitting in front of her was Ruith, true, but he was suddenly somehow much more than that. He was his house in the mountains, built from rock that had sent down taproots deep into the earth, immovable, stark, implacably resolute. Yet beside that house, around it, under it, were springs that should have bubbled up and flowed down to form a mighty, rushing river full of magic. She could see the place where the river should have been running through his soul, where the magic would laugh with delight as it tumbled over rock and falls, always pure and full of the birthright of generations of his ancestors who had been full of magic themselves. Aye, there was Olc as well, but it wasn't part of him. It had fixed itself to the windows of his house, crowding out the light, making things seem other than they were.

But it wasn't part of him.

She heard the door slam behind her and flinched at the riotously colored spell of protection that sprang up all along the ceiling, draped immediately down all the walls, spread out instantly over the entire floor. It was lovely, true, yet hard as steel and just as impervious.

"Damn him to hell," Soilléir snarled as he strode over to the fireplace. "I vow one day . . ." He swore a bit more, then cast himself down into a chair by the fire and let out his breath slowly. He put his fingers over his eyes. "Hate is unhealthy."

Ruith only pursed his lips.

Sarah found she couldn't look at Soilléir with any more ease than she'd looked at Ruith. Whereas Ruith was relatively spartan when it came to who he was and how he'd allowed himself to grow, Soilléir was a towering thunderstorm full of power and might and magic that she couldn't begin to fathom. She blinked and found that he had suddenly changed, becoming as gentle as sunlight filtering down through spring leaves in a small, intimate glade. She supposed he was somehow, incomprehensibly, both.

She pulled herself back into herself to find him watching her with a faint smile.

"Forgive me, Sarah, my dear," he said quietly. "I could have done that better."

"Done what better?" Ruith asked sharply.

"Opened her eyes," Soilléir said. "I was, unfortunately, in a good deal of haste."

"What," Sarah croaked, "did you do?"

Soilléir rubbed his hands together as if they pained him, much as Ruith had done that first night when they'd been talking about . . . well, she couldn't remember what they'd been talking about. She just remembered how Ruith had looked, as if his hands had wrought something that had distressed him somehow.

"It would seem," Soilléir said with a bit of a smile, "that you have a gift for Seeing."

"Is it magic?" she asked hoarsely.

He smiled briefly. "Not in the sense you're thinking, I daresay, but I suppose there is something . . . unusual about it."

"How did you—never mind." She put her hand over her eyes. "I don't want to know how you knew."

"I imagine you don't," he agreed. "I think we can perhaps simply concede that you were walking into danger and the most expedient way to get you out of it was to help you see the truth for yourself."

Sarah wasn't sure she could muster up any thanks, nor was she entirely sure what she should be thanking him for. She was too busy simply trying to breathe in and out. That didn't help the nausea she was feeling or the way the chamber was not just the chamber, but a place now filled with spells and essences of those around her and sights she had never before imagined. She jumped a little when she realized someone was standing next to her, holding out a cup of wine with his ruined hands. She accepted it, then looked up at the man still hovering there.

"Thank you, Prince Rùnach," she whispered.

Ruith leapt to his feet, sending his stool flying into Soilléir's knees and himself almost pitching back into the fire. "What did you say?" he asked incredulously.

"Well, that is his name," she said, feeling a little defensive. "I can see it woven into his soul. Can't you?"

Ruith's mouth was working, but no sound came out.

"Do you know him?" she asked. She turned to Soilléir. "Did I say something amiss?"

Soilléir only shook his head slightly, a very small smile on his face.

Sarah focused on Ruith with an effort. The blood had drained from his face, and he looked as if he might pitch forward onto her lap at any moment. He took a deep breath, then put his hands over hers to help her drink—though his hands weren't much steadier than hers—then took the cup away and set it aside. He then turned to Soilléir's servant, looked at him for several minutes in absolute silence, then lifted the cowl back from his face. Sarah couldn't say she was at her best, but even she could see well enough to mark the astonishing resemblance between the two.

And then she realized the truth.

They were brothers.

She realized she was pitching forward only because she heard Ruith bark something at Soilléir that sounded remarkably like, *I'll see to her myself this time, Master Soilléir, thank you just the same.*

Or words to that effect. Sarah wasn't sure of anything until she felt softness against her back. She looked up to find Ruith leaning over her. His expression of devastation almost matched what she felt. She reached up and put her hand against his cheek.

"I understand," she managed, her voice sounding as harsh as a crow's cry in her ears. "About the magic."

He blinked. "What do you mean?"

"About Olc," she whispered, finding that the chamber was starting to contract around her. "Why you don't want to use your magic. Why you want none of . . . that."

He only looked at her in silence, his eyes full of what she'd seen.

She now understood. He had, more than once, put himself between her and that evil for no other reason than to protect her.

"This is why you said those things to me in Ceangail," she murmured, feeling her eyes close relentlessly. "To spare me that."

"Aye," he said very quietly.

"I wish I'd never gone inside in the first place."

"You can blame that fully on me," he said in a low voice. "I should have left you behind, but I didn't because I am an idiot. Because I thought I needed you to find the spells. Because I thought you'd be safer with me than with Franciscus. Because I am, again, a fool of the first water."

She almost managed a smile. "That's more than you've said to me in a fortnight."

"You told me to keep my mouth shut."

"Only when we're facing black mages with your death on their minds."

Which, she supposed, hadn't been that day. She'd come face-to-face with a black mage, but it hadn't been Ruith's death he'd had on his mind.

It had been hers.

She felt herself falling into blackness and surrendered to it willingly.

Nine

Ruith watched Sarah slip into what he hoped was a peaceful, dreamless sleep, then straightened and turned to face
the other occupants of the chamber. Soilléir was standing near
his hearth, watching him gravely. Rùnach, the one who had been
masquerading as Soilléir's servant, was standing next to Soilléir,
his cowl pushed back from his ruined face, his expression equally
grave. Ruith wondered if his brother would have revealed himself
if Sarah hadn't done it for him, or if he would have remained in the
shadows.

The thought of that was, he had to admit, absolutely devastating.

He walked over to his brother, put his arms around him, and
fought the urge to break down and bawl like a bairn. Rùnach
returned the embrace, slapped him a time or two on the back with
hands Ruith had already seen were not up to that task, then pulled
back and kissed Ruith on both cheeks.

"Ruith," he said, sounding enormously pleased.

Ruith dragged his sleeve across his eyes. "I can't believe you said nothing."

"I'm discreet," Rùnach said, shooting Soilléir a look. He turned back to Ruith. "I thought you were dead, you wee fool," he said, in his voice that sounded quite a bit like branches scraping against a sheet of glass. "Léir, of course, has said nothing to me during these long years to dissuade me from such an assumption."

"Predictable," Ruith said darkly. "And nay, I'm not dead, but 'twas a very near thing. And at the moment I think I'm very near to falling upon my arse from shock. Perhaps we could sit until I'm recovered."

Rùnach stepped back. "I'll fetch chairs—"

"Of course you won't," Ruith said. "I'll see to it." He started to walk away, then looked at Soilléir. He had to take a careful breath before he trusted himself to speak instead of doing his host bodily harm. "Thank you."

"You're welcome," Soilléir said quietly.

"I don't suppose you have anything else to say to me, do you? Siblings to reveal, censure to offer, reminders of my inability to face anything but supper and come away the victor?"

Soilléir smiled faintly. "I believe my work is done with all three. I'll go pace through the halls and stir up mischief. You and your brother have things to discuss, I imagine."

"You could have told me about him," Ruith said in a low voice.

"Rùnach is not my servant," Soilléir said with a shrug. "I do not reveal secrets that aren't mine."

"It would be so much easier to dislike you if you would just be wrong. Once."

Soilléir clucked his tongue. "Unkind."

"But poetically just. I would like to see it, perhaps when you're undone by a woman, or trying to win a woman, or finding yourself turned about by a woman."

"I'll watch you a bit longer and see how the solving of that tangle is managed," Soilléir said before he clapped Ruith on the shoulder and walked away. "You might consider taking her for a walk later, Ruithneadh. She'll no doubt want to be free of the university for a bit."

Ruith wasn't about to ask him how he knew that, or exactly what he had done to make her see what she'd walked into, or what that meant for her now. He would ask before the day was out, but he supposed even Sarah wouldn't begrudge him a moment or two with a sibling he'd thought was dead.

He drew chairs up to the fire, then sat and looked at the brother he hadn't seen in a score of years.

"What happened to you?" he asked, when he thought he could speak without weeping.

"After?"

Ruith nodded.

Rùnach shrugged. "Mother covered me with her power as she died, so the well didn't kill me, but it rendered me senseless. By the time I regained my wits and managed to get my hands free of the stone, the bodies, save Mother's, were gone." He paused for a rather long moment. "I had no power—Father took it, of course—and no strength. I crawled away and hoped I could find a place to hide."

Ruith understood completely. What he couldn't bear to think on, however, was his brother having lost his power. Rùnach had been a master mage, endlessly searching for spells, continually testing them, improving upon them, making them more than they had been before. Elegant, powerful, resistant to evil—

He took a deep breath and looked at his brother. "Why didn't you go home or to Lake Cladach?" he asked, realizing Soilléir had asked him the same thing.

Rùnach's laugh was faint and humorless. "To have those at Seanagarra pity me my ruined hands and lack of magic? To have Grandmother Eulasaid fret over how to restore either—or both? Nay, Ruith, both places were closed to me."

"But why here?"

Rùnach looked at him seriously. "I wanted the seven rings of mastery."

Ruith felt his mouth fall open, and he laughed a little in spite of himself. "Surely you jest."

Rùnach shook his head slowly.

"But you never wanted those," Ruith said in surprise. Indeed, he and Rùnach had had numerous conversations about the folly of subjecting their magic to the scrutiny of masters who couldn't possibly hope to wield the same power and might. Ruith supposed, looking back on it now, that they had been a little arrogant about it all.

How things changed.

"I wanted to walk through the doors the rings would open for me," Rùnach said with a shrug, "so I would have lowered myself to make the attempt. But Léir wouldn't allow it."

"What a woman you've become," Ruith said. "Surely you could best him and his pitiful spells in order to do as you saw fit."

"Perhaps before," Rùnach said, smiling faintly, "but not now. I suppose in his own way he was attempting to keep me safe. In Mother's memory, no doubt."

"Does no one know you're here, then?" Ruith asked in surprise. "Even after all these years?"

"Not even Droch, who would likely turn me into a pawn without hesitation should he learn the truth," Rùnach said with a snort. "Nay, brother, there are advantages to masquerading as Soilléir's servant. I live and breathe, for one thing. And I have the run of the library downstairs, which you will readily admit is something to envy."

And for Rùnach, that was no doubt indeed the case. Ruith studied his brother for a moment or two in silence, then shook his head. "I still don't understand why you ever would have wanted any of those bloody rings."

"Can't you?" Rùnach asked, sounding faintly amused.

"To have Soilléir's spells?" Ruith asked, not at all surprised to watch Rùnach nod. His brother might have lost his magic and his hands, but his ambitions had obviously not changed. "Which ones?"

"I would have taken all of them, but I was willing to settle for two."

"And those would have been?"

"Return and Alchemy."

Ruith began to smile. "You can't be serious."

"Oh, I am," Rùnach assured him. "And just so you know and can be envious, Léir gave them to me."

"Good of him," Ruith grumbled.

Rùnach's face was, the poor lad, as scarred as his hands, but that didn't stop him from managing a look of supreme smugness. "He was more than generous, actually, for he gave me all his spells."

"Damn you," Ruith said with an uneasy laugh. "Very well, you have what Father would have killed for. What, pray, did you intend to do with any of them?"

"Bring Father back to life, then turn him into a rock."

Ruith smiled. "Your problem, brother, has always been your lack of imagination." He ignored the fact that he'd thought exactly the same thing. "Rather you should have turned him into a truffle, exposed perilously in a forest full of insubordinate pigs, perhaps. Or a large, hairy spider sent into a chamber full of feisty ladies' maids with heavy court shoes. Or a target pinned to a haystack for use by Meithian archers who are, you will remember, simply unparalleled for their accuracy and ability to practice for all the hours daylight allows them and often into the night when torches can be fetched. But a rock?"

"As if you could have invented anything more interesting," Rùnach said with a snort.

"I believe I just did."

"And I believe *you* don't have the spells to do it, so, little brother, 'tis naught but speculation with you."

Ruith wanted to laugh, but his brother's words hit too close to home.

He decided, for the third time that day, that he didn't like being less than he was. He didn't like it at all.

Nay, if he was going to be truthful with himself, he would have to admit that he hadn't liked the fact that his magic was buried and unused for quite some time now. Since he'd been in the great hall at Ceangail and found himself completely unable to protect Sarah.

Nay, that wasn't true either. He'd known, on a night a month ago when he'd sat against the wheel of Franciscus's ale wagon and held Sarah in his arms so he could wake her if she dreamed about his father's spells burning like lamps all over the world, that if he'd been half the man his mother had expected him to be, he would have not run but instead turned and faced his demons squarely.

Actually, his father would have agreed with that as well, but Ruith preferred not to think about that.

"And at least you have the magic to do what I cannot," Rùnach mused. "If only you had the spells."

Ruith pursed his lips and remained silent.

"You should, if I might offer an opinion," Rùnach began carefully, "be grateful for what you have."

Ruith smiled wearily. "Am I so easy to read, then?"

"I just know you, Ruith," Rùnach said quietly. "I know your demons."

"Because they're yours as well?"

Rùnach nodded. "I'm simply fortunate I'm not forced to confront them."

"You have always led a charmed life."

"Haven't I, though?"

Ruith smiled. "I've missed you."

"And I you, but if you fling yourself in my arms again and slobber all over me like a woman, I'll stick a knife in your gut."

"Do you ever talk this much to Soilléir?"

"Oh, aye. He begs me to be quiet."

Ruith smiled, then looked down at his hands for a moment or two. He could feed himself, clothe himself, and keep himself from freezing to death in the mountains. He could wield a sword, make arrows for a bow, and extricate himself from situations not requiring a sword but instead a tactfulness his mother would have been satisfied with.

But that wasn't enough to do what he had to.

"Tell me of the pages you've been hunting."

Ruith looked up. "What—oh, those. I've been finding pages of

Father's book—well, Sarah's been finding them. We had a few, but I lost them." That wasn't exactly the case, but the truth was too unsettling to look at presently. "I suppose I don't need those, though, given that I could write at least most of them from memory."

"Could you?" Rùnach asked in surprise.

"Couldn't you?" Ruith asked, feeling equally surprised.

Rùnach shook his head slowly. "I had the entire bloody book memorized . . . before. When I lost my power, I lost those memories as well." He smiled grimly. "Blow to the head and all that, I suppose. I have over the years, however, found most of the spells I think he drew from."

"Where are those?"

"I gave them to one who needed them."

"Do I want to know who?" Ruith asked unwillingly.

"I don't think so today."

Ruith dragged his hands through his hair and sighed deeply. "What do you think I should do now?"

"Oh, nay," Rùnach said, shaking his head. "I wouldn't presume to tell you how to stop making a complete arse of yourself. Unless you'd like me to echo the suggestion that you take your lady for a wee walk. I, however, would suggest that you do so in Grandfather's garden."

Ruith wondered why it was he was continually being caught off guard. He didn't remember his last visit to Buidseachd having been so taxing. "An interesting thought."

"You can't tell me it hasn't crossed your mind before."

"It has," Ruith managed. "And I made certain the thought continued on into the darkness where it belongs. I'm quite happy pretending to be something I'm not and ignoring things that make me uncomfortable."

"You're a terrible liar," Rùnach said sadly. He shook his head. "How have you managed without me all these years, Ruith?"

"Poorly," Ruith admitted, then steeled himself for the better part of an afternoon spent listening to his elder brother point out to him just where he'd gone wrong. Instruction on how to go about winning a woman he wasn't at all sure would want to be won would no doubt figure prominently in Rùnach's conversation.

Ruith supposed that whilst he was listening, he would think more than he should have about the fact that whilst he would happily have retreated to his mountain sanctuary, his brother would have shouldered his burden and marched doggedly into the battle that lay ahead.

But Rùnach couldn't.

While Ruith realized with a start he most certainly could, but he wouldn't.

Fadaire is smothered by Olc more often than not, he had said to Soilléir that first night.

If you believe that, Ruithneadh, then you do not give your mother's power its due.

He wondered, casually lest the thought become more important than he wanted it to be, what would happen in truth if he sauntered down to his grandfather's garden, released all his magic, then attempted entry, just to see what Fadaire in its strength would think of him.

Aye, he wondered, indeed.

The thought burned in his soul like a raging fire, leaving him fighting for breath until the sun began to set and Sarah woke. She didn't look any better than she had before, but Soilléir promised her a walk would do her good. Ruith would have happily avoided the bloody expedition until the next day—or never, if he could have managed it—but Soilléir handed him a rucksack full of supper, assured him that Droch was shut up in his chamber, raging at his current crop of spies, and held open the door for him. Never mind that Ruith had already opened it, perhaps in spite of his better judgement. Sarah didn't seem opposed to being liberated from a nest of mages, so there was no rescue coming from that quarter.

He supposed he would just have to carry on down a path that was so full of thorns he could scarce put his foot to it.

He slipped out the kitchen door with Sarah, then heard her sigh of relief at the reprieve from being inside a keep full of spells. He wished he could have shared the feeling, but what he dreaded lay in front of him, not behind. He walked quickly with her along sidewalks just the same, keeping to the shadows as much as possible, following a path that even he could see was laid out before his feet.

The way to the garden of Gearrannan hadn't changed at all in a score of years. He found the place without trouble, then stopped in front of the gate. He wondered, absently, if he should have brought a lamp. He knew there was a path whose head lay just inside, but he wasn't sure they would manage to find the end of it.

He reached out toward the gate, then froze as memory washed over him. He could see his father's hand there on that latch, the flat black onyx stone in the ring he always wore glinting dully in the moonlight. But his father had drawn his hand back immediately, as if the gate had stung him. He'd laughed off the moment, then pleaded a sudden thirst as reason not to accompany his family inside the garden. Ruith had thought little of it at the time; he'd simply been relieved to be free of his father's oppressive presence.

Now, though, he didn't feel any relief at all.

He stood there with *his* hand on the latch, unable to move. He heard Sarah call his name, but he couldn't speak—partly because he was still so damned tired he could hardly stand up and partly because he had, at some point during the afternoon, turned into a blubbering . . . something. It would have been an insult to call himself a woman because the women he knew didn't blubber. They wept, when appropriate, or drew steel, or wielded spells. But they never blubbered.

And still he stood there, motionless, wrestling with things he couldn't see but definitely couldn't ignore.

"I'm going to go."

That surprised him out of his stupor. He looked at Sarah. "What?"

"I appreciate the refuge for a bit," she said quietly, "but I know you have things to do. I do too. I should be about them sooner rather than later."

He was still struggling for something to say when she brushed past him. He caught her hand before she went three paces.

She stopped, but she didn't turn around.

He looked down at her hand in his. It was her right one, the hand with his father's spell burned into her flesh, tangible proof that there was evil in the world that would stop at nothing in attempting to destroy what was beautiful and whole. And she, Sarah of Doìre, had set out from the ruins of her home with nothing more than a drooling hound, a fierce-looking kitchen knife, and an unquenchable desire to do good in order to try to stop that evil.

And he had shut his door in her face.

Never mind that he'd followed after her within hours. He should have offered to help her immediately. He should have told her who he was from the start, then he should have taken back his magic from the ghost of his father and used it to keep her safe.

He feared it was too late.

He took a deep breath. "There is a pleasant garden beyond this gate."

She still wasn't moving. "How do you know?"

"'Tis my . . . grandfather's garden," he said, having to take another deep breath or two. "His glamour is laid over it, but I don't think that will trouble you. Fadaire is a beautiful magic."

She turned slowly and looked at him. She was silent for so long, he wondered if she was wondering how best to stab him and be free of him, or if she was looking for something particularly cutting to say to put him in his place, which he supposed he would have deserved. Or perhaps she, like he, was wrestling with things that for all their innocence were very serious indeed. Such as her sight. Or his ability to survive the evening without his grandfather's garden snuffing out his existence.

"It would be a safe place to linger," he added.

She hesitated, then let out her breath slowly. "Perhaps for a few minutes."

"An hour," he countered.

Her eyes narrowed. "Very well, an hour, but then I *will* go."

It was a start, but only half the battle had been won. He would have to get them both inside the gate—alive—before safety would be theirs. He took a deep breath, then very carefully released his magic. He felt Sarah catch her breath.

"What are you doing?" she asked.

He looked at her in surprise. "What do you mean?"

She gestured helplessly at him. "What you just did. I saw it. The riverbeds are now full to overflowing."

He didn't mean to gape at her, but he couldn't help himself. "Riverbeds?" he echoed.

She waved away the words. "Don't ask. Let's just go."

He promised himself a goodly bit of speech with her later—hopefully he would still be alive to do so—then nodded. He hesitated, then cast caution and pride to the wind. He put his hand on the gate, then looked at her.

"We have a bit of a problem here."

She looked over her shoulder immediately, as if she expected Droch and a contingent of his vile minions to be standing there, then back at him with a frown. "What sort of a problem?"

"The garden is not without its safeguards," he said slowly. "To keep out undesirables who might attempt entrance where they shouldn't."

She stared at him blankly for a moment or two, then a look of profound pity came over her face. "Oh, Ruith."

If he hadn't been finished before, he was then. He didn't dare reach for her, simply because he found he did have a bit of pride left and he couldn't stomach the thought of her knowing how badly he was trembling. He attempted a casual shrug.

"There's nothing to it, truly," he said, tossing away the words as if they touched him not at all. "Just a feeble spell that keeps out what the garden doesn't want in or, more insultingly, allows the refuse in but doesn't acknowledge it. If my grandfather were here, the trees would make light of their own for him. Actually, I think they would do it for any of his family. But for me, assuming the gate doesn't fell me on the spot the moment I open it . . . well, I imagine I won't be welcomed."

Sarah's expression was very grave. "Because of Gair?"

"Because of Gair."

She shrugged. "I don't mind the dark."

He most certainly did, and she was lying. He knew the dark bothered her even more than it bothered him, but there was nothing to be done about it now. He wanted to mutter a casual *nothing ventured, nothing gained, eh?* but he found he could do nothing but stand there and breathe for several minutes in silence, like a poor, spooked nag facing what terrified it the most.

Sarah squeezed his hand, just the slightest bit. "You are not your father."

He laughed a little. "So we could hope." He started to open the gate, then paused and looked at her. "If something happens to me," he began carefully, "the garden will let you inside, I'm sure. If you can bear to, wait for Soilléir. He will know if I perish. He won't leave you here alone."

The last galled him to say out loud, but more galling would have been the thought that he'd left Sarah unprotected.

Which, he supposed, was why he was willingly trying to find the place where his soul would shatter and doing so by presenting himself to a place that judged mercilessly, just to see if it would reject him.

Sarah said nothing. She merely squeezed his hand again and waited.

Ruith took a deep breath, then reached out with a trembling hand and opened the latch of the gate.

He didn't feel anything amiss, and he still drew breath. It was promising, but not overly. His grandfather, it could be said, was nothing if not imaginative whilst about the happy business of tormenting miscreants.

Ruith walked inside, drawing Sarah behind him. He shut the gate and felt his grandfather's glamour drape down behind him and seal itself with a click. Sarah shivered, but he supposed that came more from the twilight mist rather than the spell.

"Still breathing," he said, a little more breathlessly than he would have liked. He looked at the path beneath his feet, trying not to think about the last time he'd walked up it. It had been with his mother, Rùnach, and Gille. In fact he could almost see them hurrying up the way in front of him, laughing, heedless of the magic that protected them as only lads who'd enjoyed its benefits for the whole of their lives could be. The path had been lit, of course, because of his mother and his brothers.

"What now?" Sarah asked.

"We carry on." He nodded toward the path. "That leads upward to a bower. A lovely place, truly. Happily secluded and undeniably safe." He hesitated. "I would make light—"

"We'll manage without it."

He supposed they'd both managed over the years with less light than they would have liked. He promised himself a decent bit of werelight at the top of the hill, but until then . . . well, until then, he would just make do.

A bit like he'd been doing for the past score of years.

He squeezed Sarah's hand, then started up the path. He felt as if he were walking into a battle, just waiting for the first blow to fall, the first arrow to find home in his chest, the first sound of a knife slicing through the—

Sarah gasped.

He looked up, then froze.

Lights had begun to appear in the trees, faintly where he stood, but more brightly as the path wound upward. The flowers on either side of the path began to glow as well, as if they were, well, *pleased* at something. Ruith struggled to breathe normally.

"They're doing it for you," he managed.

"Don't be daft," she said without hesitation. "They're doing it for *you*."

He wanted to curse, but he thought that might be inappropriate in his current location. He supposed Sarah had seen him at his worst—or very near to it—so there was no shame in a very minor display of emotion. Unfortunately, by the time they reached the top of the hill, he feared he'd wept more than a stray tear or two. He dragged his sleeve across his eyes and looked around himself.

The trees were singing a song of Fadaire in which his name was whispered over and over again, as if they not only recognized him, but had longed to see him and wondered why he had been away. The lights sparkled, clear and warm, casting a beautiful light over the bower. He turned around in a circle, stunned at what he was seeing, then looked at Sarah.

"I can't believe this," he whispered. He started to say more, but he couldn't. All the years he'd spent with his back turned on himself, denying himself the pleasure of family, the beauty of his mother's magic . . . all years apparently wasted. He looked at Sarah helplessly.

"Regret is a terrible thing," she said very quietly.

"Are you reading my thoughts now as well?" he managed.

"Your face, rather."

He dragged his sleeve across that face, then attempted a smile. "Well, at least we have light. What do you say to a game of cards?"

"Ruith, surely not—"

"Please," he interrupted. "I'll weep in truth if I must think on this any longer. Please let's discuss food, or steel, or the many and varied flaws of a certain master of Buidseachd who talks too much about some things and not enough about others."

"I would join you in that," she said, dabbing at her own cheeks with the hem of her sleeve, "but I haven't the heart for it." She looked at him seriously. "I'll play cards with you, but for every time I win, I want a memory of yours that's beautiful. Franciscus didn't know very many tales, but I loved the ones he told me. Despite my loathing of all things elvish, of course."

"I know many tales—"

"Memories, Ruith. Good ones."

He took a deep breath, looked over her head at the trees behind her with their lights swaying delicately in their boughs. "Very well. And from you, I'll have an hour more of your company for each hand I win. Here in the elven king's garden where his spells will keep you safe."

"I don't belong—"

"And I do?" he asked with as much of a careless laugh as he could manage. He felt his smile fade. "Please, Sarah. I'll help you in the morning if you still want to go. You shall choose a place and I'll *make* it safe for you. But tonight, I want you to stay."

"Why?" she asked, pained.

"Because I don't want you to go, and I'm putting off the misery of it as long as I can," he said, before he thought too much about it and talked himself out of being honest.

She closed her eyes for a moment or two, then looked at him. "I'm terrified."

He didn't need to ask her why. Of course she was terrified because she had an enormous amount of good sense and a very long list of things to be terrified by.

She swallowed. "I've been blustering before about it all, but I'm not sure I can . . . that I can face . . ."

He drew her into his arms before she could reach for blades to place delicately in his gut. When she continued to shiver, he took off his cloak, wrapped it around her, then pulled her close again.

"We'll put it aside for the night," he said, hoping he sounded more confident and hopeful than he felt. "You can decide what you'll do in the morning."

She didn't want to give in, he could sense that, but she did. Eventually.

"Be thinking on my prizes," she said, pulling away finally and dragging her sleeve again across her eyes. "Now, Your Highness, stop dawdling and conjure us up a deck of cards and a place to sit before I turn off your lights with my salty language."

"Don't call me that," he said quietly.

Her smile faded. "I said it before to hurt you. But not now. Not here."

"I still don't like it."

"What shall I call you, then?"

"I suppose *darling* is out," he said, struggling to capture a light tone, "as is *Your Handsomeness*. I suppose you'll just have to settle for Ruith."

"Very well, *Ruith*," she said, waving him on. "Stop talking and start thinking."

He had, as it happened, an enormous store of lore in his poor head, most having to do with Heroes trotting off on their trusty Angesand steeds to do marvelous deeds with their swords, but he supposed if he tried hard enough, he might be able to remember a few things he'd read in his grandfather's library. Or manage a few decent memories of his own for her.

He made them a place to sit, enjoyed the supper Soilléir had packed for them, lost badly at cards, then didn't argue when Sarah said she thought she could perhaps lose a game or two to save his pride if she stretched out and played with her eyes closed. She was asleep long before the game was finished.

He pulled her cloak over her, but she shivered still. He considered what he might do to remedy that, but realized it could only be solved with magic. He sat up and took a very deep breath. The trees seemed to be waiting for him as well.

"Well," he said reasonably, "I'm just thinking about her."

The lights only sparkled pleasantly and the boughs began to sing again, a sweet song of peace. Ruith looked down at his very sensible hands, thought about what they could do, then thought about what they *could* do if he allowed them to.

If I had been Gair, I would have kept my family safe.

He had said those words to Sarah on their journey toward Ceangail. And he had meant it. If he'd had a family, a wife he adored, sons he wanted to show how to be honorable men, daughters he wanted to keep safe, he would have protected them to the very limits of his endurance and power. That he hadn't done so for Sarah on their journey was inexcusable.

He took another in a very long series of deep breaths, then put his hand out into the darkness.

He could have sworn he felt his mother's hand there, waiting for him.

He dragged his sleeve across his eyes one last time, then very carefully conjured up a cloak fit for a princess and spread it over Sarah, then set spells of ward, Fadairian spells that the garden approved of, just inside his grandfather's glamour.

Which had been refreshed quite recently, as it happened.

He would have considered that a bit longer, but he realized with a start that he wasn't going to manage to stay awake long enough to do so. He stretched out next to Sarah, then put his arm over her and contemplated the events of the evening.

He had walked in his grandfather's garden and found himself accepted.

He felt years fall away as if they'd never been there, leaving him with his magic and his memories and a freedom from the burden of hiding he hadn't realized he'd been carrying. He supposed if he'd had any sense at all, he would have been terrified.

But he wasn't.

He closed his eyes and fell into the first dreamless sleep he'd had in twenty years.

Ten

Sarah woke to singing.

It wasn't the sort of singing she was accustomed to, that off-key bit of warbling her mother had engaged in, peppering the ends of her phrases with curses and snorts. This was glorious, a hint of something she couldn't quite hear, as if it lingered on the edge of memory or dreaming.

It was definitely elvish.

She opened her eyes and looked up at the canopy over her head made by those trees that no longer twinkled with lights not of this world but were no less beautiful in spite of it. They were beginning to bloom with fragrant white flowers that were particularly lovely. And all through their rustling flowed their song, one of magic, woven with names she didn't recognize—and some she did. Sìle, Brèagha, Làidir, Sorcha, Athair, Sarait, Ruithneadh: the list was endless and spoken with love.

Fadaire was draped over everything like a particularly lovely snow, intertwined like ivy around the trunks and through the boughs of the trees. She stared at it for quite some time, watching the colors of not only leaf and flower shift with the gentle breeze, but the magic as well. She allowed herself to wonder, as she rarely did, what it would have been like to have been an elven maid with that loveliness to call one's own every day. To have had that sort of magic to string on a loom made from air and fire and use to weave tapestries of such beauty and perfection—

She sat up abruptly, because it was either that or weep over what she could never have, a sentiment which she realized she was suffering from enough without any sentient botanical aid. She looked at the cloak draped over her. It was spectacular, fashioned of a green silk the color of her eyes and lined with the softest white wool she had ever put her hand to. She thought at first that perhaps the garden had conjured it up for her, then she remembered that Ruith had released his magic the day before at the gate. She had seen him do it, which had surprised her, then watched it wash over his soul like a river over dry, cracked earth, healing it.

She envied him.

She knew she should have gotten up and walked or run or done something to escape her useless thoughts, but she couldn't bring herself to. She was sitting in a garden more beautiful than even her rampaging imagination could ever have conjured up, and she was being serenaded by trees. If she'd had any sense at all, she would have sat for another moment or two and committed the moment to memory.

Which she did. She smoothed her hands over the silk of the cloak spread over her, watched the threads of Fadaire it was fashioned with shimmer as she touched them, and listened to the names that trees continued to weave in and out of their song. She became familiar with them, though she found herself growing slightly amused, as time went on, that the trees seemed particularly fond of Ruith's mother's name for they whispered it again and again.

And then she frowned, for the name that figured so prominently into their song wasn't Sarait.

It was Sarah.

She found her hands were buried in her cloak, clutching it in a way that would likely take a hot iron to smooth over, but there was nothing to be done about it now. She looked up at the trees, feeling hot tears stream down her cheeks.

They knew her.

Hard on the heels of that realization came another one.

She couldn't run. Not away from her past, or her present, or her future, because if she ran, the time would come when places like the garden she was in would be overcome. She had no doubt that Daniel was alive—he'd always had an uncanny ability to land on his feet— and she knew what he could do. He wasn't Ruith's half brothers, of course, but he wasn't a village whelp either. If there was something she could do to stop him, she had to.

No matter the cost—

She had to turn away from that thought before it robbed her of the last of her breath. She crawled abruptly off Ruith's cloak, then picked it up and shook it out. She hesitated, then picked up the cloak he had made for her and pulled it around her shoulders. She knew she would pay for it eventually, but for the moment she would allow herself the very great pleasure of wearing something she never would have dared weave for herself, and damn the consequences.

Ruith was nowhere to be found, but she didn't imagine he had left her to herself. She found a handy bench sitting under the trees at the edge of the little glade and made herself at home on it. She wished she'd had something useful to do, such as wind yarn or knit, but as she didn't, she simply sat with her hands folded in her lap and tried not to think. That was difficult given that she was in a place where her entrance had been granted thanks to a man she was try- ing to forget.

I want more than an hour, Sarah.

She closed her eyes and bowed her head, partly to shut out the almost overwhelming sight of the magic-drenched garden in front of her and partly to shut out his words. He wanted her for what? To find his father's spells for him? To keep him company as he plunged into darkness? She couldn't imagine it was for any more romantic purposes, not that she was interested in anything of that nature with him. He was an elven prince—

Who was, she discovered as she opened her eyes, walking toward her.

He was dressed as he had been the day before, in his usual simple homespun. If she'd been looking at his clothes alone, she would have thought him nothing more than a man from some rustic mountain village, hardened to the labor of carving a living from where it didn't want to be carved.

But she made the mistake of looking at his face. She supposed that by now she should have become accustomed to the perfection of it, his flawless features, his bluish green eyes that had seen more than they should have, his dark hair that looked for a change as if he *hadn't* been dragging his hands through it in frustration, but she hadn't. As much as she wished she could have denied it, the truth was she was startled every time she looked at him.

He looked up from his contemplation of the grass beneath his feet, saw her, then stopped.

And she knew, with a finality that rivaled what she'd felt thinking about Daniel, that her task was not limited to finding her brother. She would have to help *that* man there with his task, no matter where that task led him. Because she could see the spells and he couldn't. Because he had been willing to accept his birthright the night before. Because his mother had been willing to turn her back on all the beauty Sarah was surrounded by, been willing to risk leaving her children behind, been willing to sacrifice her very life to try to keep the world safe.

Sarah could do no less.

The trees sang their approval.

Ruith cocked an ear and listened to them for a moment or two, smiled faintly, then continued on his way toward her. Sarah felt her breath catch, again. She wondered if there would ever come a day when she could look at him and yawn.

The truth was, it wasn't because he was handsome, even though he was. It wasn't because he was skilled with a sword and could protect a gel against any number of thugs in a tavern, even though he certainly could. It wasn't even that she could see that those rivers that ran through him were now full of Fadaire, sparkling, laughing, delighted to course through a soul that had been born to their power. Nay, it was none of those things.

It was that he, an elven prince from a house of elven kings, had wanted her to stay with him.

It was also possible that she was still trying to breathe normally after having been faced with a doom she now knew she couldn't avoid, but perhaps that was something better left for examination at another time.

She watched Ruith approach and found it in her to scowl. He might have wanted her to keep him company for the moment, but that wouldn't last. The world would discover that he was alive, and then he would have scores of princesses falling over themselves to be first in line to court *him*. He would spend his days in glittering elven palaces, taking tea with other princes and princesses, exchanging royal pleasantries with kings and queens—if he lowered himself to do so.

She had no illusions about the elves of Tòrr Dòrainn, for Franciscus had taken particular pleasure in telling her their tales. They were an exclusive lot, finding themselves superior to the inhabitants of Ainneamh, surely, and especially to the other elves and half elves Franciscus had told her about who lived in the east and were dwindling in number in the north. Nay, once Ruith stepped back out onto the world's stage, he would have no use for her, which meant she would be wise to escape whilst she could—

"Oh, nay, not this," Ruith said, catching her.

He had to catch her because, she realized, she was in mid-bolt through the bower.

He turned her to him and looked down at her gravely. "You promised to stay."

"I promised to stay the night," she managed, never mind what sort of unwholesome agreement she'd come to with the trees just a handful of moments past. "The sun is up."

His expression didn't change. "And what must I do to win another day?"

Deny your birthright and let's go hide would have been the first sensible thing she'd said in two months, but that was as impossible as the thought of his even looking at a mortal woman, which she most definitely was.

Do elves ever marry ordinary gels? she had asked Franciscus one evening in her youth as she'd sat at his worktable and watched him sort lavender from the widow Fiore's garden.

Some do, he had conceded. *But never the elves from Tòrr Dòrainn. Their king, Sìle, is particularly adamant about that.*

He's not much of a romantic, is he?

Franciscus had laughed. *Nay, gel, he isn't. He's proud and protective of his family and so gloriously elvish, a body can hardly look at him without his eyes catching fire.*

She hadn't thought to ask him how he possibly could have known that, though now she wondered why not. It wasn't possible Franciscus had known Sìle of Tòrr Dòrainn himself . . . Then again, she'd never considered it possible that Franciscus might be some sort of mage, but now she knew differently.

And she was looking at Sìle of Tòrr Dòrainn's grandson, who was almost leaving her eyes catching fire himself.

Or, rather, trying not to look at him. Because it hurt her to do so.

"Your sight bothers you," he said quietly.

She nodded, because it was easier than giving him the list of all the things that bothered her.

He reached out to pull her into his arms, but she stepped backward so quickly, she almost tripped. She turned away from him because she honestly couldn't think clearly when she was looking at him. She was almost to the point where she was seriously considering marching back up to that horrible keep and demanding that Soilléir put back whatever he'd ripped off her eyes. She was finished with seeing too much.

She stopped at the edge of the circle of trees and looked down into the city. The trees were quieter than they had been earlier, as if they too held their breath.

Sarah felt rather than heard Ruith come to a stop behind her. He freed her hair from the collar of her cloak, then ran his hand lightly over it.

"Will you answer one question for me?" he asked quietly.

She didn't want to, but she supposed the trees would drop a branch on her head if she didn't, so she sighed heavily. That was as much an assent as anyone could expect from her.

"If you had never known my parentage, or if I had simply been the grandson of Sgath of Lake Cladach, would you feel differently?" He paused. "Did you feel differently a pair of fortnights ago?"

"It makes no difference—"

"Aye, Sarah, it does." He turned her around to face him. "It does."

She dragged her sleeve across her eyes. The whole situation was profoundly ridiculous. She had a quest to manage, mages to elude, her conscience to somehow satisfy before she turned her back on it once and for all—again, her bargain with King Sìle's garden aside. Her tally was full with no room for elven princelings.

"It doesn't change anything, Ruith. And I'm not sure why we're discussing this anyway. It isn't as if you will be interested in me— not that you were to begin with—once word gets out."

"I assure you, Sarah of Doìre, I will still be very interested, no matter what word gets out."

"And just how could you possibly know that?" she said, trying to bolster what was left of her pride. "You don't know what's available."

"I have been off my mountain," he said. "Many times, in many places, in many guises."

She looked at him before she thought better of it. It was like look-ing into the sun, but she supposed if she was going to blind herself, she might as well enjoy the process. "You?" she asked with disbelief. "In disguise?"

He lifted one eyebrow. "Once I wore an eye patch."

She shut her mouth when she realized she'd allowed it to fall open. "You didn't."

"I did. Another time my hair was long enough to catch up with a black ribbon."

"And I imagine that impressive disguise left everyone completely baffled as to your identity—and not that it matters. You have your quest and I have my . . . well, whatever it is I have." She looked at his pulse beating in his throat for quite some time before she managed to meet his eyes. "I'm thinking about running, if you must know."

He reached out and tucked a stray strand of hair behind her ear. "I think, love," he began slowly, "that you could run for a bit, but things would find you. I would, of course, follow you to keep you safe."

"I was planning on running away from *you*," she said, even though it was quite possibly the last thing she wanted to do. Well, the *very* last thing she wanted to do was meet Droch of Saothair in a darkened pub, but running from Ruith was fairly high on that list as well. "I don't want the darkness," she managed. "And if I stay another day, that's what awaits me in your vicinity."

He fussed with her cloak, then clasped his hands behind his back and looked at her gravely. "And if I said I would use magic to keep you safe?"

"I won't be responsible for that choice," she said promptly. She took a deep breath. "The fact is, Ruith, we are fish and beast, water and air, fire and oil."

"Potent combinations," he said mildly.

"And doomed ones," she retorted. She took a step backward. "I have things to do, important things, and no time for dalliances."

"Why would you think I was interested in a dalliance?"

She viciously suppressed the urge to burst into tears. "Even I am quick-witted enough to know that elves do not wed mortals, *especially* elves of Tòrr Dòrainn. Perhaps you forget what I am and who you are."

"And you think I would feel any more comfortable in their glittering halls?"

She scowled. "I'm not sure you'll have a choice."

"I *always* have a choice."

She tried to walk past him, but he caught her hand. Her left one, fortunately. She turned toward him slightly, looked down at his hand around hers, his hand that could work any magic he wanted surrounding her hand that could do nothing but weave string into cloth. She looked for quite some time before she managed to look up at him.

"I have spent my entire life being less," she said finally. "I don't want to spend the rest of it that way."

He tilted his head slightly. "Have I added to that? Well, apart from what I said in Ceangail—and on the plains—but that was the only way I could think of to take attention off you. But in other ways, have I?"

"Nay," she admitted reluctantly.

He smiled faintly. "The trouble is, love, that I'm fairly besotted. I'm just not sure how to go about winning your affections."

"You're mad," she said, because she could think of nothing else. He didn't look mad, or unserious, or daft. He looked all too serious. "I can't believe the world is falling apart and this is what you're discussing."

"I would actually prefer to be discussing where you would like me to build you a house after my quest is finished, but I thought you mind find that . . . presumptuous."

"Your quest?" she echoed. "It's *my* quest."

He only smiled, as if he'd expected her to say nothing else.

She scowled at him, turned, and walked into a tree she was fairly certain hadn't been there before. She cursed it, had a shower of white petals on her head as a reward, then turned and backed up until the tree wouldn't let her go any farther. She surrendered with another curse and looked at Ruith. He was still watching her, grave and so beautiful she could hardly look at him.

"An elven prince," she spluttered, gesturing inelegantly in his direction.

"And a weaver of destinies," he said with a very faint smile. "A tale for bards to sigh rapturously over for years to come."

"I've never heard a bard spin tales before."

"I vow you will, when this is all finished." He paused. "I think, though, that despite it all, you should wait here with Soilléir, for I think him best suited to protect you."

"I'm not waiting anywhere," she said, though just the saying of it felt as if she'd just taken a step off the edge of a cliff into thin air. "You can't see the spells."

"I'll manage."

"You can't be serious," she said, realizing that she'd already said that, perhaps more than once. She looked at him and realized he was all too serious. "You can't go without me."

"I'm not taking you with me," he said mildly.

She drew herself up and glared at him. "You most certainly are."

He set his jaw. "We will not argue about this."

"You're right," she said shortly. "Argument finished. This is *my* quest and I'll decide if I'm going on it or not."

He frowned.

"And another thing," she said, supposing it was best she get the rest of her terms of engagement out whilst he was still digesting the first one and before she lost her courage about continuing on with something she had to finish, no matter how the very thought of it chilled her to the marrow, "I want you to court other women."

His mouth fell open. "I will not."

"Then I want you to meet other women."

"I've *met* other women," he said, beginning to sound faintly exasperated. "I don't want to meet any more."

"And they should be princesses."

He looked at her as if she'd lost all sense. She wasn't entirely sure she hadn't. A blindingly handsome man had professed . . . well, he'd professed something, and she wasn't swooning with pleasure?

Perhaps she was the one who was mad.

Ruith began to scowl. "And then will you be satisfied?"

She pursed her lips. "You're humoring me."

"You're damned right I'm humoring you!"

"Ten of them," she said, because it seemed like a goodly number, and because he'd shouted at her. "And if you bellow at me again, I'll make it eleven."

He looked as if he were torn between engaging in another bellow or a laugh. He seemingly settled for a heavy sigh. "Very well."

"And until then, 'tis strictly a quest between us, nothing more."

"Strictly a quest?" he repeated almost soundlessly.

"Aye," she said, rubbing her hands together briskly. "I'll dream your spells, we'll find my brother and avoid all yours, then we'll gather everything up in a neat and tidy package and set fire to it all. Then you can go look for your princesses, and I'll go off and look for a place to settle in and work. I'll send you a present for your nuptials."

He looked at her narrowly. "What familiarities am I allowed in this madness of yours?"

"The same you would have had with Franciscus."

He pursed his lips. "And what will you give me in return for my agreeing to all this?"

Nothing was the first thing that came to mind, but she supposed she should at least offer something in return for his agreeing to all her terms. "What do you want?" she asked warily.

"Full forgiveness and a new beginning."

"Done," she said, feeling rather relieved the price hadn't been higher. Her relief, handily enough, was enough to help her ignore the fact that she'd just committed herself to a quest that would send her into darkness alongside a man she was unwholesomely fond of and couldn't have, no matter how many princesses he squired about. She wasn't quite sure how she'd landed herself in that sort of mess, but she supposed it was a little late to be changing her mind.

She found herself suddenly in an embrace that was altogether too comforting for her peace of mind. She put her arms around Ruith's waist because it helped her keep from sinking to her knees in fear. No other reason.

"I'm not sure," she said, her voice muffled against his shoulder, "that this falls into the purview of what comrades at arms would share."

"You're not a soldier and neither am I," he said, running his hand briefly over her hair, "so those rules do not apply."

"You're taking advantage of my terror at the thought of what lies in front of us."

"I might be." He was silent for a moment or two, then he pulled back and looked at her seriously. "Sarah, I don't want you to come along."

"You can't find those spells without me."

"I know," he said reluctantly. He looked over her shoulder for a moment or two, presumably at the city laid out beneath them, then back at her. "If I allow you—"

"Allow?" she mouthed.

"*Allow* you to come with me," he said seriously, "then when I pull you behind me and tell you to stay there, you will do it without question. No sneaking off into the night without me, no marching off into the fray alone. And if I leave you behind at some point, behind you will stay or we go not one step further in this bloody venture."

"I—"

"Don't have the magic to fight what we'll face," he said seriously. "But I do, and I will use that magic to keep you safe. As I should have from the beginning."

She had to take a deep breath or two before she thought she could speak without her voice trembling. He was right, of course, and she had certainly seen over the past few fortnights just how cold-blooded and indifferent black mages could be. She didn't like to give up her independence, though, nor admit her limitations. She looked up at him.

"I have knives, you know."

He pulled her back into his arms and held her so tightly, she almost believed he did have a few fond feelings for her. She allowed herself the safety of it for a moment or two, then pulled away.

"Very well," she agreed. "Unless I change my mind."

"Nine princesses," he said solemnly.

She scowled at him. "Ten and done."

He rolled his eyes and reached for her hand. "Let's go back to the keep and find breakfast. We'll need to make our plans, pack our gear, then sleep a bit. I also have a few pointed questions to ask Master Soilléir before we go."

She supposed holding his hand wasn't a too terribly romantic thing, so she wasn't going to argue with him at the moment. She would, later, when they weren't in a place that seemed so happy to have him there.

He walked with her down the path, then stopped with his hand on the gate. He looked at her. "We'll come back."

She nodded, because she was sure *he* would be back. She was equally sure she wouldn't be with him. He would find a princess, wed her, and she would weave them something lovely for their wedding.

He squeezed her hand, then opened the gate. She walked with him out of light—

And into darkness.

Eleven

The spell slammed into Ruith so hard, he lost his breath. He staggered, then caught himself. He pulled Sarah behind him out of sheer instinct alone, then turned to face his foe.

Droch of Saothair.

He heard his grandfather's gate click shut behind him and the spell drop to the ground so quickly, it sounded as if half the hill had come down with it. At the same time, he realized that something else had fallen over him, a spell of protection that fortunately gave him enough time to gather his wits about him. That was Soilléir's doing, he knew immediately. He would have to thank the man, if he managed to overcome the first test of his resolve, a test he hadn't thought would come so quickly.

Droch smiled, then hurled a spell of Taking at him that flew through the air with the swiftness of a bolt thrown from a crossbow. Ruith used his own spell of protection—augmented as it was by Soilléir's—without thinking. Just as Keir had trained him to do, testing him a score of times a day, every day, for as much of his youth as he could remember.

Thankfully, it held.

Droch swore at him.

Ruith clucked his tongue. "Still haven't ironed all the wrinkles out of that one, have you?"

He felt Sarah's hands tangled in his cloak clutch him all the more tightly. He supposed she would have called him an idiot, if she'd had the breath for it. He would have agreed, if *he'd* had the breath for it. He'd come to terms with fully claiming his birthright from *both* his parents, but that didn't make his power any less heavy or unwieldy. Having it come lightly to his hand would take time, time he didn't have at the moment so he would simply make do.

He put one hand behind him and around Sarah on the off chance that she might lose all sense and decide to bolt. He didn't suppose she would, though. Soilléir's spell was actually quite a lovely thing from what he could see, steel covered by illusion and underpinned by an imperviousness that Ruith suspected not even all the masters of Buidseachd together could have breached. Thankfully.

He looked at Droch again, listened to him spit out a spell of death, then watched as it was absorbed by Soilléir's spell, gathered together, then flung back toward Droch with a speed so furious Ruith blinked in surprise. It reminded him sharply of what had befallen Amitán, with his spell of death repulsed by the Olcian spell of protection Ruith had been covered with. But why would anything of Soilléir's resemble anything made by someone who, from all indications, had been a master of Olc?

Yet another question to ask Soilléir when he had the time. At the moment, though, he was rather less at his leisure than he would have preferred to be.

Droch, however, was not a master of his craft because he was a fool, nor because he would ever be caught unawares. He sent his own spell that returned with a bit more added to it into the ether with a disgusted flick of his wrist. He looked at Ruith calculatingly.

"I demand a duel," he said. "With spells."

"Dueling is forbidden," Ruith said promptly, "which you well know, my lord."

Droch looked down his nose at him. "The youngest son of Gair of Ceangail, unwilling to fight when called upon? Your father would be embarrassed by you."

Ruith only shrugged. "He's too dead to have an opinion on the matter. Not that *your* opinion would have mattered to him, of course."

Droch's face grew very red. "Even the archmage of Neroche wasn't above defending his honor. Does that not gall you, Ruithneadh? That Mochriadhemiach would venture where you dare not?"

"He has more courage than I have," Ruith said with another shrug, refusing to be baited.

"He certainly has more power." Droch studied him for a moment or two. "Or perhaps 'tis that he has a more worthy companion to want to protect."

Ruith gritted his teeth and reached for his nonexistent sword only to be greeted with laughter.

"Surely you jest," Droch mocked. "Steel against my spells? I believe, my boy, that you have been out of decent society for too long. I wouldn't waste the effort to conjure up such a pedestrian weapon, much less trouble myself to use it." He smiled unpleasantly. "Perhaps your sister is fortunate you aren't the one protecting her, though I will admit I was a bit surprised by her choice of guardsmen."

Ruith managed to keep his composure only through sheer will alone. "My sister?"

Droch's look of triumph was hard to watch. "Ah, something you don't know," he said, coming very close to purring. "Obviously you haven't been hiding with her all these years."

Ruith chose not to answer, but the truth was, he could hardly maintain a neutral expression.

Mhorghain?

Droch's eyes narrowed. "And just so you know, I'm not finished with you. Perhaps we'll meet again when I have your little coquette there in my garden again where you can watch her finally take up one of the lesser spots amongst my chess pieces."

Ruith forced himself to concentrate as Droch turned on his heel and walked off, his boots clicking against the cobblestones.

Mhorghain? Alive?

"Ruith?"

He looked at Sarah standing next to him, watching him with frank concern on her face.

"Nothing," he said immediately. "'Tis nothing." He took her hand. "Let's go back to the keep."

"Eleven."

He stopped and looked at her. "What?"

"You just increased your number of princesses to eleven. Do you care to make it twelve?"

He retrieved his jaw from where it had fallen, then realized what she meant and why. He stopped, turned her to him, and pulled her into his arms. He let out a breath that was rather less steady than he would have liked. "I'm too accustomed to keeping things to myself."

"I know."

He pulled back far enough to smile down at her. "Are you telling me I was taciturn on our journey here?"

"That's one way to describe it." She wouldn't meet his eyes. "You needn't tell me anything, of course—"

"Of course I will," he said without hesitation. "If you want the entire truth, it galls me to have Soilléir's spell protecting us. I fear I wasted a score of years hiding in the mountains when I should have been honing my spells so I might face what I must—"

"Ruith, we're still breathing," she interrupted. "And you are responsible for that."

He suppressed the urge to shift uncomfortably. "Aye, well, perhaps, though Soilléir—"

"Gave you time to catch your breath," she said seriously. "The rest was your doing. And now that I've made you blush, you may tell me the rest."

He laughed uncomfortably. "You are a heartless wench, though I thank *you* for the time to catch my breath at present." He helped himself to another. "What has startled me the most is that the master of Olc just hinted my sister might be alive, and I'm wondering if Soilléir knows."

"You can't kill him if he does," she said seriously. "He saved my life."

"Aye, yet another reason to be annoyed with him. And myself."

She looked at him gravely. "You cannot call back the river that has already flowed past you, Ruith. All you can do is be grateful for where you are in it."

He dragged a hand through his hair. "I feel as if I'm dreaming."

"I understand."

"I imagine you do." He put his arm around her shoulders. "Very well, we'll return to the keep—alive, thanks to Master Soilléir—then you'll keep me from killing him until after I've put a few pointed questions to him."

"Is it your younger sister, do you think?" she asked quietly.

He looked at her in surprise, then shook his head. "I haven't even told you their names, have I?"

"You're a private man, Ruith."

"And a fortunate one that I have you now to trust with my innermost thoughts."

She smiled a little. "Comrades in arms, and all that, no doubt."

If she wanted to believe that, she was welcome to it. He supposed it might be for the best, given the task that lay before him and the inescapable fact that in order not to kill them both, he would have to concentrate on something besides her very fair face, her glorious hair, and the fact that even though he could feel her trembling, she was doing her damndest to carry on in spite of it.

Besotted?

Nay, he was lost.

"Names, my friend," she prodded.

He continued on with her up the way to the keep, without haste only to give himself time to calm his fury so he didn't flatten Soilléir the moment he saw him. First Soilléir, then Rùnach, then perhaps

Soilléir for another dose of his anger. Rùnach might not have known Mhorghain was alive, but Soilléir most certainly should have—and likely did.

"Keir was the eldest," he said, before he wound himself up again. "He was followed by Rùnach, whom you know." He frowned. "I think his hands must have become caught in the well when my mother tried to shut it."

"They did," Sarah said. She looked up at him quickly. "The marks from the stone are still buried in his flesh. And in his cheek."

Ruith felt a little faint. "Bloody hell, Sarah, what *don't* you see?"

"Many things, most notably the path laid before me," she said faintly, "but I don't want to think about that. Let's talk about things that make you uncomfortable."

"Are you saying I'm the only one in this companionship who must bare his soul?" he asked lightly.

"Consider it penance for your very bad behavior on our journey from Shettlestoune."

"Your turn will come, Sarah," he warned. "There will come a time when you'll need to face what you don't want to now."

"Spoken like the recently enlightened," she said darkly.

He laughed in spite of himself. "Aye, I daresay. Very well, I give you at least a pair of months to growl at me every time I bring up what you can do, as repayment for all the growling I did on the way here."

"Fair enough," she said, "and you've used up your allotment of diversions for the day. After Rùnach, who came next?"

He continued up the way with her, looking at the castle as it rose up before them, unrelentingly grey and massive. He supposed no one would have faulted him for keeping a sharp eye out for Droch, though he imagined the man had retreated to his solar to vent his anger on whatever fool had agreed to be his servant at present. "Can you not read the names written on my soul?"

She stumbled. "Don't ask me to do that."

He squeezed her shoulders briefly. "Forgive me." He could only imagine the discomfort she'd suffered in Droch's garden and how her sight troubled her presently. Vexing her over it was something he never would have tolerated had it been directed at him. He supposed he was fortunate she was of a much better temperament than he possessed. Perhaps he would ask Soilléir about it when Sarah looked less likely to do damage to anyone who brought it up.

He took a deep breath. "After Rùnach, came Brogach, Gille, and Eglach. All dead, I'm certain, for I saw them fall." He attempted a shrug, but failed. It was impossible to speak with any degree of carelessness about what had come next on that fateful morning. "I was to keep hold of my sister, Mhorghain, after my mother sent us to hide in the trees. But when I saw my mother fighting my father, unsuccessfully . . ." He let out his breath carefully. "I let go."

"I don't think they would blame you for it, Ruith," Sarah said quietly. "Either of them."

He could only nod, because speaking of it was beyond him.

She walked quietly with him until they were almost to the gates. "Do you think she's alive?"

"Droch would lie as soon as he would breathe, but I'm not sure he would see any benefit in lying here." He shrugged. "We'll ask Soilléir and see, I suppose."

The gate guards recognized them, thankfully, and only waved them through the barbican. Ruith continued on into the courtyard with Sarah, then found himself suddenly in the middle of a circle of swords pointed at his chest. Alarm bells were ringing wildly in the distance. He cursed succinctly, then looked at Sarah.

"I'm distracted."

"And no longer anonymous, apparently," she said, wide-eyed.

He wanted to say that it could have been her setting off alarms with her seeing—indeed, he wondered if that might have been that single, delicate bell they'd heard their previous trip through the front gates—but he thought silence might be the wisest course of action at present. He attempted to use what was left of his poor brain to invent a reasonable-sounding tale, but came away empty-handed. All he managed to do was watch as black-robed bodies came flying out of doors and across the courtyard, Ceannard in the lead.

The headmaster came to a skidding halt, then his mouth fell open, and he looked at Ruith in astonishment.

"Prince Ruithneadh," he managed. "Yet another lovely familial surprise."

Ruith suppressed the urge to scowl at the words. Aye, Soilléir had several things to confess. He exchanged pleasantries with Ceannard, but kept his eyes open for Soilléir, who had apparently decided the comfort of his solar was preferable to braving the brisk winter breezes—and irritated houseguests, no doubt—outside. Damn him anyway.

"What an honor," Ceannard said breathlessly. "And to have seen your grandfather not a fortnight past! We are delighted to welcome you, of course."

Ruith was happy to note Ceannard was too flustered to ask him how he'd managed to get himself and Sarah inside the gates without announcing themselves properly. He kept his mouth shut and simply listened to the headmaster continue on breathlessly.

"I'll see a chamber prepared for you befitting your exalted and quite royal station. And, of course, one for your guest, who is . . ." he trailed off, looking at Sarah expectantly.

"Worthy of your finest accommodations," Ruith said without hesitation, "but we won't be trespassing on your graciously offered hospitality."

Ceannard's expression was one of alarm. "But surely you don't intend to stay in an *inn*," he protested.

"I've business with Master Soilléir," Ruith reassured him. "I imagine he'll find a scrap of floor for us tonight."

"I cannot argue with that," Ceannard said, sounding as if he very much wished he could have. "You must at least allow us to provide a luncheon for you and your, er, guest. The honor would be ours, of course."

Ruith would have extricated himself from that delight without the slightest hesitation if he could have, but he wasn't at his best, so he conceded the battle with as much graciousness as he could muster, then accepted an escort fit for a king to Soilléir's chamber. He gave

Ceannard assurances of his presence—and Sarah's in spite of how hard she elbowed him in the ribs—at a meal befitting his exalted station a pair of hours hence, then escaped into Soilléir's chamber happily and looked at Rùnach who shut the door behind him.

"What a collection of imbeciles."

Rùnach laughed. "Grandfather would agree, of course."

Ruith reached for Sarah's hand only to find her with both hers firmly clasped behind her back. He frowned at her. "What is it?"

"I'm not hungry."

"What—oh, that." He shrugged. "'Tis simply a meal."

"Which you'll enjoy on your own, Your Highness," she said briskly. "I have other things to do."

He was tempted to fight her, but he had the feeling he would be wise not to. That she had come back inside the keep was a large concession on her part. Being willing to continue on a quest he was certain terrified her to the core was something that would leave him in her debt for quite some time to come.

Besides, the necessity of being polite would be a misery. She would be miserable surrounded by curious eyes, and since one of those pairs of eyes would likely be Droch's, there were at least three good reasons for her to remain safely out of sight.

He folded his arms over his chest. "If I leave you behind, I want you to remain inside the chamber where you'll be protected by Soilléir's spells."

"Gladly," she muttered.

"And," he said, because apparently he just couldn't keep his mouth shut, "the next time we're summoned to a torturous function such as what I'm about to be subjected to, you *will* come along."

She glared at him. "Twelve."

"Ten," he said firmly. "And you may have three."

She blinked. "Three whats?"

"Three instances where you beg off from a formal meal. You've just used one."

Her mouth fell open, but she shut it soon enough. "I need to weave. And I want ten as well."

"Three."

She glared at him. "Are we to spend the entire morning haggling?"

"Nay, I agreed to ten, you'll agree to three. Which is now two."

Rùnach laughed, a hoarse sound that was nonetheless full of good humor, and walked away. Ruith folded his arms and looked down at Sarah. "Well?"

"I'm humoring you," she warned.

"Done." He found her hand, took it in his own, then pulled her across the solar to find Soilléir sitting in front of his fire, looking perfectly at peace.

Ruith found Sarah a chair, saw her seated with a cup of wine at her elbow, then sat down and fixed Soilléir with a pointed look.

"Droch said Miach was here recently."

"Had a little chat over tea, did you?" Soilléir asked mildly.

"Don't make me do damage to you, my lord," Ruith warned.

Soilléir smiled. "Perish the thought. And aye, Miach was here recently."

"With Mhorghain."

"Don't know what you're talking about," Soilléir said with a discreet yawn. "But I see you've made a few changes in yourself since last we spoke."

"Thank you for the spell this morning," Ruith said shortly, "and aye, I have stopped being a fool and embraced what I am, so thank you for that as well, and what is this about my sister!"

He realized he was very close to shouting, but perhaps he could be forgiven for it considering the circumstances.

Soilléir looked at Sarah. "How are you, my dear?"

"Unable to protect you against him," Sarah said, a smile in her voice. "He's had a long winter so far, my lord, and I'm not sure he slept well last night, so perhaps you shouldn't torment him anymore."

"Wise," Ruith added shortly. "So I beg you, my lord Soilléir, please do me the favor of telling me what you obviously knew and couldn't see your way clear to telling me before."

"You wouldn't have enjoyed the tidings before," Soilléir said with a shrug, then held up his hand quickly. "Nay, do not growl at me, Ruithneadh. I'll tell you the details that are mine to give. Your sister is indeed alive and well. She's with Sìle and Sosar."

Ruith could hardly believe it, but Soilléir never lied, and his own ears worked perfectly well. "Is she at Seanagarra, then?"

"I didn't say that," Soilléir said, "and you won't care for some of what I am about to say, so hand your knives to your lady—"

"Comrade in arms," Sarah corrected without hesitation.

Soilléir smiled at her. "Take his blades away from him, Sarah, before he loses control during the tale and uses me for a handy place to stow them."

Ruith handed Sarah his knives only because he thought it might purchase him a bit more time to control his rampaging and quite useless emotions. If he'd had any idea his magic would have wrought such a foul work on his good sense, he would have left it where it was. He tried to refill Sarah's cup that needed no refilling, cursed silently as his hands shook, then looked at her in consternation when she took the bottle away from him. He sat back and wished for something to carve at with a knife.

Sarah's hand appeared in his line of sight. He looked at her quickly only to find her watching him gravely.

"A friendly gesture," she said. "Nothing more."

"Are you reading my thoughts as well, lady?" he managed.

"Your face, Your Highness," she said quietly.

It said much about how unsettled he was that he couldn't muster up the energy to chide her for her choice of address. He simply took her hand in both his own, gratefully, then turned to Soilléir.

"Very well. Now that Sarah's unbent enough to keep me from throwing myself into your fire in a fit of pique, tell me everything."

Soilléir sighed. "If you must know—and I'm not certain these are tidings you should have, I want it noted—Mhorghain has embarked on a quest to shut your father's well."

Ruith was on his feet without knowing exactly how he'd gotten there. He glared down at Soilléir. "She most certainly—"

"*Is,*" Soilléir finished for him. "And there's nothing you can do to stop her, so you may as well sit down and spare my floor your stomping. Sìle isn't happy about it, but you've seen the monsters the evil is producing. They're created by a spell of Lothar's, or so I understand."

"And they're hunting those with Camanaë," Rùnach said, from his accustomed position against the wall. "And Father's get, more particularly."

Ruith shot his brother a look—equally irritated with him for not having said anything—paced for a moment or two more, then cast himself back down into his chair. He pulled Sarah's chair closer to his without asking permission, then reached for her hand again.

"I refuse to believe that Sosar and Grandfather are going to go to that bloody well with her," he said. "They never would have agreed to such a thing, especially Grandfather."

"Believe it or not, they did," Soilléir said, "and they are very concerned with keeping her safe, as you might imagine. She has other companions as well, to aid her with her task."

"Who?" Ruith demanded. "They'd best be decent ones."

"Turah of Neroche—"

"Turah?" Ruith interrupted incredulously. "And what is *he* going to do? Sing a lay to all the monsters there and hope to distract them?"

"I heard—" Soilléir paused, then sighed. "Very well, I *saw* her with Keir. They're currently in Léige, if you're curious, preparing their assault. And reforging the Sword of Angesand, which Mhorghain broke in the fall."

Ruith felt his mouth fall open. "She did *what?*"

"She was . . . angry," Soilléir said carefully.

Ruith rubbed his free hand over his face, exchanged another pointed look with his brother, who he was quite certain knew many things he hadn't seen fit to share, then glanced at Sarah. "Wake me when the nightmare is over."

She smiled gravely. "You'll manage."

"I'm not sure how," he said honestly. He turned back to Soilléir. "I can't believe any of this. To start with, I'm stunned she's alive because I saw no sign of her after . . . well, after. I should think she would have sought out one pair of grandparents, but she was very young so perhaps she found refuge in a place I don't want to think about. Last of all, I can't fathom why she would touch Mehar of Angesand's sword, much less destroy it. What in the hell has she been doing all these years?"

"I'll leave the intimate details of her life for her to give you when next you meet," Soilléir said carefully, "but I'll tell you as much of her tale as you need to know now. She found herself, through a series of fortuitous events—"

"Orchestrated by someone, no doubt," Ruith interrupted darkly.

"There have been those interested in keeping her safe," Soilléir agreed, "which shouldn't surprise you. She was taken in by mercenaries after they found her near the well, then deposited on the doorstep of Nicholas of Lismòr where she proceeded to turn the university upside down until she made her way to the opposite side of the island for studies that didn't include books."

Ruith wished he could keep his mouth from continuing to fall open. *"Gobhann?"*

"The very same. And she bears Weger's mark, so I'd be careful about challenging her to any sort of contest with steel. After her release, Nicholas sent her on a quest to take a knife, which happened to be one of Mehar's, to the king of Neroche."

"And why would Nicholas . . ." He found himself considering things he hadn't before. "Something isn't right there. Why would the head of a backward university on a provincial island have one of Queen Mehar's blades?"

Soilléir only waited, silent and watchful.

Ruith suppressed the urge to scratch his head and instead settled for keeping his jaw from falling yet again to his chest. "He's Lismòrian's Nicholas. The wizard king of Diarmailt." He looked at Soilléir in surprise. "I'd never considered that before."

"I believe he counts on that sort of thing to protect his anonymity," Soilléir said. "I also understand that your mother asked him to watch over you all if something happened to her. He looked after Mhorghain as best he could."

"Then why in the *hell* did he allow her to go into Gobhann?" Ruith asked, incensed.

"I don't think he had a choice. You'll find that your sister is very determined when she's chosen a path for herself."

Ruith pursed his lips. "I'm surrounded by stubborn women."

"Necessarily so," Soilléir said, "to keep you from running roughshod over them." He smiled briefly at Sarah, then continued on. "And to continue, Mhorghain couldn't refuse Nicholas's request to take the blade to Tor Neroche, though I understand she wasn't overly fond of the knife, having no knowledge of her own parentage and a healthy disgust for all things magical."

"She didn't know?" Ruith asked. "Anything?"

"I daresay she blocked most of it out, for reasons you would understand. Once on this quest, though, she began to remember things about her past. It would also seem that during the journey she also became rather . . . fond, I believe is the word . . . of a certain member of a company she acquired on her way north. When she found out he was not the simple farmer he'd claimed to be, she took the Sword of Angesand and slammed it against the edge of the high table in the great hall of Tor Neroche, shattering the blade into countless shards."

Ruith looked at him evenly. "You can't mean Adhémar. If you tell me my sister has fallen in love with that great horse's arse, I will—" He spluttered a time or two before he could manage further coherent speech. "I'm not sure what I'll do, but it will be dire and it will include departing immediately for Léige to bring her to her senses."

"It wasn't Adhémar, but you would know that if you remembered our discussion in the library below. He is wed to—"

"Adaira of Penrhyn," Ruith interrupted with a sigh. "I'd forgotten."

"Any other guesses, then?" Soilléir asked with a smile.

"Not Cathar," Ruith said immediately. "Nor Rigaud, I daresay. I can't imagine she would have patience for his preening. Nemed she would grind under her heel inside a se'nnight. That leaves Mansourah, but he hasn't the wit to see to her."

"Nay, he does not," Soilléir agreed.

Ruith considered other brothers, then realized there was only one left to consider. He looked at Soilléir in surprise. "Miach?"

"It would seem so."

"But, he's a *child*!"

"He's a score and eight," Soilléir said calmly. "Almost a score and nine. A scant year and a bit younger than your own ancient self, if I'm counting it aright."

Ruith sat back and shook his head. "How in the *hell* did she meet *him*?"

"As I hinted, he was a member of her company. He had been following Adhémar, who was supposed to be looking for a wielder for the Sword of Angesand but was instead studying the inside of as many taverns as possible. I believe that for Miach it was love at first sight. Your sister, I understand, resisted her feelings for a bit."

"I'll help her resist them a bit longer," Ruith growled.

"Too late for that, I fear," Soilléir said cheerfully. "Your grandfather betrothed them whilst they were here. In the garden of Gearrannan, if memory serves."

"He did," Sarah said helpfully. "The trees were singing about it this morning."

Ruith shot her a dark look. "You didn't say anything."

"At the time I didn't know who the names belonged to," she said. She paused. "They were singing about quite a few people, truth be told."

Ruith looked at her sharply. He'd heard the trees singing as well, but the only names he'd heard had been his own and Sarah's. He frowned, promising himself a goodly think on it later, then turned back to Soilléir.

"I'm surprised Grandfather agreed to it."

"He offered it," Soilléir said pleasantly, "which I think surprised Miach as well. The runes are actually quite lovely. I'm not sure you can gouge them off, but I suppose you might try."

Ruith scowled. "The last time I saw the youngest prince of Neroche, he was hiding under a table in my grandfather's library, memorizing spells and eating figs. I'm sure he hasn't improved since then."

Soilléir laughed. "I think you'll find he has. And how is it you saw him there?"

"Because I was sitting next to him, eating figs and memorizing spells. We were hiding from my grandfather, who had threatened to take a switch to us both for spending the morning flying in dragon-shape." He looked up at his brother lounging against the wall, his expression inscrutable. "You didn't say anything."

"I'm discreet."

Ruith snorted.

"I said nothing to Mhorghain, either," Rùnach added. "Because of . . . well, I said nothing." He shrugged. "Miach knew 'twas me, of course, but he always was a clever lad."

Ruith had to admit that he'd been very good friends with the youngest prince of Neroche, having spent more time than his grandfather would have been happy about appropriating with him spells from various places they shouldn't have been lurking in. But he'd been driven to find things to stop his father and Miach had, well, he'd simply been driven. Perhaps he'd assumed he would one day be facing Lothar of Wychweald.

He looked at Soilléir. "I understand he was a guest in Lothar's dungeon for a bit. Sgath said as much."

Soilléir nodded. "It didn't damage Miach permanently, if you're worried. And he loves your sister to distraction, if that worries you as well. She'll never lack for whatever he can give her. I understand, though, that it took him a bit to convince her that he loved her. And you can imagine what Sìle had to say about it all. Miach had a difficult path to walk with the two of them."

Ruith felt, rather than heard, Sarah fall silent. He released her hand when she seemed to want him to, though he shot her a look at the same time. He would have asked Soilléir for more tales, but a knock sounded on the door and he knew his doom had arrived. He looked at Sarah.

"Please come with me."

"Thank you, Your Highness, but nay."

Ruith sighed, then looked at Soilléir. "I don't suppose you would come to luncheon downstairs and save me from my bad manners."

"Or is it a saving from Droch you're looking for?"

"I don't engage in duels of magic with neophytes, though I understand Miach was fool enough to do so."

"Miach wanted a look in Droch's solar," Soilléir said. "He thought he might find something useful there for Mhorghain's use in closing the well."

"My father never would have used anything of Droch's," Ruith said with a sigh. "I still cannot believe she intends to go to that horrible place and attempt anything at all. If I had any sense—"

"You would leave her to her task and carry on with yours." Soilléir looked at him seriously. "Yours will not be any easier, I assure you."

Ruith chewed on his words for a moment or two. "Are you going to offer any hints, my lord?"

"I wouldn't dream of it." Soilléir put his hands on his knees and rose. "Sarah, I found a pair of books you might be interested in. Luncheon is waiting for you on the table whenever you care to have it. Make yourself at home, of course. Nothing is private, so investigate all you like."

Ruith listened to Sarah thank Soilléir, then waited until Soilléir had gone off to confer with Rùnach before he caught her by the hand.

"Don't open the door," he said in a low voice.

"I won't." She took a deep breath and looked at him. "If I knew how, I would try to see the other pages of Gair's spells—"

"Don't," he said quickly. "Let me be here when you attempt it, lest you need me."

She nodded, though he wasn't sure how serious she was. He was half tempted to set a spell inside Soilléir's that would let him know if she attempted anything untoward, but decided that was perhaps more invasive than he wanted to be. He waited until she'd walked away toward her loom before he looked at Soilléir.

"I'm ready," he grumbled.

"Be polite."

"I have manners. I would just rather save them for that woman over there."

"Who doesn't seem to want anything to do with you. Still."

Ruith shot him a dark look, then followed him across the solar and out the door. He felt Soilléir's spell close behind them, then looked at his host.

"You couldn't add a little extra to that, could you?"

"An alarm?" Soilléir asked mildly.

"Aye."

"I'm her host, not her jailor."

"This will be an extraordinarily short luncheon, then."

Soilléir only smiled at him and walked away.

Ruith looked behind him, on the off chance that Droch was lurking in the shadows, paused, then set his own spell across Soilléir's doorway, one that would alert him if anyone but Rùnach or Sarah walked through it. He took a deep breath, then followed Soilléir.

And he hoped he wouldn't regret it.

Twelve

Sarah watched Ruith and Soilléir leave the chamber, trailed by Rùnach, then saw a spell fall down like a curtain over the door. She knew she should have felt safe, but she was too restless to feel safe. She was tempted to have another bath, but even that didn't appeal. She was cold, so she stood in front of the fire for a bit until she was then too hot and was left with no choice but to pace a bit more. She had no stomach for the very lovely luncheon Soilléir had provided, and she wasn't sure she could sit at a loom and produce anything that wouldn't need to be ripped out and begun again.

She began to pace. Far easier that than simply standing in one place where her thoughts could catch her up. She found herself eventually standing in front of Soilléir's desk, looking down at the books he'd obviously left there for her. She was sure they were nothing out of the ordinary, but somehow even looking at them made her uncomfortable.

Which was, of course, ridiculous. They were simply words on pages. How dangerous could that be?

She took her courage in hand and had another look at them. If they were of a magical nature, she couldn't see it. She picked them up, then carried them back over to the fire and sat down. The silence that fell around her like a cloak was warm and comfortable, Soilléir's doing, no doubt. She concentrated on the books in her hands, happy to have something to do besides ignore the things she'd learned over the past pair of days.

Such as the fact that she could see things she didn't want to. Or that she had, before she could stop herself, agreed to carry on with Ruith on a quest she was sure would lead to places she didn't want to go. Or that she had left Ruith no choice but to at least have a look at ten other women before she would allow him to look at her—and those gels were to be princesses, no less.

She opened the books, just to distract herself. The world was, she was quite sure, full of places she'd never heard of, and apparently the tome she held in her hands was from one of them. It was poetry, she suspected, but she wasn't equal to even beginning to decipher it. The other book was a lexicon, which she supposed would be useful in time in translating the runes on her knife. What she needed first, though, was perhaps a child's primer to help her become acquainted with letters and simple words.

She kept the books in her lap and simply stared into the fire, grateful beyond measure for a bit of peace where she didn't have to think about anything more serious than how she would stay awake.

It was destined not to last much longer, she knew, but for the moment, she would enjoy it and not wish for anything else.

She woke to the sound of the door opening at the opposite end of the solar. She jumped briefly, then realized it was just Ruith and Soilléir, arguing in a good-natured way about how things had gone below. Rùnach, she realized with a start, was standing in his accustomed place at the window, but with his back turned to her, no doubt to give her a bit of privacy. She wondered how long he'd been there and how deeply she'd slept. Long enough for the books to grow warm under her hands, which was odd, but she set the thought aside in favor of watching Ruith. He smiled, then turned back to his discussion with Soilléir as they continued across the floor.

He was, as she had noted on more than one occasion, exceptionally handsome. He looked as though he'd spent the whole of his life doing physical labor, though without the roughness of it having aged him before his time. Then again, he was an elf—only three-quarters, as he would have said—so perhaps he had no reason to worry about having his face prematurely lined.

There was something about him, though, that she hadn't seen before. She rested her chin on her fist and studied him as dispassionately as possible. She wasn't sure if it was the Fadaire that shimmered in his veins or if it was merely that he was in a place where, for a change, he was accepted for who he was.

He looked happy.

His expression didn't change as he pulled up a chair next to her and dropped down into it with a sigh. He looked at her and then smiled.

"How are you, l—er, I mean, my friend?"

She supposed she couldn't complain about what he called her when she had been the one to insist on the terms of their relationship. He might think he wouldn't indulge in a dalliance, but he also hadn't seen what would be rushing his way like a mighty river all clad in silks and tulle once those finely dressed lassies discovered he was alive.

He smoothed her hair back from her face. "You think too much."

"The future requires much thought," she said, parroting her mother's favorite saying before she realized what she was doing.

"Yours shouldn't," he said, his smile fading. "It should be full of nothing but happiness, beautiful yarns to please your hands, and the laughter of children to please your ears." He stopped abruptly, as if he feared he'd said too much, then leaned closer to her. "What do you have there?" he asked, pretending great interest in the books she held.

She put her hand over the cover of the topmost one. "One is a book of poetry written in a language I don't recognize. The second is a lexicon, but I can't even begin to read the runes on my knives, so I'm not sure where to start with it." She looked at Soilléir, who had come to sit in the chair across from hers. "My lord?"

He smiled. "The language is Mórachd, the tongue of Cothromaiche. We are a very small place in the grander scheme of things, a land full of lovers of good wine and pleasant poetry. Your knives bear the runes of my country, though I can't imagine who would have forged them."

He blinked owlishly, which led Sarah to immediately suspect he was attempting a lie. She might have pursued that more thoroughly, but she had other questions for him. She supposed politeness suggested that she tread lightly in asking the question that had nagged at her even in her dreams, but perhaps Soilléir wasn't one to offend easily. She cleared her throat and looked at him.

"Do you all see?" she asked. "Or is it just you who possesses not only sight but magic enough to undo the world?"

"Both, though you flatter me with the latter," Soilléir said with a modest little smile. "I would tell you of my people, but the history isn't very interesting and likely too violent for your peace of mind this afternoon. Instead, if you'll hand me the book of poetry, I'll read to you from it. The fair Sarait was unwilling to listen to my words of love, but even she would humor me through a heroic poem or two."

Sarah handed him what he'd asked for, even though she would rather have known what he'd done to her eyes so he could reverse it, but perhaps she could talk him into that after supper.

She leaned her head back and closed her eyes as Soilléir read. Though the verse was nothing but words at first, it soon became something far different, a picture that slowly came to life in front of her eyes. The rivers ran, a breeze set the trees to whispering secrets she was sure she could hear if she listened closely enough, and the flowers swayed as they sang in the heavy summer grasses. It was as beautiful in its own way as what she'd seen of Fadaire in the garden of Gearrannan, though somehow less elvish. Less glittering. Elegant, but not intimidatingly magnificent.

She liked it quite a bit.

"Sarah?"

She opened her eyes and realized that Soilléir was watching her. "Aye, my lord?"

"What did you think of it?"

"Rustic," Ruith said with a snort.

"I don't believe I asked you, whelp," Soilléir said darkly. He turned a smile on Sarah. "What did *you* think, my dear?"

"I liked it very much," she said, but that seemed inadequate somehow. "I could see what you were reading, as if it were happening afresh as the words were read." She paused. "What do you think?"

He only smiled, then closed the book and handed it back to her. "Would you mind if I had a small game of chess with Ruith?"

Sarah pursed her lips. "You aren't going to answer me, are you?"

"Timing, my dear. It is all about timing."

And she imagined her time at Buidseachd would run out long before he managed to answer anything at all. She waved him and Ruith on to their game, happy to simply sit in front of the fire and be warm. She supposed she should enjoy that whilst she could.

She watched as Soilléir set up a chessboard between the two chairs.

But he didn't pull out pieces.

She looked at Ruith in surprise, but he was only watching Soilléir with an expression she couldn't quite identify at first. She wouldn't have said it was resignation and it certainly wasn't annoyance. It was as if he'd expected nothing less than what was coming his way and was almost resigned to his fate.

She wondered, briefly, what it would be like to walk into a place and be known, even after a score of years. She supposed she could have walked into the pub in Doìre and had Franciscus—

Nay, he wouldn't have been there any longer. And if he had been, she would have had some very pointed questions for him as well.

There would come a day when she had the boldness to demand answers from recalcitrant mages when she wanted them.

She turned back to what apparently passed for a game of chess at Buidseachd. Soilléir was very calmly setting up his board with traditional-looking pieces, though Sarah could easily see they were not fashioned from wood or marble. Ruith sighed deeply, then began to people his side of the board. They marched themselves out quite sedately, those creations of his imagination, beginning with the pawns, then moving on to the major and minor pieces in the back row. His queen he dressed in exquisite robes of emerald and his king in gold and sapphire. He paused, glanced at Soilléir, then placed fire-breathing dragons atop both his rooks.

He lifted an eyebrow in challenge.

Soilléir answered by changing his knights' steeds into even larger, jewel-encrusted, fire-snorting beasts that hovered in the air just above their places, beating their wings impatiently.

Ruith looked at her. "You might want to move back a bit, love."

She was happy to decamp for a stool a goodly distance away from the board.

"Your move, Ruith," Soilléir said placidly.

Sarah was sitting behind him, but she could hear the suppressed delight in his voice, as if he were about to engage in something he'd savoured in the past and missed for far too long.

"Happily, my *lord*," Ruith said pointedly.

A burly-looking toad hopped forward, hesitated, then belched. Soilléir laughed and the game was begun. Sarah had imagined it wouldn't be all that sedate a match, but she realized quite quickly she had underestimated the skill and imagination of the players involved.

A mighty battle ensued, replete with fire and smoke and flashes of lightning cast down by clouds that sprang up over the board—and beyond, truth be told—and drenched all involved. Insults and weapons were hurled—and not just from the pieces—then chairs were pushed back from the board to give the combatants—mortal or not, as was the case—a bit more room to manage the fray.

And then Soilléir looked over his shoulder at her. "You might want to move," he suggested.

Again? was almost out of her mouth but she didn't have time for it. She watched as a spell sprang up to the ceiling, spread out, and dropped to the floor like a curtain. The board went skidding across the floor, its pieces clinging to it like a raft, only to immediately increase in size until it filled almost all the solar. The struggle continued, but this time it was life-sized and limited, apparently, only to the resourcefulness of the mages in charge of their armies. It was no sedate game full of dignity and Nerochian rules of fair play. It was a glorious brawl with swords, spells, and creatures from myth. She didn't recognize half the beasties she saw nor the spells she heard. It was also quite obvious to her that Soilléir and Ruith had been at this sort of thing before.

In time, the game finished with a spectacular amount of shouting and spells.

And then Sarah realized that all that had come before was just a skirmish before the true battle began. The board disappeared, and it was just Ruith and Soilléir facing each other, fighting with spells.

Rùnach stepped in front of her suddenly.

"What are you doing?" Sarah asked rather breathlessly.

"Protecting you," he said faintly, "though I'm not sure with what." He looked over his shoulder at her. "I thought I'd best attempt something as not."

She peeked around his shoulder, then took her courage in hand and moved to stand next to him where she could see a bit better. "Soilléir won't kill him, will he?"

"I don't think so," Rùnach said, sounding none too sure about that, "but I suspect my wee brother might wish he had after they've had done with their sport."

Sarah swallowed with difficulty. "Why is Soilléir doing this?"

"Why do you think?"

Sarah imagined she could come up with several reasons if she gave it enough thought. Perhaps Soilléir thought to test Ruith's resolve, or strength, or ability to encounter spells that made her flinch when she saw them being flung his way. In the end, she decided that Soilléir was hell-bent on showing Ruith just where he was lacking.

She also decided, after what had to have been half an hour of spectacle, that it was going to be a very long afternoon. She fetched her loom's bench, then sat down and offered Rùnach the other half of it. He considered, then went to procure a bottle and two glasses. He poured wine for them both and handed her a glass before he sat down. Sarah watched the skirmish for a bit longer in silence, then looked up at Ruith's brother.

His face bore marks that could have come from falling against unyielding stone, but surely Soilléir could have healed those well enough. Perhaps they were trails of something left behind by his father stealing his magic.

Odd how her arm bore the same sort of wound.

She looked into Rùnach's eyes and smiled. "A sister and a pair of brothers," she said quietly. "I'm glad for you."

"Family is a good thing," he agreed. He nodded toward Ruith. "He has become everything our mother would have wished for him, despite his years masquerading as a curmudgeon."

"He wasn't happy about giving up the disguise," Sarah said with a smile, "but I think he needed to. Not, of course, that I know him well enough to judge that." She shifted uncomfortably. "It's just an observation."

"An apt one," he agreed. He studied his brother for several minutes in silence. "Whatever else he's done, he's become a good swordsman."

Sarah had to agree. Though Ruith was using spells and not a blade, he moved as if he parried steel and fought as if he'd had a sword in his hands. She supposed he might think differently, but to her eye, the years of defending himself with his hands alone and no doubt looking for weaknesses in opponents that might not have been plain to a mage's eye had certainly not harmed him any.

Soilléir flinched at a particularly pointed spell he had to stretch to counter, then laughed. "Damn you, Ruith, what spells *didn't* you filch?"

"I told you my library was extensive," Ruith said, his chest heaving.

"Aye, well, so is mine," Soilléir said.

Rùnach sighed lightly. "Ruith is in for it now."

Sarah couldn't bring herself to speculate on what he might have meant by that. She was far too busy watching Soilléir throw apparently more than the usual complement of spells at Ruith. They began as swarms of beelike things that Ruith countered easily enough, then changed to mighty winds, which Ruith fought off much less easily, then enormous waves that beat down on him, which left him finally on his knees, simply struggling to fight off Soilléir's attack with an ever-weakening magic of his own.

And then Soilléir cast a spell of Olc over him.

Sarah watched it, shocked at its vileness—and that was saying something given the rather gory battle she'd just witnessed. She wouldn't have been surprised if Ruith had caught it, then thrown it back accompanied by a spell of some sort of terrible harm.

He didn't. He simply watched it fall over him, obviously exhausted by the battle, then with a single word sent it scattering in shards that slid across the floor to encounter Soilléir's spell of . . . well, Sarah wouldn't have called it protection. Containment, perhaps. Then again, what did she know? It had kept their battle within its confines and apparently absorbed what came its way. It treated the Olc no differently than it had anything else.

The Olc disappeared as if it had never been there. Ruith leaned over with his hands on the floor, gasping for breath. Soilléir's spells disappeared completely, leaving no trace of the chessboard, the pieces, or the magic that had so recently filled the solar with such terrible noise and lightning. Instead, there was just Ruith, shaking with weariness, and Soilléir.

Who was breathing with a little more enthusiasm than usual, truth be told.

Rùnach started to rise, but Sarah put her hand on his arm. "I'll fetch wine for them."

"Thank you, my lady," Rùnach said quietly. "I think I may have my hands full with carrying my brother over to a chair."

Sarah declined to offer him any advice on that, even though

she'd been the one to get Ruith on his horse and away from the well after his battle with the trolls there. She looked at him critically. He was grey, but not senseless, which she supposed was something of an improvement. He didn't decline the aid, however, when Soilléir pulled him to his feet and Rùnach drew his arm over his shoulders to help him over to a chair in front of the fire.

Sarah fetched two glasses and a bottle from the cabinet where she'd seen Rùnach go before. She walked over to the hearth, poured the wine, then set the bottle down. She handed Ruith his cup and would have happily walked away to take Rùnach's place in the shadows, but Ruith caught her by the arm before she could.

"Sit, please," he said, sounding rather breathless. "And forgive my condition. I'll bathe later."

"Not on my account," she began, but he shook his head.

"I do have decent manners now and again," he said. He had a long drink of his wine, spent another moment or two trying to catch his breath, then looked at Soilléir. "I'm not sure if you deserve wine or curses—especially for that last gift."

"I wanted to see what you would do," Soilléir said tranquilly. He cast himself down into his own chair and blew his fair hair out of his eyes. "Though I suppose I was more interested in what you *wouldn't* do. Thank you for the wine, Sarah." He smiled at her. "Shall we play a game, you and I?"

"After that spectacle?" she asked without hesitation. She pushed herself to her feet immediately. "I have too much weaving to do for a relaxing game of strategy, though I thank you just the same."

Soilléir smiled at her as she passed by him, which led her to believe he'd had no intention of treating her as he'd treated Ruith. Still, she had no stomach for chess pieces that weren't fashioned of inanimate substances.

She wove in relative peace for almost an hour, perhaps a bit more, before she could no longer escape what had been nagging her. She sat at her loom and simply held the shuttle in her hand. Ten princesses? She shook her head at her own shortsightedness. She should have insisted on a hundred of them. Ruith was an elven prince with the power to match his title. The thought of him—

"You think too much," Ruith whispered loudly as he walked unsteadily past her.

She looked at him, had a smile as her reward, then watched him disappear into a chamber where he was presumably going to tidy himself up. She looked the other way and watched Soilléir and Rùn-ach leave, presumably to go fetch supper.

She sat there, alone, and considered what she'd seen. She had wondered, now and again, if she might, at some point, lay claim to even the tiniest bit of magic, inherited from her mother. She would have been satisfied with calling fire or a handy spell of un-noticing.

But now that she had seen what Ruith could do and what she suspected was the very beginning of what Soilléir could do, she realized that making a fire and hiding her best skeins of wool was a very meager wish indeed.

Worse still, she wouldn't manage even that.

She put her shoulders back and recaptured her good sense. She would find her brother, help Ruith find his father's spells, then she would do the most sensible thing of all.

She would help him off on his merry—and marriageable—way.

It was, as it happened, the most she could do.

Thirteen

Ruith dreamed.

He walked down unfamiliar streets of Beinn òrain looking for some-thing he couldn't name. That in itself was unsettling given that he always recognized the landscape of his nightmares. Then again, they usually had to do with his past, his father, and being unable to save his family. The current torment, however, was full of things he didn't recognize, seen in a way that he wasn't accustomed to. Layered over it all was a feeling of urgency that was less a raging fire than it was a slow, relentless pushing that left him feeling as if he were nearing the edge of a precipice and would soon be going over it whether he willed it or no.

Without warning, he was no longer walking down the street. He was on wing, flying away from Beinn òrain. He looked down from an impossible height and saw the twinkling lights of cities and villages beneath him.

He descended toward the earth in swooping circles until he found himself flying along the edge of the plains of Ailean. It was then that he realized he wasn't looking at twinkling lights from welcoming homes.

He was looking at fires.
And they hadn't been caused by lads with flint and dry tinder . . .

Ruith woke with a start and sat up so quickly, he had to lie back down until his head stopped spinning. He put his hand over his eyes and simply breathed in and out for a moment or two until the dizziness passed. He looked to his right to find Sarah lying on the pallet in front of the fire, still sleeping. He stared at her for a moment or two, then it occurred to him that he hadn't been dreaming his dreams.

He'd been dreaming hers.

He realized with another startling bit of clarity that his sight in her dreams had been magnified far beyond what he ever saw in his own nightly visions. He put his hand over hers, then had her clutch his fingers so tightly that it pained him, though she slept still. He reached out with his free hand and smoothed the hair back from her face until she finally let out a deep, shuddering breath and her dream receded.

He considered all the fires he'd seen and wished that he'd been able to see them more clearly. He wondered if Sarah had, or if she knew what they were—

He froze. They hadn't been fires; they had been his father's spells.

He pushed himself to his feet without delay, groaning in spite of himself and regretting quite thoroughly the twenty years he'd spent without using his magic. He had certainly been no portly trader reclining on his spoils, but there was a difference between weaving heavy spells and engaging in a more pedestrian sort of labor. A pity he had no time to shoulder the burden of the former. He would just have to carry on as he could.

And hope Sarah didn't pay the price for it.

He had no idea what time it was, but it was still dark in Soilléir's chamber, so perhaps sunrise was still a distant hope. He turned to look at the windows only to find Soilléir standing there. Ruith walked quietly over to join him. Soilléir said nothing. He merely stood, still as stone, and looked out over the city. Heaven only knew what he was seeing. Ruith was quite certain he didn't want to know.

But curiosity was his worst fault, so he asked the question he'd been wondering about for quite some time.

"How do you bear it?"

"Centuries of living," Soilléir answered, not looking at him.

"Tell me of it, if you will," Ruith said very quietly. "That seeing."

Soilléir shrugged. "If one is fortunate, it comes to one's hand slowly, sight by sight, until the sight of everything together isn't so overwhelming. For others, it comes all at once and they're fairly incoherent for several months until they learn to manage what they see."

"It comes all at once?" Ruith asked. "Or it's forced upon them?"

Soilléir looked at him then. "And what else should I have done, Ruithneadh? Allowed our gel to long for Droch's garden every moment of every day until it either drove her mad or left her offering to be one of the pieces on his board simply so she could wrap Olc around her in hopes that it would ease her craving for it? Or should I have made the choice for her I did, which was to force her to see the truth and hope you would help her through the pain of it?"

"I fear I won't be the one she turns to for comfort," Ruith said grimly.

"An elven prince and a witchwoman's get with no magic," Soilléir mused. "An interesting pairing."

"She said exactly that."

"She is a very wise gel. And to answer the question you haven't asked, Seeing is usually a bloodright magic, but not always—just as there has been the occasional farmer standing out in his pasture, examining his hay, who wakes to realize he's just become the archmage of Neroche. I have it because my father had it, and his father before him for as long as our line stretches back into the dreams of our forebearers. The magic itself comes from Bruadair, where the dreamweavers wander through their forests of spells and visions. But I have met those who have it gifted to them with no apparent connection to that birthright."

Ruith looked at him. "Then you understand what she's suffering?"

"I wouldn't call it that," Soilléir said with a pained smile. "She will find it useful, in time. As for the pain she endures now, how should I ease it for her? The work must be done, whether 'tis done slowly or quickly. Just as your work must be done, be it slowly or quickly."

Ruith supposed that with Soilléir, he had no pride left. "My thanks for the game last night."

"You look to have recovered well enough."

"Not quickly enough," Ruith said with a sigh, "but that will come in time."

"Aye, it will."

Ruith turned to study the few twinkling lamplights in the city below. "Why are you here?" he asked, finally. "Instead of in Cothromaiche?"

Soilléir's breath caught, then he laughed very softly, if not a bit uneasily. "That is twice you've had me off balance over the past few days. How do you manage it?"

"I lie awake at nights working on it."

Soilléir shot him a faintly amused look. "I daresay." He folded his arms over his chest. "Only one other person has ever asked me that, not finding the usual reason of keeping Droch in check to be sufficient."

"Not my mother," Ruith said with a shake of his head.

"Nay, not your mother," Soilléir agreed. "She had far too much on her mind to worry about the twists and turns of my life. It was Desdhemar of Neroche. She and Miach are cut from the same cloth, you know, relentlessly seeking to know things they likely should leave alone."

Ruith had his own thoughts on things Miach should leave alone—namely his own sweet sister, who was definitely not old enough to be making decisions about her future without him, no matter what Soilléir or Sìle thought—but he kept those thoughts to himself. He studied Soilléir for a bit longer. "Is there an answer?"

"Not a very interesting one," Soilléir said with a shrug. "To be the youngest son in a house full of sons . . . let's just say my work is best done here. My family is not overly large, but my great-grandfather did have several children, which you may or may not know, having had your own share of things to think on that didn't include Cothro-maichian genealogy. The magic in my family, as you also may not know, is a capricious thing."

"Dangerous, you mean," Ruith corrected.

Soilléir laughed softly. "And just how many times did you hear Sìle of Tòrr Dòrainn say that in your youth?"

"Every time my mother mentioned your name," Ruith said without hesitation. "He would roar, 'Sarait, you will *not* associate any longer with that young rogue full of dangerous magic!'"

"There are those of my family to whom that description might apply," Soilléir agreed, "though I am more inclined to settle for capricious. It manifests itself differently throughout our lines."

"But always with great discretion," Ruith said dryly.

Soilléir slid him a look. "Are you mocking me, Ruith?"

"And find myself turned into a rock when I've still a stubborn, beautiful, impossible woman to convince to look at me twice?" Ruith asked with mock horror. "Of course not."

Soilléir studied him for a moment or two in silence. "You know that you could have any lass from any house of the Nine Kingdoms— or, I imagine, from any house whose ruler would very much like to sit on the Council of Kings."

Ruith shook his head. "I don't want a life at court."

"You won't escape it—and you'll force Sarah to be a part of it."

"She walked into Ceangail with nothing but her courage in order to rescue me. I think she can manage the odd supper at Seanagarra."

"But does she want to?"

Ruith pursed his lips. "When you find yourself in love, my lord Soilléir, just know that I will be there to aid you precisely as you're aiding me now if I have to crawl to where you are in order to enjoy the spectacle of you wallowing in your longing. I might, out of gratitude for the current safe haven, toss you a rope or something else quite pedestrian to keep you from drowning in the swamp."

"You have a very generous heart, Ruith."

"I doubt Sarah would agree, though I extended the courtesy of three no-need-to-justify-the-reason begging offs from social functions in return for her having placed on me the burden of becoming acquainted with ten princesses before I am allowed to pursue her wholeheartedly. She used one yesterday. I imagine she'll be more judicious with them in the future."

"Pray she doesn't use one to avoid being at your wedding."

Ruith laughed uneasily. "I hadn't considered that, though I should have."

Soilléir turned and leaned against the wooden window frame. "What will you do now?"

Ruith sighed. "I thought to make for Léige, to see if Keir might have remained behind, or returned there . . . after."

"Will Uachdaran let you in his gates, do you think?" Soilléir asked with what could have been charitably called a smirk.

"I'll approach on bended knee," Ruith said darkly. "King Uachdaran might allow me in if he knows I've just come to look for my brother. And after I've pried what I need to from Keir, I suppose we'll continue to look for spells and search for Sarah's brother." He paused. "I thought perhaps we should leave tonight."

"Agreed," Soilléir said. "There is mischief afoot in the world."

Ruith would have given much for a peep inside Soilléir's head, but there was no point in asking for it. There was no harm in asking a few questions, though, never mind that he didn't imagine he would have answers that would ease him any.

"I'm curious," he said slowly, "and I didn't have time to search in the library below for anything useful. I don't suppose you know a mage called Urchaid, do you? Or Franciscus?"

"Franciscus is a fairly common name in the north," Soilléir said with a shrug. "Unless you've more specifics for me than that, I can't help you. Urchaid, on the other hand, is a fairly *un*common name, of

which only a handful of men come to mind. There was Urchaid of
Srath, who fought against Cuideil of An-uallach, though I believe
he was slain by a serving girl who poisoned his wine. That shouldn't
come as much of a surprise knowing the cantankerous nature of the
inhabitants of An-uallach."

Ruith had no experience with them, so he remained silent.

"There was an Urchaid of Tòsan, who was one of the wizards
who argued against casting Lothar of Wychweald from the schools
of wizardry, but your grandmother Eulasaid would know more
about him than I would." He paused and considered. "The only
other Urchaid of note that comes to mind is Urchaid of Saothair."

Ruith blinked. "Who?"

"Droch's brother."

Ruith felt something slither down his spine. "I'd heard that there
was another one roaming the world besides Wehr and Droch."

"And where did you hear that?"

"In a pub," Ruith said with a snort. "Some drunkard was delight-
ing his companions with gruesome tales of how Dorchadas of Saothair had looked on his eight sons to decide which was the strongest
so he might slay the rest. There was universal agreement that he
hadn't been able to choose between Wehr and Droch, but the teller
of very tall tales was convinced that another son had escaped whilst
his father was otherwise occupied with that decision."

"'Tis possible, I suppose."

Ruith considered for a moment or two. "What of Dorchadas?
Does he live still?"

Soilléir shrugged. "He's still alive, I imagine, weaving his webs
of evil in some forgotten corner of the world."

Ruith thought about the Urchaid he knew for a moment or two,
then shook his head. For one thing, Urchaid looked nothing like
Droch, and the other . . . well, he was fairly sure that when Dorchadas of Saothair killed something, he made sure he'd done the job
properly. Tales heard in a pub were best relegated to just that. He
considered other things for a bit longer, then looked at Soilléir.

"If my father's spells are out in the world, loose, would Droch want them, do you think?"

"Assuredly," Soilléir said. "Droch was—is still, I daresay—incoherently jealous of your sire's power. And to have a collection of his most treasured spells and Gair not be able to stop his using them? Aye, I daresay he would have them if he could lay his hands on them. But you can be sure he is but the start of a very lengthy list of those who would want the same."

Ruith leaned back against the opposite window casing. "We can be thankful then, that Droch has no idea what I'm looking for."

"I doubt he'll be in the dark about that for long," Soilléir said dryly, "particularly if your half brothers exercise their notoriously loose tongues about it."

Ruith sighed. "I wish he'd never written that book."

"Could you write down what you remember of it?"

Ruith shot him a look. "I could, but I will not."

Soilléir smiled. "Just testing."

Ruith found himself being studied in a way he didn't particularly care for, but it was Soilléir after all, and there was nothing he could do but endure it and swear a bit to make himself feel better.

"Were all his spells contained in that book, do you suppose?" Soilléir asked.

Ruith looked at him sharply. "What do you mean?"

"I just wonder if he was working on other things that perhaps weren't quite perfect enough to write down. It was your father, after all."

Ruith looked over his shoulder to see if someone had opened a door or a window or if the fire had gone out. Surely that was the only reason for the sudden chill that brushed against his neck. "He was forever honing spells into something vile, which you well know. What sort of other things do you think he was contemplating?"

"I don't know," Soilléir said, looking at him with clear, innocent eyes. "What do *you* think?"

Ruith pushed away from the window and walked away, because

he didn't like what he'd heard and he liked even less the thought of having to contemplate what madness his sire had been considering during the last days of his life.

Other spells?

He shuddered to think.

He paced to the doorway and back before he stopped again in front of the window and looked at Soilléir.

"The list could be long."

"Or very short."

Ruith swore. "Why are you pursuing this?"

"Because I fear," Soilléir said quietly, "that there are things out in the world that truly *will* undo it unless they're found and destroyed. Things loosed that should be contained. Spells and thoughts and schemes that I cannot see and couldn't—wouldn't—stop even if I knew where to look."

Ruith turned to stare out the window until the faint light of dawn stretched across the sky. "There are times," he said finally, "when I profoundly regret walking out my front door and putting my foot to the path waiting for me."

"I imagine you do. But then you wouldn't have met Sarah."

Sarah. Ruith blew out his breath. It was one thing to contemplate taking Sarah along with him when the journey was comfortably far away; it was another thing to be facing that moment and realize what it would mean. He looked at Soilléir. "I'm going to leave her here."

"Nay, Your Highness, you are not."

Ruith closed his eyes briefly, shot Soilléir a warning look, then turned to find Sarah awake and standing behind him, watching him with her arms folded over her chest.

"Sarah," he began, dragging his hand through his hair.

"I'm almost finished with my cloth," she said briskly. She looked at Soilléir. "I might need needle and thread, if I could trouble you for both."

"I think I can do better than that and even dredge up a seam-stress or two," Soilléir said with a smile.

She glared at Ruith, then walked off to her loom. Ruith watched her go, then turned to Soilléir and lifted an eyebrow.

Soilléir shrugged. "She's formidable. And you need her, for more things than just her sight. You'll just have to keep her safe."

"I don't want her to come along," Ruith said grimly.

"And what is your other choice?" Soilléir asked. "Leave her behind with me? You have the power to protect her. I daresay even your father would find you a difficult opponent now."

"My mother was his equal," Ruith said, "and yet she failed to stop him."

"And she failed because his power had been augmented by your brothers' magic, which you well know. If you could turn back the wheels of time and face him as a man, I think you might be slightly more cynical about what he might do than your mother was and act accordingly. Though, in her defense, she was balancing trying to stop him with trying to keep her children safe."

"I regret that she had to face that," Ruith said quietly.

"As do I."

Ruith imagined Soilléir would have stopped the entire thing if he'd been able to—and he was equally sure it hadn't been a lack of capability so much as a self-imposed vow of discretion that included not interfering in the choices of others.

"I can't imagine," Ruith said quietly, sure Soilléir would know what he intended by it.

"I sincerely hope, my friend, that you never have to," Soilléir said.

Ruith sighed, then caught sight of Sarah sitting at her loom. He could safely say that any regret about his current path lasted only as long as it took him to look for her in any given chamber.

And the rest of the truth was, he had spent a score of years hiding, but also pacing in place, as if he'd waited for a task he'd somehow known he was destined to take on. And if that task sent him into his father's darkness, so be it. He supposed it hadn't been happenstance that the majority of the books in his library had been books of spells, gathered from obscure sources, and for the most part incomplete. He had passed the years stretching his mind in directions it hadn't perhaps been meant to go, pushing himself to think in ways he'd never anticipated he would even want to.

He was, he could admit with a fair bit of distaste, a bit like his sire when it came to that sort of thing.

But to consider things his father had been creating near the end of his miserable life?

It would take an event of monumental proportions to inspire him to do that.

He thanked Soilléir for the pleasant conversation, paced about the solar a score of times, then came to stand next to Sarah. She paused in her work, scowled at him, then shifted just the slightest bit so he would have a place to perch. He did, with his back to her work but still so he could see her face.

"I want you to stay here."

"You don't," she said without hesitation. "Not in truth."

He had to sigh a little. "Very well, I don't in truth, but I also don't want you to come where I fear we'll need to go."

"You need me."

"Well, that is true as well," he agreed. "But for more than just your sight."

She elbowed him rather firmly in the ribs. "Concentrate on what route we'll take." She continued to work, though a bit more slowly. "I dreamed last night."

"I know," he said quietly. "I was caught up in it."

She almost dropped her shuttle. "Then you saw the spells?"

He shook his head. "I saw fires, but I couldn't tell you where they were."

She took a deep breath. "I could."

"I suspected as much." He watched her continue on with her cloth, a greyish green that he imagined would blend in quite well in whatever landscape they found themselves. It shimmered with something that wasn't precisely earthly, so he imagined that the yarn had been enspelled somehow. "I was thinking we should retrace our steps," he said slowly. "North."

Her hands stilled for a moment, then she continued her work without speaking.

"I would like to find Franciscus, if finding can be done," he ventured. "I have a few questions for him, which I imagine you do as well."

"Very pointed ones," she agreed.

"The other person I would like to find is Urchaid. Soilléir gave me an idea or two about lads with that name, but he doesn't seem to be any of them." He couldn't bring himself to wonder if Urchaid the fop might have somehow escaped the heavy hand of his father's filial jealousy. He certainly wasn't going to speculate aloud with Sarah listening. "Whoever he is, he is up to no good, I daresay."

"I daresay," she murmured. "What do you think he want—nay, never mind." She looked at him. "They all want what Gair had, don't they?"

"I'm afraid so. And I fear we've only begun to unravel the web being woven." Which was why he wanted her nowhere near any of that web, but as Soilléir had once said, Soilléir wouldn't be her jailor. Better that she be where he could protect her than trapped in the schools of wizardry where she didn't dare venture out into the passageway.

"How will we travel?" she asked. "On foot?"

He pulled himself back to the task at hand. "I'll find horses somewhere and pay the seller with a few spells. Perhaps Soilléir will gift us food for the start of the journey. We'll make do as we travel."

She concentrated on her weaving for a bit longer, silent. Ruith didn't interrupt her. He merely sat next to her, considering the women of his family, powerful in their own right, endowed with magic that commanded respect even among the mighty ones of the world. He wondered, absently, what his grandfather would say when he brought home the very unmagical daughter of the witchwoman Seleg and announced that he'd inspected the required ten princesses, and would Sìle mind putting on three luxurious banquets so Sarah could only refuse two of them before she was forced to attend and listen to a proposal of marriage. Surely Sìle wouldn't roar at a woman. Ruith imagined that his own ears would be ringing for quite some time.

Somehow, he rather thought he would have preferred to take her to Lake Cladach where Sgath dressed in homespun and Eulasaid tended her gardens herself and had a great appreciation for what two hands could fashion from finely spun yarn.

Sarah finished with her cloth, then paused and looked at him. "We'll leave tonight?"

He nodded.

"I'll draw as much of a map as I can manage," she said briskly. "And see about finishing these cloaks for us."

He nodded, ignoring the way her hands trembled slightly as she took one of her knives and began to slit her warp threads. He wondered what the runes said and wondered further why Soilléir hadn't seemed to find time to translate them for her.

"Are you napping?"

He smiled faintly. "Just thinking."

"You look more at peace, if that pleases you."

"Do I?" he asked in surprise. "Was I not peaceful before?"

She rolled her eyes and slid off the bench. He was fairly certain he'd heard her mutter that what he had been before was in great need of a lengthy soaking of his head. He watched her walk away to confer with Soilléir about seamstresses, then found himself joined on Sarah's bench suddenly by his elder brother, who also seemed to find the sight of an elegant weaver of lovely cloth to be worth his study. Too close a study, actually.

"Mine," Ruith said distinctly.

"She might have an opinion about that."

"I'm planning an extended campaign to sway that opinion my way."

Rùnach smiled, a crooked thing that hadn't lost any of its wryness. "I would happily stand along the edge of the road and offer any assistance I could."

"Aye, by seeing if there might be a team of horses coming along which you might invite to crush me underfoot," Ruith said darkly. He looked at his brother assessingly. "You like her."

"Very much. Unfortunately, she seems to be looking at you more than is polite. I thought to warn her of the inadvisability of such a practice but didn't want to burden her with anything unpleasant." He shot Ruith a look. "I've tucked a few friendly notes into the book of Cothromaichian child's verse I found for her downstairs."

"Got to it before Soilléir did, did you?"

"I thought it prudent."

"Find your own wife."

"I'm trying to."

"Well, you can't have that one," Ruith said, realizing quite suddenly that his brother was serious. "I saw her first."

"She might like me better."

"Which is why we're leaving tonight," he said, then he shut his mouth as Sarah walked over to them to retrieve some pieces of thread for her seamstress.

She found it, then stopped and looked at them both with a frown.

"What mischief are you two combining?"

"Nothing," Ruith said promptly. "Just a friendly discussion about—"

"Love," Rùnach interrupted smoothly.

"A brotherly, comradely, platonic sort of love," Ruith finished, elbowing his brother rather firmly in the ribs. "Nothing more."

She looked at them both as if they'd lost their wits, then turned and walked away. Rùnach sighed wistfully.

"She is exceptionally charming."

"I'll invite you to her wedding," Ruith said. "To me."

Rùnach lifted his eyebrows. "That remains to be seen. I believe I'll go see to a few luxuries for her pack." He slapped Ruith companionably on the back of the head, then heaved himself to his feet and walked away.

Ruith watched him go, then smiled to himself. He would have given much to have simply lingered where he was, enjoying the company of his brother, the tartness of a certain lovely woman, and the tales of a man who had loved his mother.

At least he might continue on with one of the three, though he imagined there would come a time when he would wish she had been safely left behind with the others.

Other spells that Gair of Ceangail had been working on?

He shuddered to think.

Fourteen

Sarah stood near the fire, holding her hands to the blaze and purposely ignoring the fact that her fingers were well past the point
where any fire could warm them. She wasn't afraid, never mind
that she was leaving a place of safety and comfort—and that she
should have found either in a clutch of mages was alarming in and
of itself—or that she was walking into a future filled with no safety
and likely very little comfort—also filled with mages, but of a different sort entirely.

Nay, she wasn't afraid.

She was speechless with terror.

It was one thing to sit at a loom of such quality she half fancied
she could have woven spiderwebs into something that would have
been sung about for centuries to come and know that taking up the
task of looking for her brother, stopping his stupidity, and aiding
Ruith in whatever small, inconsequential thing he contemplated was
still comfortably far in the future.

It was another thing to know that future was now waiting just outside the door.

She didn't want to think about that future or where it might lead her, so to distract herself, she began a list of things that seemed to be in her favor. She was still without gold or home, but she was wearing very sturdy boots, warm leggings and a tunic, and the cloth she had woven had been gifted—no doubt by Soilléir himself—a measure of glamour that she was confident would hide her if necessary. She was wearing a pack that she hadn't filled herself, but had been assured by Rùnach would contain all she needed for at least the beginning of the trek. She had drawn a map of what she'd seen in her dream, which Ruith had studied as well and nodded over.

So, if she were to look at the quest without putting herself in the middle of it, it was a simple one and easily accomplished. She would lead Ruith from spell to spell, he would stuff them in a safer place than his boots, then when they had them all, he would destroy them. That would leave his bastard brothers nothing to want to kill him for and leave her free to imagine Daniel attempting to convince some poor village he was equal to being their local wizard.

She couldn't think any further than that. She didn't want to think about which of the ten princesses Ruith would learn to love, want to wed—

"Sarah?"

She looked up from her contemplation of the fire to find Ruith and Soilléir standing to her left. Ruith was dressed as she was and looked as if he too might have been contemplating his assets. She supposed he had a few more than she did, but then again, he had a larger burden to bear.

She couldn't think about that either.

She smiled at them both—or attempted to, rather—then took a deep breath. "Ready?"

"Almost," Soilléir said. He pulled up a chair for her, then motioned for Ruith to sit in the one next to her. He sat, then looked at them with a grave smile. "Before you go, I have gifts for you both."

"Nay," Ruith protested. "Soilléir, you have already given us more than we needed already."

"That was done willingly," Soilléir assured him. "However, there are other small things you'll need that I can provide." He looked at Sarah. "My dear, I have a spell for you."

Sarah looked at him in surprise. "A spell? What would I need with that?"

He smiled gravely. "'Tis a spell of Discernment. It may serve you when things before you become unclear."

"But surely it would be of more use in someone else's hands," she protested. "Someone with magic."

"The spell comes with a sort of magic wrapped around its warp threads, if you care to think of it that way." He shrugged. "Many can wield spells, some can wield weighty spells, but the truth is, most mages are blind because of it. It is easy to use a spell and affect a destiny without thought. More difficult is to see how the patterns of lives are woven and how they might be bettered. It takes a certain sort of magic to offer naught but a single word or a simple thought, then stand back and allow things to progress as they will."

Sarah supposed trying to convince him she wasn't even equal to putting her oar in occasionally was futile, so she listened to the spell, memorized it, then repeated it dutifully when Soilléir asked her to. She felt nothing, but she hadn't expected anything else. Soilléir obviously had more faith in her abilities than she did, but the words were pleasant, so she was happy to tuck them away.

"I fear I've loaded you down with books," he said apologetically, "but in addition to the poetry and the lexicon, I left you a very small history. It contains two other spells and a bit of my genealogy, if you're interested. One of those spells will be useful to you if your Sight begins to trouble you. The other . . . well, the other you'll find a use for in time."

She took a deep breath. "Are you offering single words and simple thoughts now, my lord?"

He laughed a little. "How quickly you see through my attempts at doing nothing. Aye, I'm offering you nothing more than that, which is enough for now. We'll see, though, how your friend there reacts to something more than single words."

Sarah looked at Ruith to find him watching Soilléir carefully, as if he wasn't precisely sure what to expect. He glanced at her, smiled, then looked back at their host.

"Advice?" he asked.

"You don't need any more of that," Soilléir said. "I thought you might find a use for a spell or two."

Ruith was suddenly very still. "And which ones would those be, my lord?"

"Return and Alchemy."

Ruith pushed himself back in his chair as if he didn't care for what he'd heard and wanted nothing but to be away from it.

"Don't," he said harshly. "Léir, don't."

"You could stick your fingers in your ears, I suppose," Soilléir said with a shrug. "You wouldn't be the first one to do so." He paused and frowned. "Though truth be told, I can only think of one other person over the centuries who begged me not to give him a spell."

"I'm not sure I dare ask who that was," Ruith managed.

"Yngerame of Wychweald," Soilléir said with a smile. "Perhaps he feared he would use it on his son."

"Which he didn't."

"Which he didn't," he agreed. "I have confidence that you'll exercise the same sort of control. And if you're interested in the whole tale, Yngerame only pretended to stick his fingers in his ears."

Sarah shivered. They were speaking of things that could truly undo the world, yet Soilléir seemed to find them simple enough. Or perhaps that wasn't the case. He might have been affecting a casual air, but she was quite sure he'd given his offer a great deal of thought.

She shifted so she could look at Ruith without seeming to stare at him. He was sitting with his elbows on his knees, his hands clasped, watching the floor as if it might provide him with better answers than he could find elsewhere. He finally sighed, smiled at her wearily, then looked at Soilléir.

"I won't say I don't want anything you'll give me," he admitted slowly. "I will say that I won't use your spells on my sire."

"I know."

"At least I hope I won't."

"I know that too."

He took a deep breath. "Very well. If you must."

Soilléir smiled a little, then gave him the spells. Sarah listened to the words, then watched them hanging in the air, shimmering there between Ruith and Soilléir for a moment or two, each spell in turn, before they simply winked out of existence, as if they'd been sparks cast from a fire.

Ruith considered them for quite some time before he looked at Soilléir seriously. "Could I heal Sarah's arm with Alchemy? I assume you've tried it on Rùnach."

"I have," Soilléir said gravely. "Unfortunately, there is something in both their wounds that a change of essence won't touch." He paused. "I fear it has to do with your father's spells, though I'll admit to being thoroughly baffled as to what. 'Tis another mystery to add to your tally, I suppose, for I certainly don't have the answer."

Sarah was tempted to say she would have rather had that answer sooner rather than later, simply because her arm pained her more often than not, but she was also fairly certain that answer didn't lie in a pleasant place. Ruith was watching Soilléir thoughtfully.

"Alchemy wasn't what you used on Sarah's arm that first night."

"It wasn't," Soilléir said mildly. "That was a spell of Confinement. Also a very useful thing to have under one's hands."

"That makes three of your spells I now know."

"And yet the world continues to turn."

Ruith smiled, apparently in spite of himself. "I suppose that leaves us no choice but to march into the fray and see that the rotation continues."

"I daresay you have that aright. But, if you don't mind, I do have a favor to ask."

"Anything," Ruith said, then he shut his mouth abruptly. "Or perhaps not. It depends on what you want."

"Nothing too taxing," Soilléir said with a smile. He rose and walked over to his desk, then fetched a sword Sarah hadn't noticed there before. He came back over to the fire and held it out to Ruith. "I need this carried to Uachdaran of Léige. I thought since you intended to travel his way, it might not be too much of a burden."

Ruith took the sword slowly. "Do you have a message to send as well?"

Soilléir shook his head. "The blade is message enough. You could, if you needed to, use the blade yourself. It has suffered from inattention, I daresay."

Sarah watched Ruith draw the blade halfway from the sheath, then felt her mouth fall open. The blade was covered with the same sort of runes as her knives, but there was something else there, something that looked remarkably like a layer of spells. She looked at Soilléir in surprise, but he only lifted an eyebrow briefly in answer.

She shut her mouth and put on her most unaffected expression. Already she could see where discretion was useful for more than just his spells, though that feat was made a bit more difficult by the fact that she suspected what was written on that blade might have as much to do with her as what was written on her knives. She watched Ruith resheath the blade as if he saw nothing especial about it. He thanked Soilléir in a rather perfunctory fashion.

Interesting.

Ruith looked at her. "Ready?"

She nodded, though her mouth was substantially more dry than it should have been. She tucked her hands into her sleeves to try to warm them, but that was fairly useless as well. She walked with Ruith over to the door, then turned to bid farewell to their hosts. Rùnach took her hand and bent low over it.

"Fare you well, my lady," he said in his hoarse, ruined voice. "It has been a tremendous pleasure for me to watch you weave. I will always be a grateful recipient of any of your castoffs."

"I'm sure I'll manage something for you in the future," she said, feeling a bit more flustered than she likely should have been. She wanted to point out that he had all the glories of Tòrr Dòrainn at his disposal and needed nothing from her, but perhaps he preferred the genteel luxury of Buidseachd.

Ruith scowled at his brother before he embraced him, patting his back several times in a manly fashion.

Rùnach pulled away. "I've been invited to Mhorghain's wedding. Perhaps you'll be there as well."

"We will, if we manage what we must," Ruith agreed. "If we're late, don't let them wait for us. We'll make the journey to Tor Neroche to see them. Afterward."

Rùnach didn't ask what Ruith meant by afterward, and Sarah wasn't about to volunteer any opinions on what might come before— or if she would still be part of Ruith's life then. She merely thanked Rùnach again for his lovely manners, then followed Ruith and Soilléir from the chamber and down the passageway. And if Soilléir went first and Ruith followed behind her, as if she needed to be protected, she pretended not to notice. She considered the spell Soilléir had given her and was tempted to just repeat it aloud whilst wishing it might work for her, but she didn't want to potentially set alarm bells to ringing. Better that she save it for another time.

Soilléir led them down to the kitchens and through a door that led outside the keep. There were stables set just a bit away from the castle, which were apparently his destination. Two horses stood there already, saddled, and behaving quite nicely. Sarah looked up at Ruith quickly, but he only frowned.

Soilléir took the reins from a stable lad and sent him off with a nod, then turned to them. "These are yours."

"But I haven't paid—" Ruith began.

"Consider them a gift," Soilléir said, "and consider that gift when you're overseeing my wallowing."

Sarah wasn't sure why that made Ruith smile, but there had obviously been conversations she had missed out on at some point during their stay.

"Very well," Ruith relented. "You have my thanks."

"And mine," Sarah added fervently. "I wasn't looking forward to walking."

Soilléir handed her a set of reins. "I will admit, my dear, that I was mostly thinking of you when I considered these fine lads here. They are actually gifts from my father to me, stallions I assure you the good lord of Angesand would salivate to have in his stable, so keep a close eye on them lest you find some enterprising son of Hearn's stalking you. Yours is Ruathar and Ruith's is Tarbh."

Sarah looked at Ruathar and was fairly surprised at the look he gave her in return. Either she had only ridden dim-witted nags before or those ponies in front of her were an entirely different breed of horse. Ruathar didn't chafe at the reins or try to bite her. He merely stared at her, then turned his head just so, apparently so she might better admire him.

She laughed as she reached out to stroke his neck, then realized Ruith was having an entirely different experience with his mount. There was a battle of wills going on there, one that looked to be breaking Tarbh's way for a bit, before he grudgingly lowered his head and blew out his breath.

Soilléir smiled, looking pleased. "I thought they might suit. And in case neither of you has noticed, these steeds not only have minds of their own, but shapechanging magic of their own. All you must do is tell them what shape you require and they will assume it."

"Shape?" she echoed incredulously.

"Dragon, hawk, eagle." Soilléir shrugged. "I imagine they would suffer through the indignity of masquerading as milch cows if necessary, but I would suggest you limit yourselves to more heroic sorts of things to save their pride."

"Dragon?" Sarah knew there wasn't any sound to the word but didn't bother trying to remedy that. She was too busy gaping at her horse and wondering how she was possibly going to manage the rest of her quest when she couldn't bring herself to put her foot in the stirrup.

Soilléir put his hand on Ruathar's neck, had some sort of mage-ish conversation with him, then reached down and picked up the miniature statue that suddenly stood where Ruathar had been. He held it out.

"Put him in your pack, Sarah, my dear, then call to him when you need him and he'll resume his proper shape. He agreed to travel in this shape as often as you need him to."

"Handy, that," she managed faintly, accepting the minuscule statue gingerly. "How did your father teach them to do this?"

"He didn't," Soilléir said. "There is, you might say, something in the water at home."

"Hearn of Angesand would agree, no doubt," Ruith said with a snort. "I'm equally sure he's been trying over the course of his very long life to divine what that particular something is."

"He tries," Soilléir agreed, "but fails, repeatedly. He's not much for the shapechanging of animals, but he would readily accept their fleetness of foot, which I daresay will please you two as well."

Sarah had to admit that that would, though she hoped she would survive whatever else they did long enough for her to enjoy that speed.

Ruith led his pony off a ways, then stopped and looked at it. Tarbh tossed his head, then in the next heartbeat, became a dragon from dreams, glorious, glittering, and absolutely ferocious-looking. If he'd swooped down from the sky toward her, she would have looked for the first handy clutch of brush and dived underneath it to hope for the best. Soilléir only laughed.

"Pray there are no archers in the area. They'll shoot you out of the sky for the value of the gems encrusting his breast."

Sarah was less worried about that than she was staying on his back, but perhaps that was something she could think about later, when she was safely back on the ground.

Ruith left the dragon stretching his wings and came back across the little courtyard to embrace Soilléir.

"Thank you," he said, with feeling. "You have saved us countless hours of dangerous travel on the ground."

"I did it for Sarah, of course," Soilléir said smoothly.

"I never doubted it," Ruith said with a snort, "but I appreciate not being forced to trot along after her, as it were."

"But," Sarah protested, because she could hardly believe she was being faced with a saddle that belonged on something far more equine, "I don't see any, um, reins."

Ruith shot her a look. "Then 'tis fortunate we're such good friends," he said with hardly a hint of a smirk, "that you won't be unwilling to hold on to me."

"Did you plan this?"

"Believe me, Sarah, I couldn't possibly have dreamed up a scheme so perfectly suited to my lecherous preferences as this one. Blame Soilléir."

Sarah was tempted to, but he'd gifted them things kings would have willingly begged for, so she instead embraced him, thanked him sincerely for all his aid, then watched him walk back inside the keep with the ease of a man who wasn't currently contemplating a trip off the ground where no sensible soul would wish to be. She was appalled to realize there was a part of her—an alarmingly large part—that wished she were walking back inside with him.

She took hold of her terror, shouldered her pack with her horse inside, then turned to Ruith. "What now?"

"We'll be off."

She'd been afraid he would say that. She couldn't think of any reasonable-sounding reason to dawdle, so when Ruith walked over to their mount, she dragged her feet behind him. He looked over his shoulder, then stopped and put his arm around her shoulders.

"I won't let you fall."

"I wasn't worried about what you would do," she managed. "I was planning on holding on very tightly and concentrating on not screaming."

"Already my plan yields benefits," he said with a small smile. He nodded toward the dragon, who seemed to sense that he was about to be carrying at least one rider who wasn't precisely thrilled about his shape. "The view will be spectacular, I promise."

"How would you know?" she asked faintly.

"How do you think I know?"

"What I think is that you are not at all who I thought you were," she said with a shiver. "But since that seems to be the usual fare where you're concerned, I likely shouldn't think anything of it."

"Consider me your very dear friend with a tumultuous past," he said, turning her toward him. "And since we are such dear friends, perhaps you'll indulge me in a friendly embrace to settle my nerves."

"Your nerves," she huffed, then found she couldn't say anything else. It was a miserable start to what she was now convinced would be a miserable journey. If she couldn't even set foot to the path, how was she to continue on it when things became truly dangerous?

She didn't want to hold on to Ruith so tightly, but she did *not* like heights of any sort and the thought of clambering onto that dragon's back and not screaming when he leapt up—

"I could clunk you over the head with my sword and spare you any undue anxiety," Ruith offered.

She was more tempted by that offer than she wanted to admit. "I don't think Soilléir's sword would care for that treatment—oh," she said in dismay. "I left without the bow you made me. And you forgot yours."

"Both are stowed in my pack," he said. "Slightly altered in form for the moment."

She shivered again. "You have become appallingly accustomed to magic in a very short time."

"The truth is hard to deny," he agreed ruefully, "but I'll admit that if my magic serves us, I'll use it without hesitation." He pulled her hood up over her hair. "Shall we go?"

She couldn't spew out anything that sounded like an assent, but she managed a nod, because the way was clear there before her feet and she had no choice but to walk it. She supposed she might have been forgiven legs that felt like noodles straight from the pot under her. Ruith pretended not to notice, and he did her the enormous favor of hooking her pack onto what was apparently going to serve them as a saddle. Then he helped her up and onto that saddle as if she'd been a feeble old woman.

She realized, as he settled himself in front of her, that she couldn't breathe. She suspected that if the choice had been between facing his brothers, his father back from the dead, and Droch himself, or facing the thought of that dragon leaping into the air, she would have chosen any of the former three—or all of them together—without hesitation.

Ruith hesitated, then swung suddenly off the dragon. She looked at him in surprise.

"What is it?"

"You steer. I'll clutch."

She forced herself to make a noise of humor—it couldn't have been even charitably termed a laugh—instead of sobbing like the terrified woman she was. "You are a lecherous knave," she managed.

"But a *friendly* one," he said, motioning for her to move forward. "Hurry up, gel. I'm envisioning all sorts of groping whilst you're busy being terrified."

She shifted to sit on the forward part of the saddle, which she wasn't sure was an improvement as it left her looking over the dragon's neck and . . . down. At least the pommel was rather high, which might prevent her from tumbling off the front. Ruith's arms around her made things better still, but not by much.

"You know, Tarbh would consider it an appalling blow to his dignity if you were to fall off."

"How do you know?" she asked, her teeth chattering.

"He told me so, of course. He said that all you need worry about is not flinging yourself off his back. He will make certain to keep you in the saddle."

"Are you trying to be helpful?"

His laugh rumbled in his chest against her back. "We'll both keep you safe, Sarah."

"Ah," she began, then she had no more breath for speaking because Tarbh had apparently decided it was time to take off, as it were, whilst she was otherwise distracted by Ruith's babbling.

She supposed he was doing his best not to terrify her, but even so, she imagined she was going to consign the first handful of moments of that very bumpy ride to the place where she put her nightmares when she was finished with them.

She was fairly sure she hadn't wept, but she wasn't at all sure she hadn't screamed a time or two and laughed hysterically the rest of the time. Or at least she did until Tarbh leveled himself out and began to flap his wings in a less frantic manner.

"It wasn't frantic," Ruith said loudly. "It was measured."

"Are you reading my thoughts now?" she managed.

"You were shouting them aloud, I'm afraid."

She imagined she was. So to keep herself from doing so any further, she who hadn't clutched a pommel in a score of years clutched the pommel of her saddle, because she didn't dare let go of it. She did manage, after what seemed like a small slice of eternity, to open her eyes. She realized with a bit of a start that they were covered in some sort of spell. It didn't seem to trouble their steed, flowing as it was around them as they flew. She found the presence of mind to see what it was made of.

Fadaire.

It was one of protection first, then comfort second. She could see the strands woven into it, glittering in the faint starlight, strands of such beauty she could hardly look at them. Then again, it was elven magic, so she supposed she shouldn't have been surprised.

She squeezed Ruith's hands. "Thank you."

"You're welcome."

She took a deep breath. She could hardly believe it, but apparently they were off on their quest, again—in quite a bit more style than the first leg of it. She sincerely hoped riding a dragon into the shimmering twilight was going to be the worst of what happened to her.

But she didn't imagine it would be.

Fifteen

❧

Ruith closed his eyes and simply enjoyed the feel of the wind in his face. It had been years since he'd last flown, and he'd never thought he would miss it. He'd been wrong. It was glorious, that soaring above the earth, made all the more glorious by the lack of it over the years. He didn't imagine Sarah was enjoying it, so he tightened his arms around her. He supposed the fact that he didn't have an elbow in his ribs for the familiarity told him all he needed to know about her opinion of their mode of transportation.

He also supposed he would be wise to enjoy the brief moments of pleasure he might have in doing something besides encountering what he was quite sure he would find along their quest. He didn't want to say as much to Sarah, but he feared those moments would be few. Soilléir had given him nothing but abstruse hints about nothing in particular. Rùnach had been more specific about his aid, having given him earlier that morning a list of black mages to consider. He had a fair idea of who was still roaming through the world, but he would be the first to admit he hadn't kept up with it as he should have.

He jumped a little at the feeling of Sarah's elbow in his ribs. He bent his head over her shoulder.

"What is it?" he said, loudly to be heard against the wind.

"There's something down there."

He could see nothing at all, but that didn't mean anything. He steered Tarbh where Sarah pointed, then smiled, pained, at her acerbic curses. Unfortunately, he suspected events were going to worsen before they improved. He put his mouth to her ear.

"See the lad there?"

"Chasing the other?" she managed. "Aye, 'tis Daniel. I don't know who the other one is."

"Can you see him?" Ruith asked in surprise. "Or can you, ah, *see* him?"

"I can't tell the difference any longer," she said with a shiver. "I'm going to have words with Soilléir after this is all over. I want him to put back whatever he took off my eyes."

Ruith didn't want to tell her that he suspected it was far too late for that. He simply cast a spell of un-noticing over them, asked Tarbh to consider a rather quiet landing, then waited until Tarbh had put talons to earth before he carefully swung down off his back.

He looked at Sarah, intending to tell her to stay where she was, only to find her clambering inelegantly off the saddle.

"I needed to stretch my legs," she said hastily.

He might have believed that if she hadn't stumbled and fallen into his arms. It was a fortuitous turn of events, but one he didn't dare take advantage of. He waited until she was steady on her feet before he pulled away.

"I won't be long."

"You're not going anywhere without me," she said breathlessly, taking hold of his arm. She looked over her shoulder. "What is that fool doing?"

Ruith looked over her head. "Continuing his chase, I daresay. I wonder if gold is involved."

"*My* gold," she grumbled, "though I imagine he's after spells." She looked up at him. "I forgot to tell you, but that morning I found myself in Droch's . . . ah . . ."

"Garden," he supplied. "If you can call it that."

She nodded, once. "Aye, there. I had actually been following a pair of men who were talking about the buying and selling of spells. To Droch, as it happened." She paused. "I thought I should follow them."

"Brave."

"Stupid," she conceded, "but what else was I to do? I'm sure one of them was Droch's servant that we saw at the front gates that first morning. The other—" She shrugged. "I don't think I'd recognize his voice if I heard it again, but he said he was working for a mage from Shettlestoune. I'm assuming that had to be Daniel."

Ruith frowned. "Why would Daniel want to make a bargain with Droch?"

"For a ring of mastery, I imagine. His messenger said he'd torn the spell he was attempting to sell to shreds, even though he'd been instructed merely to tear off a small piece and bring it along as proof of having the entire thing."

Ruith watched the spectacle in front of him. He perhaps wouldn't have been able to see the unknown man throw a fistful of shredded parchment up in the air if it hadn't been for Daniel's rather useful werelight. At least the fool could do that much.

He didn't think, however, that Daniel was capable of slicing through any Olcian spell of protection, which left him still with questions he didn't care for, namely who *had* made the rent in that particular spell and how Daniel had come by another spell of Gair's. He considered that for a bit longer, then looked at Sarah.

"Your brother doesn't look happy."

"Nay, he doesn't."

"I could make him substantially less happy."

She watched her brother for a moment or two, then looked up at him. "Well, if you're interested in fighting my battles for me."

"Endlessly," he said. "With magic, or without, however they come."

She closed her eyes briefly, then looked as if she might have considered a brief embrace. She seemed to stifle that readily enough, then settled for taking his hand and shaking it firmly. He somehow wasn't terribly surprised.

"I don't know what it cost you," she said seriously, "that first step into . . . well, into this whole business of magic and spells. It couldn't have been easy."

It had been made much easier by knowing just exactly what he was protecting with that magic, which was the woman standing in front of him, holding his hand in hers in most comradely fashion, but he didn't suppose the time was right for telling her as much.

"You wouldn't kill him, would you?" she asked.

"I would certainly end his life to save yours," Ruith said, "but for now, perhaps I'll limit myself to helping him along to his just desserts." He took her hand and pulled her behind him. "I'll go first. He won't see us until we're ready for—"

He stopped in mid-sentence because in spite of all the times he'd seen his father leave mages as nothing but lifeless husks, he'd never seen his sire kill someone in white-hot anger. Daniel of Doìre apparently didn't have any reticence about the like, for he shouted at his messenger, then suddenly thrust a sword through the man's chest.

"I think, Sarah my love," Ruith said seriously, "that I may be taking those words back sooner rather than later."

"He's not a nice man," she agreed.

Ruith suspected that was a bit of an understatement, but he wasn't sure he dared find out the truth of it lest the tidings lead him to act more rashly than he would have otherwise. He stopped a score of paces away from Daniel, removed the spell of un-noticing, and conjured up his own ball of werelight bright enough to have woken a drunkard out of a stupor.

Daniel didn't notice.

Ruith would have said something to help him with that, but before he could, Sarah took matters into her own hands. The fact that she trusted him to keep her safe was quite possibly one of the more humbling moments of his life, even coming, as it did, whilst dealing with her ridiculous brother.

"Daniel."

Her brother stopped frantically searching the ground for the pieces of whatever spell lay there, then leapt up and spun around, an expression of astonishment on his face. Scraps of parchment fluttered to the ground.

His astonishment only lasted a split second before what Ruith had come to recognize as his usual smirk appeared and a spell came tripping out of his mouth. Ruith didn't even stop to consider what to use. He simply dissolved the spell without fanfare and waited for the reaction he fully expected. Daniel gaped first at Sarah, apparently reminded himself she had no magic, then scowled at Ruith.

"How did you do that?"

"'Tis a secret," Ruith said solemnly, "known only to mages with a decent amount of power."

Daniel's eyes narrowed. "Who are you?"

"Ruithneadh," Ruith said casually, "the youngest son of Gair of Ceangail."

Daniel blinked in surprise, seemed to consider whether or not he should run, then threw a spell of death at Sarah. Ruith caught it easily, crushed it, then did far less to Sarah's brother than he deserved. He wrapped him securely in a spell of fettering and left one end of it waving tantalizingly near the man's face.

Sarah looked up at him and smiled.

He smiled in return, feeling a little winded. "I forget that you can see so much."

"I never forget," she said, her smile faltering. She nodded at her brother. "What will become of him?"

"Nothing will eat him, if that's what you're worried about. If he has two wits to rub together, he'll figure out how to unravel the spell. I think, given what I have seen of his wits, that it may take him a bit of time. He might die of hunger first." He provided Daniel with an endlessly filling waterskin he could reach if he tried, then looked at Sarah. "We should gather up the pieces of my father's spell, I imagine, and be on our way."

"I will," she said without hesitation. "Perhaps you can use the time to lecture that fool there on the evils of slaying messengers."

Ruith supposed he could do no less. He fashioned a shield of Fadaire, then covered it with a spell of un-noticing, poached from the solar in Léige. He would have offered to help Sarah, but he hadn't been indulging in false modesty. He couldn't see a damned thing but the moon darting behind clouds and his werelight that followed Sarah as if it had been designed specifically to cast its light lovingly around her—and that wasn't because of anything he'd done.

Though he heartily agreed with the sentiment.

He stood next to Daniel and watched with him as Sarah gathered up the pieces of spell. He looked at her brother and had to shake his head. How the two of them could possibly have been related . . . well, it defied even his well-developed powers of imagination. But since he had the lad within earshot, there was no point in not asking him a pointed question or two.

"Where did you find that spell?" he asked politely.

"I'll never tell you," Daniel spat.

Ruith lifted a finger and the spell of fettering tightened. Daniel only cursed him. Ruith was happy to torment him by degrees, though it only took another handful of moments before Sarah's brother was gasping out things he no doubt didn't want to.

"Found it on the ground," he squeaked. "Had to replace what was taken from me, didn't I?"

Ruith supposed there was no point in telling Daniel he'd been the one to make off with the other spells. He was still left with the unpleasant question of who had taken the spells from his boot, but he supposed he could safely exclude Daniel from any list of possible suspects.

He tried to consider that list, but Daniel's cursing became distracting enough that he was forced to slap a spell of silence over his mouth. He loosened the lad's bonds because he wasn't completely heartless, but he certainly had no intention of setting him free. He indulged in a few minutes of instruction on the proper way for

Daniel to comport himself in the future, then smiled at Sarah when she came walking toward him.

"Ready, love?"

Sarah nodded as she shoved the fragments of parchment into a pocket of her cloak, then studied Daniel for a moment or two before she spoke.

"You were a bad brother," she said.

Daniel gurgled in response.

"I should have liked someone to watch over me now and again, which you never did." She looked at Ruith. "I don't suppose I could borrow Rùnach."

"Absolutely," he said without hesitation. "He would be an ideal older brother for you—and nothing but, if you want my suggestion." He leaned closer to Daniel. "Come within twenty paces of that woman there and you'll wish you hadn't. If you're tempted to disregard my advice, remember who my father was and think on all the things I likely learned at his knee."

Daniel looked at him in horror for a moment, then his eyes rolled back in his head. His head lolled to the side, and he began to drool.

"That doesn't look very comfortable," Sarah remarked.

"It isn't meant to be very comfortable."

"I think your chivalry is showing."

"That, or my depravity," Ruith agreed, taking her by the elbow and turning her back to their mount. "I can scarce believe I invoked my father's name."

She smiled up at him faintly. "What is the use of being related to a black mage if you can't use his reputation to intimidate now and again?"

"I'm not sure we would want to know what my grandfather Sìle would say to that," he said dryly, "so perhaps we'll keep it to ourselves."

He walked with her over to Tarbh, realizing only then that he was feeling a sense of urgency he hadn't felt before. Or perhaps he simply hadn't noticed it before.

"I suppose I could have spent a bit more time being careful that I didn't miss anything," Sarah said slowly.

"You're simply looking for a way to avoid flying again," he said, struggling to keep his tone light.

"I might be," she muttered. "Unfortunately, I don't think there's anything else here. No spells, no magic. Just darkness made by ordinary things." She swallowed, hard. "Though I'm less sure of the last than I'd like to be."

He was too, but he wasn't going to say as much. "You're certain there's nothing else on the plains of Ailean?"

"Absolutely."

"Then we'll make for Slighe," he said. "We could be there by dawn if we flew hard. It would give us the chance to see if the lads were there before we turned north."

"Will Tarbh agree to it?"

He nodded toward the dragon, crouched and watching them with his glittering eye. "He doesn't seem opposed to the idea. I gather his only regret is that you don't much care for his takeoffs and landings."

She started forward, then stopped and simply shook for a moment or two before she looked at him. "I'm not going to be much help if I don't get over this."

"You'll accustom yourself to it," he promised her. "I will admit that I too suffered a bit of . . ." He paused, then supposed there was no point in not being honest. "Very well, the first time I threw myself off my grandfather's battlements and changed into dragonshape, I thought I wouldn't manage it before I hit the ground and died."

"Which thrilled you so much that you immediately tried it again."

He smiled sheepishly. "I was a lad."

"Who were you with?"

"Miach of Neroche and, if you can believe this, Rùnach."

"How old were you?"

"Five."

"Your poor mother."

He smiled a little at the memory. "Aye, I daresay. She spent the evening convincing my grandfather that beating us soundly for our cheek would only drive us to do it again. *Elves do not shapechange!* he bellowed periodically that evening at supper until the lot of us were simply bundles of nerves."

"And what do elves do?" she asked. "Though I hasten to add I'm only asking out of polite and friendly curiosity."

"We admire flame-haired weavers of exquisite cloth and always hurry about our business on the ground so we might fly with them again."

She scowled at him. "I'm not going any farther on this quest of yours if you don't stop that."

He smiled and put his arm around her, because she was trembling. He imagined it wasn't from the cold. "Where—" he began, then he stopped. The moonlight had broken through the clouds and cast the whole of the tableau in front of him into sharp relief, making his werelight unnecessary.

There was something standing twenty paces behind Daniel.

"Let's go," she said quickly. "I'll try not to scream so much this time."

He was happy to acquiesce. He climbed onto his horse-turned-dragon's back, then pulled Sarah quickly up onto the saddle in front of him. He put his arms around her and held on as Tarbh leapt up, beating his wings against the chill air. He looked over his shoulder but saw nothing untoward following them. If someone had shapechanged to chase after them, he certainly couldn't tell. He didn't imagine Sarah would be willing to open her eyes long enough to look. Perhaps later, when she felt more secure.

He started to pull Sarah's hood up over her hair only to have her shriek.

"Don't let go!"

"I never plan to," he assured her. He wrapped both arms around her again, then rested his chin on her shoulder. "I won't let you fall. I promise."

She didn't relax, but she did pat his hands briefly before she went back to clutching the pommel of the saddle. He closed his eyes and enjoyed the feel of the chill wind against his face.

"I left my cloak behind," she said suddenly. "The very lovely green one you made for me."

"I know."

"It was too fine for a journey such as this will be."

He tightened his arms around her briefly. "We'll fetch it after we're finished. Soilléir will keep it for us."

She nodded, then fell silent for quite a while. Ruith would have thought she had gone to sleep if it hadn't been for the way she flinched every now and again, as if she'd almost fallen asleep but reminded herself unhappily of where she was. She finally leaned back.

"Ruith?"

"Aye, love?"

"I can't help but wonder about that spell of Gair's. The one of Diminishing. I tried not to listen too closely when Connail was speaking of it on our way north, but it was hard to avoid."

"Given Connail's unfortunate familiarity with its effects, I can understand why he was obsessed with it."

"That was the spell that Daniel had half of, wasn't it?"

He nodded. He could scarce believe he'd lost that half he'd had, which was indeed his fault. Perhaps he shouldn't have been so fastidious about not using magic—

"I wonder why someone would want it so badly," Sarah said, interrupting his thoughts.

He leaned up a bit so the wind wouldn't carry away his words. "There are mages out in the world who aren't satisfied with their limits. In the beginning of the world, I think there were boundaries set—by good taste, if nothing else. Over the years, though, there have been many who sought to cross those boundaries and do the unthinkable."

"Taking someone else's power?" she asked faintly.

He nodded. "Neònach of Carragh was the first to attempt it, but it went badly for him. He began with inanimate, enspelled objects that rendered him, in the end, quite inanimate himself."

"So it is as Connail said," she said. "When Gair took his power, he took his madness as well."

"No one ever said it came without risks," he said. "Lothar has his spell of Taking, but it is, from what I understand, a crude and inelegant thing that might siphon off half another mage's power. Droch has his own variation of the same thing, loftily called Gifting, which produces about the same result."

"But Gair's?"

"Every last drop," he said with a sigh, "as Connail also said. It is a spell that never should have been conceived, much less refined and certainly not written down. Why my father allowed such a thing to be let loose, I'll never know."

"Perhaps he never intended it be discovered."

"I imagine he didn't," Ruith agreed. "He guarded it jealously, never uttering it in the presence of anyone but those whose power he took."

"Then how do you and your brothers know it?"

"I was very young when Keir first determined that it was something we all should know," Ruith said slowly. "He eavesdropped first, but refused to pass along what he'd heard—to his credit. He and Gille argued bitterly about that, for Gille thought the only way to counter my sire's evil was to know how to name it thoroughly, but Keir feared the spell would somehow corrupt us."

"Did it?"

"Nay," he said simply, because he couldn't blame her for asking. "Keir insisted that if we wanted it, we would have to have it for ourselves and watch with our own eyes what it could do. We all then made it a point to overhear my father using it, though we certainly never would have used it ourselves."

"You were never tempted?" she asked casually.

He pursed his lips. "Never, you heartless disciple of Soilléir of Cothromaiche. Not even when my father was opening that damned well, though perhaps I should have been." He sighed. "I'd never heard him spew out so many spells in such a short time. First he used his spell of Diminishing on my brothers, then, with their power in hand, he opened the well. He then turned his favorite spell on the well itself only to realize that he was sadly out of his depth. By the time the evil had raced up into the sky and was headed back down toward him, he was frantically trying spells of containment and closing. 'Twas too late for that, I fear."

"I'm sorry."

He shook his head. "'Tis in the past, fortunately. I feel somewhat better about it, knowing that I'm doing something to stop his evil from spreading instead of merely sitting in the mountains, fretting over it."

She fell silent. He wasn't sure if she contemplated all his years hiding away in the mountains or wondered if he now had the power to protect her. Perhaps, in the end, it was just better not to know.

"Ruith?"

"Hmmm?"

She leaned her head back against his shoulder and turned toward him slightly. He had a difficult time concentrating on what she was saying. If he'd been a less gentlemanly sort of man—or one with more sense, perhaps—he would have kissed her right then, professed his undying love, then begged her to wed with him. But that might have caused both of them to fall off, so perhaps that was better left for another, less perilous perch.

"Are you listening to me?"

"Trying to."

"Try harder."

"The wind is fairly loud," he said. "And you, if I may say so, are extremely distracting."

She elbowed him firmly in the gut. He grunted, then wrenched his thoughts away from where they would have lingered quite pleasantly.

"What?" he asked.

"I was wondering," she said loudly, "given that your father was so interested in taking the magic of others, if he ever worried about someone taking his?"

"Never," Ruith said automatically, but then he found he couldn't say anything else.

In truth, he'd honestly never considered it. His father had

always seemed all-powerful, a towering figure full of arrogance and strength. The thought of anyone being able to do anything *to* Gair of Ceangail instead of running *from* him had certainly never crossed his mind as a child.

But now that he didn't have his mother and brothers to protect him and he was exposed to the full brunt of whatever black mages wanted to throw at him, he certainly thought about his own mortality more often than he cared to. Surely his sire must have at least considered in passing the same sort of thing.

He tightened his arms around Sarah briefly. "Nay, he never would have, but I'll think on it just the same, if you like."

"At least it will keep you awake."

He smiled. "I won't fall asleep."

"I know I certainly won't," she said with a shiver.

He wrapped his arms more securely around her, then rested his chin on her shoulder and gave some thought to things he hadn't considered before. His father, who had spent more time than he would have admitted to looking over his shoulder, wouldn't have left himself unprotected, in spite of his belief in his own invincibility. Surely.

What if he had created a spell to counter Lothar's spell of Taking and Droch's attempt at the like?

Or what if he had suffered a spontaneous and quite unwholesome bout of altruism and created a spell to restore what had been taken with his own spell of Diminishing?

The thought was intriguing, but Ruith wasn't certain it was worth thinking on too seriously. His father never would have let his magic be taken, so he had likely never thought seriously about needing to find a way to have it restored. He certainly wouldn't have given such a spell to anyone else. As for using it himself, *on* himself, he wouldn't have had the magic to use it had all his own power been taken.

Then again, perhaps even if another mage managed to find and use the spell of Diminishing, anyone but Gair of Ceangail might not have managed such a thorough result—especially on Gair himself.

Which would have left Gair with perhaps enough power to save himself with a spell of Anti-Diminishing.

Ruith rolled his eyes at the thought. His sire was dead and gone. Whatever fools might have been left in the world were not his equal and would never harness the full power of the original spell.

Still, they might manage a good bit of damage, which left him with his original task, which was preventing the meeting of those two halves before someone with a decent bit of power put them together.

And in the meantime, he supposed he might be wise to actually do the unthinkable and create something of his own to fight whoever might be canny enough to have the entire spell at his disposal, though the thought of that was a bit like walking over his father's grave.

He shivered, and not from the chill. That wasn't a path he wanted to put even a single foot to.

Though he supposed he might not have a choice.

Sixteen

Sarah walked down the muddy street with Ruith, grateful she had him to duck behind if things became too dodgy. She'd never been in a place that was so overtly unpleasant, not even when compared to a few of the seedier villages in Shettlestoune she'd traveled to with her mother to hunt for new customers. The buildings had quite obviously taken their fair share of abuse from the weather, which was particularly nasty and had consisted of, over the past half hour, a driving rain that had turned to a painful sort of hail that had abated into a sleet that stung her face and gathered on her eyelashes until she could hardly see where she was going. If she hadn't known better, she might have suspected it all to be the work of some vile mage.

"Why does anyone live here?" she muttered, not entirely under her breath.

"Last bit of civilization for leagues," Ruith said with a shrug, "such as it is. There isn't anywhere of note between Slighe and

Ceangail or, for that matter, between Slighe and Léige. You've seen for yourself what lies on the plains of Ailean—or perhaps you weren't watching whilst we were flying."

"I kept my eyes closed," she said, mustering up a glare.

"I imagined you had," he said wryly. "As to what lies to the south, there is nothing of any decent size for a few days' travel at least. If you want supplies for even a modest journey, this is your last chance to purchase them."

"I'm not sure I would stop here for supplies," she said, wishing she had a sword and the skill to use it. "And that because I would most likely be robbed of them on my way out of town."

He smiled. "I would disagree, but I think you have it aright." He studied her briefly. "Are you concerned?"

She pursed her lips. "I think if your sword didn't frighten any and all ruffians off, your knives would, so nay, I'm not overly concerned. I won't say that I won't be happy to leave the place behind, though, no matter how intimidating you are."

Though why putting Slighe behind her would be an improvement, she couldn't say. At least in Slighe it seemed fairly obvious where trouble might be coming from—any doorway that opened onto the street, actually—but out in the wilderness? Enemies lurking there would be more difficult to see, especially given the possibility that the mountains and forests were full of Ruith's bastard brothers. It was difficult to accept that she felt more comfortable in Buidseachd, but there was no denying it. At least there, she knew to distrust most everyone she met.

She let her mind wander as she walked and it wandered right to the first unpleasant thing she'd seen on her current journey, which was her brother flinging a sword into his messenger's chest. Obviously the double cross the messenger had attempted had gone horribly awry. She didn't want to content herself with knowing the man would have suffered a much worse fate at Droch's hands, but the truth of it was also difficult to deny.

At least she'd had the time to gather up the pieces of spell, and she and Ruith had escaped without harm. She supposed Daniel would free himself eventually, and whilst he might consider Ruith's parting words to him, he wasn't one to learn lessons easily. If he thought he could have even a fraction of Ruith's sort of power, he would risk everything to obtain it. She sincerely doubted they had seen the last of him.

"Why did Soilléir give you that sword, do you think?" Sarah asked, dragging her thoughts away from things that bothered her but finding only other bothersome things to think on.

"I have no idea," Ruith said. "King Uachdaran certainly doesn't need another blade given the quality of work his own smiths produce."

"Would you want it?" she asked.

He shot her a quick smile. "I would be lying if I said nay. I'm not sure where Soilléir came by it, but it is a very lovely blade. Well balanced and discreetly made."

"None of the flash and pomp of the Sword of Neroche?" she asked with a smile.

"With a gem in the hilt large enough to blind you?" he said. "Nay, fortunately none of that. Unlike Adhémar, I prefer my weapons to be unembellished."

"At least the spells won't bother you—ah, I meant the runes." She cursed herself silently, but 'twas too late. Ruith was already looking at her with the same sort of sharp look he'd turned on Soilléir a time or two, as if he intended to have answers even if he had to wait days on end to have them. She attempted an owlish blink, but she feared she'd been no more successful at it than Soilléir had been.

"Spells?" he echoed pointedly.

"I meant runes."

"That isn't what you said."

"You heard me awrong," she said promptly. "Too much wind in your ears, no doubt. Or in mine. I'm not sure which, but I'll give it some thought and let you know later." She tried another innocent look. "I'm weary and speaking out of turn."

"What you're going to be out of, woman, is one of your begging-off-from-unpleasant-courtly-affairs excuses if you don't elaborate on what I heard awrong."

She shrugged, vowing to be more careful in the future with her single words and simple thoughts. She was beginning to see that it would be more difficult than it looked. She yawned hugely, then wiped the tears from her eyes.

"Are we here for a meal or sleep? I can't remember."

He pursed his lips at her. "I know what you're doing and I won't press you now, which isn't to say that I won't later." He slid her a sideways look. "Runes, my arse."

"I don't think that's where they're inscribed, but I could be wrong."

He blinked, then laughed. "Very well, you've very saucily avoided any more pressing questions until the proper time. As for our immediate plans, whilst I'm not sure I want to trap us in a chamber here in town, we do need to sleep for at least a handful of hours. I think Tarbh will be safe enough where we left him."

"In the trees," she said with a smile. "Not exactly where I would think to look for a horse, were I a villain."

"Well, an owl is a mighty bird, given the right breed," he allowed. "As for anything else, I had originally planned to return here after our little foray to Ceangail and regroup with our good alemaster. I don't know if Franciscus will choose this as a place to roost, but the rest of our lads might. It seems as if we should at least make the effort to find them."

"Will they have dared wait here?"

"We'll soon know, I imagine," Ruith said, "given that Oban isn't easily hidden. If he's even set foot in town, someone will have noticed him." He slowed. "We'll try this tavern first. I suggest you keep your face covered and a knife up your sleeve."

"And just where will you be?" she asked, eyeing the particularly unpleasant-looking place in front of them.

"Asking a question or two of the barkeep." He frowned at her. "You couldn't try a bit of a manly swagger, could you?"

She opened her mouth to tell him she would not only swagger but be happy to brawl with him if he needled her much longer, but he laughed before she could and pulled her hood farther over her face.

"Let's go, wench. You can spew out all your missish grievances later."

She walked with him across the boardwalk and into the tavern. It was just after sunrise, but already there were a few lads hard at their day's labor. Or perhaps they were still finishing up their night's work. Sarah wasn't sure and didn't care to investigate. She found herself deposited at a table near the door, then summarily abandoned.

She looked at the sign over the bar that tersely proclaimed that magic was not tolerated. That was something she certainly agreed with in principle, so she settled back in her chair and supposed the worst she could expect was the flash of a blade in the dim light from the fire.

Ruith stood at the bar for several minutes, a tall, intimidating figure cloaked and hooded. She watched the other patrons watch him, but apparently they didn't care to investigate him more closely for none of them moved. She didn't blame them in the slightest. She certainly wouldn't have attempted polite conversation with the man if she hadn't already known who he was.

He came to her table finally with two mugs in his hands. He set them down, pushed one toward her, then sat down with his back against the wall.

"Tidings?" she asked.

"Nothing of note," he said with a sigh, "but I'm not sure we could have expected anything else. I wasn't about to bring up the subject of mages, and the barkeep didn't seem inclined to offer any hints of the same." He had a sip of his ale, grimaced, then leaned back against his chair. "I think even a few hours' sleep here would serve us, though I imagine we'll be safer on the floor than whatever flea-ridden thing passes for a bed."

Sarah drank only because she was desperate, but had the same opinion of the brew Ruith had. *Vile* wasn't the word she would have used, for it didn't begin to describe the disgusting nature of her ale.

She supposed Ruith might manage to enspell what was in her cup, but she wasn't about to ask him. She simply set her mug aside, then agreed with him that perhaps it was time to go. She followed him from the tavern and back up the street until he paused in front of an inn that looked slightly less disreputable than everything surrounding it.

The chamber they were shown to was no less squalid than she'd expected it would be. Ruith set his pack down in front of the fire, tossed more wood onto the blaze, then turned and walked back to the door.

"Lock it behind me, if you would."

"Are you going out?" she asked in surprise. "Alone?"

He turned and leaned against the door, looking so casually lethal that she almost caught her breath. The women would fall all over themselves to get to him and the men would fall over themselves to get out of his way.

She held up her hand. "Never mind. You'll be fine."

"No one will enter," he said, "if you're worried."

He said nothing, but suddenly a spell of protection fell down over the door. She could tell there were two sides to it and the pleasant-looking side was facing her. She didn't imagine she would be lifting it up to see what lay on the other side.

"Will I be able to leave?" she asked uneasily.

"I am not your jailor, Sarah."

"Just my protector."

"There is a difference," he said dryly, "though if you would be willing to take my advice, please just stay here."

She sighed and walked over to him. "Very well, be off with you, then. I'll lock the door behind you and stay to do womanly things."

"Is that so terrible?"

She realized he was quite serious about the question. She met his very lovely pale eyes and shook her head. "Honestly, Ruith, I would much rather you go trudge in the muck and hobnob with seedy sorts whilst I stay here and sit in front of the fire. I'm just trying not to be a burden."

He reached out and tucked a strand of hair behind her ear. "Is it a burden for a man to do unpleasant things to keep safe the woman he l—er, I mean, *likes* rather well?"

"I don't know," she said quietly. "Is it?"

"If I could fulfill this quest without your aid, Sarah, my love, I would do so without hesitation. I regretted every step you took with me to the glade and to my father's keep and was frantic with worry when we were inside the walls. If I had thought it would have kept you safer, I would have brought the entire place down upon myself, killing the lot of us in the process."

She caught her breath. "Surely you didn't consider it."

"I did," he said. "But I am a selfish lout, so I was ecstatic—well, after I moved past wanting to wring your neck, of course—to have you rescue me so I could spend the rest of my life convincing you that I l—er, I mean *like* you very much indeed and would be honored to spend equal amounts of time making sure your life was full of whatever you loved most that I could provide." He paused and smiled briefly. "Put simply, that is."

She took a step backward because it was either that or throw herself into his arms, which she most certainly couldn't do. She held out her hand in her most manly fashion. "Thank you."

He looked at her hand, looked at her, then took her hand and shook it slowly. "You're welcome."

"You should go now," she said, pulling her hand away and tucking it and her other one under her arms so they didn't do anything untoward. "You know, to do those manly unpleasant things you need to do."

He nodded, then opened the door. "I'm not sure how long I'll be."

"I'll wait."

He smiled briefly, then slipped out the door. Sarah locked it, then heard his spell lock as well, much as the spell had done in his grandfather's garden. She stood there with her hand on the door, tangled in the spell he'd wrought, and thought about the magic she'd seen in that garden. Poor Sarait, who had lived no doubt for centuries in that sort of loveliness, then found herself in Ceangail. Sarah wondered if she had known ahead of time just what Gair was, or if he had simply presented her with what he thought she would want to see. She pitied Ruith and his siblings for what they had seen and Ruith for what she feared he might see in the future.

She couldn't say she was looking forward to seeing any of it herself.

She looked at the magic in front of her and trailed her fingers through the strands of Fadaire she could see, strands that were woven with the faint sound of snow as it fell through bitterly cold air and the soft fall of rain as it fell in the spring. Ruith had done that, she was sure, for no other reason than to please her.

And she had insisted he chat up ten princesses before he looked at her.

She was daft as a duck.

She was also weary beyond belief. She left the spell whispering softly behind her and walked over to the fire where she could dig in her pack and see what Rùnach—another very lovely son Sarait had no doubt been very proud of—had packed for her.

She didn't go far, simply because she didn't have the energy to. Fortunately a polite foray into the pack produced a child's primer, written in what she assumed was Soilléir's native tongue, a set of knitting needles, and several particularly lovely skeins of yarn packed tightly into the side of her pack. She fingered the yarn for a moment or two, then set it aside and opened the book.

She couldn't say with any confidence that she was pronouncing correctly what she was attempting to sound out, but she continued on in spite of that. She had to pause after a few pages because there was something about the sound of that tongue against her ear that tugged at her in a way she couldn't identify. She couldn't say it made her uneasy, for it didn't. There was something attached to the words, though, something that tinged them with a sadness she couldn't shake off.

She attempted another handful of pages, then had to shut the book because she thought she just might weep. She put her hand over the worn cover, then stared into the fire for a moment or two.

It occurred to her, with a start, that she had recognized a few of the words, not because she had seen them before, nor because she had heard them in Soilléir's poetry.

She had heard them somewhere else.

She frowned. There was a mystery there that only became deeper the more she looked at it. It would have been so much easier for Soilléir to have simply translated the runes on her knives for her, especially since it was obvious he had recognized them as ones coming from his native land, but he had chosen not to. Why hadn't he just told her what she needed to know instead of sending her off on a journey with books in hand and no one to help her?

Well, he was a mage, and they were unpredictable. Perhaps he'd foreseen the fact that Ruith would disappear for hours at a time and leave her without something to occupy her time. She imagined, however, that he hadn't been the one to tuck yarn into her pack, so she thought pleasant thoughts of Rùnach as she considered a skein of dark blue wool.

She thought about Ruith's hands, then began a pair of mittens for him. She'd done the like so many times that she hardly needed to think about what she was doing, so she reopened the child's book and kept it on her lap as she knit. The first poem there wasn't difficult and the more she attempted to sound it out, the more easily it seemed to come to her tongue. She wasn't entirely sure she hadn't heard her mother mutter something in those same words, but that seemed so fanciful, she could scarce credit it.

She saw something out of the corner of her eye, dropped her knitting, and flung her knife at it before she thought better of it.

Ruith reached up and stilled the knife quivering near his ear in the wood of the door—the *closed* door, as it happened. Her blade had torn through the hood of the cloak she had so carefully woven for him, which seemed to trouble him more than the fact that she'd almost put a knife through his eye.

"I hereby resign the position of your guardsman," he said faintly. "I'm hiring you to protect me."

"Don't be daft," she said, setting her things aside and pushing herself up out of her chair. "You frightened the bloody hell out of me!"

He pulled off his cloak and looked at the rent in the hood. "My most abject apologies, I assure you."

She jerked her knife free from the wood of the door and glared at him. "Knock next time."

"I will." He looked at his cloak. "Shall I fix—"

"Nay, I will," she said, taking his cloak out of his hands. "It will keep me from doing damage to you. And you may as well come have something to eat since you're alive to do so."

He nodded and followed her across to the pair of chairs set in front of the fire. Sarah set to work on his cloak, simply because he had frightened her quite badly and she thought if she had something to work on, her hands might not tremble so. Or at least she did until Ruith reached out and covered her hands with his.

"I'll do that."

She wanted to protest, but found she couldn't. She allowed him to take his cloak away, then watched him heal the rent with a spell. She happily accepted not only food from her pack but drinkable wine from his. Once she'd had a restorative sip or two, she set her cup aside.

"Well?"

"I asked a few questions," he said carefully, "but not so many as to garner undue attention. I'm fairly sure the lads aren't here."

"Did Franciscus come fetch them, do you think?" she asked, reaching for her needles and holding them, just to give herself something to do.

"It would seem logical," Ruith agreed. "Oban wouldn't have gone with anyone else, and I don't imagine Seirceil would have allowed himself or the rest of them to be carried off against their will. He isn't powerless."

She looked up at that. "Did Seirceil know you, do you think?"

"He certainly recognized the Camanaë spell I used on him." He shrugged. "He knew my mother and he knows Sgath. I would imagine at least the thought of who I might be crossed his mind."

She put her knitting down in her lap. "That must have been difficult for you. Healing him, I mean."

"I've done more difficult things since," he said, "though I will concede it wasn't pleasant."

"Because of the magic, or what it meant?"

He smiled faintly. "You sound like Soilléir. And if you want the truth, it was both, though just using magic was surprisingly unpleasant. It was the first thing I'd done in twenty years. It about flattened me."

"You did look a little weary."

"Your tea helped."

"I have no idea how," she said, pursing her lips. "It was nothing but herbs."

"Brewed skillfully."

She picked her knitting up again, then looked at him suddenly. "Could we go back to that farmer's house where we left the horses and our gear?"

"We're not terribly far from it," he conceded. "Is there something in particular you want?"

"The herbalist in Firth gave me an entire sack full of things. They were definitely enspelled, but with wholesome things."

"How do you know?" he asked casually. "See something?"

"Aye, thank you, I did," she said shortly. "I thought I was losing my mind."

He laughed a little. "We were quite a pair, then, for I daresay I thought the same thing about myself. And aye, if you want them, we'll fetch them. Perhaps I can talk the man back out of my bow, though I think my sword has likely already been melted down for wagon parts."

"Did it have especial meaning for you?"

He shook his head. "'Twas just a blade. The arrows I would have again, though, and the bow." He frowned suddenly as if he considered something truly dire. "I daresay we'll need to fly there, if Tarbh is willing. Just to save time."

"If we must," she said with a shiver.

"I think it is the only way I'll have more out of you than a hand-shake."

"You scoundrel."

"I'm determined."

She pushed her hair back from her face with the back of her hand. "Ten women of rank, Your Highness. I'm sure you'll find one among them to suit."

"Have I ever told you the tale of Tachartas of Tòrr Dòrainn?"

"Did he fall in love with a milch maid?" she asked sourly.

"Even worse: a shieldmaiden whose only claim to magic came from what was spoken reverently about her swordplay."

"Must you?" she asked, pained.

"I'll tell you another about Fearail of Cothromaiche afterward if you can refrain from throwing something at me during the telling of the first."

"How do you know so many tales—nay, don't tell me. Your library was extensive."

"And your mother's wasn't?"

"My mother's was full of spells I couldn't bear to look at, even in Doìre. I spent most of my time down at the alehouse, reading Franciscus's books. I will admit he had more than his share of tomes for a simple alemaster." She hesitated, then asked the question she hadn't been able to bring herself to before. "Who is he, do you suppose?"

"We'll ask him when we see him next."

"I don't like things that turn out to be what I didn't think they could be."

"Which is why I'm always so straightforwardly ardent. So you aren't surprised later when I fall to my knees and beg you to look at me twice."

She threw her ball of wool at him.

He laughed at her as he caught it, then reached over to hand it back to her. "Two tales, then a bit of a nap for the both of us, I think. I'll go out again after dark to see what I can learn after the lads have tucked a few strong ales away. Then I think we'll go. We would be wise to travel under the cover of darkness."

She supposed there was sense in that, as well as the added benefit of not being able to see clearly just how far off the ground they might have been. She listened to Ruith begin his tale, then closed her eyes, because she couldn't help herself.

She lost the thread of his tale, but couldn't muster up the energy to ask him to backtrack. She fell asleep almost before she knew what she was doing.

She woke to a kink in her neck. Ruith had covered her with his cloak, but he was nowhere to be seen.

She looked around, feeling slightly panicked, only to find him standing at the window, motionless. She set his cloak on his chair, staggered to her feet, then managed to get herself across the chamber. Only a day into her quest and already she needed more sleep. She didn't suppose that boded well for the rest of the journey.

Ruith turned his head and smiled at her. "Sleep well?"

"Terribly," she croaked. "And you not at all, I imagine."

He shrugged. "I had things to think on. That and I supposed you could keep me in the saddle tonight if necessary."

"I wouldn't count on that," she said uneasily. She started to elaborate on the fate that would await him did he trust her with his life on the back of a dragon, then she had a decent look at his face. "What is it?"

He seemed to chew on his words a bit before he turned and leaned back against the window frame. "I'm curious about a few things."

"I hesitate to ask which ones."

He considered a bit longer. "I wonder where Franciscus is."

"With the lads," she said in surprise. "Don't you think?"

"I'm not sure what to think," he said slowly.

"What else would he—" she began, then felt her mouth fall open. "What are you suggesting?"

"Nothing," he said carefully. "I just find several things rather too . . . convenient."

She had to lean against the opposite side of the window to keep herself upright. "Such as?"

"Such as why it was he was at Ceangail when we needed him the most," Ruith began, "or why he was waiting with his wagon in Bruaih on the same road we were taking, or why he found himself as the alemaster of Doìre—pretending to be what he was not—when he obviously could have been loitering anywhere else in the world." He took a deep breath. "Or why he befriended a perfect stranger masquerading as a mage on a mountain when the stranger was a boy, yet kept his secret as he became a man."

"Happenstance," she said, but she doubted the truth of it the moment the word left her mouth.

"Happenstance, or contrivance?" Ruith asked grimly.

"To what end?" she managed.

He looked at her steadily. "Because that stupid boy on the hill was the youngest son of the black mage of Ceangail."

"Ruith," she breathed, "you can't be serious. Franciscus couldn't possibly have known—well, if he's a mage, I suppose he could have known. But you can't believe he would want any of Gair's spells."

"Someone took them from me," he said in a low voice. "Someone who knew I had them. Someone with a power that sliced through Olc as if it had been naught but flimsy spiderwebs."

She put her hand over her mouth. "Impossible."

"Sarah, that spell of protection was the most aggressive thing I've ever seen. It captured a spell Amitán threw at me, changed it into something quite different, then flung not only Amitán's spell but something of its own make back at him. If he's not dead by now, he likely wishes he were. Yet the mage who braved that same spell to steal the spells from me obviously suffered no ill effects. He would have been left writhing on the ground otherwise."

"But you can't think he took the spells," she managed. "Not Franciscus."

"As I said, I'm not sure what *to* think."

"I've known him for the whole of my life. There is no guile in him."

"Nor any magic?" he asked carefully.

She felt her face grow uncomfortably warm. "Very well, perhaps I am not a good judge of mages, but I'm not so poor a judge of men."

He sighed and reached out to pull her closer to him. He kept his arm around her shoulders and sighed. "Nay, love, you aren't. I'm speculating where I shouldn't." He rubbed his free hand over his face. "I have spent too many years looking for shadows in every corner, expecting them to be full of more than they should be." He shrugged. "I'm just curious about who has the spells your brother so thoughtfully collected for us and what it is we found shredded last night near that poor fool out there on the plain. And I'm frankly terrified that that someone will find the half of my sire's spell of Diminishing we know is out there in the world."

"Is that all?" she asked.

"Well, I'm a little unnerved at the thought of someone finding the other half," he said wryly. "Or the possessors of both halves finding each other."

"Perhaps they'll do each other in fighting over the privilege of putting it all together."

"We could hope," he said with a humorless smile. He shook his head. "I've never regretted more not having been out in the world. I have no idea who is alive or dead."

"I thought Rùnach gave you a list."

"I looked at it whilst you napped. It is lengthy, but somehow I just have the feeling the lad we're looking for isn't on it."

"Is there someone who might know of other wretches out to destroy the world?" she asked reluctantly.

"The witchwoman of Fàs," Ruith said with an uneasy laugh. "She is renowned—or infamous, depending on your point of view—for keeping meticulous notes on the happenings in the Nine Kingdoms. I would imagine she knows every mage with any magic at all in their veins. Unfortunately, I don't think I'd be welcome to tea."

"Trample her garden during your youth, did you?"

He cleared his throat uncomfortably. "Let's just say that I wasn't

particularly kind with my observations about the wartiness of her
nose."

Sarah smiled. "You were a child. Surely she would forgive that."

"She might, but there is the matter of my mother earning a
proper wedding where she merited nothing more than the honor of
my father's company from time to time, long enough to conceive a
few sons."

"Ah," Sarah managed. "That complicates things a bit, doesn't it?"

"A bit," Ruith agreed. He looked at her. "Are there any of my
father's spells at Ceangail, do you think?"

She shook her head. "Nay, and I'm fairly sure that's an honest
opinion and not just my intense desire never to return there."

He smiled ruefully. "I daresay, love." He studied her for another
moment or two. "If you wanted to piece together that spell we found
on the plains of Ailean, I'll make it whole when I return."

"Short of stitching it together myself, I think that's our only
alternative."

He nodded toward the fire. "Let me see you settled, then I'll go.
Briefly. Then we'll take whatever direction you think we should."

She wasn't particularly happy about the thought of leading the
charge, as it were, but she supposed it wasn't any different than the
place in which she'd found herself at the beginning of her quest—
which had been stepping off into the darkness with absolutely no
idea what she was doing.

Only she'd found aid along the way in the person of Ruith, and
Oban . . . and Franciscus, all of whom had turned out to be mages.

She couldn't bear to think about what else might turn out to be
something she hadn't expected.

Seventeen

Ruith sat in the seediest tavern he'd been in all evening—and given that it found itself in Slighe, that was very seedy indeed—and eavesdropped with abandon.

He wasn't an eavesdropper by nature, his lengthy and frequent youthful bouts of it aside, but as he'd discovered that morning, trying to chat up bartenders wasn't going to get him anything besides potentially a belly full of daggers as he lay in a heap behind some ramshackle pub.

Nay, better that he simply sit, listen, and watch. Sarah was perfectly safe in the best chamber he could find, protected as she was by the spell he'd left behind, and hopefully doing the sensible thing of taking another rest. He was happy to wait for what the loose tongues around him would eventually produce.

Unfortunately, there was no talk of an alewagon full of mages, though he supposed no one with any sense would have dared speak of magic within Slighe's borders. He hadn't even been able to manage any tidings about fresh ale with delicate essences of apple and lavender. The lads in Slighe apparently didn't particularly care how their brew tasted as long as it rendered them profoundly intoxicated with as little fuss as possible.

Ruith pretended to nurse his very vile ale and continued to watch the clientele surreptitiously, wondering when one of them would drink himself far enough into a stupor to say something useful.

And then he suddenly realized he wasn't the only one in the pub with an interest in the goings-on.

A pair of lads sitting in the opposite corner seemed equally concerned. He wondered why he hadn't noticed them at first, then had to struggle to mask his surprise when he realized why not.

They were both wearing elvish glamour.

It was very faint, not enough that it would have been visible to a mortal drunkard, but to one who had spent a good portion of his formative years beneath its shadow, it was clear. He leaned back against the wall behind him and studied the men as unobtrusively as possible. He couldn't see their faces—they were sitting in the shadows just as he was—and he had no means of even beginning to identify who they might be. The glamour was nondescript and could have come from either Fadaire or Ciaradh, or a happy combination of both magics, though he couldn't imagine who in his family would have mixed Fadaire with what they would have considered the lesser magic of Ainneamh.

Whoever the men were, they were definitely watching him. He didn't imagine he would be wise to go over and demand their names. He supposed the only thing he could do was get up, walk out, and see if they followed him.

He tossed a coin onto the table, then did just that. He supposed his sword was an unnecessary burden, though he had brought it along partially out of habit and partly because it made him look at least on the surface like an ordinary lad out for a mug of courage after a long day. It would be of no use against the two he hoped would follow, but then again, they likely wouldn't dare use any magic openly if they ever wanted to walk the putrid streets of Slighe again.

He started down the street where the only relief to the darkness was provided by light that spilled out of doorways and windows. He continued on his way without haste, as if whatever business he might need to see to demanded no especial consideration. He knew without looking that someone was following him—actually more than a single someone—which led him to believe he'd drawn the attention of the right souls.

He continued on his way, then suddenly stepped into an alleyway, turned, and waited. There was a lamp on the street, but the flickering flame there did little to relieve the darkness where Ruith stood. He hadn't spent a score of years alive without magic because he was a fool, nor because he didn't have the patience to wait to see which way the wind would blow, but there was no reason in not being at least somewhat prepared. He drew a spell of protection over himself as a concession to what magic he suspected he would soon be facing. He waited for the first spell to slam into him as his followers rounded the corner and almost ploughed him over.

The men facing him were obviously not novices at the practice themselves. They pulled up short, though so quietly that he wouldn't have noticed if he hadn't been watching for the like, then simply stood there and stared at him in silence. The man on the left broke first, after several very long minutes. He pushed his hood back from his face, then folded his arms over his chest.

"Looks like a bit of a storm tonight," he said in a low voice. "I wouldn't think you would want to be out in it, friend."

Ruith blinked in surprise, for the elf facing him was no stranger. Perhaps that shouldn't have surprised him. The elves, at least of Ainneamh and Tòrr Dòrainn, weren't exactly a numerous lot. It was, however, a bit startling to see a cousin where he hadn't expected to.

"Thoir," he said calmly, pushing his own hood back and revealing his face. "A surprise to see you here."

Thoir's mouth worked for a moment or two, as if he were bungling his way through a long list of names, looking for the right one. *"Ruithneadh?"*

"Back from the dead," Ruith agreed. He nodded to his right. "Who is your friend?"

"Ardan of Ainneamh," the other said haughtily, apparently not inclined to show his face. "And you are Gair's whelp, I presume. I suppose I shouldn't be surprised to find you haunting this sort of place."

Ruith felt one of his eyebrows go up before he could stop it. "How troubling it must be for you then, Your Highness, to find yourself in similar straits."

"You have no idea," Ardan said, the disdain plain in his voice. "I don't suppose I dare hope you took the trouble to pay for a chamber here. Perhaps you are simply living up to your appearance and rolling yourself in a tatty blanket as you pass your nights under the stars."

Ruith exchanged a look with his cousin, who only laughed a little and reached out to clap a hand on his shoulder. "It has been many years, cousin. I imagine you have quite a tale to tell."

Ruith realized with a bit of a start that his first instinct was to immediately distrust the two standing in front of him, though he had no reason to. Thoir was his first cousin, son of the crown prince of Tòrr Dòrainn. He was the youngest son of half a dozen, true, but he had wealth and status and, from what Ruith could remember of his youth, dozens of elven maids sighing over him everywhere he went. In spite of that, he had never seemed inclined to take any of it too seriously, though Ruith supposed he hadn't been, at the tender age of ten winters, particularly adept at determining that sort of thing.

He wasn't unfamiliar with Ardan either, for the elven princeling's reputation as an unpleasant and profoundly pretentious fop preceded him everywhere he went. He and Urchaid would have made a formidable pair if ever they had decided to mount an assault on the salons of the Nine Kingdoms. They would no doubt send every hostess of note into frenzies of effort to appease them.

He wondered why it was Ardan and Thoir happened to be in Slighe whilst he was. Coincidence? Somehow, he couldn't bring himself to believe that.

But if coincidence wasn't responsible, what was?

Or who?

He decided that knowing the answer to that sooner rather than later might serve him rather well. He nodded at the street behind the two. "I do have a comfortable spot," he said with a casual shrug, "if you're interested in a hot fire and fairly serviceable chairs. My traveling companion is guarding a very lovely bottle of wine."

"Is he another of our kind?" Ardan asked doubtfully.

"Nay," Ruith said easily, "but a soul worthy of your best manners just the same. Follow or not, as you choose."

And with that, he parted the pair and walked between them. He didn't look over his shoulder to see if they would follow. Curiosity would be too much a temptation for Thoir. As for Ardan, perhaps just the hope of a decent cup of wine would bring him along.

He made his way without haste to the inn, then continued on up to his chamber. He suffered a moment of unease because, truth be told, he cared very much how Sarah was treated. Thoir would behave himself, but bore watching. It was possible that Ardan would be his usual self—relentlessly unpleasant and impossibly arrogant—but Ruith didn't hold out much hope that he would keep all that arrogance to himself.

He looked at Ardan. "Watch yourself," he said shortly.

"Ah," Ardan asked, his eyes widening. "A lady of quality inside, is there? No wonder you're trotting out your best courtly manners."

Ruith ignored him, announced himself, then dissolved his spell as Sarah opened the door.

"Friends, not foes," he said reassuringly.

Her expression didn't lighten, but he understood that. He took the door and had to force himself not to slam it on the elves following him. He kept them behind him and entered slowly once he realized Sarah had the fragments of spell laid out on a table. She quickly scooped them into her hand and deposited them into a bowl she then set on a trunk under the window. She turned and looked at him, silent and wary.

"This is my cousin, Thoir of Tòrr Dòrainn," he said, gesturing to the appropriate interloper. "And Ardan of Ainneamh, who is another cousin of sorts. Gentlemen, this is Sarah of Dòire."

Thoir murmured something polite and complimentary. Ruith couldn't blame him for that. Sarah was, as he would happily have told her endlessly, a very beautiful woman. A currently quite unsettled woman, but a beautiful one nonetheless.

"Dòire," Ardan said doubtfully. "What is there in Dòire?"

"Sagebrush and criminals," Sarah answered without hesitation. "For the most part."

"Well, it produced one thing beyond compare," Thoir said, taking a step forward.

He didn't take another because Ruith put his hand out and stopped him. He shot his cousin a warning look, then saw Sarah seated comfortably in front of the fire. He looked for and found two more poor excuses for chairs, then happily relegated himself to an evening of standing in front of the fire, which would make it a very short evening indeed.

"Who was your mother?" Ardan asked, looking at Sarah down his very long, very aristocratic nose. "I don't recognize you."

Ruith wouldn't have blamed Sarah if she'd glared at him for his part in bringing two elves home with him, as it were, but he also supposed she knew by now that he couldn't stomach pompous fools any more than she could. He only watched her steadily, catching just the briefest glance from her before she looked at Ardan.

"My mother was the witchwoman Seleg," she said calmly. "As to the identity of my father, your guess, Your Highness, is as good as mine."

The reaction was predictable. Ardan spluttered for a moment or two, coming close to an animated case of the vapors. Thoir only smiled at Sarah, seemingly unfazed by her lack of pedigree.

"You are obviously her finest work."

"Thank you," Sarah said with a polite smile. She looked at Ardan. "Would you care for something to drink, Prince Ardan? To ease your suffering?"

Ardan looked for a moment torn between choking to death and accepting, but apparently his instinct for self-preservation was very strong because he accepted a cup of wine with only a small grimace of distaste. Ruith watched him for a moment, then turned to Thoir, who had said something to him he hadn't marked.

"I'm sorry," Ruith said. "I was distracted."

"Understandable," Thoir said with a nod at Sarah. "I had simply asked why you found yourself here in Slighe."

Ruith shrugged. "Looking for companions we had a month or so ago, but seem to have missed. And you?"

Thoir shrugged as well. "I've heard rumors of things let loose in the world. Spells and that sort of rot."

"Slighe seems a strange place to be looking for them," Ruith offered. "Doesn't it?"

Thoir shrugged. "As likely as any, I suppose. I've been other places recently, but joined forces again with Ardan earlier in the day. As for the other, one does what one must. My father usually frequents these sorts of places in an eternal hunt for the unpleasant and unsavoury, but since Grandfather is on an adventure and my father sits the throne, I was selected to be off and doing. I would prefer to be anywhere else—Tor Neroche even, watching the steady stream of lovely young gels searching for a prince to wed—but one does what is required."

Ruith knew what sort of adventure their grandfather was off on, but he imagined Thoir didn't and he had no intention of enlightening him. He looked at Ardan.

"And you, Your Highness?"

"Slumming," Ardan said crisply. "Spending most of my days keeping your wee cousin here from falling into his stew part of the time and trying to keep the horse manure off my boots the rest of the time."

Ruith supposed Ardan couldn't have been more disgusted with his lot in life if he'd suddenly found himself without magic and wallowing in some depraved port town like Istaur.

"Keeping an eye out for tidings as well?" Ruith asked politely.

"To my eternal horror, aye," Ardan said. "And all the while endeavoring to remain unsullied by the commoners of very low birth I'm forced to associate with."

The look he gave Sarah simply dripped with contempt.

"Are you intimating something?" Ruith asked.

Ardan looked at him. "Aye, that your choice of whores—"

He didn't finish his sentence. Ruith supposed that might have been because he had reached over, pulled Ardan up to his feet by the front of his cloak, and acquainted his distant cousin's mouth quite abruptly with his fist. Ardan went sprawling, then climbed inelegantly to his feet and spun around, a spell on his lips.

A very unpleasant spell of death, as it happened, that left Sarah gasping. That apparently startled Ardan enough to keep him from spewing it out. He looked at her in surprise.

"What did you think you saw—"

"Something you shouldn't have thought about uttering." Ruith put his hand on the back of Sarah's chair and looked at Ardan evenly. "I should be very careful, Your Highness," he said, lacing his tone with a heavy layer of the disdain his grandfather always used whilst referring to anyone of the house of Ainneamh, "that I didn't overstep the bounds of polite conversation, were I you. My lovely companion is under my protection. Any slight directed at her will be repaid."

Ardan pursed his lips, then winced. He put his fingers to his mouth, examined the blood he found them covered with, then looked up at Ruith with fury plain in his eyes. "Would you rather I burst into tears at the thought of your mighty power, Ruithneadh my *boy*, or shall I simply sit in the corner and tremble?"

"*Prince* Ruithneadh," Sarah corrected sharply.

Ardan glared at her, then turned back to Ruith. "Well, *Prince* Ruithneadh, how shall I satisfy you?"

"An apology first," Ruith said pointedly, "and then perhaps either an unaccustomed display of manners or simply a bit of silence. Either would be acceptable."

Ardan blew out his breath, then seemed to let go of his anger. "Very well, I can see I'll have no pleasure in tormenting anyone here." He looked at Sarah. "My most abject apologies, my . . . lady."

"Accepted," Sarah said coolly.

Ardan looked up at Ruith. "While I am ascertaining the damage you've done to me, why don't you entertain us by telling us what you're doing here—beyond a very unbelievable tale of looking for companions you lost."

"That much is true," Ruith said. "We might also be looking for a black mage or two."

Thoir's ears perked up. "Indeed," he said. "And why would you want to do that?"

"So I can kill them, one by one."

"Barbaric," Ardan said, "but I must say I approve." He looked at Thoir. "He's no doubt looking for a few of his half brothers. We should aid him in his task."

"Happily," Thoir agreed. He looked up. "Where have you been so far, Ruith?"

"Ceangail, most recently," Ruith lied without a twinge of guilt, "to stir up a hornet's nest full of them."

"With your lady?" Thoir asked in surprise. "Are you mad?"

Ruith pursed his lips before he could stop himself. "I was," he conceded, "but I am mad no longer. As for the results of our visit, the keep is mostly destroyed, I daresay, but the inhabitants aren't." He paused. "I would be glad to know of any rumors you might hear."

Thoir and Ardan exchanged a look, then Thoir shrugged. "Neither of us has been hunting mages, but we could for a bit, if you like. Where are you headed now?"

"We haven't decided on a course yet," Ruith hedged. "But perhaps north."

"We had contemplated a northerly direction as well," Ardan said with a heavy sigh, "given that I certainly don't want to return to the south any time soon. It seems to hold nothing but ruffians and the rather pungent smell of farm animals—though I honestly can't fathom why I find myself out in the wild instead of home—"

"Where you could do what?" Thoir asked with a snort. "Elbow your sire out of the way so you might catch King Ehrne's crown should it fall from his hoary head?"

"I have very sharp elbows," Ardan retorted. "Unfortunately, I find myself cravenly bowing to my father's wishes and traveling the length and breadth of these rustic countries in search of tidings he would never lower himself to seek." He looked at Ruith. "We could meet you in a fortnight's time, if you like. Perhaps in Léige."

"But would Uachdaran let you inside his gates in your current condition?" Ruith asked, finding himself as unable as he usually was of keeping his mouth shut in the presence of fops. "Or would you need to tidy up a bit first?"

Ardan drew himself up. "What condition?"

"I think," Thoir said, his eyes twinkling, "he's suggesting that you smell, Ardan, and that not even a change of clothes will hide the fact that you've seen more of the outdoors than is polite."

Ardan looked at Thoir. "He is as insufferable as your grandfather. And here I hoped he would take more after his sire, who was not exactly a paragon of virtue and goodness."

Thoir shrugged. "Apparently not." He looked at Ruith, then rose. "I thank you for the hospitality and the opportunity to admire your lovely companion, but we should be off. If we find anything interesting, we'll find you. If not in Léige, then somewhere farther north."

Ruith considered. "That is very good of you. And unusual, to find such a joining of forces."

"What else were we to do?" Ardan asked curtly. "We needed some way to pass the time and we grew weary of trying to kill each other. Tossing in our lot together occasionally seemed a welcome relief from the monotony of it all."

Ruith could only imagine how unrelenting the monotony must

have been to inspire such a thing. He watched Thoir bow low over Sarah's hand, then walk to the door. Ardan looked down his nose at the both of them, muttered something under his breath, then turned and walked to the door, holding a suddenly produced lace handkerchief to his nose.

Unsurprising.

Ruith followed them just the same, helped them out with no small bit of relief, then shut the door and dropped a spell over the entire chamber. He returned to the fire and dropped down into the chair opposite Sarah.

"Interesting," Sarah said faintly.

"Wasn't it, though," he said. "I saw them in a pub, allowed them to follow me here, then thought I'd best talk to them rather than ignore them. Break bread with your enemy rather than leave him in the shadows, as my father would have said."

"Enemy," she echoed in surprise. "Don't you trust them? Well, that Ardan would give you reason enough not to, I suppose, but what of the other one?"

"Thoir?" Ruith asked, then shrugged. "He is my uncle Làidir's youngest and undistinguished either by accomplishment or reputation, unless you're considering his ability to leave every poor gel within a three league radius swooning whenever he chooses."

"I don't feel faint."

He smiled at her. "Prefer a more rugged sort of lad, do you?"

"Aye—" She shut her mouth. "If I were looking for a lad, which I'm not. The quest and all, you understand, taking up the bulk of my energies."

"Of course," he agreed easily. And the sooner the bloody quest was over, the sooner he could see if he couldn't convince her to turn her energies to other things. "As for what the pair is doing out in the world, I imagine 'tis just as he says: Làidir is at Seanagarra, sitting on the throne, and Thoir is out collecting tidings for him. Ardan is the crown prince of Ainneamh's youngest son, which leaves him taking on all manner of unsavoury tasks given how far away from the throne he finds himself." He sighed deeply. "For all we know, they'll see something we might miss. But trust them? Not as far as I could heave either one."

"How will they find us, if finding us is what they want to do?"

"I suppose we'll see if they have any skill in tracking," he said. He paused, then shrugged. "I'm not particularly worried about either one of them, actually. They're annoying, but harmless." He paused, then looked at her seriously. "I'm sorry for what Ardan said to you."

She only smiled faintly. "You repaid him well enough, I daresay. I'm not overly concerned with having his good opinion."

"Nor am I," he agreed. "Now, love, what of you? Did you pass the time pleasantly whilst I was gone?"

She blew her hair out of her eyes. "I'm not sure pleasant is the word I would use, but I at least had a hot fire at my feet over the past pair of hours." She paused. "I put the fragments together for you."

"Which I gave you no choice but to undo," he said, rising to fetch a table. "I'll help you, if you like."

She shook her head. "You nap whilst I see to it."

He couldn't deny he needed even but a quarter hour's rest, so he accepted the offer and closed his eyes. He wasn't sure he slept, but even sitting still without having to watch his back was a welcome relief. He opened his eyes to find Sarah watching him.

Without undue disgust in her expression, it should have been noted.

He smiled. "You didn't bolt."

She shook her head. "Not yet."

"You'll tell me before you decide to, won't you?"

"If you like."

"I like," he said, then he straightened and shook the sleep out of his mind. He looked over the scraps of parchment laid out on the table before him. "Find anything interesting?"

"Put it back together, then I'll tell you."

He looked at her sharply, but she was only watching him steadily. He nodded, then restored the page to what it had been. He turned it toward him and sighed at the sight of his father's spell of Unnoticing. He did what he always did when faced with that sort of thing, which was to roll it up and stick it down his boot. Hopefully it would stay there this time. He looked at Sarah only to find her still watching him expectantly.

"Well?" he asked.

She slid a small piece of parchment toward him, torn on two edges and scorched on the other two.

"This didn't fit," she said.

He picked it up, looked at it, then felt the blood drain from his face.

"Ruith?"

He shook his head. "I am well." He realized too late that she was halfway out of her chair to come over and presumably keep him from falling out of his. "For the most part," he said faintly, "though should you still feel the need to aid me, you might go ahead with it."

She sank back down into her seat. "I think you'll manage without my holding you up. What is that a piece of?"

"I think," he said slowly, "that it is from my father's spell of Diminishing."

"Then we've found a clue as to who took it from you," she said with relief. "Perhaps Daniel found a way to cut through that spell—"

He shook his head. "Nay, this isn't the half your brother had—the half we took from him, then I lost." He paused. "It's from the first half."

Her mouth fell open. "The *first* half?"

He could only nod.

She suddenly looked as winded as he felt. "And how did it find itself on the plains of Ailean?"

"I have no idea," he said, "but I imagine we should find out."

"How would Daniel have come by it?"

"That, my love, is perhaps the most unsettling question we've had to answer yet."

"It could have been an accident," she said promptly. "Perhaps Daniel was being followed by someone and he—this unknown mage—feared discovery and left it behind in a fit of panic."

"'Tis possible," he conceded. That was, in truth, the most obvious answer.

But who could that panicky mage be and where was he now? And what if the scrap of spell hadn't been dropped accidentally?

"I don't like the thoughts crossing your face," Sarah said suddenly.

"See them, can you?" he asked uneasily.

"I'm surprised to find that I can." She sat up and rubbed her arms briskly. "You should sleep in truth. I can keep watch for a bit."

"We could," he said slowly, "or we could press on and see if you notice anything as we fly. I imagine we daren't ride given what the surrounding forests are likely full of."

"And flying will save us from them, is that it?"

He managed a smile. "My bastard brothers are vicious, but they don't have any imagination. If they were looking for us—especially given that they wouldn't think we would be using magic—they wouldn't be looking up in the sky. And should they suffer any sort of untoward kinks in their necks and look up in spite of themselves, I'll have hidden us from view."

"Flying," she said, with hardly any sound to the word. "Well, I suppose we don't have much choice."

"I won't let you fall."

"You haven't so far."

"Not recently, at least," he agreed quietly. He rested his elbows on his knees and rubbed his hands together. "We could first make for the farmer's house where we left your herbs, if you like. Then I think we should head for Léige."

"To look for your brother?"

Ruith nodded. "I need him to make a proper list of spells. I think I remember most of them, but only Keir would know for sure. If he's not still there—which he very well could be, with Mhorghain and the rest of them—we might learn where he's gone."

She fussed with her pack. "And will the king allow us entrance? I mean me, actually—"

"I was counting on you to sneak me in," Ruith said with a smile.

She pursed her lips at him, then rose and began to gather her gear together. "I very much doubt I'll be of any help in that, but I will bribe him with a bit of weaving if possible." She glanced at him. "I hope your brother is there."

"I do too," he said, with feeling, and for more reasons than just Keir's memory. After having spent even a pair of days with Rùnach, Ruith realized just how much he'd missed his brothers.

"Ruith?"

He looked up. "Aye, love?"

"Thank you."

"For what?"

She took a deep breath. "For defending my honor." She held out her hand. "I appreciate it."

He walked over to her, took her hand, then bent and kissed it. "It was very willingly done, my lady."

She attempted a smile, but didn't succeed. "That's quite a title for the bastard daughter of an obscure witchwoman."

"Given by the legitimate son of the black mage of Ceangail," Ruith said with a huff of a laugh. "We're a delightfully matched pair." He squeezed her hand, then released it. "Let's be off. You know how much I love the opportunities that flying affords me where you are concerned."

"Lecher."

"Aye," he agreed pleasantly, then went to fetch his own gear. It took him longer than it should have. Troubling thoughts did that to a man, he supposed.

It wasn't possible that someone other than Daniel had left behind a fragment of his father's spell of Diminishing, a fragment from the part that he himself *hadn't* had his hands on less than a month ago.

Was it?

The thought of it was enough to make him feel rather ill. He didn't suppose he dared hope that the two halves of that spell wouldn't find each other. The only thing that eased his mind in the slightest was that he felt certain if someone had put the two halves of the spell together, the world would have ended already.

That life carried on was a bit of a relief.

He busied himself with packing up their gear and making sure

Sarah was distracted from thoughts of flight. If he was also distracted in the process, so much the better. There would be time enough for thinking terrible thoughts later.

Perhaps whilst he was about the unenviable task of convincing Uachdaran of Léige to allow him inside the gates instead of slaying him on the spot.

Eighteen

❧

Sarah wondered if another day would come when she felt as though she were walking in something other than a waking dream.

She would have happily trailed along behind Ruith and avoided having to look at dwarves with very sharp swords—and a few with very pointed pikes, truth be told—but he had tucked her hand under his arm and seemed determined to keep her next to him. She wasn't going to argue. She was too busy hoping they wouldn't be thrown in the dungeon for attempting entrance into a place so fortresslike it made Buidseachd look like a pitched tent. Whatever the dwarves hid in their palace, they wanted it kept safe.

She supposed she would have felt quite comfortable with all the stone and guards and well-crafted steel—and the spells which were enough to give any woman with wit to spare pause—but she wasn't entirely sure those things wouldn't be barriers to her escape, should she need to make one.

They were ushered and not pushed—a good sign, she thought—through passageways and up and down stairs that whispered with tales of glorious riches and their discovery by only the most canny and persistent. Perhaps the people of Léige were more concerned with their exploits than they were using their spells on uninvited visitors—yet another promising sign. All they had to do was find out if Keir was there, have a little chat with him, then be on their way into other places that she was quite sure would be even more unpleasant.

Without warning, they walked out into an enormous hall, cavernous and intimidating, with a floor so polished, she had to look twice to make sure she wasn't walking on glass. The walls bore carvings of the same sort of heroic scenes that the passageways had seemed eager to tell. She saw those only because, despite the darkness of the stone and the blackness of the polished floor, the entire place was full of scores of lamps and candles and other sorts of lights that weren't entirely of this world.

"Oh," she breathed.

Ruith looked a little winded himself. "I've never been in here. We were always accorded the lesser greeting hall."

"Your reputation precedes you, then."

"I think it might have been the chance to admire our horses more closely," Ruith managed. "It was probably wise to ask them to resume their proper shapes well away from the walls, though I imagine Uachdaran's scouts saw everything anyway."

"Perhaps they're afraid you'll do the same to them," she whispered.

He looked at her, then smiled. "We'll speak of dwarvish magic later, when we have some privacy. They have no fear of me." He looked around him for another moment, then shrugged. "I have the feeling it was the sword that earned us this. And I believe I'm going to owe Soilléir a fortnight or two of mucking out his stables as repayment."

She would have agreed heartily, but they had come to a stop some thirty paces away from the thrones set on a dais, and she thought idle chatter might be out of place.

One throne was empty, but 'twas obvious that the king was occu-
pying the other. She remembered Franciscus having told her that
the dwarvish queen had lost her life in some tragic sort of fashion, but she couldn't remember the details. She stopped with Ruith
and wondered if she should bow or curtsey. She decided upon the
latter and attempted it whilst Ruith made the king a very low, very
long bow.

A guilty conscience was keeping him there longer than he might
have been normally, no doubt.

"King Uachdaran," Ruith said, straightening. "We bring you our
deepest gratitude for your hospitality, as well as a gift from Soilléir
of Cothromaiche. I am—"

"I know who you are," Uachdaran grumbled loudly. "Gair's
youngest brat save one."

"Um," Ruith said, sounding nonplussed, "well, aye. I am that."

"You've missed an entire contingent of your relations," Uachdaran said, looking at Ruith calculatingly. "If I didn't know better, I
would think the entire house of Seanagarra was determined to make
itself at home in my hall. *And* in my private solar."

Ruith at least had the grace to blush. "I can understand why you
might think that, Your Majesty, and I apologize for any past forays
into places not usually accessible to visitors."

Uachdaran grunted. "I don't want to know how many forays you
made, but at least you apologized. When that young upstart from
Neroche arrived at my gates recently, he only flattered me in a rather
restrained fashion, then retired to my solar for a very long morning
of no doubt continuing to look for things he shouldn't have."

"I'm sure he had his reasons."

"He always does," Uachdaran said severely. "And I'll have it
known that the only reason I allowed it was to reward him for his
eye for a beautiful woman."

"My sister?"

Uachdaran smirked. "Bet you didn't know that until recently, did
you, Ruithneadh?"

Sarah pursed her lips to keep from smiling. Whatever bluster

Ruith had possessed on the way into the palace—which she had appreciated, in truth—had apparently left him abruptly. He seemed only capable of looking at Uachdaran as if he'd just been rapped smartly on the nose with a stick.

"Nay, I didn't, Your Majesty."

"Ha," Uachdaran said, then he frowned. "I should enjoy this more, but your grandfather was uncommonly—and uncustomarily—pleasant to me recently. I suppose you'll benefit."

"Your Majesty's generosity knows no bounds."

"Don't think it'll earn you another trip into my solar, boy."

"Of course not, Your Majesty."

"Your sister has very pretty manners, for a soldier," Uachdaran continued. "No taste in lads, but decent manners."

"I plan on speaking to her about both, Your Majesty."

The king scowled at him, then turned his scowl on her. Sarah felt a little faint, but since Ruith was obviously not going to be of any help, she stiffened her spine and returned the king's look steadily.

He grunted at her. "Sarah of Doìre."

"Aye, Your Majesty." She had given her name at the front gates, so it was no surprise that he knew it already.

He squinted at her from a steely eye. "I daresay I should have kept young Mhorghain here a bit longer. Would have saved me time in advising you both of the wisdom of avoiding entanglements with mages—*especially* such a pair as you both seem to have taken up with."

"I'm not entangled," Sarah protested, though she found herself squirming under the words. Nay, she wasn't entangled, but that wasn't because she had other entanglements to contemplate, nor because she wouldn't have had anything to do with Ruith if things had been different.

Uachdaran only snorted at her. "You shouldn't hedge, gel. You're not good at it." He pushed himself up off his throne and bounded down the steps with the energy of a youth, which he most assuredly was not. "Show me the sword you've brought, young Ruithneadh, and let's see what Soilléir has foisted off upon me."

Sarah watched the king's face as Ruith drew the sword and laid it across both his palms where Uachdaran could see it plainly.

The dwarf king froze, just as Soilléir had done.

And then the moment was gone, just as it had been with Soilléir, as if it had never been there and nothing about the blade had startled the king. He stroked his chin thoughtfully, then looked up at Ruith.

"Nice steel," he said.

"Not as fine as something you would make, of course," Ruith began respectfully.

"You would be surprised at what comes from my forge," Uachdaran said. "Including this blade."

"Indeed?" Ruith asked in surprise.

"Indeed," Uachdaran said, in a perfect mocking imitation of Ruith's tone. "There isn't a blade that leaves my smithy without my inspection and my mark. Even the Sword of Neroche," he added with a twinkle in his eye. "And that gel's blade that Mehar of Angesand is so fond of. I added a little something of my own recently while the interested parties were off having tea."

"I had no idea," Ruith managed.

Uachdaran snorted at him. "You would think with all the prying into my private affairs you did in your youth that you might have learned a few details about my most powerful magic, but perhaps not." He pointed with his nose to the darkness behind them. "Go have a rest, children, then come to supper—if you're not too high for simple fare."

"We would prefer it," Ruith said promptly, "but, Your Majesty—"

Uachdaran stopped in mid-step and turned back around. "Eh?"

"Don't you want the sword?"

"It served its purpose," Uachdaran said with a shrug. "You keep it."

Ruith frowned. "Then there was a message you understood . . . or . . ."

Uachdaran pursed his lips. "If you haven't the wit to discover that on your own, little lad, then you're not worthy of that blade. Go put your wee thinking cap on, Ruithneadh. The answer will come to you in time."

Sarah waited with Ruith as Uachdaran turned and strode out of his grand audience chamber. Ruith resheathed the sword, then turned to her. He still looked a little winded.

"The king loves a good riddle."

"Apparently," she agreed. She managed a smile. "Are you going to solve it?"

"Among other ones, aye, if I have the chance." He took a deep breath, then let it out slowly. "We have dinner and a bed for the night, at least. We'd probably best take advantage of both whilst the offer still stands. I might do a little investigating—"

"Don't," she interrupted quickly. "Please."

He smiled and drew her hand through his arm. "I won't—at least not until we're ready to leave. For now, I think we should take the king up on his invitation for a nap and something to eat."

Considering we're likely not to enjoy the like again for some time was what he hadn't said, but she was sure he'd thought.

She walked with him as they were escorted back out of the hall and through other passageways that were no less full of tales of glory and glittering things than the first set had been. She would have paid more attention, but the truth was, she hadn't slept well, even at Buidseachd, and she hadn't slept much at all for the past two days. She saw a quite lovely bed near the hearth in the very lovely chamber she was shown, managed to stagger over to it, and fell into its softness before she could even attempt a stab at good manners or thanks to the serving maids she had noticed.

Her last thought was that she hoped Ruith would shut the door so no one would watch her drool in her sleep.

Several hours later, she sat in front of a mirror and wondered if it would be rude to put her foot down and demand back her traveling clothes which seemed to have disappeared along with her used bathwater.

She was wearing a black dress that she learned, after sifting through profuse apologies for not having had something ready just for her, had been worn very briefly by Ruith's sister Mhorghain before she'd demanded her leggings and tunic back.

Sarah thought she and Mhorghain might get along very well indeed.

Her hair had been washed and combed out and left hanging in a riot of curls down her back. She was rather paler than she would have thought she would have been given all the traveling she'd done, but perhaps her face was a reflection of the unease she couldn't seem to shake, even protected as she was inside impenetrable walls. She watched as the maid, a rather tall, exceptionally lovely girl of obviously dwarvish descent, reached for something else to torture her with.

"Absolutely not," she said, eyeing the item suspiciously.

The girl held a circlet of gold in her hands. "But, my lady, 'twas fashioned especially for you."

Sarah scowled in spite of herself. The seamstresses had been too busy to aid her, but the goldsmiths had been lounging about with time on their hands? She revisited the idea of putting her foot down.

"'Tis a modest thing," the girl added, holding it out for inspection. "Hardly anything to be seen, don't you agree?"

Sarah had to agree that it was very discreet, but that was beside the point. "I'm not worthy of a crown," she protested.

"Well," said a voice from the doorway, "that's a matter of opinion."

Sarah looked around her maid to find Ruith standing just inside her doorway, leaning back against the wall, watching her. She wondered just how long he'd been standing there and how much of her complaints he'd heard. He was smiling, though, so perhaps he hadn't been bothered by them.

"Are you responsible for this?" she demanded.

He only shook his head slowly. "I'm not, though I would certainly take credit for it if I dared." He tilted his head to one side and studied her. "You look lovely."

She stood, because she thought it might be easier to bolt that way. "You look lovely as well," she said, because it was true, though something of an understatement.

He had obviously succumbed to the same pressure she'd been put under to dress properly for supper, though his clothing was still very discreet. No baubles, fine embroidery, capes hanging from his shoulders, or fancy court shoes. He was wearing black boots, black trousers, and a deep green tunic that she imagined would do quite lovely things for his eyes. She noticed immediately that even though he wasn't wearing a crown, he'd been given one because he'd stuck his arm through it as if it had been a very large bracelet.

"I understand," he began slowly, "that there is to be a formal sort of entertainment tonight."

"How fortunate for you," she managed. "You'll have the chance to audition a princess or two."

"Perhaps," he conceded, "but since my first thought was that I would have the opportunity to pass the evening with you, I wanted to rescue myself from complete embarrassment and see if you would humor me by practicing a dance step or two."

She sank back down onto the chair she'd recently vacated. "But I can't dance," she protested.

"And I can?" he asked, with an uncomfortable laugh. "We have half an hour to remedy that before supper. I suggest we take advantage of the dancing master I bribed and left out in the passageway to await our pleasure."

"I think I should just sit and watch—"

He walked over and pulled her up off the chair. "Nay, my lady, you will not."

She looked up at him. "You arrogant, autocratic—"

"State dinners include dancing."

She pursed her lips for she knew there was no escaping her fate. She conceded the battle, but not the war.

"Very well," she said with a sigh, "I will dance, but I will not wear—" She managed to point vaguely toward the serving girl. "I won't wear that."

The girl looked at Ruith for support. He looked fully prepared to give it to her, so Sarah left them to their scheming and retreated to stand in front of the fire where she could attempt to warm her hands that were far colder than they should have been. She heard Ruith's soft laughter, listened to him usher the girl out the door, then heard his footsteps approach. He stopped behind her and waited silently, but Sarah couldn't bring herself to help him along into hitherto unexplored realms of uncomfortable conversational topics.

He apparently had more patience than she did, though, because he outlasted her easily. She finally gave vent to a gusty sigh and turned to look at him.

"I've changed my mind. I want to use one of my remaining beg-off-from-supper tokens."

"Can't," he said cheerfully. "Even my grandfather doesn't refuse supper here—when he manages to get himself inside the gates."

She had to force herself to breathe normally. "I don't belong here."

"And given the long history of prickly relations between my mother's people and Uachdaran's, I would say I didn't either. But since the king has been good enough to offer us shelter and a meal, I imagine we should accept and see if we can't improve the goodwill a bit."

"How politic of you, Your Highness."

"It is, isn't it?" he asked, frowning as if he wasn't quite sure where the impulse had come from. He walked over to rest his hand on the enormous stone mantel. "Lovely gown."

"Your sister wore it when she was here."

He flinched. "Touché, love."

"The difference is, the crown they tried to stick on her head was bigger, I understand, though she balked at wearing it as well." She tucked her hands into her sleeves, wincing as she grazed her right arm.

"It sounds as if you'll get on famously," he said.

She nodded, then turned to look at the fire again, because it was easier than looking at him. She knew she was stalling, but it seemed the only thing to do out of a sense of self-preservation. "Ruith—"

"We'll be late if we don't hurry," he said, taking her arm suddenly and pulling her across the chamber. "Dancing lessons. But first the appropriate *accoutrements*."

Sarah watched him, unable to speak, as he plopped his crown on his head with an adroitness that bespoke a youth in a palace, then took hers, turned her toward him, and gently placed it on her head. Then he met her eyes.

"This is freshly forged."

"Mistakenly—"

"Purposely," he corrected, "for you, which means you should wear it."

"But I am nothing," she protested.

"You are something to me," he said seriously, "and Uachdaran perhaps honors you for that reason. I suspect, however, that since he obviously ordered this made for you, he has other reasons we can't yet divine."

"I'm not sure I want to know what they are," she muttered.

"Delving too deeply into the dwarf king's motives can be dangerous," he agreed, "but always yields interesting results." He paused. "If nothing else, you could wear this very lovely bit of work and give a goldsmith who will likely be sneaking a look in the great hall tonight a measure of delight at seeing his creation atop the head of the most beautiful woman there."

She looked up at him, but found she couldn't see him very well. She was weary; that was it. It had been an extraordinarily long winter turned spring so far with no sign of any of it abating any time soon. She blinked rapidly.

"I'm not a weeper."

"Nay, love, you aren't."

She took a deep breath. "I still don't want this, but I will endure it to please that very shy smith." She paused. "I'm not sure I can keep it on my head."

"I'll see to it." He fetched a pair of pins from the dressing table, then frowned thoughtfully as he attempted to use them for their intended purpose. He examined his work, then reached up and brushed two stray tears from her cheeks. "You need a distraction. Allow me to offer myself."

"Altruistic of you."

"Self-serving," he admitted, "but you can think of it how you want." He took her left hand. "Let's be off to see what we can learn before supper begins."

Their dancing master, a small, elfin creature, had endless amounts of patience and an infectious amount of good humor. He taught them three dances, pronounced them quick studies, and promised to have a quiet word with King Uachdaran's musicians after supper so she and Ruith would have something familiar to dance to. Sarah felt absolutely ridiculous walking into a great hall full of royalty and important guests, but Ruith had promised her he would chase her if she bolted, so she concentrated on the very necessary task of making sure her crown stayed on her head.

She found herself sitting on Uachdaran's right hand in a place of honor, with Ruith on her right. She was very grateful for the king's single-minded concentration on his supper, which gave her the chance to attempt to do the same. She gave up the effort after a bit, not because the food wasn't superb but because she was too distracted by what she was seeing in the hall.

Soilléir had much to answer for.

Whilst the hall itself could be properly described as stately, it wasn't the heavy beams in the ceiling or the marvelously designed and fashioned tapestries draping over the walls from floor to ceiling that she couldn't look away from.

It was the tales being told by the flames flickering in the massive hearths set on either side of the hall.

She felt as if heroic epics were being reenacted for her benefit alone, mighty deeds wrought by dwarves throughout the ages, battles fought against darkness and evil when men and elves were otherwise occupied with less weighty matters of their realms. Sarah could only watch, speechless, at what she saw, things she had never once considered might be occurring under her nose—or under mountains

she had never laid eyes on in her life—things that had quietly, relentlessly, absolutely kept the inhabitants of the Nine Kingdoms sleeping safely.

She looked at the king to find him watching her with a small
smile as if he knew exactly what she was seeing.

"Do you see too?" she asked, because she couldn't help herself.

"Oh, aye, lass," he said with another knowing smile. "Not many
others do, though. I daresay your lad there isn't seeing anything in
my hearths but a flame to warm his backside on a chilly night."

"See what?" Ruith asked politely, leaning forward. "Your strings
warming up, Your Majesty? My lady owes me a dance or two."

Uachdaran winked at her, then looked at Ruith. "While I understand your enthusiasm, lad, first I think we must humor my bard.
He keeps our genealogy, as you may or may not know, and while
that is a worthy task, he never misses the chance to have a peep in
someone else's family tree. Your grandfather, I'm afraid, didn't have
the time to attend him at all, to his great distress. I hope you children don't mind if he at least comes to greet you. I imagine neither of
you will escape without divulging a few details he'll want to record
in his books."

"I don't think my heritage will come as much of a surprise to
him," Ruith said dryly, "but I'll gladly humor him. I might have
an unsavoury connection or two to delight him with, if he has the
stomach for it."

"He does," Uachdaran said mildly. He nodded to one of his pages,
who ran off without hesitation.

Sarah would have liked to have distracted herself with the fire a
bit longer, but the tales had ceased. That might have been because
they felt they were competing with what the musicians were creating, music she could see hanging in the air, forming itself into proper
patterns of dance. She blinked, but the notes remained long enough
to make their appearance, take their place in the song, then slip off-
stage, as it were.

She looked at Uachdaran in surprise.

He was still simply watching her with that half smile, as if he

knew exactly what she was seeing—which she suspected he did—
and was pleased to enjoy it with her.

"Didn't expect this, did you, lass?" he asked gently.

"I'm finding, Your Majesty, that that has become my lot in life."

He smiled, a smile full of good humor. "I hope, my gel, that you
will one day be able to leave that saying behind, but I fear that day
is not near. Ah, here is Master Eachdraidh."

Sarah looked at the man hurrying across the hall, his arms full
of papers and the voluminous sleeves of his robe flapping with his
haste. He was tall, for an inhabitant of Léige, and very thin, looking as if he spent the majority of his time holed up in some chamber
or other, looking through books. She supposed she could have been
accused of hiding herself in a place or two to weave, but she somehow didn't think she looked quite that pale.

Master Eachdraidh skidded to a stop in front of the high table,
made the king a very low bow, which sent his pages scattering, then
spent a few minutes trying to gather everything back up. Ruith, the
good-hearted soul that he was, walked around the table and bent to
help him. They chatted amicably about the unpredictability of pages
that weren't sewn properly into a book—Sarah caught the look Ruith
sent her and smiled in understanding—then Ruith straightened and
left the historian to his own devices.

Eachdraidh clutched his papers to his chest, then made the king
another low bow. "Your Majesty, I have come to, of course, first
delight you with the retelling of a tale or two unearthed from the
vaults below, then I thought . . . to . . ."

Sarah watched the man lose his ability to speak. His mouth
worked soundlessly, as if he'd just seen a ghost. She looked over her
shoulder to see if that might be the case—she was fully prepared to
see more things than she would have *ever* wanted to in the past—but
there was nothing behind her. She turned back to Uachdaran's genealogist and realized he wasn't looking at someone behind her.

He was looking at *her*.

His papers fluttered to the floor.

He joined them with substantially less grace.

"Interesting," Uachdaran said, then he clapped his hands together. Guards strode across the hall, gathered up the fallen bard, then carried him and his things off to points unknown. The king looked at Ruith. "Dancing, lad?"

"Of course," Ruith said smoothly. He pushed his chair back and held down his hand. "Sarah?"

She wasn't opposed to holding his hand, though she was beginning to think she should hold it, then continue to hold it as she fled with him out the front gates. She stopped in the middle of the hall and looked up at him.

"And just what was that all about?" she asked.

"The bard?" He shrugged. "He's excitable. I wouldn't give it another thought. I imagine you're finding enough to think on without worrying about the antics of an overwrought keeper of histories."

It was just one more thing to add to a very odd evening, so she set it aside. She couldn't set aside the other things as easily. "What is this place?" she managed.

"You tell me."

"The fire tells stories and the king is unsurprised by that."

"Love, I daresay the king isn't surprised by much."

"The music makes patterns in the hall," she added. "As if the notes were dancers themselves."

"Fascinating."

She glared at him. "You're making sport of me."

"I'm not," he said frankly. "I'm intrigued by what you can see. And willing, as always, to suggest that if your sight of other things bothers you, you are more than welcome to look only at me. Indeed, I think that might be just the thing for you tonight. I promise the view will be—"

"Ruith," she warned.

"Very well," he said with a smile, "I'll leave off with the feigned arrogance, though I want it noted I indulged in it simply to ease your nerves."

She grumbled at him, though she had to concede that his

technique had been rather successful. She forgot about the things in Léige that apparently only she and the king could see, forgot about what lay beyond the walls, and even managed to forget about Uachdaran's bard, who had looked at her and then fainted.

"I think you're forgetting about me," Ruith said in a singsong sort of voice. "Though how you could, I don't know."

She smiled at him in spite of how hard she fought not to. "Thank you."

"A stroll in the garden later, whilst you're feeling so charitable toward me?"

"I think your time would be better spent dancing with a handful of Uachdaran's granddaughters," she said with a snort.

"And then a walk?"

"Aye, to my chamber where I will thank you for the lovely dances, then climb into bed and pull the blankets over my head where I need not see anything else this day."

He smiled. "Very well, I'll concede the battle. Tonight. But I think you would find the garden very interesting. Nothing there but trees and a handful of stone benches for those who need a rest."

She imagined it would contain quite a few more things than that, but she wasn't going to argue the point. She would fight him about it on the morrow, after she'd spent a peaceful night not dreaming. Retiring early would give her a chance to get her crown off her head, allow Ruith some time to pry useful details out of the king, and provide her with a place to close her eyes and block out more things she didn't want to see.

Such as the bard, Eachdraidh, who was now clinging to one of the hall doors, still watching her as if he'd seen a ghost.

"I'm more interesting than he is," Ruith remarked.

"That you are, Your Highness," she agreed, happy for once to look at him and no one else.

Though it was rather more hard on her heart than she suspected it might be.

Ten princesses, indeed.

But at least thinking on that gave her a reason not to think on all the other very odd things she'd seen since she'd walked through Uachdaran's heavy front gates. Surely Soilléir would have known what he was sending them into, but he'd done it anyway, without a twinge of remorse or hesitation.

She couldn't help but wonder why.

Nineteen

Ruith woke to screaming.

He thought at first that he was still trapped in a dream and he had been the one crying out, but he sported no crushing headache, nor could he remember anything that would have wrenched that sort of sound out of him.

Nay, it wasn't him. It was Sarah.

He threw back the covers, pulled on clothes, then sprinted out of his chamber and down the passageway, blessing Uachdaran for having put him next door to Sarah. He unbolted her door with a spell, pushed his way inside, then lit every candle in the place, along with the fire, as he rushed across the floor. He came to a teetering halt next to the bed, suddenly unsure what he should do. He didn't think he had the skill to go into her dreams, though his mother had managed it often enough for him, but he also couldn't allow her to fall deeper into where she was. He understood all too well the perils of that.

He leaned over, intending to take her by the arms and gently shake her, only to jerk aside when he saw the flash of a dagger in the candlelight. Obviously, he was not at his best, something he noted as he looked at the blade buried to the hilt in his arm. Feeling rather grateful that had been his arm and not his chest, he sat down on the edge of the bed and called Sarah's name, repeatedly.

It took longer than he would have supposed, likely because he hadn't thought to use a spell until she had stopped shrieking and had descended into racking sobs. He cast a spell of Camanaë over them both, a spell guaranteed to drive out all but the sweetest of dreams, then found his arms full of her. He tried not to wince as she jarred the blade on her way to throwing her arms around his neck, but he feared he hadn't managed it very well.

She pulled back and looked at him in surprise, then gaped at his arm. "What befell you?"

"Ah—"

She blanched. "I did that?"

"I shouldn't have leaned over you."

"Did you?" She blinked, as if she couldn't fathom why he was where he was and she had stabbed him. "Was I dreaming?"

"Don't you remember it?"

She took a deep breath. "Only darkness." She looked at his arm dripping blood down onto the bed. "I'm sorry I can't fix that. Well, I could sew it—"

"Not to worry," he said, ripping off his other sleeve and tying it above the wound. "Take your blade back, love."

She pulled the steel free of his flesh, and he swayed in spite of himself. He rolled his eyes at his own inability to tolerate a small prick of a wound, then rose. He cleaned her knife on his shirt, then handed it back to her. "Bring your blades, and come with me. You'll have my bed, and I'll take the floor."

She crawled unsteadily out of her bed, then accepted the dressing gown he handed her. She pulled it around her, then padded behind him on bare feet. He would have to remedy that sooner rather than later, but perhaps she wouldn't mind if he attended to his arm first of all. He extinguished all he'd lit on his way in, held open her door for her, then followed her out into the passageway.

And into Uachdaran of Léige.

"Your Majesty," he said, a little off balance.

Uachdaran looked at his arm, frowned, then looked at Sarah. "I don't suppose," he said in a tone that said he very much hoped he wasn't supposing, "that you made that wound fighting off the wee princeling behind you."

"I was having a nightmare," she said faintly, "and stabbed him by mistake."

Uachdaran peered at Ruith's arm, then looked up at him. "Need a surgeon, do you?"

"A spell would be just as welcome."

"Happily, I might have one or two of those," the king said. "Put your lady to bed in your chamber, lad, then you'll pull up a scrap of floor in my solar—though I can't believe I'm inviting you into my private sanctuary."

"If it's all the same to you, Your Majesty," Ruith said, because he had spent the last night of Sarah's life without her in the same chamber as he found himself, "I would prefer to keep Sarah within reach."

Uachdaran made a noise of disapproval. "I don't hold to these newfangled ideals of too much togetherness before marriage. A visit or two is sufficient, to my mind, to check for crooked teeth and knobby knees."

Ruith wasn't at all surprised, but he managed not to smile. "I vow I will be, as I have been until this moment, a perfect gentleman where Sarah is concerned. I wouldn't want to face my mother's disapproval."

Uachdaran considered. "Well, she did manage to raise six lads without any of you going off to follow your sire in his madness, so I suppose she instilled some decent character into you. Very well. Bring your lady along. I'll have a look at her arm while we're tending yours."

Ruith didn't ask how Uachdaran knew about the trail of spells in Sarah's arm. There was little—perhaps nothing, actually—that passed within the dwarf king's realm that he didn't know. He took Sarah's hand, spelled a pair of soft slippers onto her feet, then walked with her after the king. He was a little surprised to find he did indeed remember the way to the king's solar, but he supposed that was something he should keep to himself.

The king opened the door, entered first, then held the door for them both. He saw Sarah seated in front of a fire that leapt to life at his approach, then motioned for Ruith to help himself to the stool next to her. Ruith did, smiling a little at being put in his place. Uachdaran went off to putter amongst things that smelled like herbs, so Ruith took the opportunity to look at Sarah.

Sleep had obviously fled from her, which he couldn't blame her for in the least. He'd never been able to sleep again after waking from a nightmare.

"Sing her a lay, Ruithneadh," Uachdaran said, holding a glass bottle up to a candle. "Take her mind off the darkness. There's a lute somewhere in here. I'd lay odds you know where it is."

Ruith would have preferred to stick hot pins in his eyes rather than embarrass himself by demonstrating his lack of ability with anything bearing strings, but he could at least carry a tune. Perhaps Sarah would forgive him his very poor accompaniment.

He did indeed find a lute, tuned it, then looked at Sarah who was watching him in surprise.

"I had no idea you had so many courtly skills, Your Highness," she said.

"Having them is perhaps a matter for debating later," he said, "but I will concede that my mother did insist we all learn a few useful things. I do not play well, but if this could count as wooing, I might play better."

"You seem to be lacking those ten princesses closely examined, Prince Ruithneadh," she said pointedly, "before you begin to think of anything akin to that."

"I believe we recently decided it was ten princesses *danced* with—and I believe that is much more than I agreed to at the start," Ruith said, frowning as he plucked at the strings, "and I believe I danced with not one but two of our good king's granddaughters this past night. That makes my remaining tally eight, not ten."

"Well," Uachdaran said, sounding as if he were trying very hard not to laugh, "the boy can do his sums. You must accord him that, Sarah, gel."

"And I'm playing under enormous duress," Ruith said, "with an arm that still bleeds. Surely that should earn me a concession or two."

Sarah hadn't begun to offer her opinion on that before Uachdaran had walked across the floor, slapped a dwarvish spell of binding on Ruith's arm, then grunted at him before he returned to his work.

Ruith winced at the spell, but found its thoroughness to be quite admirable. He took a deep breath, then trolled back through his memories to things he'd learned as a lad. That repertoire was exhausted quite quickly, which left him attempting things he'd heard in other locales over the past decade, things he rendered quite badly. He looked at Sarah occasionally to find her watching him with a faint smile.

"I warned you," he said simply.

She shook her head. "It's charming."

"Do you play?"

"Franciscus taught me a little, but my repertoire is limited to raunchy pub songs."

Ruith laughed. "He should be ashamed of himself."

"He should," she agreed. "I much prefer to listen to you. It's lovely."

He was happy to humor her a bit longer, though equally pleased to set aside his lute when Uachdaran finished his work, crossed back to Sarah, and pulled up a chair in front of her.

"Let's try this on your arm," he said.

Sarah pushed up her sleeve and didn't wince as he applied the salve he'd either found or made. The red that had faded with Soil-léir's spell had returned, leaving terrible trails up and down her arm. Uachdaran's mix made no difference in the black, though the redness

receded. He sat back, studied Sarah's arm for another moment or
two, then looked at her.

"Something has delved deeply into your flesh, my lady," he said
gravely. "It is difficult sometimes to undo too much digging, be it
mountain or flesh." He looked at Ruith. "What have you tried?"

"Camanaë," Ruith said. "Master Soilléir attempted an essence
change, but even that failed." He paused. "Have you any sugges-
tions, Your Majesty?"

The king shook his head slowly. "Thoughts enough, but no sug-
gestions. I'll consider the matter further, then see if another attempt
might be made. Put away that lute, my boy, and go fetch your lady
a pallet. We'll put her here by the fire and watch over her until she
sleeps."

"If it's all the same to you, Your Majesty," Sarah put in, "I'm not
sure I could sleep. Close my eyes, perhaps, but not sleep."

The king nodded. "As you will, gel, for I can understand your
apprehension well enough. Darkness that doesn't abate can be quite
terrifying. Ruith, fetch that blanket there and we'll at least wrap her
up well. Then you and I will discuss the state of the world."

Ruith did as requested, then met Sarah's eyes as he laid a blanket over her. "You've spent your last night without me within arm's
reach, my lady."

That she didn't protest said quite a bit about her distress. "As you
will, Ruith."

He reached out and tucked a lock of hair behind her ear. "I'm
sorry for what will drive you there, but not unhappy to have you
nearby."

She smiled faintly. "I daresay you aren't, but I shouldn't expect
anything else."

He smiled in return, then moved his stool closer to her and sat
down. He waited until she had closed her eyes before he spoke again,
though he didn't dare hope she slept.

"Thank you, Your Majesty," he said quietly, "for the attempt."

Uachdaran watched Sarah for a moment or two in silence, then
looked at Ruith. "How did she come by that?"

Ruith had to let out a long, slow breath. "Her brother had come by my father's spell of Diminishing. Well, half of it. She reached out to touch it and the spell assaulted her."

"Diminishing," Uachdaran repeated with a grunt. "That was just a fancy way of saying hello to a man before taking what he prized the most. Your father did have a way with words."

"He did, Your Majesty."

Uachdaran fixed him with a look. "You're going to have to do something about what's buried in her flesh, lad. If I can't heal it, nor can Soilléir with all his mighty power, there's something to worry about. Since the injury came from your sire, though, I think you may have to give more thought to trying something of his to remedy it."

"I'm trying to discover the proper spell."

"Not filched from my library, you aren't," Uachdaran said pointedly. "And you'll need more magic than you have at present, if you want the entire truth."

"I've recently become reacquainted with it," Ruith said with a sigh, "which I'm realizing hourly was a score of years too late. Though the sources are powerful enough, I daresay."

"They are indeed, my boy, but the sad truth is, your grandfathers on both sides are mighty oaks with centuries of magic making to their credit. You're naught but a twig by comparison. When the wind blows—and it will blow, son—you won't stand long against it."

"Thank you, King Uachdaran," Ruith said dryly. "Unfortunately there is no easy way to remedy that, so I fear I've no choice but to simply soldier on as best I can."

Uachdaran sized him up. Ruith watched him do the like and felt something slide down his spine. He might have called it unease if he'd been the sort of lad to worry about that sort of thing.

"I believe," Uachdaran said slowly, "that I'll see you in the morning. In my lists."

Ruith blinked. "Do you have lists?"

"Don't you already know the answer to that?"

Ruith smiled. "I fear, Your Majesty, that your lists might have been the one place Prince Mochriadhemiach and I didn't investigate."

"Which is why seeing you there later this morning will give me an added measure of delight," Uachdaran assured him. "We'll spend a day or two honing your magic. It won't build all the strength you'll need for your task, but it will be a start. You'll have to do the rest on your own."

"Thank you, Your Majesty," Ruith said. It was a very generous offer, though he imagined his gratitude would only last as long as his strength—which he suspected Uachdaran would ravage within a pair of hours.

Uachdaran fetched mugs that turned out to be full of a deep, rich ale. Ruith enjoyed a few sips without hesitation. He imagined his respite wasn't going to last long. He had his own questions for the king, but he didn't dare blurt them out until the proper moment—and he was quite sure that moment wouldn't come until he'd satisfied the king's curiosity.

It took perhaps a quarter hour before Uachdaran seemed to be satisfied that Sarah had fallen into at least an uneasy sleep. He looked at Ruith.

"I've heard rumors that trouble me."

"Tidings of the well?" Ruith asked.

Uachdaran shook his head slowly. "I'll not diminish the gravity of that, but there are things in this world—old things—things that should have passed into the realm of memory but haven't."

Ruith took a careful breath. "My father's spells, for instance?"

"Those, and other things. Mages, magic, mischief wrought by both." He shrugged. "Things you might want to look into as you're off roaming through these parts. But first tell me how it is you slipped out of the world's notice for so many years only to reappear along with these unsettling rumors. Not," he added, "that I'm accusing you of being the reason for any of it. You may be your father's get, Ruithneadh, but you are not your father's son. If you can appreciate the difference."

"I can," Ruith said, with feeling. "And I thank you for according me the benefit of the doubt."

Uachdaran waved away his words. "Lad, I knew your father well.

Not only do you not look particularly much like him—you look much more like your mother's kin—you haven't his heart. His damnable curiosity, of course, but not his heart."

"Curiosity is what makes a good mage."

"It also gets that mage's fingers singed more often than not, but we'll leave that for now. You were hiding who knows where—most likely in Doìre given your good fortune in finding that beautiful gel there—and something woke you out of your stupor and convinced you to move about in the world again. Go on from there."

Ruith nodded, then gave him as much of the tale as was polite. He had no reason not to trust Uachdaran, though he couldn't have said that about other members of the Council of Kings. He didn't imagine he would have many more hints from him than he'd had from Soilléir, but each one might add up to something useful in the end.

He was completely frank about what he'd loosed in Ceangail, the fact that he'd discovered there that Franciscus of Doìre was a mage and that Urchaid, of places unknown and no doubt unpleasant, was a darkness that Sarah had seen clearly.

"And that was before Soilléir worked whatever magic he had upon her and opened her eyes," Ruith said with a shrug. "I'm actually surprised at the things she was able to see before then."

Uachdaran didn't look at all surprised. "Shettlestoune is a place souls go when they don't want to see. Or be seen."

"I will admit it was a good place to hide," Ruith said.

"I imagine you aren't the first one to think that," Uachdaran said, a little dryly. "So, you came to your senses in Beinn òrain, then decided you would pay me a little courtesy visit, is that it?"

Ruith smiled briefly. "Actually, Your Majesty, I was hoping to find my brother Keir." He paused. "He is the only one left who remembers what spells were in my father's book."

Uachdaran stuck his chin out. "He was here, true, well over a se'nnight ago, with your sister and Mochriadhemiach." He paused. "He went to see to their business with them."

Ruith felt a chill descend, though there was no reason for it. The fire was hot and he had warm ale still in his hands. He looked at

Sarah, expecting to find her asleep, but she was not. She was watching him gravely, as if she too felt his unease. He lifted his eyebrows briefly, took a deep breath, then turned back to the king.

"And have you had word of him since, King Uachdaran?" he asked.

The king set aside his cup and returned Ruith's look steadily. "He is no more, son. From what I've been told, as he was holding the cap of the well open for your sister to find the final word of closing, he was struck from behind by an enemy." He paused. "Prince Keir then perished inside the well, drawing its evil inside with him where it is now contained."

Ruith bowed his head, because it was either that or make a noise of grief he couldn't bear to. He hadn't realized Keir was alive until recently, of course, so losing him should have been no great thing.

Yet somehow it was.

He lifted his head and took a deep breath. "I see."

"He died so your sister—and the rest of us, I daresay—could live." Uachdaran paused. "Your mother would have been proud of him, I daresay."

Ruith nodded shortly. "She would have been."

Uachdaran rose. "I'll go fetch a bit of sweet wine," he said quietly. "I'll return shortly, children."

Ruith was grateful for an old man's discretion. He rose, then turned and put his hand on the warm stone of the mantel, grateful for the privacy to fall apart. He wasn't sure he had wept, but he'd considered it. He looked up, after a time, to find Sarah standing next to him, watching him gravely.

"I'm so sorry, Ruith," she said quietly.

"Nay," he said thickly, "don't be. Keir, of all of us, most wanted to see my father's evil stopped. He was willing to give his life in return." He managed a smile. "Indeed, I thought he had a score of years ago. This shouldn't affect me."

"But it does, because your heart is not made of stone," she said. She stepped forward and put her arms around him. "I'm sorry for it, Ruith. No matter what your brother would have wanted."

Ruith wrapped his arms around her and held her happily for several minutes in silence, then laughed a little. "I have been trying to get you into my arms for days, yet my late brother manages it for me with ease."

"Ruith," she said, sounding slightly shocked.

"He would agree, trust me," Ruith said wryly. "He was nothing if not a realist."

She lifted her head from his shoulder and looked at him. "What will we do now without him?"

"Make do," he said with an attempt at lightness. "I had counted on his memory, but perhaps that was badly done. I think I can manage the feat myself." He paused. "Thoir might be of some use there, actually."

"Your cousin?" she asked in surprise. "Why?"

"He was interested in my father," Ruith said with a shrug. "He and Keir had many conversations about my father's intentions, if not his spells. It's entirely possible that he might remember things I've forgotten. At this point, love, it might be our last hope."

She patted his back. "I can see the spells, Ruith. We'll find them all."

He looked down at her. "Taking care of me now, are you?"

"Even the mightiest mage needs a nap now and again."

"A quote from Soilléir?"

"My mother, if you can believe it. Usually said as she was drifting off to sleep in front of her fire after a morning full of mischief making."

He laughed a little. "You had an interesting childhood, I daresay."

"You don't know the half of it," she said wryly. She looked over her shoulder, then pulled away. "Here is the king with pallets. You sleep; I'll keep watch."

Ruith had no intention of that, but he wasn't going to argue with her. He helped Uachdaran's servants set up beds in front of the fire, then watched in surprise as the king pulled up a comfortable chair and sat.

"No sleep?" he asked.

Uachdaran shook his head. "I'm an old man, son, and don't sleep much any longer."

"Not even when contemplating a morning in the lists?"

Uachdaran snorted. "Take your rest, little twig. I'll see to you well enough, I imagine."

Ruith imagined he wouldn't see to himself without at least a bit of rest, so he happily pitched his tent, as it were, with Sarah in front of the fire.

He didn't want to think about the loss of Keir or Mhorghain's success in closing the well. Both were simply too overwhelming for a proper contemplation at the moment. He couldn't bring himself to even look at the possibility that he was the last hope for finding his father's book in its entirety.

But he would have to look at it, and soon. He would, if he survived what he was certain would be an absolutely brutal stint with Uachdaran in some underground cavern where no one would hear him scream.

He felt Sarah take his hand and lace her fingers with his.

Sleep did not come easily.

Twenty

❧

Sarah stood at the door of the king's private solar and reminded herself that she'd been instructed to treat it as her own. Considering the fact that she was keeping company with a notorious spellpoacher, that was likely saying something.

She walked inside, and found that she was still breathing and hadn't been overcome by a nefarious spell designed to keep her immobile long enough for the king to come collect her and deposit her wherever he took thieves. Down to his lists, no doubt, to relentlessly show them where they had room for improvement in their magic.

She had to sit down, even though she'd been sitting for the better part of three days. She'd been offered a variety of locales where she could take her ease whilst Ruith was about the heavy labor of being shown where he could make improvements in his own magic. She had passed a bit of her time in the library, reading obscure books that the king had personally selected for her, or pacing through the passageways, listening to the tales the stone had to tell her. She'd also sat on the edge of what served King Uachdaran as some sort of training field, though she wasn't sure anyone would have marked it as such without aid.

If the great hall had been cavernous and the king's throne room enormous, the lists eclipsed them by sheer size alone. Well, that and the fact that once a body entered through the stone doorway, the stone sealed behind him and left no indication of having been there.

She'd felt a little claustrophobic, truth be told.

But she'd decided that if Ruith could bear the work, she could bear the watching. She'd occupied a tidy little stone bench near that doorway that came and went capriciously, and never lacked for food or drink. She had watched Ruith train during the morning on that first day, if training it could be called, building his strength without complaint.

Actually, it hadn't been done without complaint; it had been done with an attitude of thankfulness that she'd been sure hadn't been lost on Uachdaran, though he'd not gone easier on Ruith because of it. He had tested Ruith in a thousand different ways, relentlessly, ruthlessly, far, far past the point where she would have begged for mercy. She had asked Ruith, when he'd been released to find water after countering ever-increasingly complex and weighty spells, why he was doing it. She had fully expected him to say it was so he could fight the mages out in the world who wanted his father's spells.

She'd been rendered speechless by his answer.

"For you."

He'd made her a low bow, then turned away to walk back out into the middle of the uneven stone floor.

She might have thought he was simply flattering her, or angling for another dance, but each time she'd had that thought creep into her head, she'd caught a look he'd sent her way, as if he'd known the precise moment she'd begun to disbelieve him.

For you.

It was almost enough to make her believe he was serious in his professions of, well, affection.

There had come a point, somewhere during the afternoon of that first day, when she had no longer been able to soldier on so well. King Uachdaran had dredged up from some unpleasant well in his mountain home an entirely new collection of very vile spells. They had made her ill to watch them. Even Ruith had paled a time or two. He had called for a halt, then walked over to her. He'd pulled her to her feet, opened the door, then pushed her through it wordlessly.

He'd shut it in her face.

One of Uachdaran's granddaughters, Dreachail, had seemingly been waiting for just such an occurrence. She had introduced herself, then offered the comfort of her private chamber for the afternoon. Sarah had accepted the offer and the distraction gladly. Ruith had appeared for supper, looking very much worse for the wear, but apparently having had the energy to arrange for a pair of gowns to be fashioned for her. She'd worn the flaming red one in spite of what she thought it might do for—or to—her hair, because she'd learned he had chosen the color himself. She hadn't protested the crown, nor had she argued with him when he'd announced, after two dances with Dreachail, that he was down to seven.

Never mind that he'd already danced with Dreachail the night before when she had been number nine.

She pushed herself to her feet and began to pace, because if she sat too long, she began to think about what Ruith might be doing below, and she didn't want to see any vision of the depths to which he'd no doubt been forced to descend. She wandered about the solar with her hands clasped behind her back until she found herself standing in front of the king's map table.

She wondered, as she studied it, if it was there for his own amusement or if he ever found it necessary to use it to plan battles. It was of the entire Nine Kingdoms, though the eastern part of the world seemed to have been given short shrift. She started in Doìre and retraced her steps to where she now found herself. It was surprising to realize how far she'd come and how much longer it took to ride a horse than to fly on a dragon.

Ruith would have agreed.

She noticed a collection of markers in two bowls, little carved stones for which she couldn't see any especial significance save they were small enough to use for all sorts of representations. She held a pair of them in her hand for a moment or two, their chill rather soothing all things considered, then put the first one in Doìre, where she had first seen one of Gair's spells.

The world shuddered.

She didn't enjoy the feeling, but she had to admit she reacted to the otherworldly sensation better than she had in times past. She took her courage in hand, then considered the next place they'd seen a spell—or, rather, the imprint of one, in Lord Connail's solar. It was with hardly any flinching at all that she marked the spot where they'd found a spell in that farmer's barn. Marking the spot on the plains of Ailean was easily done as well.

But it was then that things began to take a turn she hadn't expected.

She placed markers on other places where she'd seen spells in her dreams; that didn't trouble her. What bothered her was realizing that she was seeing fires on the map in front of her without the buffer of a dream.

She covered those fires with the little stones, because she couldn't bear to look at them and the stones seemed to extinguish the flames. That, and she was obsessed with apparently marking every damned place in the Nine Kingdoms where Gair's spells resided.

Once she was finished, she set the rest of the carved stones down on the table and walked away.

And almost into someone poking his nose through the crack she'd left in the doorway where she hadn't managed to shut the door.

It was Eachdraidh, that bard masquerading as a historian. He'd been watching her for three days now, both when she hadn't been looking for him and when she had been. He seemed to be everywhere she was, peeping at her. She'd had enough.

She started toward him.

He squeaked and fled.

Thrilled beyond measure for something useful to do, she ran after him. He was speedy, she would give him that, but she had been either walking, running, or riding for the past two months and she was hardened to the labor. She caught him just as he was attempting to slip inside his door.

"Why do you keep following me?"

He tried to shut the door on her, but along with her newfound stamina, she had apparently gained a bit of strength as well. She shoved the door open, sending him stumbling back into his chamber. He scuttled behind a table piled with scrolls and pots of ink and piles of quills.

"Ah, nothing," he said nervously.

She looked at him narrowly. "I don't believe you."

"'Twas a mistake," he said. "My eyesight isn't what it was a millennia ago, but perhaps that is to be expected."

He continued to spew out a lengthy bit of nonsensical excuses for his bad behavior, but she had long since stopped listening to him. She found a marginally sturdy chair, dusted it off, then sat down and looked at him expectantly.

His hands fluttered like nervous butterflies up and down the front of his tunic, finally coming to rest briefly on his cheeks before he seemed to gain some measure of control over himself. He took a deep breath, then put his hands down. They continued to twitch nervously, but perhaps that couldn't be helped.

"How may I serve you?" he asked, only half sounding as if he were choking to death.

"You can tell me why you've been following me," she said sternly. "It's been three days now."

"You noticed."

"I've become accustomed to looking for things in the shadows."

He looked as if the very thought might have induced a bout of terror he wouldn't soon have recovered from. He sank down on a tall stool behind his table, wrapping his arms around himself. "I see."

"And I've seen as well—you, following me. I want to know why."

"I mistook you for someone else," he said promptly. "My apologies."

She had no reason not to take him at his word, but she had to admit it was a little unsettling to find a king's bard following her. Then again, the entire journey had been unsettling so perhaps this was just another in a long series of things that would unbalance her.

Or perhaps he was lying through his teeth.

She decided that since she was so comfortable, perhaps she would take a few more minutes and determine which it was.

"You were prepared to favor the king with an heroic tale or two," she said smoothly. "I am a very sympathetic listener, should you care to relate those tales just to me."

He looked at her suspiciously for a moment or two. "In truth?"

"In truth," she promised. "I am always interested in a good tale."

Especially if those tales might lead to the odd bit of truth slipping out unnoticed. Perhaps during the course of the afternoon she might even manage to pry from him a detail or two about Soilléir's kin. Finding someone to undo what he'd done to her eyes might be very useful.

Eachdraidh eyed her suspiciously for another moment or two, then sidled around his table and took up a chair a goodly distance away from her.

"I'm not sure you'll find them interesting," he said slowly.

"I don't know many dwarvish tales," she said, which was mostly true. Franciscus had only told her a handful, and she hadn't paid the attention to them she likely should have, having been more interested in torturing herself with tales of elves. "I would hear yours quite happily."

That seemed to put him at ease. He settled a bit more comfortably into his chair, looking quite a bit like a hen settling onto her roost, then he began spinning a tale that featured several dwarves in the thick of heroic deeds. She nodded in what she hoped were the right places, made the appropriate noises of shock, horror, and appreciation, then waited a bit longer whilst he was about the happy labor of providing refreshments for them. She accepted a small square of cake, a cup of tea, and the invitation to direct him to other things she might be interested in.

"What do you know of Cothromaiche?" she asked.

He spewed out a mouthful of cake all over his finely embroidered robe. He looked at her, a few crumbs clinging to his chin.

"What?" he asked, his eyes darting about nervously as if he looked for an escape.

"Cothromaiche," she said. "The country, if that's what one calls it. I met someone from there recently, but I couldn't seem to pry anything interesting out of him besides a book of poetry and a lexicon."

Eachdraidh's ears perked up. "A lexicon?"

"It isn't mine, or I would give you a peep at it. I might anyway, if the inducement is sufficient."

He looked horribly torn, over what she couldn't imagine. She waited, then waited awhile longer as he struggled to apparently overcome his aversion to telling her what she wanted to know. He leaned closer.

"What do you want to know?" he whispered.

"Everything."

He looked as if she'd just handed him a bag of gold—or manuscripts, rather. Before she could catch her breath, or finish her tea, he had launched into a recounting of things she couldn't keep pace with. Perhaps he was a good historian for Uachdaran, but as a raconteur of tales he hadn't planned in advance, he was like a mouse darting across a kitchen full of hungry cats. She had scarce attempted to determine who one set of players might have been before he was off recounting the exploits of another. There seemed to be a great many wars and more bloodshed than a single, small country merited, but a good deal of that seemed to stem from their neighbors to the southwest.

Sarah would have asked for a map, but she didn't have time before Eachdraidh leapt to his feet, sending his tea and a cake that hadn't made it into his mouth crashing to the floor.

She looked behind her to find Ruith leaning against the door-frame, watching her solemnly. She lost her breath—an alarmingly regular occurrence where he was concerned—then managed to find enough of it left to speak.

"What are you doing here?" she managed.

"Shadowing you."

"I thought you were training."

"I finished."

He looked impossibly tired, but he was still standing, so perhaps it had all been a success.

She gestured helplessly toward the historian. "He kept following me. I followed him instead to find out why."

"Did he answer you?"

"Not yet."

Ruith pushed away from the doorframe and walked—slightly unsteadily, truth be told—across the chamber to lean against the edge of Eachdraidh's table. He looked down at the historian.

"Well?" he asked politely. "Why were you following her?"

Eachdraidh's hands recaptured their former inability to remain still. "I, er, I . . . ah . . . I thought your lady reminded me of someone, but I was mistaken."

"It is easy to be dazzled by her beauty."

Eachdraidh sank back down onto his chair and nodded enthusiastically.

Ruith glanced at what was behind him on the table. "Working on something in particular?"

Eachdraidh leapt to his feet and hurried around his table to show Ruith just what that had been. Sarah couldn't bear to listen to any of it. She realized at that moment that she had simply listened to too many tales—told by mortals or stone, as the case was—to be interested in yet another. She busied herself cleaning up the tea things and tidying up Eachdraidh's floor. She put everything to rights, then looked for something else useful to do. She would have stacked books, but that seemed a bit too invasive, so she settled for sitting in front of the fire. She put her fingers over her eyes to stave off the headache she could feel coming on.

Too many tales of bloodshed and woe, no doubt.

Surely only a moment or two passed before she felt Ruith's hand on her head.

"Let's be off," he said quietly.

She looked up at him in surprise. "Are you finished already?"

"I think you are," he said wryly, "and actually I only came to fetch you." He held down his hand, then pulled her to her feet. "Thank you, Master Eachdraidh, for the pleasant conversation."

Eachdraidh was profuse in his returning niceties, but fortunately Ruith had apparently dealt with that sort of thing before because he politely extricated them from the stuffy chamber without delay. Sarah didn't feel her headache ease any, but her brow definitely unfurrowed.

"He is well suited to his life's work," Ruith remarked as they walked down the passageway.

"He was full of all manner of tales, none of which answered the question of why he kept spying on me."

"Your beauty overwhelmed his good sense."

"And too much time in the lists has overwhelmed yours."

Ruith laughed. "I am in full possession of my good sense and all my wits. What did he bludgeon you with first? Anything useful?"

She walked with him down the passageway, rather more happy than she should have been to find his arm suddenly around her shoulders. She leaned on him a little, which she likely shouldn't have given that he was the one who had been wrung out for the past three days, but she couldn't help herself.

"I encouraged him to talk by asking him for the tales he'd intended to give the king that first night. After that, I attempted to learn details about Cothromaiche since I seem to have been given the task of translating the runes on my own knives."

"The runes that match my sword."

There was no point in denying it. "Aye. I thought that perhaps he could enlighten me."

"And did he?"

"Unfortunately not. He blurted out some ridiculous tale about a renegade dreamweaver—whatever that is—and an equally dreamy lad from Cothromaiche who wed her."

"It sounds like a love match."

"I think it was, but it didn't end well for them. Apparently, one of their neighbors was convinced they had a mighty power between them and wanted it. When they wouldn't do as he bid, he slew them."

"Tragic," Ruith murmured.

"And not at all what I was looking for," Sarah said grimly. "It isn't as if I can travel to meet this pair and have answers from them that Soilléir won't give me, is it? I am left to myself to learn what I can from the books Soilléir gave me."

"I could attempt to intimidate Eachdraidh for you tomorrow, if you like."

"I'm not sure you'll have any more success than I did, but you're welcome to try." She looked up at him. "Are you finished with your training in truth?"

"I could spend a year here and not be finished," he said with a sigh, "but Uachdaran was afraid any more of his tender ministrations might kill me."

She smiled. "You're not serious."

Ruith smiled in return. "Those were his words, and he was certainly serious. For myself, I'll say that . . . well, I'll say that it was time well, if not pleasantly, spent."

"I'm not sure I want to know what you've been fighting the last three days."

"You don't," he agreed, "which is why I wouldn't let you back through the door after I pushed you out of it." He shivered, no doubt in spite of himself. "I do *not* want to know where he's learned what he's learned and if I meet one of those spells again, it will be too soon. But," he said brightly, "'tis done and I'm the stronger for it. The king has called us to his solar for a parley and then I believe we'll have the opportunity for more dancing tonight."

"If you can stay awake for it."

"I wasn't asleep last night. I was resting my eyes."

"I saved you from planting your face in your soup, Your Highness."

"A feat for which I am most grateful, my lady," he said politely. "Even if I'll bear the bruise from your elbow in my ribs for some time to come."

She laughed a little, then felt her smile fade abruptly. "I'm not sure the king will be pleased with me."

"And what terrible thing have you done?" he asked gently.

"I fear I made free with the king's map."

"I know. That's why I came to fetch you. Well, other than I missed you."

She looked up at him quickly. "Is he angry?"

"Curious," Ruith said. He slid her a look. "You've marked the locations of the pages, haven't you?"

She could only nod.

"Have you been dreaming them?"

"I don't have to any longer."

He closed his eyes briefly, then stopped and pulled her into his arms. "Ah, Sarah," he said, his voice full of pity. "I'm so sorry, my love."

"'Tis a gift, or so says Soilléir."

"He would say as much, being who he is." He held her close for several minutes in silence. "I'm sorry I haven't attended you as I should have recently."

"I don't need a keeper, Ruith."

"A betrothed, then?"

"Not when he might be a man who has eight princesses left to seek out," she said, pulling away from him and feeling profoundly flustered.

"Seven."

"Oh, very well, seven, then," she said, grumbling because it was easier than facing the fact that he seemed to be quite serious about his offer. She took him by the hand and pulled. "Let's go."

He didn't argue. He also didn't let go of her hand as he opened

the door to the king's solar and led her inside. Sarah found Uachdaran standing at his map table, studying it. He looked up and smiled
when he saw her.

"Sarah, gel," he said. "I trust you've passed your time pleasantly
today."

"Forgive me," Sarah said, gesturing toward the table. "I was restless. I should have asked leave to trim your map before I took the
liberty."

"Of course you shouldn't have, as I gave you leave earlier to be
free with my things. The map was simply sitting here, waiting for
some fierce strategy to be planned upon its surface." He shot her
a quick smile. "In case you're wondering why I have this here, I
believe 'tis always best to be prepared when you have a world's ran-
som in gems hiding in your cellar. Wouldn't you agree?"

"Absolutely," she said faintly.

"I'm curious, though, what sort of battle you have planned here,"
he said slowly. "You seem to have chosen two kinds of stones, which
I'm assuming represent two different things? I hesitate to ask the
details of you, but I think it might be of some use to your lad there."

Sarah looked at Ruith, who only watched solemnly. She knew he
wouldn't push her, but then again, he didn't have to. She was under
no illusions about the critical nature of their task that lay before
them. She took a deep breath and looked at the king.

"They're Gair's spells," she said. "The black stones represent the
spells we've either found or I've dreamed." She had to pause for a bit
before she thought she could finish. "The others are ones I've seen
whilst . . . whilst not dreaming."

Uachdaran motioned to her left, and Ruith fetched the stool that
waited there and brought it to her. She sat, because she suddenly felt
very close to being ill. It was ridiculous, actually, because she had
been all alone in the solar with the map and the stones and hadn't
suffered any ill effects before.

She realized Uachdaran and Ruith were speaking in low voices
but didn't understand at first what they were saying. There was an

annoying buzzing in her ears, which she realized was her headache ascending into new and hitherto unexplored heights of pain.

"Are you seeing what I'm seeing?" Uachdaran was saying.

Sarah squinted to see Ruith's face. He was absolutely grey.

"Aye," he said. "A pattern."

Uachdaran stroked his chin thoughtfully. "The first thing to decide," he said slowly, "is whether the pattern comes from the spells themselves, or if someone has placed them purposely in that particular order. Or is someone merely using them to lead an inquisitive mage on a merry chase?" He looked up at Ruith. "What do you think, lad?"

"I don't know," Ruith said hoarsely.

Uachdaran lifted his eyebrows briefly. "I suppose if a mage wanted to gather a certain collection of spells, he could hope enough foolish wizardlings would happen upon and become enspelled by them, then march off with them to a predetermined place without knowing why they'd done so."

Ruith didn't answer. Sarah couldn't blame him for that. Some of his color had returned, but not enough to leave him looking anything but shocked. She understood. She'd wondered, as they'd hunted the spells, why it was her brother had looked so, well, *mesmerized* in his bedchamber that day he'd destroyed their mother's house.

"I think that part's true," she said, realizing then that she hadn't said anything to Ruith about it. She shrugged helplessly when he looked at her in surprise. "After I touched that spell on his table, Daniel appeared in his doorway. I hadn't been expecting him or I wouldn't have dared enter his chamber. He was very angry with me, but once he saw the spell, he completely forgot about me. I didn't think much of it at the time, but now I would definitely say he had been . . ." She paused. "Well, *enspelled* is as good a word as any. "

"And afterward?" Uachdaran asked.

"He wanted more spells, as Ruith will attest, but I wouldn't say that was anything more than his own greed driving him." She paused. "I could be wrong."

Ruith shook his head. "I think either answer is perfectly reasonable, which doesn't aid us in determining the truth of it." He looked at the king. "Why would anyone want to lure a mage—*any* mage—to a predetermined spot? And who would attempt it?"

"The only reason I can think of," Uachdaran said slowly, "is that someone who wants these spells very badly has no other way to gather them to himself." He paused and looked at Ruith. "Perhaps he can't see them himself. In that case, it would certainly be useful to know someone who *could* see them."

Sarah felt the chamber begin to spin. It spun even more violently when Ruith picked her up, carried her over to a chair in front of the fire and sat down with her in his arms. She heard, through the thunder rushing behind her ears, the dwarf king settle into a chair across from them.

"Someone wants my father's spells very badly, then," Ruith said.

"I agree," Uachdaran said. "Unfortunately, even knowing that much doesn't solve the riddle of why someone would tear a piece from a very valuable spell and leave it behind. It wasn't *un*intentionally done, I can almost guarantee it." He paused for a rather lengthy bit of time. "Unless the mage knew, again, that there was someone in the world who could see them and *would* find them."

"Then perhaps the spells themselves aren't the pattern," Ruith said, unwillingly. "Perhaps the pieces of the spell of Diminishing are."

"Possibly," Uachdaran agreed. "I suppose you'll only know that when you find other fragments of it, I daresay. Of course, I could be wrong. It could simply be someone with a rather offensive sense of humor who has the time and means to see if anyone will bite at such bait."

Ruith grunted. "It sounds like something my father would do."

"It does, my boy."

Sarah felt silence descend, a silence that was only broken by the rushing in her ears and the beat of Ruith's heart in his throat where she rested her forehead.

"He's dead," Ruith said quietly.

"I don't doubt it, son."

Ruith took an unsteady breath. "I'll think on other possibilities."

"I believe I would if I were you. I am not much out in the world, and I don't know as many mages as I should, but I would think that the lad we're looking for will be a mage who wants your sire's spells the most. Wouldn't you agree?"

Ruith shifted. "Your Majesty, I didn't think anything could possibly be worse than those unrelentingly, torturous hours in your lists, but I was wrong. Even giving thought to this makes that work pale in comparison."

"But you'll find the answer."

"I will."

Uachdaran rose. "I'll leave you to rest for a bit, children. Don't be late for supper. I think we'll spend another day together, thinking on your route, but no longer."

"Thank you, Your Majesty, for your hospitality," Ruith said sincerely.

"Oh, don't think I'm throwing you out the front gates," Uachdaran said with a brief laugh. "I'd keep you both a bit longer and not regret it—and will in the future if you're ever wandering close to my hall. I think, however, that time grows short to solve this tangle, and you may not be the only ones who stumble upon these spells. Best to find them sooner rather than later, eh?"

Sarah listened to Ruith agree that that would be best, heard the door soon shut, then remained with her head on Ruith's shoulder for far longer than she likely should have.

"Who wants those spells?" she murmured finally, when she could chew on the question no longer.

"Only those who know about them," he said with a deep sigh. "Franciscus—"

She lifted her head so quickly, she had to put her hand to it to keep from being ill. "Ruith, you can't be serious."

"I'm not accusing him," he said wearily. "Just making a list."

She let out her breath slowly. "Very well. List away."

"Franciscus," he said slowly and seemingly unwillingly. "Your brother. All my bastard brothers, as well as Rùnach, Soilléir, Miach of Neroche, and Uachdaran."

She closed her eyes, because she couldn't look at the names hanging in the air in front of them.

"Droch," he continued grimly, "and his brother Urchaid, half a dozen kings on the Council I haven't even considered, and last of all, me."

"And what would you do if you had the spells, Ruith?" she asked quietly.

"Destroy them," he said without hesitation. "Wrap them in illusion and rot and impotence, then drop them into a bottomless well before capping the thing, then burying it under a score of things that would take millennia to even begin to unravel."

"A simple fire wouldn't do?"

He smiled, apparently in spite of himself. "Nay, love. A simple fire wouldn't do."

She put her head back down on his shoulder. It was appalling how accustomed to it she had become over the past three days and how just the thought of his going off with some other perfectly pressed and mannered princess vexed her.

"Seven left," he murmured, dragging his fingers through her hair. "And may they all descend at once."

She smiled. "I loved the red gown, if you were wondering."

"I wasn't sure about the color," he admitted, "but you were glorious in it."

"You have excellent taste."

"You're proof enough of it," he said, a smile in his voice. "What say you to a quarter-hour nap, then a final push to supper? I think if we last through it, we might both be weary enough to sleep."

She had to agree. She closed her eyes and tried to let the sound of the steady beat of Ruith's heart soothe her. In time, she could have sworn she heard the trees from the garden of Gearrannan begin to whisper their names across her mind.

Sarah . . . Sorcha . . . Athair . . .

She frowned, for the last two names sounded uncommonly familiar, but she couldn't bring to mind why. Perhaps on the morrow, when her head had ceased to pound.

She closed her eyes again and fell asleep to the feeling of a remarkably persistent man carefully combing his fingers through her hair.

Twenty-one

❧

Ruith looked at the map on the table in front of him and struggled to commit it to memory. It was difficult, which it shouldn't have been given that he had slept well the night before. He had spent a lifetime memorizing spells and lore and endless lists of names, in the beginning because it had been expected and later because he had found the discipline of it to be rather bracing.

Now, though, his discipline—and his wits—were failing him at a most inconvenient time. He couldn't imagine Sarah wouldn't remember everything she'd seen, but in a moment of duress, it was always wise to have more than one person in a company with the journey's route at their fingertips.

He looked up, then jumped a little. King Uachdaran was standing on the other side of the table, watching him with his dark, shrewd eyes.

"Forgive me, Your Majesty," Ruith said wearily. "I didn't hear you come in."

"I planned it that way," Uachdaran said, "on the off chance you were rifling through my private books."

"I will admit, King Uachdaran, that I've been too tired to even contemplate the like."

"Don't expect any pity from me," Uachdaran said with a snort. "You'd sleep better if you allowed that lass of yours some peace, but I can see why you want to keep her close." He considered, then reached inside the purse hanging from his belt and pulled out a scrap of parchment. He held it out. "I thought you might be interested in this."

Ruith took it, though he knew before he touched it what it was: another piece of his father's spell of Diminishing. He looked at the king. "Where was it found?"

"Outside my gates." He handed over another. "This was brought back by one of my scouts last night. Someone, I daresay, knows you're here."

Ruith accepted the second offering with even less enthusiasm. "And the direction this was found in?"

"North," Uachdaran said, "and a bit east. Toward An-uallach."

Ruith chewed on his words until they became dust in his mouth. "Then I'm being led."

"I would say aye," Uachdaran agreed. "You and that gel of yours."

Ruith considered. "Why her?" he asked, finally.

"Because she sees, for one thing," Uachdaran said without hesitation. "As for the rest—" He shrugged. "You of all people should know that things are not always as they seem."

Ruith leaned gingerly against the sideboard behind him and considered things he hadn't had time to before. "Your historian seemed surprised to see Sarah."

"He's skittish."

Ruith couldn't argue, because he'd said much the same thing to Sarah. "But he's been following her, as if he couldn't tear his eyes away from her. She is exceptionally lovely, I'll admit, but he must know she is . . . ah . . ."

"Spoken for?" Uachdaran asked politely. "You could only hope, my boy."

"I do," Ruith said fervently, "but that still doesn't clear up the mystery of his interest. And whilst we're about the happy work of discussing things that puzzle me, why do the runes on the sword I brought you match the runes on Sarah's knives that I found for her in Gilean? Why was there no message attached to the blade, yet you understood what Soilléir had been trying to tell you?"

Uachdaran only looked at him steadily. And silently, damn him.

"Master Eachdraidh seems to be unusually interested in the histories of Cothromaiche," Ruith continued. "He told Sarah several of their tales, I believe."

"He's always interested in a good tale. Or an intriguing mystery."

Ruith frowned. When that didn't help him any, he frowned a bit more. "I didn't realize they had any mysteries in Cothromaiche."

"Only one," Uachdaran said with a smirk, "which would be how that young rogue Soilléir managed to slip out with all those spells of essence changing before his great-grandfather was the wiser."

Ruith tried another tack. "I understand that the runes on our blades are theirs, but they aren't a simple rendering of their tongue."

"Are the runes of Tòrr Dòrainn any different?" Uachdaran asked pointedly. "Even ones on a simple blade would take a body years to unravel—being, as they are, unnecessarily complicated—then a lifetime to understand. Yet somehow your grandfather and his get seem to use them easily enough."

"But they've been taught what they mean."

"Then I suppose you'd best look for someone to teach you how to read what's on your blade, hadn't you? But don't look at me. I've no patience for that sort of rot. I prefer my blades to bear words of power and might in a tongue that's easily recognized as it finds home in a lad's gut."

"There is a certain beauty to that sort of simplicity," Ruith agreed. He considered a bit longer, then made Uachdaran a small bow. "I believe, Your Majesty, that whilst Sarah is happily occupied

with your granddaughter this morning, I will make a little visit to
your bard."

"Don't render him unfit for supper."

"I won't." Ruith made him another bow, then took up his quest
for answers he hadn't thought he would need but now found himself
quite anxious to have.

He knocked on Master Eachdraidh's door, then opened it before
the man could escape out some hidden passageway. The historian
was sitting in front of the fire, poring over a book he subsequently
dumped into the fire in his surprise. Ruith rescued it, restored it,
then handed it back to him.

"Thank you," Eachdraidh said faintly. "I'm grateful—"

"How grateful?"

Eachdraidh eyed the door, but Ruith sat down in the chair across
from him and affected a pose he hoped bespoke plans for a long
visit. Eachdraidh hesitated, then sighed.

"Grateful enough for several tales," he said. "If His Highness
wishes."

"I wouldn't trouble you for that much," Ruith said smoothly. "I
would simply like to have the one you told Sarah yesterday, the one
about the lovers from Cothromaiche whose romance ended badly."

Eachdraidh looked as if he would rather have been facing Uachdaran in his lists, but he'd apparently resigned himself to being
trapped.

"They were slain," Eachdraidh said hollowly, "so it wasn't exactly
that the romance ended badly, it was just that it ended prematurely."
He paused and seemed to be looking for the right thing to say. "They
were terribly happy, or so I understand, for as long as they were
wed."

"What befell them?"

"They were slain."

"By whom?"

"By a neighbor."

Ruith considered the countries that bordered Cothromaiche.

There was Gairn to the west, then Bruadair to the northwest where the forests were full of dreams and spells and things that sensible souls avoided. There was nothing to the east but endless plain claimed by no one at all. But to the south . . .

An-uallach.

Ruith rubbed his arms suddenly, wishing Uachdaran could do a better job at keeping the bloody place warm. He looked at Eachdraidh.

"Which neighbor was responsible?"

Eachdraidh shifted uncomfortably. "Ah," he said, "I'm not sure . . ."

"You led Sarah to believe it was a king, but there are no kings in Bruadair or Gairn—at least none who would sit on the Council. That leaves Morag of An-uallach."

Eachdraidh fidgeted, then let out a deep, shuddering breath. "So it does, Your Highness."

Ruith stared into the fire for a bit. Interesting that Eachdraidh should feel compelled to tell Sarah a tale of Cothromaiche. Uncanny that to An-uallach he was apparently being led, for reasons he couldn't see.

He looked at Eachdraidh. "What were the names of this hapless pair?"

"Athair and Sorcha," Eachdraidh said nervously. "They had a wee gel. Don't remember her name, though."

A lie, Ruith thought. "And what did this unfortunate pair look like?" He paused. "Did you ever meet them, Master Eachdraidh?"

Eachdraidh looked profoundly miserable. "Athair was a great friend of King Uachdaran's granddaughter Dreachail's husband, so aye, I knew him. And his bride, Sorcha. Athair was tall and fair-haired. Handsome enough for a lad, I suppose."

"And his lady?"

Eachdraidh swallowed convulsively. "Flame-haired. Green-eyed." He swallowed again. "About your lady's height."

Ruith caught his jaw before it fell to his chest. He wasn't one to engage in idle speculation—his long bouts of it during his youth accompanied by Miach of Neroche as they speculated on the caches of spells they might plunder if given the opportunity aside—but in this instance, he couldn't stop himself.

Soilléir of Cothromaiche had given Sarah not only a book of his people's poetry but the means to learn his language, ostensibly to read runes that Uachdaran himself had said could only be read after considerable teaching from one who knew more than just the language. He himself had been sent to Léige to deliver a sword inscribed with the same runes only to have the king shrug it aside whilst his bard followed Sarah about as if he were looking at a ghost.

Further, Uachdaran had made Sarah a crown. Ruith had supposed it had been for his sake, but he wondered now if he had been wrong. Soilléir had treated them with a level of care that had been far above what Ruith could have reasonably expected even given Soilléir's undeniable affection for his mother, going so far as to give them horses that were truly beyond price.

Why?

He was beginning to consider things that couldn't possibly be true, but then again, the world was full of impossible things. Such as an elven prince who had denied his birthright falling in love with a weaver of cloth who could see things in broad daylight that eluded even the most powerful.

He leaned forward and looked at Eachdraidh seriously. "How old was the wee gel when her parents were slain?"

"Not yet two summers, or so I've been told."

"Are you telling me you never saw the child?"

"N-n-nay," Eachdraidh managed. "I mean, aye, Your H-highness. I-I never saw h-her."

Ruith sat back. Another lie, but he suspected if he pressed the man, Eachdraidh would burst into tears. "I don't suppose you have any books on Cothromaichian genealogy, do you?"

Eachdraidh shook his head nervously.

"I see," Ruith said, and he did. And he also knew where he might find just such a thing.

A pity it was in Sarah's pack.

And then something utterly unthinkable occurred to him. He looked at Eachdraidh sharply. "What was the name of Athair's father?"

Eachdraidh opened his mouth to speak, then shut it with a snap. He stood up suddenly and looked behind Ruith. "My lady," he said, inclining his head.

Ruith looked over his shoulder, expecting to see one of Uachdaran's granddaughters.

He was mistaken.

It was Sarah.

He rose immediately and walked over to her. He reached for her hand and smiled at her. "I didn't expect to see you here."

"I was afraid you had snuck off to Uachdaran's solar," she said quietly. "I was coming to save you from yourself."

"I was just intimidating Eachdraidh for you," he said lightly. "Work's done, but with enough of him left to entertain his liege lord later. Shall we go have another meal, then see to our packing?"

"If you like," she said slowly.

He started off with her, then heard Eachdraidh call his name. He turned in the doorway. "Aye?"

"You forgot something, Your Highness," Eachdraidh said, looking as pale as Sarah did.

Ruith squeezed Sarah's hand, then released her to walk over to the bard. Eachdraidh handed him a sheet of paper.

"Franciscus," he whispered under his breath, then straightened. "A good journey to you, Prince Ruithneadh," he said loudly. "And to your lady, as well."

Ruith looked at what he held in his hand. It was nothing but a blank sheet, but Ruith supposed it had been useful enough as an excuse for a quiet word. He rolled up the sheaf and stuck it down his boot, because it was all he could think to do. He thanked Eachdraidh again, then turned and walked over to the door to collect Sarah.

Sarah, that gel from a no-name town in the midst of ruffians and thieves who had been guarded by an alemaster named Franciscus— a man far better educated than the average alemaster—who had suddenly discovered the ability to see, and who looked so much like a woman from a land of legend that a dwarvish bard had fainted the first time he'd seen her.

"Ruith?"

He stopped in the middle of the passageway, turned her to him, then gathered her into his arms. It wasn't possible that all those things could pertain to her. It wasn't possible that she was the granddaughter of Franciscus who was apparently the grandson of Seannair of Cothromaiche, the original keeper of the spells of Caochladh.

Was it?

"You're shaking."

"I'm cold," he lied without hesitation. "Let's go find a fire and I'll sit on your lap where you can comfort me."

She laughed a little and pulled back to look up at him. Her smile faltered. "You look terrible."

"Thank you. At least you're so beautiful no one will notice me." He put his arm around her shoulders and pulled her along with him. "Perhaps Uachdaran has something to eat in his solar. It will give me one last chance to poach a spell or two, to make him feel as if I've made a proper visit."

She only nodded and walked down the passageway with him, her arm around his waist. She finally cleared her throat. "Something occurred to me this morning."

He wasn't sure he wanted to know what. "Did it?"

"I've heard those names before, the ones Eachdraidh told me about yesterday." She looked up at him. "Athair and Sorcha."

He managed not to catch his breath only because he had self-control developed over years of austerity. "Have you? Where?"

"In your grandfather's garden," she said. "The trees were singing about them."

He imagined they were, damn them to a hot fire. "Interesting," he managed.

"Do you think so?"

"Aye, and look, here we are at the king's solar. Something to eat, love?"

She frowned at him. "Are you changing the subject?"

He sighed, then turned toward her. He put his hands on her shoulders and bent his head to rest his forehead against hers. "I am," he said quietly, "but not because I'm not interested. I would love nothing more than to find a grassy spot beneath the most beautiful fruit trees in Sgath and Eulasaid's garden, stretch out with you, and in a perfectly safe place have you tell me everything you've seen and heard." He lifted his head and looked down at her. "But here—"

"You don't have to say anything else," she said, taking a deep breath. "I understand completely."

He stopped her before she pulled away. "I promise you an afternoon there, Sarah, when we're finished with this. As many afternoons as you'll gift me."

"Are we going to spend them with one of your eight to-be-wooed princesses?"

"Seven, and they are to be merely admired, not wooed, so don't make yourself too comfortable with your bargain," he warned. He stopped himself just before he kissed her—which he wasn't entirely certain wouldn't have resulted with her fist in his gut—and settled for a chaste peck on the end of her nose—which only earned him a scowl she couldn't seem to put any energy behind. "Food?"

"Please."

He knocked on Uachdaran's solar, then entered when commanded to do so. He greeted Uachdaran pleasantly, saw Sarah seated, then made himself page and served both king and ordinary gel the luncheon that had been brought. He finally sat down next to Sarah and looked at the king.

"Thank you, Your Majesty," he said seriously. "For all your many kindnesses. I'm sorry we've trespassed so long—"

"Don't be daft, boy," Uachdaran said gruffly. "Haven't had such pleasant conversations since I saw your grandpappy a pair of fortnights ago." He squinted at Ruith. "But don't think I'm going to make a present of any of my spells."

"I wouldn't dream it."

"And don't think I won't be checking your pockets for the same before you leave."

Ruith laughed. "I would expect nothing less."

"And so you don't have to ask, I shot Mochriadhemiach of Neroche a stern look or two on his way out my gates."

"Very wise."

Uachdaran chewed on his words for a moment or two. "I don't like to poke my nose in where it doesn't belong," he began slowly, "my having ground you to powder in my lists aside." He looked at Ruith briefly. "I give asked-for advice even more rarely."

"And if I were to ask you for advice, King Uachdaran?"

Uachdaran seemed to wrestle with something—either his good sense or his conscience. "Then I'll say this—unwillingly." He looked at Sarah quickly. "We discussed your route this morning, gel, whilst you were with my granddaughter. You might have an opinion on it."

She shook her head. "If it leads to a spell, that's all the opinion I have."

Uachdaran conceded the point with a nod, then turned back to Ruith. "I'll say this much: I don't like those at An-uallach, and that doesn't come from Queen Morag's, er, her—"

"Commanding presence on the Council of Kings?" Ruith finished for him delicately.

Uachdaran laughed a bit. "Inherited your dam's gilded tongue, did you? 'Tis for damned sure you didn't get it from Sìle."

"My mother would be flattered."

"She was a lovely gel, and I took great pleasure in sending the odd spy off after your father for her sake, but that isn't what concerns us here. I would advise you to tread lightly. *I* wouldn't go at all, but I haven't your burden. Be careful with our young miss. I wouldn't leave her alone there."

Ruith considered. "Queen Morag has six daughters, doesn't she?"

Uachdaran shot him a look. "That, my boy, is only part of the problem. The only saving grace for you is that Morag cannot shapechange. 'Tis the only thing about her your grandfather approves of, I daresay." He opened his mouth, then shut it just as quickly. "I'll say no more. Just be careful." He put his hands on his knees, then rose. "I know you've packed your own gear, but I have a few things to add—to make your journey a bit easier, if you will. I'll go see to them."

Ruith watched him go, then waited until the door was shut before he looked at Sarah. "Gifts and friendships where we didn't expect them."

She shivered. "Why do I have the feeling this may be the last outpost of both?"

You might be surprised, he wanted to say, but he forbore. In truth, he had no idea what the future would bring, nor where he dared travel save where his sire's spells were to be found. For all he knew, Sarah was right, and they would never see the inside of another decent inn until their quest was finished—or they had perished in the attempt.

Which, he supposed, was entirely possible.

He rubbed his hands over his face and suppressed the urge to curse. He had received aid, but not what he had been hoping for. Keir was no more, Mhorghain wouldn't remember their father's spells even if he dared take the time to follow after her to ask, Rùnach knew even less, and the rest of his siblings were dead. It was just him, struggling to fight against things he couldn't see and wasn't sure he could master.

It was a pity his father wasn't alive. He could have walked up to him and asked him frankly if he was missing something. Perhaps the lad who was calling the spells had an accurate count of them. If he hadn't known better, he might have thought that that someone was a man who had a particular use for those spells.

Someone like his father, for instance.

Which was impossible, of course. He had watched that wave of evil fall down on his father and crush him beneath it. No one could have survived it. His mother hadn't. His brothers had all been washed away save Rùnach, who had been spared only because his hands had been trapped under the cap of the well—

"Ruith, you should rest."

He considered the floor at her feet and thought it might do quite well for a brief closing of his eyes. He kissed her hand, thanked her kindly for the suggestion, then stretched out in front of the fire.

She reached down and smoothed the hair back from his face. "We'll find what we need to," she said quietly.

He reached up and caught her hand, held it for a moment, then released it. "Aye, I daresay we will."

She sat back, but not before he'd seen the book she was holding in her hands. It was the child's primer that Rùnach had found for her.

He sincerely hoped that all that lay within was children's verse.

The sun was setting as he stood in the courtyard of Léige and bid farewell to the king. He and Sarah were wearing the cloaks she'd woven for them, but their saddlebags had been stuffed with warmer clothes and footwear. He watched Uachdaran hand Sarah a spindle as a parting gift.

"Thank you, Your Majesty," she said, surprised. "'Tis very finely wrought."

"And doubles as a dagger if you touch that wee lever there and release the blade," Uachdaran said, sounding absolutely delighted by the thought. "Very handy for a weaver in a tight spot, I'd say."

"I'm not sure where I'll ever find roving to use on it," she said with a smile.

"Oh, you'd be surprised what you can spin into warp and weft with it," he said seriously. "Not that I know anything about making cloth. We would have our behinds bared to the cold stone if it weren't for that young rogue from Neroche."

"Miach?" Ruith asked in surprise.

"Carrying on his mother's tradition of supplying me with bolts of useful things, aye." Uachdaran looked at him mildly. "I think she felt guilty for having poached one of my spells in her youth. I wonder if her son suffers from the same affliction?"

"I daresay," Ruith managed. He took a deep breath. "I'm not sure I could ever repay you in like manner, my liege."

"Ha," Uachdaran said with a snort. "My liege, my arse. The deference—which would grate on your grandsire endlessly, I'll warrant—is a good start. As for the rest, I'll say that there's something trickling under my mountain that I can't seem to stop. When you're finished with your task, come plug the leak for me. That'll be payment enough for that quite useful spell of hiding you've been using so freely all these years."

"That is a very light repayment," Ruith said, "for it is a *very* good spell, Your Majesty."

Uachdaran pursed his lips, then looked at Sarah. "If he ever convinces you to wed with him, child, and you fashion sons between you, make certain that they know that stealing is wrong."

"I will, Your Majesty."

Ruith watched as Uachdaran's granddaughters came to wish Sarah a safe journey and found himself pulled aside. Uachdaran looked up at him gravely.

"I don't know if you've noticed anything particular about your lady's knives," he began bluntly. "Or dare I hope you're as canny as you look?"

"Outside of bearing interesting runes, they slice through spells rather nicely," Ruith said with a frown. "Why do you ask?"

"Because you should know that the man who crafted those knives for his daughter-in-law first crafted that blade you carry for his son, as a coming-of-age gift."

"Did he, indeed?" Ruith asked in surprise.

Uachdaran glanced at Sarah, then turned back to Ruith. "Ofttimes daughters look like mothers," he said. "Your wee sister couldn't look any more like Sarait had she been Sarait. I almost fell off my chair the first time I saw her." He chewed on his words, then stuck out his chin. "Morag of An-uallach wanted what Sorcha of Cothro-maiche had—or what she *thought* she had."

Ruith felt his mouth go dry. "And just what sort of power does a dreamweaver have?"

"It depends entirely upon the soul in question, for their magic is capricious in a way only those from Cothromaiche could admire." He paused. "If you could go any other way and do what you must, I would advise it."

"Sarah believes there is more than one spell in An-uallach's keep," Ruith said, suppressing the urge to drag his hand through his hair or give some other sign of his distress. "I cannot see them myself, and I dare not leave her to fend for herself whilst I go make an endless and potentially fruitless search."

"Then you'd best keep her nearby, hadn't you?" Uachdaran asked, though there was no sting in his tone. "And remember what I've said."

"I will," Ruith said with a grim smile. He had the feeling he was going to be spending quite a bit of time thinking about all the king had hinted at. "You've done much more for us than I ever could have asked for."

"Well," Uachdaran said with a small smile, "I didn't want to say as much, but aye, I've been exceptionally generous to you, all things considered."

"I have the feeling you did it for Sarah."

"You might be right. And for your mother. And your wee sister, whom you'll have to tread lightly around."

Ruith imagined that was true. He thanked the king again for his exceptional generosity, bid farewell to all others whom polite-ness required him to, helped Sarah put her horse in her pack, then watched as Tarbh changed himself into a fabulously bejewelled dragon.

Uachdaran only shook his head and walked back into his hall.

Ruith saw Sarah situated comfortably, fashioned reins for her because he could, then put his arms around her as Tarbh leapt into the air and carried them off into the night.

And he thought about a sword with no message, magic worth killing for, and tragedies that involved other families besides his. They were all things he had never considered before and now wondered why not.

He tightened his arms around Sarah and closed his eyes.

And hoped he wasn't flying them into a trap.

Twenty-two

❧

Sarah walked alongside Ruith and contemplated the twists and turns of her life, things her mother never could have imagined, much less enjoyed.

She was traveling in style at least. Not only were her traveling clothes made of the finest material, her boots were sturdy and warm, and her cloak apparently imbued with not only a bit of glamour but the ability to repel even the most unpleasant weather. Given that she was walking through a torrential storm up to the gates of an enormous castle that had suddenly appeared in the midst of equally enormous trees, she thought she might have been in a position to offer an opinion on that.

Her method of travel hadn't been without its discomforts, though she supposed she was the only one who thought so. The flying didn't bother Ruith, though she wasn't sure there would ever come a point in her life where she could attempt it and not shriek.

Their mounts, or more particularly, Tarbh, had informed Ruith

that he would wait for them outside the gates. He'd changed himself into a mighty owl and flown up to perch majestically in a tree.
Ruathar, who had continued the journey whilst residing in her pack,
had apparently been content to remain there. Ruith had been happy
not to argue, pointing out the handiness of having a shapechanging
horse nearby for potential emergencies.

Sarah had had no desire to know what sorts of emergencies he
might be anticipating, though she could speculate readily enough.
She knew how King Uachdaran had felt about An-uallach and the
queen who apparently ruled there with an iron hand. If there hadn't
been a pair of Gair's spells there—and very powerful ones, if her
sight could be trusted to determine such a thing—she was convinced
Ruith would have gone another way.

Sarah put her head down against the rain, then noticed something she hadn't before. She put her hand out on Ruith's arm to stop
him. She would have happily credited that small slip of parchment
that seemed to glow on its own to merely lantern light glinting on
wet cobblestone, but she couldn't. She reached down, retrieved what
she'd seen, then handed it to Ruith.

"Do I want to know what that is?" he asked as he pocketed it
without looking.

"I imagine not." She swallowed with difficulty. "Have you
invented something for us here? Identities, I mean?"

He sighed. "Queen Morag is a hard, shrewd woman with a very
long memory. I'm not entirely sure she would recognize me, though I
fear I look enough like the men of my mother's family that she would
infer some relation. I don't think I can hide who I am."

"And who will I be?"

He hesitated again, only briefly. "For your own safety, I think
you'll be a cousin, related to my grandmother Eulasaid. She had six
sisters who reproduced prodigiously. You do look a bit like my aunts
and cousins from that side and a pair of them were flame-haired, so
the possibility isn't out of the question." He looked at her seriously
from inside his dripping hood. "There are times when a title comes
in handy."

"I'm beginning to realize that."

"Then Sarah of Aireachan shall you be and we'll at least have a decent meal before we go off to ransack their bedchambers. And now that I think about it, the queen has six daughters." He looked at her in mock surprise. "How fortunate for me that I might tick so many off my list in one locale. A dance with each won't take more than an hour, leaving me well on my way to pursuing other, more interesting things."

"You would think," she began severely, "that you would have other, more serious things on your mind than romance."

"You would think," he agreed, "but apparently not."

Sarah supposed he was trying to take her mind off other things, but she couldn't say he'd been all that successful. They were facing yet another gate leading into yet another place she didn't want to go. Only this one, she was certain, wouldn't lead to either the loveliness of Soilléir's chambers or the security of the dwarf king's hall.

The guards were surly, which didn't surprise her. She listened with half an ear as Ruith talked their way inside the gates, but she found she couldn't concentrate on what he was saying. It hadn't occurred to her before that the keep might be covered in magic, but now she wondered why not. She hadn't felt it until she walked through the barbican gate with Ruith, but perhaps that was because she hadn't been looking for it as she should have been.

The edges of the spell fell down behind them as surely as the gates had closed, but it was a spell she couldn't quite see. She frowned thoughtfully as she walked with Ruith through the courtyard and up to the keep itself. Buidseachd had been a fortress that intimidated with sheer size alone, never mind the spells that had been layered over it to add to that impression. Léige had been overwhelming not only because of its imperviousness, but because it gave every impression of having been carved out of the mountain behind it. Anuallach was a different sort of place entirely.

The overall impression should have been one of grandeur, but despite the vastness of the land the walls enclosed and the quite impressive size of the keep rising up in front of her, there was something about the entire place that seemed a bit shabby, as if what should have gone to maintaining it hadn't. The clothing of the guardsmen was just a little tattered about the hems, their swords not exactly bright, their helmets a bit rusty in spots. The walls were sturdy—or they should have been sturdy. She found that if she looked hard enough, she could see that they were crumbling in spots, as if the noble family that lived within those walls couldn't be bothered to have them repaired—or perhaps didn't have the funds for the like.

She thought back to Ceangail with its cracked foundations and spell-stained walls, all held together with a web of absolutely vile spells. An-uallach didn't have that same reek of evil, though the spell it was covered with was unpleasant enough to give her pause.

Ruith reached for her hand and pulled it into the crook of his elbow. "We'll hurry."

"I don't like it here," she murmured.

"Neither do I, but we've no choice. See anything interesting yet?"

She could only nod, partly because she couldn't quite put into words what she was seeing and partly because she thought if she spoke any more, she would shout that they should turn around and bolt whilst they had the chance—which they couldn't do. There were spells in the keep that she had to help Ruith find. She'd known it wouldn't be easy.

She just hadn't expected the task to be so distasteful in a magical sense.

The guard led them up the stairs to the door of a keep that boasted the same lack of care shown the outer walls. They were shown into an antechamber full of formal guards, then through another set of rather weathered doors that opened onto a great hall. Massive hearths were set into the walls and a pathway was set into the stone of the floor, a pathway that led to a raised dais in the distance. Sarah wondered how she was going to walk that entire distance without her knees betraying her unease, but found that wasn't going to be a worry. A gaggle of maidens startled from their chairs on that dais much like a small flock of birds, squawking and flapping

about before they seemingly regained their composure and formed a
sedate little line that marched down the path toward where she and
Ruith had been stopped in the midst of the chamber.

She supposed, judging by the guardsmen who accompanied
them, that the lassies coming their way were Morag's daughters.
They were certainly dressed the part, as if no expense had been
spared in fashioning their garb. Sarah would have wondered what
sort of lad might have been interested in any of them if he'd judged
them by the condition of their hall, but she made the mistake of looking at the first gel who stopped some ten paces away from them. She
caught her breath.

Ruith did too, but he was a man so she supposed he couldn't help
himself.

The truth was, the foremost princess was absolutely stunning.
Sarah could hardly take her eyes off her. She was tall, slender, with
a waterfall of dark hair that fell artistically over one shoulder and
down to her waist. It was her face, however, that was almost too
beautiful to admire. She wasn't elvish, that much was clear, but she
was something else equally as splendid. The girls fanned out behind
her, giving Sarah a perfect look at the six of them, each more beautiful than the last, which left the youngest very lovely indeed.

Sarah realized, with a start, that there was nothing to the gels.
They weren't wraiths, for there was form enough to them, but they
were shadows of what they could have been, as if they had grown up
under a mighty evergreen that had stolen all their sunlight.

The eldest princess folded her arms over her chest and lifted her
chin.

"Announce yourselves before I have you thrown out."

Ruith pulled his hood back from his face. The five other sisters
made appreciative noises, which Sarah understood, but the first did
not, which Sarah couldn't fathom. Either her vision was so poor she
couldn't see what was in front of her, or she was attempting to increase
Ruith's admiration of her by perpetrating a strategy of disinterest.

Sarah decided abruptly that she had been fortunate not to have
grown up in a palace.

"We are as we said we were," Ruith said in a soothing voice Sarah was certain he'd learned at some noble house or another in his youth. "We gave our names to your gate guards, Your Highness, but I will happily give them again to you, if it pleases you."

The dark-haired princess's chin went up a notch, allowing her perhaps a better view down the length of her perfect nose. "They mentioned Ceangail, but that is full of naught but bastards, and we'll have none of them here."

"I am no bastard," Ruith said with absolutely no change in his tone that might have reflected the taking of offense. "I'm sure your genealogist could delve further into it, should you care to ask him." He made the princess a very slight bow, which was perhaps all that a prince of Tòrr Dòrainn could possibly be expected to offer in such circumstances.

Sarah felt a bit like a small, brown mouse standing there next to him, insignificant and plain. She was, as usual, sadly out of her depth.

But she was equally sure she would drown in that depth if she gave any indication of it, so she put her shoulders back as unobtrusively as possible and pretended that she had some sort of noble blood running through her veins, no matter how thin it felt at the moment.

The princess's expression didn't change. "I believe until I've discussed the matter with someone whose opinion I trust, you'll wait—"

"Where you are," said a voice coldly from behind them.

Sarah wasn't one to panic, but she found she was torn between wanting to flee and being rooted to the spot where she stood. She didn't dare reach for Ruith's hand, but she couldn't help but notice he had moved slightly ahead of her, as if he wanted to be in a better place to protect her, if necessary.

It was hard not to feel a certain fondness for him over that. In fact, if she was to be completely honest with herself, it was becoming increasingly difficult not to allow herself to be more than fond of him. That she was considering that in her present straits said perhaps more than she wanted it to about her state of mind at the moment.

She watched as a woman walked around Ruith to put herself in front of the eldest princess. The girls all gave way immediately, inclining their heads respectfully.

The woman was easily as beautiful as her daughters—and as young-looking—but in a way that was so cold, it made Sarah's teeth ache.

"Well, who do we have here?" she asked softly. "One of Sìle of Tòrr Dòrainn's grandsons, perhaps, though I couldn't say for certain, not having had the time nor the inclination to keep up with the affairs of his very small realm."

She looked at Ruith expectantly, one eyebrow raised in a way that left Sarah feeling that if Ruith didn't answer, she would have to.

"I am Ruithneadh, Your Majesty," Ruith said, inclining his head slightly. "Sarait's youngest."

"Ah, the fair Sarait," the queen said in a faintly mocking tone. "Swayed by the ever-charming but not-so-gallant Gair of Ceangail."

"She would likely agree," Ruith said mildly. "Queen Morag."

"Then you've heard of me," Morag said, looking down her nose at him in a perfect imitation of her daughter. "But of course you have."

Ruith nodded deferentially. "Your presence on the Council is and always has been a formidable one. Especially for one so young."

She smiled, as if she knew he was merely flattering her, though she seemed disinclined to disagree with his assessment of her.

"We have a modest kingdom here," she said with a negligent shrug. "We're farmers for the most part, growing things that no one else seems to care about. Surely nothing your grandfather would find interesting."

Ruith made some polite comment or other that Sarah only half heard. She was too busy being the object of scrutiny. If she could have, she would have ducked behind Ruith's back and disappeared. She held herself where she was by sheer willpower alone as Morag started at the top of her head and took her measure from there down to her feet and back, her eyes missing no detail.

"And who do we have here?" she asked, cutting Ruith off in mid-flattery.

"A distant cousin," Ruith said. "Sarah of Aireachan."

Morag smiled, but it wasn't a pleasant one. "Come now, my prince, we are able to be honest with each other, are we not? If this is one of Lodan of Camanaë's great-granddaughters, then I am Yngerame of Wychweald." She pinned Sarah to the spot with a look that felt more like a blow. "Who is this gel who cowers beside a mighty elven prince of a house she surely wouldn't dare approach save on her knees?"

Sarah would have taken umbrage at that, but she was too terrified to speak. Besides, Queen Morag had it aright. She was standing beside a glorious elven prince, and she was most definitely cowering.

"She is who I say she is," Ruith said. "And she is under my protection."

Sarah was startled enough by his tone to look at him, though she realized immediately that she shouldn't have. It was dangerous to look away from a coiled snake. The queen laughed, a cold, hard sound that reminded Sarah of the stinging hail that fell occasionally in Doìre when a chill wind blew down from the north. Whether against her mother's workroom window or her own head out in the forest, it was unpleasant.

"You are entitled to your little dalliances, of course," Morag said with another laugh that hurt Sarah simply to listen to it. "I'll see chambers provided for you. A discreet distance away from each other."

"That won't be necessary, for what should be obvious reasons of propriety," Ruith said, in that same low, dangerous voice, "though we certainly do appreciate your hospitality, Your Majesty. We have come merely to seek shelter for the night. We won't trouble you longer than that."

"It is no trouble, Prince Ruithneadh," Morag said smoothly. "Of course."

Sarah thought it might be wise to simply keep her mouth shut and see if she couldn't stay out of Morag's sights. She listened to Ruith and Morag make a bit more small talk, then tried not to weep with relief when Morag motioned for one of her servants to come forward and show the guest and his, ah, *cousin* to their chambers. She didn't argue with Ruith when he put her in front of him as they made their way out of the great hall, then up stairs and down passageways until the servant stopped in front of a doorway. Sarah wouldn't have cared if it had been nothing more than a closet in which to discard used linens; she was simply happy to know that there would soon be somewhere for her to hide.

The servant withdrew a discreet distance and looked away, but not before Sarah saw the smirk on his face. She looked at Ruith.

"Well," she said, because she couldn't manage anything else.

Only his eyes betrayed his fury. "I will come to fetch you, my lady, for supper."

"Thank you."

"Do not leave this chamber, Sarah."

She let out a shaky breath. "I wouldn't think to."

He opened the door for her, then stood back. "Sleep if you can. You'll be glad of it later."

Aye, when they snuck out of their chambers and scurried about the keep, looking for things Queen Morag shouldn't have had in her possession. She nodded, though she didn't imagine she would manage sleep anytime soon. She walked into the chamber and closed the door behind her. A spell slid down to the floor, the same sort of thing Ruith had put over the door in Slighe. She let out a shuddering breath, then turned in a circle to look at her luxurious accommodations. They seemed nothing out of the ordinary, though painfully small. Not quite a closet for bedclothes, but close.

A knock startled her into dropping her pack on the floor. She picked it up with trembling hands, set it on a chair, then turned to open the door. A servant stood there with a gown draped over her arms.

"From Her Majesty," the girl said, bobbing a curtsey. "For your pleasure, my lady."

Sarah found the gown thrust into her arms, then the door pulled shut in her face. She wouldn't have minded that so much if she hadn't found herself suddenly in a great deal of pain. The wound on her

right arm where Gair's spell had left its mark flamed into a burning
that left her gritting her teeth in order not to cry out. Her left arm
pained her equally, which surprised her. She quickly put the gown
over the back of the chair, then stepped away from it. She realized
that she was trembling badly and that it didn't come from standing
in the middle of a stone-cold chamber. She would have made a fire,
but there was no wood. She didn't dare take apart one of the chairs.

And then she realized there was something else about the chamber, apart from its unrelenting inhospitality, that bothered her.

Something that smelled of death.

She walked over to the window, which was unfortunately not
large enough for her to jump out of, and opened the shutters. The
rain-soaked breeze was a welcome relief from the stench of the spell
she hadn't noticed at first, the spell that lingered inside the chamber.
She looked out into the mist for quite some time before she could
bring herself to face the thought that had been tugging at her mind.

She might have the means to see what sort of spell lay in her
chamber, hidden from view.

She took a deep breath of bracing spring air, then turned and
leaned back against the wall, which felt comfortingly steady beneath
her hands. It took her longer perhaps than it should have to muster
up the courage to try the spell Soilléir had given her. She wasn't sure
she believed it would do anything but hang there in the air, then
blow away like so much smoke.

Believing is seeing.

Soilléir's words, spoken offhandedly at some point during her
stay in Buidseachd, came back to her as if he'd been standing there
next to her, whispering them afresh. Her mother had always held to
the opposite view, that she wouldn't believe something until she'd
seen it with her own bloody good eyes, as she would have said.
Sarah imagined now that Soilléir had chosen his words and their
particular order with great care.

She closed her eyes briefly, gathered up all the faith in herself
she could lay her hands on, then repeated faithfully the spell he'd
given her. The words seemed to come with a power of their own,

a power she certainly hadn't felt the first time she'd said them. She took another deep breath, then opened her eyes.

And she wished she hadn't.

A spell lay in the middle of the chamber, bubbling up from some unseen source. She would have leapt out of its way, or hopped up onto the bed, or used a chair as a last resort, but she didn't have the chance. It wrapped itself around her feet before she could blink, then crept up her like a noisome vine, but more rapidly than any earthly thing ever could have.

And that was just the beginning.

She tried to move only to find she couldn't. She would have cried out for aid, but every time she took a breath, the vines tightened about her chest, stealing her air. She stood there and watched helplessly as the bubbling spring sent forth more things that grew and blossomed in a way that left her watching in horror, mute.

Morag had said she was a farmer.

Sarah had never dreamed just what sorts of seedlings she might have cultivated.

Twenty-three

❧

Ruith walked quickly down the passageway toward Sarah's chamber. He wasn't particularly concerned that he might be late for supper, never mind Queen Morag's insistence that he not be. He was, however, quite concerned that Sarah not find herself in the woman's sights again alone. Under normal circumstances, he wouldn't have given the queen's reaction to Sarah any especial thought. Sarah was a very beautiful woman and Morag had six daughters—never mind that he wouldn't have looked at any of the six even if his heart hadn't been given. The queen obviously sensed a threat and had lashed out accordingly. There should have been no mystery there.

But they were in An-uallach, and he knew very well that things were not as they seemed.

Especially given that he was sure that if Morag hadn't killed Athair and Sorcha of Cothromaiche outright, she'd seen it done by someone else. And if what Uachdaran had hinted at was true—that daughters often resembled mothers to an astonishing degree—it stood to reason that Morag might find another murder committed in the near future to be no more difficult than the first two.

He had retired earlier to his chamber and forced himself to sleep for an hour before he'd risen and been about his own investigations in another guise than his own. He had, unfortunately, turned up nothing more than what he would have expected. The keep was full of miserable servants, vicious guardsmen, and spells that reflected an old, unpleasant sort of magic that he was fortunately not very familiar with. It wasn't his father's bastardization of Lugham, nor was it of any elven derivation. It wasn't even as if it had sprung up from the wells of power he could sense lingering beneath the keep's foundations. It was as if someone during the centuries of An-uallach's existence had simply taken what was required from other magics, then created something else out of it. It was powerful, though, for all its flaws, so he didn't take any of it lightly.

He stopped in front of Sarah's door and knocked. He could see that his spell hadn't been disturbed save for the servant who had brought Sarah a gown so he was confident she was still inside, unmolested. He sincerely hoped she'd gotten a decent bit of sleep. He had hoped to find where his father's spells were by himself, but unfortunately Sarah would have to do the honors. He could only hope they weren't languishing under Morag's bed. Her husband Phillip likely wouldn't have minded his rummaging about, but Ruith suspected Morag most certainly would.

He realized that Sarah hadn't answered. He knocked again, more loudly that time, but still no answer.

"Sarah?" he called, ruthlessly squelching a sudden bout of panic. His spell hadn't been breached; he could sense it still hanging there, just inside her door.

Yet she didn't answer.

He turned the knob, broke the lock with a spell, then shoved the door open.

Sarah was standing next to the window, so pale he half feared she was dead. Tears streamed down her cheeks, though, and she was gasping very carefully for breath. He started inside the chamber only to realize why she was standing where she was. He laid no claim to any special sort of sight, but even he could see what lay inside the minuscule bedchamber.

Spells of Olc and that other rot that passed for magic in Anuallach covered every conceivable surface, hung down from the ceiling like spiderwebs, wrapped themselves around Sarah in a vile embrace.

He destroyed them all with a single word—or tried to, rather. It took him a handful of moments to wipe out everything there, which irritated him further. He slammed the door shut behind him, locked it with a spell of Wexham he'd appropriated from Miach of Neroche, then strode over and pulled Sarah into his arms.

She wasn't hysterical, but she was close. He held her tightly with one arm, then smoothed his hand over her hair again and again, whispering what soothing words he could lay hold of. It was difficult when all he wanted to do was stride off into the keep, find the queen, and . . .

He channeled his anger into more useful things, such as creating for Sarah the chamber she should have been offered. He couldn't say his was overly luxurious, but it wasn't a soot-encrusted, spell-strewn closet just one step up from a cesspit. He lit a fire, draped tapestries from the walls and laid them on the floor, then created as much light as he could. And when Sarah finally managed to breathe normally again, he swept her up into his arms and carried her over to the bed, a much more comfortable rendition of the like than what he'd found there before.

He laid her down, then perched on the edge of the bed. "Have you been standing there this entire time?"

"Aye."

He drew his hand over his eyes. "Forgive me, love. I had no idea."

"I'm afraid I did it."

He blinked in surprise. "What do you mean?"

She tried to mop up her tears with the hem of her sleeve. "I didn't like how the chamber felt, so I thought I would try one of Soilléir's spells, just so I could see what needed to be changed." She looked at him from bloodshot eyes. "I think I should have kept my mouth shut. Whatever I said woke up whatever was here before."

He smiled and put his hand over hers. "Give me Soilléir's spell again, won't you, just for curiosity's sake. I fear I didn't listen very well to it in Buidseachd."

She repeated it, but with a wince, as if she wasn't entirely sure she wanted it to work for her again. He considered the words. It was like nothing he'd ever heard before, but it had been from Soilléir and that one had a repertoire of spells which Ruith could only hope one day to acquire.

"And what happened when you used it?" he asked. "To you, I mean, not to the chamber."

She looked at him helplessly. "I saw. More than I usually see, truth be told." She paused. "I'm not sure how to turn it off."

"Perhaps you shouldn't," he said slowly. "Until we leave."

She nodded uneasily. "I daresay you're right. I hate to think of what might be swimming in the soup tonight."

Ruith looked at her, her cognac-colored hair highlighted by the flickering flames of the lights he'd made, then down at her hands, hands that could so deftly work with cloth she'd woven herself. She was, he could say with all honesty, the same sort of woman his mother had been. Fierce, courageous, profoundly stubborn. He wondered, absently, as he watched her, if he would ever convince her that what she thought she lacked didn't matter a whit to him. He had magic enough for the both of them when it came to safety and security. They could soldier along quite happily through everyday life without the benefit—or annoyance—of kettles walking off when they weren't supposed to or fires starting themselves without permission. He quite liked starting his own fires and cooking his own meals.

Though at the moment, he had to admit that he was rather more grateful for his magic than he had been before.

"I should have held to my vow never to let you out of my arms again," he said grimly. "I'm sorry I did."

"You were trying to save my reputation, though I'm not sure why we care here." She let out a deep, shuddering breath. "I am no threat to the queen, though I daresay she would like to have you as a husband for one of her girls."

Ruith had his own ideas on what sort of threat Sarah posed, but he kept them to himself. "Too late," he said cheerfully. "I am already promised."

"To whom?" she asked with a snort.

"To someone who has set for me impossible tasks to surmount before she'll look at me twice." He shuddered delicately. "The thought of dancing with those harpies below—"

She smiled. "Unkind."

"Accurate," he corrected, "but I will force myself to dance with each of those gels downstairs, so that I might appease you and the queen at the same time. Then we will quite happily march off into the gloom sooner rather than later where you will look for spells and I for the final lass to fulfill my tally. And then, my lady, you will have exhausted your excuses and have nothing to hide behind except perhaps an intense dislike of your would-be lover."

She sat up, pushing him out of her way as she did so. "That won't do, so I suppose I'll need to invent something else."

"Don't," he said reaching for her hand. "Please don't."

She looked at him quickly. "You choose the damndest times to speak of romance."

"You're a difficult case. I must take the opportunities as they present themselves." He kissed her hand quickly, then rose. "I'll leave you to think on that whilst you dress."

She hesitated. "I don't think I can wear that gown over there. I'm not proud, well, not overly, but there is something sewn into the seams that . . . hurts."

Ruith supposed he should have looked just to see what that something was, but he didn't have the stomach to. It was one thing to make Sarah miserable; it was another to endanger her, a guest in the hall. He spelled the gown into oblivion, then created another, along with shoes to match and a wrap to ward off the chill.

"I'll wait for you without," he said, holding out his hand to help her to her feet.

She nodded, looking quite a bit worse for the wear, but determined. He left her holding on to the footpost of the very lovely bed he'd made for her, then walked out into the passageway, pulling the door shut behind him. He leaned back against it, though, so he would hear if anything untoward happened inside.

It seemed only a handful of moments had passed before Sarah opened the door. He turned, then caught his breath.

He wasn't much of a designer of ladies' gowns, that he would freely admit, but he could remember a pair of them his mother had worn. Sarah was wearing one of those, an emerald thing that dripped with crystals from various appropriate parts of itself. Toes of lovely crystal-encrusted shoes peeked out from beneath the hem of her gown. He opened his hand and a necklace of diamonds lay there with another smaller circlet to go around her wrist. She looked up suddenly, her eyes full of tears.

"I didn't realize your imagination extended to sartorial endeavors."

He smiled faintly. "My mother had a gown that looked like that."

"I'm sure she was exquisite in it."

"She was," he agreed, "and so are you." He motioned for her to turn around, then asked her to hold up her hair so he could fasten the necklace for her. He slipped the bracelet over her wrist after she'd turned back to face him, then shook his head slowly. "I don't know," he said thoughtfully. "I may only manage four of the six."

She smiled hesitantly. "You're daft."

"That isn't the word I would use, but I won't argue." He heard someone calling his name loudly from down the passageway. He suppressed the urge to roll his eyes, then held out his arm for Sarah. "Shall we go?"

She put her hand on his arm, then paused. "Thank you, Ruith," she said quietly. "The gown is beautiful."

"It is a poor covering for the true gem, but it will have to do." He tucked her hand under his arm, then nodded down the passageway.

"Let's go have this over with. I suppose we would do well to insist on a food taster."

"I think I can manage well enough for us."

"Can you?"

"You may want to add your own bit of whatever it is you could add to improve the flavor," she said, "but I think I could see if there was anything vile in it to start with." She looked up at him. "Will you think about that spell later? The one I tried?"

He nodded. "I may have to borrow your lexicon. I'm not as familiar with the Cothromaichian tongue as I likely should be. Nor with what useless fluff passes for magic there."

"You're such an elitist," she said with a smile.

"Born and bred, my love," he said, trying to mirror her light tone. "Wouldn't want to disappoint my grandfather, the most elite of them all."

"Would he approve of the lassies downstairs, do you think?"

Ruith snorted before he could stop himself. "Absolutely not," he said before he realized that Sarah was asking more than just that. He looked at her. "My grandfather is a difficult sort—"

"Who will expect you to wed a princess," she finished for him. "Which is as it should be."

"He'll expect me to wed someone I love," Ruith corrected. "As will Sgath, who, if you'll know the truth, spent most of the time we were at Lake Cladach telling me to wed you before you realized what you would be saddling yourself with."

She wouldn't meet his eyes. "Surely not."

"He's saving that piece of ground he showed you, that little clearing on the shore, just for you. And I'm telling you that against my better judgement because he said he didn't much care if I came along to build you a house there or not. It's yours if you want it, simply because he saw into your soul and was pleased with what lay there."

She looked up at him then, her eyes swimming with tears. "Do you *want* me blubbering into my poisoned soup?"

"Nay, you should most certainly not, else you'll leave me doing the same thing." He took her face in his hands, then kissed both her cheeks before she could plow her fist into his nose. "Supper first, then . . ."

She nodded and pulled away, then carefully dabbed the tears from her cheeks. "I'm fine."

He tucked her hand under his arm again and walked with her down to the great hall. He put on his best courtly manners, then spent soup and the main course making certain that the spells that occasionally fell from the ceiling *appeared* to cover Sarah, but didn't. And just to further distract the queen, he rose soon after dessert and begged her for the pleasure of a dance with her eldest daughter.

The girl was beautiful, he would give her that, and she certainly danced well enough. Her conversation, however, was limited to questions about the luxuries to be found at Seanagarra and how soon he planned to wed so she—er, so his very fortunate bride might enjoy them.

The next two princesses he danced with were less interested in his treasures surely stored in his grandfather's vaults than they were in him personally, but he wasn't any more swayed by that than he had been by their eldest sister's curiosity.

He had a small sip of wine back at the supper table, then made Sarah a low bow. "If you would?"

If the servant behind her pulled her chair out a bit too quickly or the queen glared at her a bit more than necessary, she simply ignored it. She walked around the back of the table, then put her hand into his.

He was rather relieved they had taken the trouble to brush up on his dancing at Léige, no matter how much improvising they would now need to do. Perhaps he shouldn't have been surprised by how easily Sarah had memorized the steps. Franciscus had, as she had said more than once, made certain that her education was far greater than anything her mother could have offered her.

Franciscus, the father of Athair who had been slain—allegedly— by Morag of An-uallach, leaving behind a wee gel whose name Uachdaran's bard hadn't been willing to divulge?

Ruith was beginning to think he might be able to supply that name, if pressed.

"You dance very well," Sarah said, interrupting his thoughts.

"As do you."

"Which is all your doing," she said with a smile. "With, I will admit, a bit of aid from Franciscus."

"He has a surprising number of skills you wouldn't think an ale-master should have," he remarked politely.

"I seem to manage to surround myself with men who have secrets."

"I wouldn't keep the secret of where my heart would wander if you weren't so insistent on formalities that have nothing to do with what I would rather be doing, which is spending the evening danc-ing with you."

"You're not calling my requirement ridiculous any longer."

"'Tis past ridiculous, Sarah," he said with a snort, then he laughed a little. "Forgive me. We should be politely formal and dignified. I'll give you my unvarnished opinion of the undertaking you've bound me to later, when I can speak plainly."

"I did agree to dance with you, you realize."

"You're taking pity on me."

She smiled. "I might be."

He smiled in return and decided he could complain about the remainder of his tally later, when he didn't have the pleasure of Sarah and a fairly decent complement of musicians nearby.

The dance was all too short—and by design, no doubt—but he made up for that by dancing with Sarah between Morag's daugh-ters. Perhaps it wasn't wise to provoke the queen, but he couldn't help but wonder what she might reveal if pressed.

Wine and fruit were provided as refreshment during a respite and Ruith happily indulged in both after making certain they weren't poisoned. He was also quite happy to sit between Sarah and Morag lest the latter find herself clumsy enough to spill something in Sarah's direction.

"It is always a pleasure to see your grandfather Sìle on the Council," Morag said smoothly. "When he deigns to come, of course."

Ruith shrugged. "He makes no apologies for his behavior, Your Majesty. I suppose that is the prerogative of a king or queen, isn't it?"

Her eyes narrowed slightly. "When one wears a crown, Your Highness, one finds that alliances on and off the Council are taken lightly at the peril of one's realm."

"Surely not yours," Ruith said, pretending not to notice the threat. "An-uallach is a bit like silk over steel, isn't it? Subtle, yet unbreakable."

Morag shrugged lightly. "I do what I can with what I have. There is always more that could be done, of course."

Ruith imagined there was, and he was fairly certain he knew precisely where Morag thought she could lay her hands on a bit more power to do just that.

He supposed he also knew what she'd done in the past to attempt the same thing.

"The acquisition of more power doesn't come without a price, though, does it?" he asked, with a thoughtful frown. "Either in the stretching of monarchial magic, or the necessity of forging alliances one might not necessarily want to make." He looked at her innocently. "Or perhaps I don't know enough of the world to judge."

"You are young," Morag agreed, "and obviously know little of our concerns here in the north given that we don't fall within Tòrr Dòrainn's rather insignificant borders."

Ruith only sipped his wine politely and waited. He couldn't see Sarah out of the corner of his eye, though he could feel her anxiety. He turned toward Morag to give Sarah more of his back to hide behind. "Surely you suffer no danger from your neighbors," he said, "not with your power to keep your people safe."

"I don't think you know what danger is, lad," she said tartly. "I'm forever waiting for those fairies and whatnot from the mountains to flutter down and vex me. Worse still is Seannair of Cothromaiche and that rot he spreads all over his land."

"Indeed," Ruith murmured.

"He could sit upon the Council of Kings," she continued with a sneer, "if he weren't so concerned with keeping to himself and shunning the outside world. Then again, perhaps he fears 'tis too lofty a place for him and an appearance there might show his lack of power."

Ruith nodded, though he had heard a far different tale. He couldn't say he knew much of Soilléir's family, but he knew Soilléir's great-grandfather Seannair didn't sit upon the Council not because he feared it, but because he thought it silly. If he owned a crown, he had most likely forgotten where he'd stashed it. Ruith smiled to himself. He should have told Soilléir that along with *Sarait, you will not associate any longer with that young rogue full of dangerous magic,* Sìle had generally added, *who likely inherited all of it from his great-grandsire, who couldn't find his blasted crown if he sat upon it and it poked him in the arse!*

His grandfather, Ruith would admit, could venture into the earthy description now and again if it suited him.

And the thing Ruith would have pointed out to Morag now but thought discretion suggested that he not was that if Seannair took his seat on the Council, it would be the one Morag currently occupied with such grace.

"Perhaps he does fear to be shamed," Ruith conceded, reaching for his wine and toying with the glass, "or perhaps 'tis his grief that keeps him from taking his proper place in the world."

Morag looked at him, a puzzled frown on her face. "His grief?"

"I understand he lost one of his great-grandsons, Athair." Ruith didn't hear Sarah's breath catch, so she either hadn't paid any heed to his conversations with Uachdaran—which he knew she had—or she was a very good cardplayer. "A hunting accident, I believe."

"I'm not sure," Morag said doubtfully. "I've heard that the lad did perish tragically. Of course, that was likely his fault because instead of looking for a woman of rank and station as he *should* have, he wandered off to perilous locales and wed himself a commoner. More the fool was he, for there are certainly plenty of titled gels in the surrounding environs for him to have chosen from."

Aye, and six of them were sitting on her other side. Ruith frowned.

"Perhaps he should have chosen one of your daughters, Your Majesty. Indeed, I'm not sure how he could have made any other choice after seeing them."

"Perhaps you will be wiser than he was, when you choose to wed," Morag said. "It wasn't that I didn't invite him here several times to see the glories of my hall. Instead, he chose a peasant from Bruadair, where they pretend to see things they cannot." She shrugged. "Seannair did the same thing, so perhaps Athair isn't to blame for his stupidity."

"Then perhaps it is fortunate that Seannair remains in his rustic hall," Ruith said with a conspiratorial smile, "given that he obviously doesn't have the wit to take his place amongst more sensible and foresightful kings. And queens, of course."

Morag wasn't buying what he was selling. He would have wondered if it was perhaps that he had been too long out of polite society and his ability to woo and befuddle others had been sadly diminished.

Or it might have been because he had Athair and Sorcha's daughter sitting behind him.

It almost defied belief, but he found that the longer he thought on it, the more he believed it. Franciscus might have been a common name in the north, but it certainly wasn't in the south. And what were the odds of an alemaster—a painfully well-educated alemaster, at that—named Franciscus taking up residence not a quarter league away from a gel who, according to hints delivered by the king of the dwarves, looked just like Franciscus's daughter-in-law?

The only question that still puzzled him was that if Morag had done away with Athair and Sorcha, why she hadn't done away with their daughter as well.

Unless she had and he was imagining things where he shouldn't have been.

"Perhaps it was for the best," the queen said, with that smile that still didn't reach her eyes. "That Athair and his lovely dreamweaving bride disappeared without a trace, I mean. They might have produced a child, and then Seannair would have allowed her to be raised like the savage lads he has rampaging about his kingdom." She looked at Ruith. "Stupidity is the only answer I can divine."

"Fortunate it is, then," Ruith said politely, "that you sit on the Council of Kings and not a rustic from the north."

"It is," she agreed. She looked at him assessingly. "Your grandfather has met my gels, you know."

Ruith had no trouble understanding where she was leading him. "I regret that he didn't make mention of them to me," Ruith said slowly, "but it has been many years since last we met. I was too young to have appreciated the tales then."

"Have a falling out with him?" she asked, sounding rather more pleased than was polite by the thought.

"Something like that," Ruith agreed. He had a final sip of his wine, then set his glass down. "And I know 'tis terribly impolite to retire before one's host does but I was hoping that I might retire early tonight that on the morrow I might have the pleasure of passing the morning with your fair daughters? Chess or cards—or something else, if they prefer. I'm sure Sarah won't mind."

"I'm equally certain she won't," Morag said. "And I will alleviate any discomfort you might feel by forcing myself to retire first." She motioned for her servant to pull her chair back.

The rest of the table rose, then the prince consort and Morag's daughters followed her from the chamber. Ruith stood, waiting as they all vacated the hall, wondering what it was that set so ill with him. It wasn't any of the looks Morag had given him, or the glares her daughters had given Sarah—irritating though those had been. There was something . . .

They might have produced a child, and then Seannair would have allowed her to be raised like the savage lads he has rampaging about his kingdom.

Ruith frowned. Why would Morag have thought Athair and his bride would have produced a girl child?

"Ruith?"

He looked at Sarah. The thoughts tumbled over and over in his head, as if they'd been caught in a mighty wave and couldn't right themselves. Athair and Sorcha had died . . . if they had produced a girl child . . . Morag wanted more power . . .

He looked at Sarah, then *saw* her, that beautiful, obscure gel who had inherited no magic at all from the witchwoman Seleg, but had somehow acquired the ability to see, an ability augmented by Soil-léir of Cothromaiche, who had certainly taken a great interest in her.

Hadn't he?

"Ruith."

"I'm fine," he said.

"I didn't say you weren't," she said. "Shall we go?"

"Please," he agreed.

She didn't look any better than he felt. "Interesting dinner conversation."

Aye, it had been. He reached for her hand. "We need to be about our business tonight, not tomorrow night."

She looked as if she would rather have put it off a bit longer, but she nodded just the same.

He leaned close. "I'll walk you to your chamber, then come fetch you after the house settles down to sleep."

She took a deep breath. "I might try to use that spell again to see exactly—"

"Wait for me to come to you first."

"But—"

"*Wait* for me."

"I want you to understand, Your Highness, that the only reason I am submitting to your bullying now is that I'm almost too terrified to speak. It will not last, I assure you."

"'Tis for your own good."

"Why is it I'm fairly certain Soilléir said the same thing to you?" she muttered.

He only smiled and took her hand. His smile faded as he walked, though, for he knew that the unpleasantness at supper could only be intensified the longer they stayed.

Until it possibly spiraled into something he might not see coming.

He wondered why Morag had a pair of his father's spells, why she was so obsessed with Seannair of Cothromaiche, why she feared the peoples of the north who wouldn't possibly want her land or her keep. He understood the lust for power. He had spent the first ten years of his life watching it in full bloom. And though it had been dangerous, it hadn't been directed solely at him.

Or at the woman he loved.

Aye, they would be about their business and get the hell out of the castle whilst they still could, before something happened to Sarah.

Something more than what he feared had already happened to her as a wee babe.

Twenty-four

Sarah stood in front of the fire Ruith had made her earlier in her chamber that still seemed to be smoldering from the spells he'd used to rid it of what had been there before, and looked around her. He had changed the closet into a rather lovely place, all things considered, with enough light to keep her from having to look into corners for unpleasant things. It was difficult to believe, sometimes, that the only reason he did what he did was that he wanted to make certain she was comfortable.

A pity there wasn't anything he could do to ease the terror she felt over the task that lay in front of them.

She tried not to think about Athair and Sorcha, that poor pair who had perished in a way no one seemed to want to talk about. It occurred to her, as she stood there and looked into the flames of the fire, that if they were descended from Seannair of Cothromaiche, that patriarch with no delusions of grandeur, and so was Soilléir, then he and Athair were cousins.

Odd that Soilléir had said nothing.

Then again, she hadn't mentioned their names after that morning in the garden of Gearrannan, so he would have had no reason to discuss them with her.

She felt rather than heard something behind her. She had scarce gotten one of her knives in her hand and turned before she realized it was only Ruith there, standing just inside her door. She replaced her knife with trembling hands, then glared at him.

"I wish you wouldn't do that."

"No choice," he said, dropping his pack onto the floor, then striding over to her. He put his hands lightly on her shoulders. "How are you?"

"About as you might think," she managed.

He put his arms around her and pulled her close. Perhaps she should have protested, but she couldn't bring herself to. She put her arms around his waist and held on, hoping he wouldn't realize how badly she was shaking.

"We should go, shouldn't we?" she asked, her voice sounding far more breathless than she would have liked.

"In a moment," Ruith said. "I don't think the spell is going anywhere."

"Spells."

He took a deep breath. "Spells, then."

She stood with him for several moments in silence, then pulled back and looked up at him. "I'm appalled by my lack of courage."

He reached up and brushed a few stray strands of hair back from her face. "A wise warrior doesn't shun the fear that prepares him for battle."

She pursed her lips at him. "Did you just invent that?"

"I believe 'tis one of the more famous strictures of Scrymgeour Weger, who you may or may not know is without a doubt the fiercest warrior of our age. I would imagine he knows of what he speaks."

"Did he face a keep full of spells tended by a queen who wanted his escort to wed one of her daughters?"

"Escort," Ruith echoed, sounding amused. "Is that what I am?"

"It seemed a circumspect thing to call you," she said, feeling altogether quite ill. She took a deep breath. "Might we go? I can't think about this any longer."

He blew out his breath, then nodded. "I'm going to cover us in a spell of un-noticing. I'm afraid it won't be pleasant, but I think it best to use a magic the queen won't think out of the ordinary."

"Olc?" Sarah asked uneasily.

He only nodded. "I've been studying the spells slathered all over my chamber and found one that I'll use to cover the Olc. Morag wouldn't see us if she stood between us."

Sarah closed her eyes briefly. "Don't wish that on us."

"I wouldn't," he said fervently. "Just trying to reassure you." He reached for her hand. "In and out, Sarah. A trivial exercise."

She nodded, then steeled herself for the sight of his spell falling over her. She found, to her dismay, that the reality of the spell was far worse than the thought of it. She didn't doubt that Ruith was right about using it, though, so she closed her eyes and let him lead her from the chamber. It wasn't as if she needed her eyes to see where the first spell was anyway.

"Where to, do you think?" he murmured.

"Down."

Ruith nodded, then took her right hand. She winced initially at the pain, but soon forgot it in her terror. They paused every time a guard approached and then walked past, then continued on. By the third time and after a set of stairs, Sarah flattened herself against the wall and squeezed Ruith's hand.

"Stop," she wheezed. "I can't breathe."

"Of course."

She decided after a minute or two and another pair of guardsmen tromping by that it was best they just get on with their work. She nodded in the direction they'd been going. "We should hurry."

He nodded, then continued on without comment.

She followed him through passageways, down stairs, then down more stairs until they reached the point where they could go no farther. Sarah found that after what she'd been through upstairs, waiting for guardsmen to pass now was easily done.

Sarah padded silently through the cellar with Ruith and led him without either haste or enthusiasm to the spell that lay there behind casks of grain. Ruith squatted down by it, then looked up at her.

"Well?"

"Well, what?" she managed. "I've gotten you here. You do the rest."

"I can see the spells," he said slowly, "but not as you can. Is there a flaw or a weakness that you can see?"

She gritted her teeth to keep them from chattering. She supposed she looked as if she were exactly three heartbeats away from either bursting into tears or sinking to the floor and rocking herself in misery. "Are you trying to make me feel useful?"

"I wish I were," he muttered, "but unfortunately I'm not. I'm also fresh out of time to coddle you, so be about your work quickly."

Sarah felt her eyes narrow even though she knew perfectly well he was provoking her intentionally. "You great bloody bully."

"Which is exactly what you need, you vexatious, headstrong wench."

A pity he'd said the last with a quick, affectionate smile that left her truly undone. She dragged her sleeve across her eyes. "Don't be kind to me. I can't bear it. Not now."

He reached for her hand and held it, hard. "Then let's finish this, quickly, and go somewhere where I *can* be kind to you. And to humor you, I'll tell you what I can see. This," he said, pointing to the topmost spell of illusion, "is an everyday spell of Olc, fashioned to conceal and repulse at the same time." He studied the nasty web spread across the page a bit longer. "I can't see the complete composition of what's underneath, but there appears to be a bit of Caol—" He shot her a look. "The queen's magic, as it happens. The other I can't discern." He pointed to the four corners where the spell was attached to the floor, then to a spot where other magics were oozing out. He looked at her. "Can you improve upon that, friend?"

"Olc," she said hoarsely, "holding down the four corners of the concealing spell. Suarach—or it claims it is called—is indeed coming out from underneath it on that side, for it announces itself as it does so, but you missed the Lugham underneath that and a rather vile perversion of Croxteth over there." Her hand shook only a bit as she reached out and pointed to the farthermost corner of the spell of concealment. "That is Seiche, whatever that is. There is Wexham and something from Léige, mixed together in an unwholesome way." She looked at him. "Not that I would recognize it as such if the language of the spell wasn't woven into the spell itself."

"Is it?" he asked, peering at it thoughtfully. "An interesting combination. The dwarves have, as you might imagine given their riches, a compelling interest in keeping things hidden from unfriendly eyes. The dwarvish bit is there, I would imagine, to leave anyone resourceful enough to get that far feeling as if they were imagining what they were seeing." He looked at her. "Clever, isn't it?"

"Diabolical," she agreed. She paused. "What do we do now?"

"You slit the spell with your knife, we pull the page out, then you tell me how to repair the damage."

She was silent for a moment or two, then she met his eyes. "You truly cannot see what's there?"

"Nay, Sarah, I truly cannot see what's there." He smiled gravely. "That's your gift."

"I think I would rather be *doing* something."

"And I would rather be sitting happily upon my arse with my feet up, watching you doing something."

She fought her smile. "A bully, and a lazy one at that."

"Aye," he agreed cheerfully, then his smile faded abruptly. "We must hurry. We've been here too long."

She nodded, drew her knife, then reached out and carefully slit a few of what he assumed were threads holding the spell to the ground. She heard no alarms go off, so she assumed they were safe enough. She pulled the page free, then looked down at it.

"There's something on it—"

"No time to look," he said.

She held it out on the tip of her knife. "You should be careful with it, unless you want the barbs going into your shin. And you'll have to patch the hole. I cannot."

He patched quickly, then rolled the spell up and stuck it down the side of his boot. Sarah supposed he was going to need to find a better place to stash spells than that, but now wasn't the time to look for it. She heard footsteps coming their way. She looked at Ruith in alarm, but he merely put a finger to his lips and pulled her behind him. He waited until the guard was within arm's reach before extending a greeting.

The guard never saw Ruith's fist coming toward him.

He fell without a noise, thanks to Ruith's catching him, and no doubt had several hours of pleasant rest to look forward to behind the ale kegs. Ruith took her hand.

"Where for the next spell?"

"Up," she said, but there was absolutely no sound to the word. It was bad enough to have descended into the kitchens. The thought of going anywhere else in the keep was nothing short of terrifying.

But it was what she'd committed herself to doing that morning in Sìle of Tòrr Dòrainn's garden, so she reminded herself that Ruith's mother had put herself in far more peril than she ever would, put her shoulders back, and nodded.

And if it was unsteadily done, perhaps Ruith hadn't noticed.

She lost count of the twists and turns they took and the guards they passed. The only thing she could say with any certainty was that the second spell that awaited them was more powerful than what they'd found in the cellar.

She stopped Ruith outside a particular door, then leaned back against the wall as he put his hand on the wood and bowed his head. After a brief moment, he looked at her.

"No one inside."

"How do you know?"

"I'm guessing."

She pursed her lips at him, but followed him inside just the same. The chamber was empty, as he'd said, but that wasn't a relief. She walked immediately over to a wall sporting shelves full of treasures.

There in the place of honor was what they'd come for. There were no strands of barbed magic laid across the glass case, which surprised her. In fact, there was nothing at all there, just a sturdy lock, as if Morag didn't think anyone would dare make it into her inner sanctum.

"Which spell is that?" she asked, because she had to do something to keep from weeping.

"Finding," he said, "which surprises me because it isn't a particularly powerful spell."

"And the other one from downstairs?"

"I didn't stop to look, but I can tell you it's burning a bloody hole in my leg—"

She would have smiled, but she had been jerked off her feet—literally—and pulled into a corner of the solar. Ruith backed her up against the wall, then pressed himself back against her. If his intent had been to crush her, he was coming close to succeeding. She put her hands on his back, closed her eyes, and forced herself to breathe silently. It was surprising how accustomed she'd become to having him put himself between her and danger.

A gel could learn to appreciate that about a man.

The door opened, bodies entered, then the door slammed shut.

"I think you should let them go," a male voice ventured.

"Are you mad? He's Gair's *son*, you fool."

Sarah forced her hands to remain flat against Ruith's back instead of clutching the cloth of his tunic in terror. Ruith didn't seem to be panicking, but, then again, he never had during the whole of their acquaintance. He simply stood in front of her, an intimidating and hopefully quite invisible barrier to the terrible storm brewing there before the fire.

"He's no good to you dead," the prince consort said.

"I have no intention of killing him. I want him for what spells he might have."

"But you don't have the power to use . . . ah . . . them—"

"I know where to have help with that!" Morag bellowed. She took a deep breath. "Let me explain this to you again, Phillip, and simply, so you'll understand. I am, as you can't help but have noticed, collecting spells."

"Gair of Ceangail's spells?" Phillip asked hesitantly.

"Aye, Gair of Ceangail's spells," Morag repeated, in the same tone of voice she might have used with a small child. "These are very desirable spells because whilst Gair was the most hated mage of his generation, he was also the most powerful. Indeed, it wouldn't be exaggerating to say he was perhaps the most powerful mage of all. To have even one of his spells commands great respect and admiration."

"But everyone respects and admires you already—"

"It isn't enough!" Morag bellowed. "Is it possible you're this stupid? I don't want respect, I want power!"

Sarah listened to Morag in fascination. Indeed, if she hadn't been cold with terror, she might have been slightly amused by the queen's tantrum. It must have been extremely frustrating for Morag to find herself trapped in a keep that no doubt seemed far below what she likely supposed she should have had, being forced to socialize with rustics, remaining unadmired for her obviously superior self. Sarah couldn't imagine that having any more of Gair's spells would help with any of that, but what did she know? She could only see spells, not use them to flatter her vanity.

"Why do you think I've been looking for these spells for so long?" Morag demanded.

"Well, not you personally," Phillip protested.

"Nay," Morag said in a deceptively soft tone, "you have been looking for me, haven't you, my love? Traveling the world for the past twenty years, trying to make up for your blunder."

"I couldn't kill a child—"

"So you left her to rot in the moors instead," Morag snarled. "At least I would have made her death quick."

Sarah felt Ruith flinch, but she had as well, so she couldn't blame him. Killing a child? What sort of woman was Morag that she could contemplate the like?

And what had the child seen, or done, or known that would have merited such a fate?

"I couldn't kill a child," Phillip repeated, sounding as if he would rather have been having a different conversation. "So I saw to her end as I saw fit."

There was silence in the chamber for so long, Sarah finally could bear it no longer and gingerly peeked out from behind Ruith's shoulder.

Morag and Phillip were facing each other in front of the fire, frozen there, as if they'd been statues. She initially suspected that Morag was angry and Phillip equally so, then she realized that wasn't the case at all. Morag wasn't angry. She was something else, something that went beyond anger.

She was mad.

Sarah could see her lunacy wrapping itself around her as if it had been a fine cloak she had reached for, swathing herself in its comfort with a pleasure that was actually quite difficult to watch.

"You didn't send her out to the moors, did you?" she asked in a soft voice. "Come, now, Phillip. You have no need to fear me."

"I don't fear you, Morag."

Even Sarah could tell that was a bald-faced lie. The poor man looked as if he might soon fall to his knees and beg his wife to kill him quickly rather than end his life in other, more painful ways.

"What did you do with the babe?" she asked soothingly. "The truth, now, after all these years."

"Why does it matter?" Phillip asked nervously. "I got rid of her."

"Why does it matter," Morag repeated slowly. "Why does it matter?" She lifted her arm and pointed back toward the door. "It *matters*, you imbecile, because of what walked through my gates this morning!"

"Gair's get—"

Morag took a deep breath. "Nay, Phillip, not Gair's son. The girl, the girl that came with him. Surely if anyone would see her for who she is, it would be you, given how often you admired her dam."

Phillip looked at her in surprise. "But she doesn't look like Sorcha—"

"Of course she looks like Sorcha!"

The prince fell silent, obviously considering things he hadn't before. "But that's impossible."

"Because you killed her?" Morag asked in a low, furious voice. "Or is there another end to this tale you haven't told me?"

"Ah—"

"What did you do with the bairn?"

Phillip swallowed convulsively. "I sold her, her and a kitchen lad I picked at random, to a gypsy—"

"You *liar*!"

"Very well," he shouted back, "I didn't sell her, I gave her to the witchwoman Seleg and begged her to carry her off somewhere you wouldn't find her because I *could not kill a child*!"

Sarah blinked. She would have shaken her head, but there were stars spinning around it already and she didn't want to add to the cluster of them. Ruith's hand was immediately around her, holding her to him. She clutched his arm and continued to look at the pair before her, because she couldn't look away. Phillip had apparently found the spine he'd been missing for quite some time, but the truth was, he wasn't his wife's equal in power or craft. Sarah watched spells gather in front of Morag, spells of death and misery and horror that sprang up and blossomed into a single something that towered over them both. Phillip watched it, openmouthed and unmoving.

But it never fell upon him.

It took Sarah a moment or two to realize that someone was pounding on the door. The spell disappeared, Phillip collapsed against the mantel, holding himself up by willpower alone, no doubt, and Morag walked over to the door and threw it open.

"What?" she snapped.

"My queen," a guardsman said, sounding thoroughly terrified, "I've heard word there was one of the night lads found on the floor of the kitchens—"

"Put a guard in front of Gair's get," Morag said immediately. She shot Phillip a look. "Guard the spell here, if you have any power at all." She sent him another withering look. "I *told* you we should have killed her."

"But she has no magic," Phillip protested. "She had no magic as a babe, which was why you wanted her in the first place, wasn't it?"

"Shut up, you fool," Morag said, drawing herself up and looking down her nose at him. "What would you know of it?"

"I know what you did to her sire—"

"Enough," Morag thundered. She swept out of the chamber and jerked the door closed behind her.

Ruith walked immediately over to the case. Sarah could only watch him, numb, as he picked the lock with an adroitness she might have admired another time. The prince consort had been staring into the fire, but when the hinges on the glass squeaked, he whirled around, his mouth open.

He watched for a moment or two, then shut his mouth.

Sarah could still see Ruith, perhaps only because she could *see*, but obviously Phillip could not. Until, rather, Ruith dissolved his spell of un-noticing. He locked gazes with the prince as he rolled up the spell and stuck it down his boot. Phillip looked around him in surprise—presumably for her, but she was apparently too well hidden by Ruith's spell. Sarah supposed that was just as well. She knew she must have looked like death.

She certainly felt like it.

Ruith continued to look at Phillip. "I have a spell for you, Your Highness."

"What sort—" Phillip licked his lips nervously. "What sort of spell, Prince Ruithneadh?"

"A spell of protection," Ruith said quietly. "I don't know if you have the power to use it, but you could certainly try."

"I'll stretch myself."

"That might be wise."

Sarah listened to him give Phillip the spell, watched the prince consort attempt to use it—badly—then watched Ruith nod briskly at him. He pulled his spell of un-noticing over himself again and walked swiftly toward her.

"Let's go."

She'd hardly gotten halfway across the chamber with him before the door burst open again and guards spilled inside.

Ruith took her by the arm—her right arm, unfortunately. She almost fainted from the pain.

"We'll need to shapechange," he whispered harshly.

She gaped at him. "But I cannot—"

"Trust me."

The next thing she knew, she was running along behind him, hugging the wall and praying no one would step on her very long tail. Either Ruith had chosen their colors well, or the guards were simply too busy shouting at each other to notice two plain brown mice skittering along underfoot. Sarah found herself almost felled by the unaccustomed smells assaulting her nose alone, but she ignored them and pressed on until she and Ruith were at her door.

Guards were there, trying to get past not only the lock but Ruith's spell he'd covered both the inside and outside of the door with. He paused so suddenly that Sarah ran up his back before she realized what she was doing.

We'll need to change again. His voice whispered across her mind.

I can't—

We'll try air this time.

She was going to kill him. If she ever had hands again, she was going to find some slow, painful, unpleasant way to do him in. She tried to concentrate on that, but it was too difficult. She found herself somehow wrapped up in Ruith as he pulled her under his spell and through the doorway with him.

She regrouped—or *was* regrouped, as it were—near enough to the fire that she was a little surprised she hadn't rolled right into it. Ruith materialized out of thin air and went sprawling half over her.

"Get off me," she squeaked, because squeaking was all she could manage. She patted herself frantically and was very relieved to find she was herself and not something for which squeaking might come more naturally.

Ruith conjured up a cloak and pulled it over her, sending sparks

flying. He looked down at her, his eyes full of wildness. It was mage-
ish delight at becoming something he wasn't, no doubt.

"I have to go," he said, sounding a little breathless. "I'll be outside
before they manage to get through my spell. Feign ignorance."

She had every intention of doing just that. She looked up at him.
"I think I'm going to be ill."

"Puke on Morag."

"You, sir, have absolutely no compassion for the unmagical."

He bent his head, kissed her cheek—rather near her mouth,
actually—then pulled away. She caught him before he could get to
his feet.

"Don't ever do that again, damn you," she warned. "You turned
me into a mouse!"

He smiled at her. "And the breath of air?"

"I still feel scattered."

"I understand, believe me," he said with a bit of a laugh. He
pushed himself to his feet. "Hold them off as long as you can."

And with that, he disappeared.

She cursed him again but had to clap her hand over her mouth.
She lay on the floor, feeling truly very ill, and listened to the pounding on the door continue.

"Coming," she called weakly.

There was a sudden silence. Sarah knew without being told that
Morag was now standing just outside the door. She could only imagine the terrible spells that would accompany the woman. She had no
way of knowing where Ruith was, how he would get himself on the
other side of the door, or what he would do when Morag realized he
had his father's spells stuck, as usual, down the sides of his boots.

She decided it was better to meet the storm on her feet, as it were,
so she heaved herself up—and almost into the fire. She clung to a
chair until a violent wave of nausea passed, then staggered over to
the door.

"Open this door," came the voice that cut through the wood and
spells as if they hadn't been there.

Sarah shuddered. She was frankly terrified to stand alone—for however long that might be—against a woman so ruthless as to take a child and order her to be killed—

That was something she was going to have to come to terms with, she suspected, very soon.

She put her hands on the door to hold herself up, then suddenly found herself stumbling backward. Morag towered over her as if she'd been a thundercloud, accompanied by a dozen spells Sarah could see surrounding her and half out of her mouth. It was one of the single most horrifying things she'd ever seen, and that included what she'd been witness to at Ceangail.

She realized abruptly that she was going to be ill.

So she did the first sensible thing she'd done in a fortnight.

She took Ruith's advice and sicked up her supper on the queen.

Twenty-five

❧

Ruith put himself between Sarah and the queen as Morag let her hand fly. She caught him full across the face, which troubled him not at all. It was rather bracing, actually, and cleared his head of the last of the shapechanging magic. He backed up a pace, only because he wanted more room to fight, if necessary.

"Where did you come from?" Morag spat.

Ruith pointed toward the passageway. "There. I believe I knocked over a pair of your guardsmen on my way in."

The truth was lying there in a heap, struggling to get back to their individual feet. Morag spun back to glare at him.

"Where have you been?"

Ruith raised his eyebrows and put on his grandfather's best none-of-your-bloody-business look. Morag was—predictably—unimpressed, but he didn't dare give her any ground.

"I was trying to rest," he said haughtily, "when I was disturbed by what sounded like the castle falling down around my ears. Knowing that couldn't possibly be the case given the perfect condition of your hall, I thought perhaps there had been an assault of some sort. How disappointing to find it was only your guardsmen disturbing my lady's rest."

"Your *lady*," Morag said, her words dripping with disdain. "You are as foolish as Athair of Cothromaiche, to look so far beneath you."

"Am I?" Ruith said coldly. "Then perhaps I should take care to make certain I don't suffer his same fate."

"I wouldn't know anything about that," Morag blustered. She tried to push past him, then glared at him when he wouldn't move. "I want to look in this chamber for something I believe was stolen from me."

"Are you accusing my lady of stealing?" Ruith asked sharply.

"Nay, I'm accusing you," Morag said without hesitation. "And unless you want me to kill you where you stand, you'll step aside and allow me my look."

Ruith held her gaze for a handful of long, highly charged moments before he pulled Sarah behind him and stepped aside, waving the queen into the chamber with an expansive, mocking gesture. The woman's gown was still soiled from Sarah's efforts, but she seemed to have forgotten that in her fury to find what she thought had been taken from her.

He could only hope she wouldn't look down his boot.

The queen was thorough, he would give her that. She delved into every cranny, every drawer, under the bed, behind the tapestries. She found nothing save Sarah's pack—Ruith had hidden his on a quickly made hook he'd driven into the ceiling—which she emptied out onto the bed. She reached out to touch the statue of the horse, but pulled back in revulsion at something she apparently saw there.

Ruith didn't want to know what that might have been, but he was quietly very thankful for a horse who apparently could still be useful even cast as he was in very fine marble.

"What rubbish," she said stiffly. She turned and swept toward the door. "Your gel there is nothing but a common strumpet."

Ruith gritted his teeth. "Your Majesty, you are obviously

overwrought by your loss, but that hardly excuses the discourtesies you've favored us with. I will not tolerate any more slurs directed toward my lady."

"And just what are you going to do about it?" Morag asked mockingly. "Intimidate me with your pitiful magic?"

"Tell tales on the Council of Kings?" he returned before he could stop himself.

Morag's fury was truly impressive. She looked at him as if he'd been a bug she intended to crush under her shoe, then turned and swept from the chamber. Before Ruith could open his mouth to ask her what her intentions were, the door had slammed shut and the entire chamber had been enveloped in a spell of containment that he could tell immediately was going to be difficult to break through.

Nay, not difficult.

Impossible.

It only took one attempt to slice through the spell with his own magic to tell him that. He dragged his hand through his hair, then turned and pulled Sarah into his arms. She didn't seem at all opposed to it, nor did she protest when he set her down in a chair, spelled the vile water she'd been left with into something drinkable, then handed her a cup so she could wash out her mouth. She handed it back to him, then looked up at him blearily.

"You told me to puke on her."

He laughed, pulled her out of the chair, then sat down and drew her onto his lap. He wrapped his arms around her and leaned his head back against the wood.

"You did a credible job of it, love."

She let out a shuddering sigh. "Are we trapped?"

"For the moment," he said dismissively. "We'll escape soon enough."

She fell silent. Indeed, he would have thought she had fallen into an uneasy sleep if it hadn't been for her hand that occasionally trembled as it rested upon his chest. "Ruith?" she said finally.

"Aye, my love."

"What is a dreamweaver?"

He'd wondered how long it would take her to ask. He had to take a deep breath before he trusted himself to answer. "I'm afraid I know next to nothing about them and what bits I do know may not be terribly accurate."

"Are you finished with your caveats?"

He might have taken her words personally, but he could feel her fighting something. Sobs, most likely. Sobs, he imagined, that didn't come from fear of being locked in their chamber for the rest of her days.

"Very well, this is what I know," he said, reaching up to drag his fingers through her hair. "They aren't mortal, nor are they elvish. They are who they are, souls that move in and out of dreams at will. I've *heard*—which is rumor only—that not only are they able to weave anything into cloth, they spend a great deal of their time stringing the looms of the world with their dreams and using our destinies as their weft threads. Unbeknownst to we poor fools who think we're in charge of our lives."

"You can't be serious."

He shrugged. "I'm repeating rumor. Now, if you want to know about Cothromaichian history, I can tell you about a bit of that with better accuracy."

"Because of Soilléir?" she asked quietly.

"Well, I always have admired him," Ruith admitted with a smile, "and my mother was terribly fond of him even if my grandfather wasn't." He paused. "I think perhaps we might find a few more of their tales in that last little book Soilléir gave you."

She shook her head sharply. "Not today."

He wasn't going to push her. He simply nodded, then continued to stroke her hair. He covered her left hand with his own and closed his eyes, feeling remarkably peaceful, considering the circumstances.

"Will we escape?" she asked.

"I'm working on it."

"And here I thought you were snoozing."

He smiled. "Just enjoying a brief respite with you in my arms." He pressed his lips against her forehead, then pulled away before she could hit him.

Though she didn't seem particularly inclined to do so.

He closed his eyes again and considered their tangle. They had horses—if they could get to them—and magic—even if it might not surmount Morag's spells. He considered half a dozen things he could throw at anyone who dared come through the door.

And then he realized, quite suddenly, that things coming through the door wasn't what he had to worry about.

The chamber was contracting.

It was almost imperceptible, which was likely why he hadn't noticed it at first. He looked up at the ceiling and watched with a goodly bit of alarm as it crept downward.

"Ruith?"

"Just thinking," he said, forcing himself to sound calm. "About our leisurely escape."

"Will Morag let us go?" she asked. "In truth?"

"Perhaps you have forgotten who I am."

"Impossible," she said. "Your haughtiness is tangible."

"I'm channeling my grandfather."

She smiled. "So I suspected, but will that manage to win our release, do you think?"

"I won't say that Morag isn't powerful," he said, watching the far wall creep toward him, "for she is. But every dragon has a soft spot somewhere on his underbelly, and she is no different. Her vanity is, if I may say so, colossal. I imagine the thought of losing her seat on the Council of Kings is more vexing to her than allowing us to leave unimpeded. That isn't to say that she won't try to kill us both and make it look like an accident. It wouldn't be the first time—" He shut his mouth abruptly. "Forgive me."

She lifted her head and frowned at him. "Why—oh."

He let out his breath slowly, then nodded. "Aye, oh." He supposed they could both spend quite a bit of time speculating on the fate of that poor great-great-granddaughter of Seannair of Cothromaiche, but the fate of her parents was indisputable.

Actually, the identity of that gel was, to his mind, indisputable as well, but he didn't imagine Sarah wanted to discuss that yet.

He reached up and touched her cheek. "I understand how it can be to find out things aren't how you thought they were," he said quietly. "Things of a parental nature."

"Can you?" she said, sounding absolutely shattered.

He nodded slowly. He cleared his throat. "I was six when I realized that my brothers were not teaching me endless numbers of spells for their amusement and my edification. It was then I realized that whilst my mother put on appearances for us, she was desperately worried that she wouldn't live to see us raised—much less save our lives. It was also then that I realized that my father was the reason for all of it and that he was most definitely not what he seemed to be. But," he added, "I will admit that at least I knew my parents were mine."

Sarah's breath caught on what might have passed for a half sob in someone else. "I'm not sure we can rely on the queen for accurate information about anything."

He smoothed his hand over her hair and continued to watch the ceiling drop. "Perhaps not, but would you trust Soilléir?"

She lifted her head and looked at him. "Why would that matter?"

"Because he sent along that little book with his genealogy in it. I don't think he would relate it inaccurately, do you?"

She closed her eyes briefly. "Do you have a spell to keep me from falling apart?"

"I might, but it would require that you spend lengthy periods of time in my arms."

She blew her hair out of her eyes. "Do you ever think about anything but that?"

He smiled. "I do, but those thoughts mostly concern how long I'll manage to keep you in my ardent embrace if I'm fortunate enough to get you there. Such as now. But as lovely as that thought is, I think we should perhaps concentrate on escape first."

"Why—" She looked at the wall behind him, then up at the ceiling. She sat bolt upright. "She's going to kill us."

"I think she would like to try."

Sarah fell off his lap, but scrambled to her feet before he could aid her. "What are we going to do?"

"Pack your gear, my lady. I'll work on the other tangle."

She shot him a look that spoke volumes about her panic, but walked quickly to the bed just the same and began to shove things into her pack.

"Not the horse."

She looked over her shoulder at him, then nodded and set him aside. Within a handful of moments, she was standing next to him.

"Well?"

He started to spew out a spell, then he remembered something Uachdaran had said to him.

The man who crafted those knives for his daughter-in-law first crafted that blade you carry for his son, as a coming-of-age gift.

He considered how easily Sarah's knife had slit through the spells Díolain had wrapped around him in Ceangail. And if his sword and Sarah's knives had been made by the same person, it was possible they enjoyed the same spell-shattering properties. And if Franciscus had made the blades for Athair and his bride, wasn't it possible there had been something woven into their forging that could be useful in countering a known enemy?

Perhaps the enemy to the south who obviously had borne them ill will for years?

Ruith drew his sword. It blazed with a golden glow that startled him so badly, he almost dropped it. He took a firmer grip on it and looked at Sarah.

"Try one of yours."

She didn't take her eyes off him. She merely reached into one of her boots and drew out a knife—with the same results.

"Well," he said, dumbfounded. "I daresay Adhémar of Neroche might just be jealous of this steel."

"Does the Sword of Neroche glow?"

"With a horrifying bloodred light, no doubt in honor of those Nerochian rules of fair play you're so fond of," he said with a snort before he could stop himself. "But these works of art . . . I'm not sure what sort of rules they abide by."

"Will they slit spells?"

"I believe we'll see presently. Resheath your blade, love, and fetch your horse."

"And just what am I to do with him?" she asked.

"Toss him out the window and hope for the best."

She laughed a little, but it sounded rather more like a gasp. "Are we flying?"

"If Ruathar has any love for your tender care of him so far," Ruith said with feeling, "aye."

He waited until she'd shouldered her pack and picked up her horse from off the bed. He took a deep breath, cast one last glance up at the ceiling that was quite a bit closer to his head than it had been a quarter hour ago, then took a firmer grip on Athair of Cothromaiche's sword. He sliced through the spell with his sword the same way Sarah had cut through the threads that had bound him in Ceangail.

The spell shrieked.

"Off we go," he said, resheathing his sword and grabbing his pack before taking Sarah's hand.

She tossed Ruathar through the small arrow loop, Ruith smashed an enormous hole into the rock with the first spell that came to his hands, then he pulled Sarah up onto the resulting ledge with him.

Ruathar hovered there in the air three feet beneath them, a glittering, jet-black dragon who looked as if he were barely restraining himself from flapping off in a tearing hurry. Obviously, he was the lad for them at the moment.

"Jump," Ruith suggested.

Sarah didn't hesitate. He followed her onto the dragon's back, sent out a mental call for Tarbh to follow, and hoped neither he nor Sarah would fall off given Ruathar's speed and lack of saddle.

Alarms sounded wildly. Ruith felt the bolt from a crossbow go through the hood of the cloak he'd just conjured up before he had the presence of mind to protect them in a more ordinary fashion.

It was not a pleasant trip, those first few moments as Ruathar carried them out of the heart of Morag's darkness. Ruith realized there were more spells there than he'd counted on, and they were more difficult to counter than he'd expected. He fought off things that leapt up and tried to wrap themselves around them, repelled spells of death that came at them in enormous, crashing waves, and countered outright assaults that perhaps would have caused Ruathar pause if he hadn't been raised on the steppes of those magical Cothromaichian mountains.

It was a very rough ride.

By the time Ruathar had driven himself up over the hills that ringed An-uallach, Ruith was shaking with weariness and thought he just might be ill. He realized that Sarah had drawn his arms around her and was patting his hands soothingly. He would have smiled, but he just didn't have it in him.

It occurred to him, when he could think clearly again, that he wouldn't have managed their escape if he hadn't spent those days with Uachdaran deep in his mountain, facing much worse things.

Which he suspected Uachdaran had foreseen.

As had Soilléir.

He would have to make a list, he supposed, of favors he owed various souls. The mucking out of stables would no doubt figure prominently in repayment at both Buidseachd and Léige.

He looked over his shoulder to see an owl flapping majestically behind them in the distance, and he relaxed just the slightest bit. Morag couldn't shapechange, which was something to be very grateful for.

He turned his mind to the future and considered a direction, but nothing useful came to mind. He tightened his arms around Sarah and simply held on for quite a while before he thought he could speak calmly.

"Any ideas on where now?" he asked.

"*Away* was my first thought," she said. "But now?" She took a deep breath. "West. But not very far west."

"I'm sorry to ask you to navigate."

"Why?" she asked, sounding surprised. "It isn't difficult."

He regretted it because he regretted that she had to be a part of what he was doing, but he supposed that ground had been covered too often already. He only sighed and closed his eyes against the wind.

West it was.

I t was dawn before Sarah told him they needed to stop. Ruathar, that endlessly energetic beast, followed her unspoken directions as if he'd read her thoughts—which Ruith supposed he could. They landed in a little glade without any undue signs of distress from Sarah. Either she was growing accustomed to flying or she was simply too tired to protest. Ruith understood both.

Ruathar turned himself into a quite ordinary-looking horse and eyed them purposefully.

"He's hungry," Sarah said. "There is a farmhouse up ahead."

"Is there?"

She looked at him. "I can see a spell in the barn."

He let out his breath slowly. "Very well. I'll see if I can't purchase us a bit of peace for the morning—and you the opportunity to do a little spell hunting."

"Where did you get gold?"

"Out of thin air." He smiled wearily. "Magic *is* useful now and again."

"Don't expect me to disagree," she said with feeling. "Especially after our escape last night." She looked behind her. "Where's Tarbh?"

"Flapping along languidly behind us," Ruith said. "I'm sure he'll catch up. Let's go find oats for this hungry beast here. I imagine my pony-turned-owl will find his own breakfast."

She nodded and waited as he gathered both their packs, shouldered them, then trudged off with her toward the farmhold he could see in the distance. Sarah was very quiet, which didn't surprise him. She had not only their rather unpleasant exit from An-uallach to recover from, but things to think on, things he'd suspected she couldn't avoid much longer.

He put that thought aside for further consideration as he saw the farmer walking across his fields toward them. He looked quickly at Sarah, but she only smiled bleakly.

"The spell is in his tack room. I imagine our good landholder has no idea it's there."

"Let's find it sooner rather than later," Ruith murmured, "then have a nap."

"Happily," she said with a gusty sigh. "I'm exhausted."

He nodded, then stopped a handful of paces away from the farmer. He nodded politely and had a nod in return.

"Looking for shelter?" the man asked.

"And stabling for our horse," Ruith agreed. "Just for the day, if possible."

"More than possible," the farmer said with a shrug, "for the right price."

"Name it," Ruith said without hesitation.

The man assessed them, then nodded. "I'll think on it later." He started to turn and walk away, then hesitated. He looked at them with a frown. "I don't suppose either of you has magic."

"A little," Ruith conceded. "What is your need?"

"There's something in my barn I don't like, but I'll be damned if I can divine what." He took off his hat and scratched his head. "Some leaking of something. Animals don't like it and the cow stopped giving milk a month ago. Can't say as I blames her, actually."

"I think we could investigate," Ruith conceded. "Before our horse has his breakfast, of course, as a good-faith token."

"You fix it, my lad, and I'll even feed you and your wife."

"We would be most grateful," Ruith said. He looked at Sarah. "Wouldn't we, darling?"

She only rolled her eyes at him, but walked with him after the farmer just the same. "One more to go, Buck," she murmured. "Your tally is not yet seen to."

"I should have danced with Morag."

"At the peril of your soul, I daresay. I'm not sure it would have been worth it."

"I believe I'll be the judge of how much peril you're worth," he said with a smile.

"You're daft."

"Again, besotted," he said, squeezing her hand. "I'll tell you of it in glorious detail if you can stay awake long enough to hear it."

She smiled at him, which eased his heart a bit. He saw to the stabling of Ruathar, then investigated the tack room with Sarah. A spell was indeed there, tucked into the bottom of an old and obviously unused saddlebag. Ruith didn't bother to see which one it was. He simply rolled it up and stuck it down his boot. He walked with Sarah down the aisle to where the farmer was waiting for them, laying spells upon the animals as he went. He accepted a basket of supper, thanked the farmer kindly for his hospitality by handing him a pair of gold coins, then shut himself inside the stall with Sarah.

He quickly set spells of protection, distraction, and illusion around them that even his grandfather might have been satisfied with, then sat down in the fresh hay with Sarah and tried to cling to his manners through what served them as breakfast.

He looked up to find that Sarah was being much more successful at it than he was.

"Not good?" he asked, his mouth full of some species of muffin.

She only shook her head slightly, an even slighter smile on her face. "I'm too tired to eat."

He considered. "Too tired to sleep?"

"Not if you have a tale for me to help me along."

"I might," he said slowly, "if you would let me read you one from a book."

She looked at him for quite some time in silence. Her eyes were very red, but that could have been from weariness, not tears she couldn't shed. She reached into her pack beside her without looking away from him, opened it, then pulled something out of the top and handed it to him.

It was a book he didn't recognize, but he had the feeling he wouldn't be surprised by the contents. There was no title embossed on the cover, but he opened it to find the title written there in a very fine hand.

A Brief History of Cothromaiche, by Soilléir, son of Coimheadair.

Ruith looked at her. "This might be interesting."

"I'm not sure I'll get through it on my own."

"Then allow me, my lady, to aid you in the task."

She dragged her sleeve across her eyes. "Ruith, I'm not sure I can bear much more of this sort of thing."

"I think this will be the worst of it," he ventured.

She blinked rapidly. Her cheeks were wet and now her nose was red. He smiled, pained, and set both the book and the basket aside. He rose, took his cloak and spread it out on the hay, then fetched the book and Sarah and brought them both with him. He stretched out, then pulled her down to lie next to him, offering his shoulder as a pillow. She put her arm over his waist and sighed.

"I feel as if I'm dreaming."

"I imagine you do," he said quietly. He paused. "You know, Sarah, you might find this isn't such a bitter pill to swallow as you might suspect."

She huffed out a very small laugh. "I'm not sure why I'm even fretting over any of it. It can't possibly apply to . . . or have anything to do with . . . ah . . ." She took a deep, shuddering breath. "You know what I mean."

He wrapped his arm around her and pulled her a bit closer. "Reserve judgement until after I finish. At the very least, this will give us a way to fall asleep. Soilléir is, as you may or may not have noticed, a crushing bore. I'm sure we won't make two pages before we're both snoring happily."

She tilted her head back to look at him. "You, Ruithneadh, are a very kind man."

"And you, Sarah, are a very distracting woman."

She pursed her lips at him. "Concentrate on the book, my lord prince. Your tally, if you remember, is not yet filled."

"Ridiculous," he muttered, but he smiled as he said it. He waited until she had settled her head more comfortably, then took up the small book with his free hand and began to read.

The tale, which Ruith wasn't entirely sure Soilléir hadn't written precisely for Sarah's benefit, began in the far reaches of time before Cothromaiche had organized itself into any collection of hamlets under a common ruler. The text devoted quite a bit of time to describing the sheer mountains and pristine lakes, rolling foothills dotted with small villages full of farmers and herders of sheep, and lovely seasons that came and went at just the right and proper moment.

"Sheep," he noted. "They make wool, don't they?"

"I believe, Your Highness, that they do."

"You like wool, don't you?"

Sarah laughed a little. "Keep reading."

He was rather more relieved than he should have been to find she wasn't weeping. He didn't imagine she was past all danger of it, but at least the beginning of the book seemed to please her.

From a description of the very desirable countryside, the author moved into a discussion of politics and a quiet revelation that the king of Cothromaiche, Seannair, was a most sensible man with an aversion to the trappings of royalty to which he was most assuredly entitled, preferring to put his feet up next to his stove at night and discuss the potential effect of the weather on his plans for spring planting—and sheepshearing.

"More wool," Ruith noted. "Your kind of people."

"Hmmm," was apparently all the response she could give to that.

The wars and contentions with neighboring countries were touched upon briefly, as well as a thorough discussion of the art, music, and other necessities of culture that seemed as well developed as their weaving industry.

And then Soilléir turned to his genealogy.

Ruith paused. "Still awake?"

"Unfortunately," she whispered.

"Feel free—" He stopped himself and sighed. "I was going to say feel free to cling to me if necessary, but I won't make light of this." He paused. "I'm sorry, love. I fear this won't be easy. But it may be worth it, in the end."

"Will it?" she asked wearily.

"If what we suspect might be true *is* true," he said slowly, "then a certain flame-haired gel of our acquaintance wouldn't be related to Daniel of Doìre."

"Well, there is that," she agreed.

"I believe the witchwoman Seleg could be discarded as a relation as well." He put the book down and smoothed her hair back from her face. "It would answer quite a few questions, wouldn't it?"

"About her treatment of me?"

"Aye, and the reason a certain alemaster took such an interest in you," he said, "or why you were taken to a place where souls don't see—and they aren't seen, if you take my meaning."

She was silent for a long moment. "Do you think so?"

"Aye, I think so."

She took a deep breath. "Read on, Ruith, if you will."

He kissed her forehead. "Brave gel." He picked up the book. "Ah, here our long-winded author now feels the need to bludgeon us with yet another retelling of his very sparse genealogy of which he is obviously very proud. We have Seannair, whom we already know, who spawned three lads whose names I won't bother to pronounce, and those three lads then sired one lad each and named them Coimheadair, Meadhan, and Franciscus, respectively."

She didn't flinch, so he carried on.

"Coimheadair, being the crown prince of Cothromaiche, wed him a gel from An Cèin—my grandmother is of that lineage—and was apparently busier than his father for he sired three sons himself, the youngest being our good Soilléir, who apparently prefers to be off tormenting Droch instead of waiting for his brothers and his progenitors to die so he can take the crown."

"He is a useful man," Sarah agreed.

"Realistic is more to the point, perhaps," Ruith said dryly. "But we'll leave that for the moment. Meadhan's children and grandchildren do not figure into our study here, so we'll leave them aside and concern ourselves with Franciscus." He continued to trail his fingers over her back, partly because he thought it might soothe her and partly because it allowed him to feel her distress. He wasn't terribly surprised when she only took a deep breath and closed her eyes. She was that sort of march-into-the-fray and do-what-needed-to-be-done sort of gel.

"Franciscus," he continued, "the youngest son, had three daughters and a son—"

Sarah lifted her head and looked at him in surprise. "Did he? What happened to the daughters?"

"I have no idea," he said, surprised himself. "It gives their names, but says nothing about their fate. But the son, he who was the youngest, was named Athair. He married a dreamweaver named Sorcha." He had to stop for a breath himself. "They had a daughter, a gel-child."

"And her name?" she prompted, when he fell silent.

"Sarah."

She continued to breathe normally, if not a little carefully. "Anything else?"

"It says here that Athair and his bride were slain by the queen of An-uallach. She had devised a way to have a mage's power on his way out of this poor world and intended to use it on Athair and his bride."

"That woman is evil," Sarah breathed.

Ruith cleared his throat. "I fear the rest isn't any more pleasant. 'Tis written in the same hand, but dated the night we were in the garden of Gearrannan." He had to clear his throat again. "I'm not sure I can read it aloud."

Sarah pulled his hand back where she could see the words as well, though she didn't seem to be any more capable than he of reading them except to herself. Ruith left Sarah holding the book long enough to drag his sleeve across his eyes, then took it again and kept it where she could read along with him.

My dearest Sarah,

I have given you the history of my people, but it is also the history of your people. Your mother was Sorcha, your father Athair, who was my nephew. Morag waylaid your parents, true, but the hard truth is, you were the true prize. She was convinced that the powerful magics they both bore would find home most powerfully in you. They were, unfortunately, merely practice for what she intended for you.

We were frantic when we found you missing. Your grandfather, Franciscus, was beside himself with worry. Perhaps you were fortunate in that our magic is capricious and your mother's gift of Seeing is not so readily apparent. Morag quickly discovered—or so she thought—that you had nothing she could easily take, which sent her into a towering rage.

We allowed Prince Phillip to give you to Seleg and further allowed Seleg to take you south to Shettlestoune. Franciscus disappeared in what appeared to be a terrible accident, visible to anyone who cared to see. In secret, he followed you to Doìre to watch over you.

It was not ideal, but we had to allow events to proceed unhindered. If Morag had known you were alive, she would have carried you back to An-uallach without hesitation, out of spite, if for no other reason. She has never realized that Seeing is not a blood magic, but a magic of the soul that cannot be given to another—nor taken from the one who sees.

I have not looked to see where your path lies from here, for that is not our way. I suspect, however, that you will walk through the halls of An-uallach at some point, which is why I gave Ruith the sword. Uachdaran will see the runes and warn Ruith accordingly, even if only in riddles. He will know you when he sees you. You are, if I might venture to say it, as much like your mother as Ruith's sister is like hers.

I grieve for you that you didn't know your mother, for she was a very lovely gel, full of laughter and joy and dreams that were easily read in her eyes. She loved you to distraction, begrudging the rest of us the fussing over you that we so longed to do. Great-grandfather Seannair held you once, Franciscus a time or two more, but only your father and mother other than that. I'm not sure your feet touched the ground for the two years they called you theirs.

I am sorry, my dearest Sarah, that the reading of this will grieve you. Know that you were—and are still—loved by those who have been watching you unseen over the years.

Your loving cousin,
Soilléir

P.S. Beware Morag and her husband. Her reach is long and her pride implacable when stung.

P.P.S. If Ruith cares to know, Franciscus was the one who planted the legend of the mage on the hill in the minds of the villagers and provided a house for him to land in. It might also interest him to know that Franciscus and Sgath have known each other for centuries and both have terrible reputations as matchmakers.

P.P.P.S. I expect your lad to treat you properly. Genuflecting would not be beyond the pale for him.

Ruith closed the book softly and set it aside. He wrapped his arms around Sarah and simply held her for several minutes in relative silence, the only sounds being the occasional wicker of a horse or the soft hoot of an owl. He waited until he thought Sarah might have gotten hold of herself before he turned his head and looked at her. He'd expected to find her weeping, or on the verge of raging about the injustice of it all.

She was asleep.

He smiled to himself and committed the sight to memory so he could needle Soilléir with it when next they met, then put his head back down and looked up at the ceiling of the stall. He wasn't sure what she had read, but it had obviously not distressed her to the point of insanity. When she awoke, if she wanted to speak of it, he would reread to her the parts she'd missed, then either weep with her over what she'd lost or rejoice with her for what she'd found, perhaps whilst slyly inserting himself into her vision of the future.

He let out a slow breath. It would have been wise to have disentangled himself from her and gotten up to do a bit of scouting. Morag had been left behind, true, but she had fleet horses and would catch them up if she thought she could manage it.

But he couldn't bring himself to. He spared one last thought for making certain that his spells were intact and their horse and owl were safe, then he closed his eyes and allowed himself a sweet, peaceful, if very brief, sleep with the woman he loved in his arms.

Twenty-six

❧

Sarah walked along a rather dusty road with her horse tucked into her pack and Tarbh walking sedately behind Ruith, and kept on with the cheerful face she'd been wearing since she'd woken two days earlier in that farmer's stall to find Ruith standing there, silent as a tree, tending what she assumed were spells and no doubt listening for things she couldn't hear.

When she'd stirred, he had pulled himself back from wherever he'd been and smiled at her. He hadn't made mention of what he'd read to her earlier that morning, and she'd avoided the topic as well, quite happily. She'd found the book tucked back in her pack, and she had left it there, perfectly content to consign it to things better left examined when she had the leisure to, say in several years, when she was comfortably far away from her current straits and was spending the winter in front of some hot fire, knitting.

She suspected Ruith would have been happy to have lingered a bit longer in that farmer's barn, but the spell she'd found had seemed rather bright for one of Gair's creations, and they hadn't wanted it to draw attention from someone who might have been able to see it.

Such as perhaps the mage who had left another scrap of the spell of Diminishing outside the stall where they'd been sleeping.

To say it had unnerved them both was a profound understatement. Ruith had remained as he ever was when faced with a crisis: calm and unfazed, though he had moved quickly and efficiently to get them out of the barn without delay. They had been running— or flying, rather—very quickly ever since. Ruith would have taken more time, but whatever horse they'd found themselves riding had never seemed to want to halt. Sarah hadn't argued, for though she couldn't see it, she could certainly feel that someone was watching them.

It couldn't have been Morag. That vicious woman would have killed them as easily as to have looked at them. She wouldn't have simply followed them to torment them.

That had, unfortunately, left her wondering just who it might be.

She looked up at the inn that had risen up quite quickly before them, happy to put the thought of her two-day-old panic behind her. She'd seen worse, so she didn't feel any need to comment on its quality. It sported a roof, no doubt had drinkable ale, and likely boasted a hot fire inside. It was perhaps all they could expect.

"You realize," Ruith said conversationally, "that I'm finished with sleeping without you within arm's reach."

Given that he'd scarce let go of her since they'd left An-uallach, she was perfectly ready to believe him. "Rogue," she said just the same, lest he feel too comfortable with the thought.

"But an honorable sort of rogue."

She looked up at him. "Those sorts of thoughts seem to continually distract from our purpose."

"And hopefully distract you from things I think trouble you as well," he said seriously. "Is it working?"

She had to take a deep breath, not because she was still overwhelmed by what she'd learned about herself, but because they had been running as if all the hounds of Riamh were after them, which, she supposed, they might very well be.

"Aye," she managed. "It's working very well."

He didn't believe her, that much was clear, but he was apparently going to refrain from pressing her. She was grateful for it, which she supposed he also knew.

He stopped her, then put himself in front of her. "I'll go first."

She didn't argue. If he wanted to save her from wearing something sharp flung in their direction, he was welcome to it. She walked into the tavern behind him and was relieved to find that the inside was much less neglected than the outside. She made her way over to a bench set against the wall near the fire and sank down onto it with a grateful sigh. She took off her pack, set it down very carefully next to her on the floor, then leaned her head back against the wall and happily watched Ruith stand at the bar and order them a meal. He accepted two cups of ale, then made his way over to her, sitting down with his own sigh of relief. He took her right hand carefully in both his own.

"Safe," he said. "For the moment."

"It won't last," she said grimly.

He laughed uneasily. "What a cynic you've become."

She looked at him, his beautiful face so close to hers, and couldn't help but smile just the slightest bit. "Can you fault me for it?"

"Aye," he said seriously, "and myself as well. You should rather be enjoying peace and—"

"Rides on the backs of dragons, hot fires provided by elven princes, and terrible moments spent scurrying about as a mouse," she finished for him, "provided as well by that same sort of lad." She started to tell him those were the least of the things that troubled her, but she realized with a start that it wouldn't have been true.

Trouble had followed them more easily than she'd feared it might.

"What is it?" Ruith asked.

She could only nod at the hooded figure who had entered the tavern and paused near the doorway. He shut the door behind himself, then walked across the floor. Sarah could scarce believe her eyes, but the man was coming toward them as if he had every intention of joining them at their table. For all she knew, he had followed them to the inn. Worse still, perhaps he had been following them all along—

"Wonderful," Ruith muttered. "A brawl before we even have a bite to eat."

"A brawl," she repeated breathlessly. "One could hope it would be with just your fists."

"I appreciate your faith in my magic," he said dryly.

She looked at him quickly. "I have absolute faith in your magic. And your sword. And your fists."

He smiled. "Woman, you are about to find yourself thoroughly kissed."

"Not until you've encountered that last elusive princess, I'm not," she said, "and not until you've solved our current problem, which is still coming our way." She would have said more, but their doom was already almost upon them. All she could do was watch and struggle to breathe normally.

Ruith didn't change his casual pose, but she knew him well enough to know he was fully prepared to fight with whatever means he had to.

The man came to a stop in front of their table and simply stood there, apparently content to wait for them to acknowledge him.

"Good e'en, friend," Ruith said, in a neutral tone. "Looking for a place to sit?"

"I might be," the shadowed man said, just as neutrally.

"There seem to be seats over there, by the door."

"I think I prefer a spot over here," the other said easily, "by the fire."

Ruith considered for a moment or two, shrugged. "As you will."

The man pulled a chair up to their table and sat. As he did so, his cloak parted—only Sarah realized it hadn't been his cloak to part, but rather some sort of spell of concealment. She realized with equal clarity that he had intended it thus. She glanced at Ruith, but he hadn't seemed to have noticed. He was too busy signaling the barmaid to fetch them another mug of ale. He squeezed Sarah's hand briefly before he released it and propped his elbows up on the table as if he merely intended to settle in for a lengthy discussion of local politics.

"So, friend," Ruith said easily, looking for all the world as if he routinely invited strangers to dine with him, "what brings you to this lovely lodge in the middle of nowhere?"

"Family," the man said simply.

Ruith nodded. "A good thing to have. Do you have any nearby?"

The man only nodded at Sarah. "Ask your lady. I believe her sight is a bit clearer than yours. *Friend.*"

Sarah shifted uncomfortably and vowed that she would at her earliest opportunity memorize the other spell she'd found in the book Soilléir had given her, the one that was supposed to dim her sight when it became too much to bear, because she could see very well who the man was.

Well, at least she could say with a fair degree of confidence that he wasn't about to draw his blades and kill them both any time soon.

Ruith elbowed her gently in the ribs. "Well?"

She looked at Ruith. "His name is written on his soul."

Ruith lifted an eyebrow. "Which you have read, apparently."

"'Tis a bit difficult not to," Sarah said. "He isn't hiding it. Or at least he isn't hiding from me. It is as if he, ah, *wants* me to know who he is. You too, I'll warrant."

"Shall you divulge his name," Ruith asked, shooting their guest a warning look, "or shall I beat it from him?"

Sarah exchanged a look of her own with their guest, had a faint smile in return, then leaned close to Ruith. "I'm not sure you would want to, Your Highness, given that 'tis your future brother-in-law who sits across from you."

Ruith's mouth fell open. He continued to gape as supper was brought and new mugs of ale handed all around. Sarah watched as Mochriadhemiach of Neroche pushed his hood back off his head and smiled at her, ah, escort.

"Ruith," he said, sounding both pleased and rather unsurprised to see him.

"Miach," Ruith managed. His mouth worked for a moment or two, then he laughed a little. "I'm not sure if I want to kiss you or kill you."

Miach smiled wryly, stood, then embraced Ruith and slapped him several times on the back before he released him and resumed his seat. "Now you need do neither. I'm starved and I've been traveling with your grandfather for the past night and day. Let us eat, then we'll have speech together."

"You've been traveling with my grandfather," Ruith repeated in astonishment. "On foot?"

"As a very bitter, very terrible wind."

"Elves do not shapechange."

"Apparently they do, which is why he came along with me on this little journey to see how things in the world were progressing."

"You are the *last* person I expected to see today," Ruith managed, "here, of all places. And that has surprised me so thoroughly that I've forgotten my manners. Miach, this is my, er, *friend*, Sarah of—"

Sarah couldn't bring herself to face what she'd fallen asleep to two days earlier, not even for the niceties of introductions. "Of nowhere in particular," she said firmly.

Ruith smiled a very small smile. "For now, anyway. Sarah, this is Miach, the archmage of Neroche and apparently my sister's bloody fiancé, though I still have things to say about that." He shot Miach a dark look. "A princess of the house of Tòrr Dòrainn lowering herself to keep company with the youngest prince of that rustic hunting lodge in the mountains? 'Tis truly unthinkable."

"So said your grandfather, more than once."

Sarah cleared her throat carefully. "Actually, Ruith, he's not the youngest prince anymore."

Ruith looked at her in surprise. "What do you mean?"

"He's not the youngest prince." She looked at Miach and smiled apologetically. "The crown that hovers over you is too robust."

Miach sipped his ale casually. "Your lady's sight is very clear, Ruith. I would imagine she has that from very interesting sources."

"What," Ruith said in exasperation, "are you two talking about?"

Miach leaned forward with his elbows on the table. "That though she doesn't want to admit it yet, I can plainly see she is the grand-daughter of Franciscus of Cothromaiche, who is Léir's first cousin once-removed. Or perhaps she doesn't want that nosed about yet."

"And you're the bloody king of Neroche," Sarah shot back, because he'd irritated it out of her, "which perhaps *you* didn't want nosed about either."

The king of Neroche only laughed and reached over to take her hand briefly. "Forgive me, lady. I fear I spent too much time with Soilléir in my youth."

"Ripping the scab off the wound quickly?" she asked sourly.

"Sometimes, Your Highness, it is the only way."

"Don't call me that," she said sharply, then shut her mouth abruptly. She attempted a smile, but when that failed, she settled for a deep breath or two. "Forgive me," she said quietly. "I didn't mean to be rude."

"Miach doesn't bruise easily," Ruith said, shooting Miach a warning look, "but he does talk too much."

Sarah wasn't going to argue the point in a darkened tavern. She was happy to accept the king of Neroche's apology, however, because he had a very lovely smile and she could see that he was sincere in not having wanted to cause her distress. She looked at Ruith, who was frowning at his childhood friend.

"Then Adhémar is dead?" he asked quietly.

"Unfortunately," Miach said with a sigh.

"How do your brothers feel about your crushing them under your dainty heels on the way to the throne?" Ruith asked politely. "Are they still blubbering into their cups?"

Miach pursed his lips. "Cathar is vastly relieved not to be sitting in the most uncomfortable seat in the hall, though that shouldn't come as a surprise. The rest are also vastly relieved, or so they say, save Rigaud, who is still raging about the injustice of it all and hiding my crown under his bed."

Sarah watched Ruith's mouth work for another moment or two before he looked at her.

"I knew that lad there when he had no manners."

"I imagine you did," she said with a smile.

"The king of Neroche," Ruith said, shaking his head in disbelief. He looked at Miach with that same expression. "I can't say I'm completely surprised, nor unhappy for your people. You'll do a credible job. Unfortunately, I suppose this happy event will make prying my sweet sister away from your dastardly clutches more difficult, but I assure you not at all impossible."

Sarah sat back and watched them discuss very quietly things that should have shaken kingdoms as if they merely discussed what sort of weather they might encounter for a brief trip out to the lists.

Which left her thinking that perhaps she should leave them a bit of peace and go check on the horses, who were reputedly crunching hay, having promised to retain their equine shape unless danger loomed.

It was also a handy excuse to avoid meeting Ruith's grandfather, who she was certain would frighten her to death before he announced that ten princesses were insufficient and no matter who Soilléir of Cothromaiche thought she was, witchwoman's get or daughter of princes, she was not at all suitable for his grandson.

She finished her meal quickly, then looked at Ruith. "I'll check on the horses."

He shot her a look that said he understood all too clearly what she was about. "Accompanied by my best spell of protection, or you don't go anywhere."

Sarah looked at the king of Neroche. "He's a tyrant."

"You seem to be managing him well," Miach offered.

"It is a constant battle," she said, scooting off the bench and not looking at Ruith. "It has been a pleasure, ah, Your—"

"Miach," he finished before she could. He smiled at her. "'Tis just Miach."

She smiled in return, because he was terribly charming and self-effacing, two things she couldn't help but like. "Very well, Miach."

"Be careful, Sarah."

She picked up her pack and left the pub before she had to look at Ruith again, made her way out to the stable, and assured herself that the horses were housed well. She looked around, then found a handy trunk to sit on, because she had to. She had assumed, mistakenly, that it would be Ruith with the more difficult path.

She wrestled with herself a bit longer, then pulled the book out of her pack, the one Soilléir had apparently written just for her. She turned to the last pair of pages and found the last thing she'd read before she'd fallen asleep.

I have not looked to see where your path lies from here, for that is not our way . . .

I am sorry, my dear Sarah, that the reading of this will grieve you. Know that you were—and are still—loved by those who have been watching you unseen over the years.

She closed the book before she could read the postscripts, sure they would only coerce tears from her she wasn't ready to shed. She closed her eyes and leaned her head back against the wall.

It shouldn't have been difficult to accept. She had always wondered, in the back of her mind, how it was that Seleg could ever have been her mother. She'd never called the woman *Mother*, because Seleg had forbidden it. Seleg had never showed her any especial affection, particularly once she'd realized that Sarah had no magic. The only place she'd felt safe or loved or valued had been in Franciscus's workroom or in the great room of his small house where she had passed most of her time. He had educated her, laughed with her, treated her as he would have a daughter.

Now, she understood why.

She contemplated that for far longer than she should have, which led her to realizing with a start that she hadn't been paying attention to her surroundings. There was someone standing a few paces away, leaning against one of the stable posts. She had scarce pulled her knife free from her boot before she realized it was Ruith. He held up his hands in surrender.

"Only me," he said.

She resheathed her knife, but couldn't manage a smile. "That was a lovely reunion inside."

"It was," he agreed, coming over to sit next to her. He held out his hand for hers, then took it gently between his own. He stared down at her fingers linked with his for several minutes before he looked at her. "I see you have your book there."

She nodded.

"How are you?"

"Trying to ignore things I'd rather not think about." She had to look up at the roof of the stable to keep her tears where they belonged. "I don't want this."

"I understand," he said, very quietly.

She gestured helplessly into the darkness of the stall facing her. "It isn't just the past," she said. "It's all of it. What I can't see in front of me. What I *can* see." She looked at him miserably. "We've only begun and already I'm unsettled almost past what I can bear."

He stroked the back of her hand gently. "Sarah, I'm not sure how to tell you this easily, but you can't change the past."

She laughed, but it was more a half sob than anything. "You would know."

"Aye, my love, I would know."

"Then what do I do?" she asked miserably. "I can't go back, but I don't dare go forward."

He wrapped his hands around hers. "What you do, my dearest love, is take the evening, retire to the safety of a chamber inside, and pitch your camp with me on the floor in front of the fire where I will tell you all manner of tales to delight and astonish," he said. "Tales having nothing to do with Cothromaichian escapades or black mages. Then, tomorrow, we will break bread with my grandfather, send the illustrious king of Neroche back to his very soft life in the west, and decide how best to continue on with our quest."

She looked at their hands together for a moment or two, then up at him. "I can do that."

"I imagined you could." He smiled. "Let's go seek out that warm place before the fire."

She nodded and rose with him. He hesitated, then turned her to him and put his arms around her. She looked up at him in surprise.

"What is it?"

"I was just curious as to where I was in my tally."

She found herself suddenly and quite unaccountably nervous. There was, if Soilléir was to be trusted about her past, no reason why she couldn't count herself as one of the gaggle of noble—well, royal, actually—lassies who would be forming a very long, very impatient line to have their turn at impressing the very eligible, exceptionally handsome grandson of the king of the elves. But it was difficult to place herself there, just the same.

"I don't remember where you were," she hedged.

"I believe I had one to go."

"Did you?" she managed. "I think that might be right."

"Perfect," he said solemnly, "given that I kissed the barmaid inside."

She fought her smile. "You did not."

"I did."

"She was no princess."

"She said she was," he said as he slipped his hand under her hair.

She put her hands on his chest. "There might be other women out there that you might want to meet."

"They can be bridesmaids at our wedding if you're so set on making them a part of this relationship."

She felt a little faint. "Wedding?"

He put his other arm around her waist. "Aye, wedding."

"What happened to comrade in arms?"

"That was your idea, not mine," he said, bending his head toward hers, "and I only agreed to it to keep you from bolting on me until I could convince you I loved you."

She blinked. "You what?"

He laughed a little and rested his forehead against hers. "Sarah, are you going to keep talking or let me kiss you?"

She realized she was wrinkling the front of his tunic. She relaxed her fingers and smoothed over the cloth. "You are who you are, Ruith, and I am . . . well, I'm not sure what I am."

He lifted his head and looked down at her seriously. "Could you," he began, then he had to clear his throat. "Could you *learn* to be fond of me?" he asked. "With enough time?"

She looked up at him in surprise. It was the first time in all their acquaintance that she'd heard him sound the least bit hesitant. "I don't need to learn anything," she said, before she thought better of it.

"Then let's discuss what it was about me you first learned to love," he said promptly. "My terrifyingly handsome face, my enormous amounts of irresistible charm, or just all of that combined so appealingly?"

"You talk too much," she said with a bit of a laugh, slipping her hands up around his neck and pulling his head down to hers. She looked into his lovely bluish green eyes and smiled before she closed her eyes and met his lips.

Halfway, as they had somehow managed to do everything so far.

Unfortunately, he lifted his head rather sooner than she thought she might have liked. She frowned up at him.

"What?"

He took her face in his hands, kissed her once more, very briefly, then looked at her grimly. "A new thought has occurred to me."

"Which one?"

"The one that suggests that if I don't present myself to one of your relatives with a list of good reasons why they should allow me to have you, I may find myself languishing in some forgotten ditch in the wilds of Cothromaiche."

"And just who would you ask?" she asked faintly.

"Franciscus seems a likely suspect."

"It might take a bit to find him."

"Which is why I think spending most of my time kissing you until I do find him is an extraordinarily unwise thing to do. Unless you want to wed me today and face his wrath later."

She sighed, then pulled out of his arms. "Very well. Comrades in arms until Franciscus is found."

His mouth fell open. "Well, I didn't mean to go that far."

"I'm saving you from yourself. And me from myself," she muttered, turning to put her book back in her pack. She slung it over her shoulder, then looked at him. "Well?"

He took the two steps toward her, then pulled her back into his arms and kissed her rather thoroughly, all things considered.

"You can't do that anymore," she said faintly when he lifted his head.

He laughed uneasily. "I fear I must agree, though 'tis most unwillingly done."

She blinked. "Wed?"

He nodded solemnly.

"Is that a formal proposal?"

"Not in a stable, it isn't." He brushed his hand over her hair. "I was in earnest about the other. I must—willingly, I might add—accord Franciscus the respect due him by making a formal request. And I will honor you with the same after the fact."

"I told you he wasn't a black mage."

"Aye, you were right," he agreed cheerfully. "Let's go find that hot fire. I have the uncomfortable feeling we'll have company in that. I left the charming king of Neroche waiting for us at the pub door, because apparently he thinks we are too feeble to get ourselves back to safety."

"Perhaps he intends to be a chaperon."

"I have more self-control than that," Ruith muttered under his breath. "And he damned well better behave himself with my sister, or he'll answer to me."

She smiled and walked with him to the door of the tavern where they did indeed find the king of Neroche, slouching negligently against the wall, watching them silently.

Ruith stopped in front of him. "Well?"

"Just waiting," Miach said easily. "To show you where your grandfather is sleeping off his stormy voyage."

Ruith looked at Sarah. "Shall we go up?"

"I haven't anything to fear," she said firmly. "We aren't, well, it isn't as if you have formally suggested, or implied, or—"

Ruith held up one finger, then turned to Miach. "Would you excuse us?"

Miach held up his hands and turned to go inside. "Far be it from me to interfere in the romantic stylings of an elven prince and his future dreamweaving bride. I'll wait for you inside."

Sarah found her arms full of that elven prince and herself quite thoroughly attended to. She felt a little faint after the fact, truth be told, but perhaps that had been his intention.

"Implied, suggested, and deferred for grandfatherly permission," he said briskly. "Understood?"

She found it in her to glare at him. "And where is romance in all that?"

He laughed a little and hugged her so quickly, she squeaked. "Deferred as well, in favor of good sense. Or until my grandfather falls back asleep."

"Ruith—"

He laughed at her again, took her by the hand, and pulled her along with him into the inn. He didn't seem overly terrified at the thought of seeing his grandfather, but she couldn't say she felt the same way. She allowed him to pull her along after him until they reached the steps that apparently led to chambers on the upper floor.

"Ruith?"

He looked at her with a smile. "Aye, my love?"

"Are you sure?"

He looked at her, puzzled, for a moment, then apparently he realized what she was asking. "How can you ask?"

"Because when a gel wants something very badly, she tends to want to avoid breaking her heart over the false hope of having it."

His breath caught. If she hadn't known better, she would have thought he was blinking rapidly from something besides the smoke in the passageway.

He pulled her into his arms and held her tightly. "This is the only thing about this entire nightmare that frightens me to the core," he murmured against her ear. "Losing you, that is."

"I feel the same way."

He pulled back, kissed her quickly, then took her hand and led her up the stairs. "Let's go find a bit of safety for the night. We'll examine that revealing admission you made in a bit more detail in a place where you can't escape."

She wasn't entirely sure she wouldn't long for a quick escape. In spite of everything, which included facing black mages, horrible spells, vengeful queens, and a dozen other things she was certain she couldn't even imagine up in the depths of her blackest dreams, what unnerved her the most was what awaited them upstairs.

The king of the elves.

She put her shoulders back and reminded herself that she was . . . well, she was a decent sort of gel with good manners whom his grandson apparently loved.

She hoped it would be enough for him.

Twenty-seven

※

Ruith walked up the stairs, following his future brother-in-law—an appalling thought in and of itself—with his future bride bravely marching alongside him, and had to suppress the urge to wipe his hands on his thighs. In spite of his bluster, he realized that he was quite a bit more nervous than he should have been.

It was implausible enough to be following a boy he'd combined all manner of mischief with only to find that that boy had become the bloody king of Neroche, though in truth, he wasn't terribly surprised. He knew all Miach's brothers and whilst each of them would have made an excellent king given the chance, there had been something about Miach from the start that had set him apart—his ability to ferret out the most irresistible spells, no doubt, but perhaps that was something to ponder later.

It was also astonishing to think he was holding on to the hand of a woman he truly, profoundly loved, a woman whose parentage he hadn't cared about—only to find out she was not at all who the world thought she was.

But strangest of all was to think that he was only a few heartbeats away from seeing a grandfather he hadn't ever thought to see again.

Miach paused at the door, then looked at him. "He doesn't know you're here."

Ruith looked at him in surprise. "You were supposed to tell him."

"I thought it best to let sleeping kings lie. He woke up just the same when I came back in, but I said nothing. I told him I would go below and fetch supper, which deference he most certainly appreciated."

"Coward," Ruith grumbled. He looked at Sarah. "I think I'm nervous."

"Don't look at me for help," she said, sounding rather ill. "I have my own reasons for wanting to go hide—not that I will."

"I never thought you would." He took a deep breath and looked at Miach. "You go first."

"I believe, brother, that is the first time in our lives you've ever said that to me."

Ruith pursed his lips and suppressed the urge to push him. Miach only smiled and opened the door. He walked inside, then paused.

"Your Majesty," Miach said deferentially, "I'm not sure how to tell you this—"

"Damn you, you dratted boy," Sìle growled, "don't you do this to me again."

Ruith took a deep breath and gathered his courage. He would have kept Sarah's hand in his, but she pulled her hand away, took both their packs off his shoulder, then pushed him inside in front of her.

Ruith stumbled into the chamber—Sarah was rather strong, after all—then came to a teetering halt. Sìle rose to his feet, looking at Ruith as if he'd seen a ghost.

Ruith understood completely.

His grandfather hadn't changed much over the years, though he seemed smaller than Ruith remembered him. But he was still as proud, still as powerful . . . and suddenly weeping.

Ruith found himself enveloped in an embrace that robbed him of breath. He had often wondered, over the past pair of months, if there would come a time when he might go back to his sensible, emotionless existence on the side of his lonely mountain. He knew now that he never would. His heart had been broken half a dozen times since he'd closed the door of his house, but he didn't regret it.

The price was worth paying.

"Ruithneadh," Sìle said, pulling back and looking at him in astonishment. "Where in the *hell* have you been?"

"Hiding," Ruith said honestly.

"Son, why didn't you come home?" Sìle asked, sounding as if the question had been torn out of him by claws. "Did you not know who you were?"

Ruith couldn't even manage a shrug. "I knew," he admitted. "And that was the problem."

Sìle closed his eyes briefly, then embraced him again. Ruith was very grateful that Sarah had seen him completely undone, for he was no better than his grandfather at hiding his emotions. It was a bitter weeping, but somehow a cleansing one. He held his grandfather, happily, until Sìle finally pulled away. He dragged his sleeve across his eyes, then laughed a little.

"I am too old for any more of these surprises. Tell me I'm finished."

"Rùnach is alive and in Buidseachd," Ruith said, supposing that it was better to have all the shocks over with at once.

"With Soilléir, no doubt, that young rogue," Sìle grumbled. He frowned. "Well, I'm almost unsurprised by that, though I am positively undone seeing you. You'd best explain yourself, lad. And since I'm assuming I don't have you to thank for bringing yourself back to the living, I'm assuming there is *someone* with sense in the area?"

Ruith fumbled behind him for Sarah's hand. He pulled her to stand next to him and opened his mouth to introduce her.

It wasn't necessary.

His grandfather gaped at her in much the same way he'd gaped at him not five minutes earlier.

"Sorcha?" he managed. "But . . . nay." He continued to look at her in surprise. "Forgive me, child, but I mistook you for someone else."

Ruith watched Sarah look at him briefly, then back at his grandfather.

"Sorcha was my mother."

Sìle's eyes again filled with tears. "Sarah, then."

Ruith looked at Sarah, but he couldn't see her very well for that dratted smoke that seemed to permeate every bloody chamber of the inn. Then again, tears were streaming down her cheeks. The only one in the chamber who wasn't weeping was that damned king of Neroche, who likely never had anything take him by surprise.

Ruith looked at his grandfather in time to watch him reach out and gather Sarah into his arms. He patted her back gently.

"Ah, you poor lass," he said gently. "I'm so sorry." He patted her a bit more, then pulled back and looked down at her. "And where have you been keeping yourself, young Sarah? If you tell me Weger's tower, I will have an attack, so take pity on an old elf and tell me something else."

"I was masquerading as the daughter of the witchwoman Seleg."

Sìle made a noise of horror. "Surely not." He drew her arm through his and led her over to the fire. "And where was that old hag hiding you? And how is it you came to know my grandson? He's a good-looking lad, isn't he?" He looked at her with sudden calculation in his eyes. "You could do worse, you know."

Ruith caught the look Sarah threw him—not precisely one of panic, but it was close—and laughed a little. He listened for a few minutes to what of his whereabouts and antics Sarah was able to relate, then realized Miach was watching him. He looked at him, then felt something slide down his spine.

He was beginning to dislike that feeling quite intensely.

He sighed and walked over to stand next to his former companion in dastardly deeds. "I'm prepared for just about anything. Spew away."

"You haven't changed."

"Neither have you and given that I know you always know things you shouldn't, I'll say it again: spew away."

Miach looked at Sarah. "She's perfectly lovely. And your grandfather seems to like her."

"So do I."

"Besotted, are you?"

"Admittedly."

Miach smiled at him. "It is good to see you, Ruith. Where in the world have you been? I'm assuming somewhere between here and Doìre, else Sarah wouldn't have encountered you."

"Shettlestoune," Ruith said with a sigh. "Hiding in a house on the side of a deserted mountain."

"You, my friend, had cause," Miach said, "though I imagine hiding isn't all you've been doing."

Ruith studied him for a moment or two. "How did you know to find me, or is this a happy coincidence?"

"Do you want the answer to that?"

"Actually, I think I might."

Miach nodded toward the window, which was a safe distance away from the fire and just made for private conversations. Ruith followed him, then stopped and looked at his—and he could hardly believe it—future brother-in-law.

"How is the crown?" he asked.

"Uncomfortable," Miach said honestly, "and a little heavier than I expected."

Ruith smiled in spite of himself. "At least you've satisfied Sìle."

"Barely," Miach said, with feeling. "It took almost dying to convince him that I loved Morgan—Mhorghain, rather."

"Is that what they've called her?" Ruith asked, finding the question surprisingly difficult.

Miach nodded. "You will like her, I imagine. She is much like your mother, but perhaps even more like your grandfather. Stubborn, fierce, and utterly loyal. And so beautiful, I can hardly stand to look at her."

"Spare me the details," Ruith said with a grimace. "If you wax rhapsodic about my sister's charms, I truly will do damage to you."

Miach only smiled. "I wouldn't blame you. Now, tell me what you're about and why you're taking Soilléir's cousin to places she shouldn't go?"

"I'm collecting my father's spells."

Miach nodded. "I wondered what had happened to them." He studied Ruith for a moment or two. "I suppose there is no one else to do it, is there?"

"Keir might have been able to, but . . ."

Miach looked at him gravely, his face full of understanding. "He died helping Mhorghain close the well." He put his hand on Ruith's shoulder. "I'm sorry."

Ruith shook his head sharply. "Uachdaran already told me, so don't fret over it. It is what he would have wanted, which you well know. He was determined to protect both her and Mother at all costs. I'm not sure he could have lived with himself if he had failed Mhorghain—especially if that failure had come because of something my father had spawned."

"A sentiment you share," Miach noted. "How are you looking for your father's spells?"

"Sarah can see them."

"I'm not surprised," Miach said quietly. "I knew her parents had been slain, but I had no idea she was alive." He shrugged. "I always wondered what it was that Franciscus found in Shettlestoune to occupy his time after his very suspicious disappearance."

"Brewing ale, watching over his granddaughter, and how the hell do you know all this?" Ruith demanded. "What *don't* you know?"

"Where you've been, apparently," Miach said with an apologetic smile. "Or where your father's spells are to be found."

Ruith sighed. "Don't worry about that. You could, however, worry about the fact that I'm also finding pieces of the first half of his spell of Diminishing cunningly shredded and scattered in my path, as if someone either knows where I'm going or wishes to lead me in a certain direction."

"And where is the second half?"

"Taken from me just outside Ceangail, but that is another tale entirely."

Miach smiled. "And you're hoping the possessors of both halves don't meet over tea?"

"That thought had occurred to me, aye."

Miach held up his hands. "Don't look at me for aid. I have enough to do without meddling in your affairs."

Ruith studied him for several minutes in silence. "Why are you here?"

Miach rubbed his hands over his face suddenly, then sighed deeply. "To give you tidings."

"What have you seen?"

"My boundaries are set," Miach hedged. "What would I know of anything in the wide world?"

Ruith snorted. "Please, Miach. Even as a lad you were poking your questing nose into places it didn't belong."

"Following your example, of course."

"Tidings, Miach."

Miach chewed on his words for several moments. "Tell me more about your plan to find these spells, then I'll tell you what I suspect."

Ruith leaned back against the wall. "Sarah made a map of them in Léige. We made note of where they lay, and we're collecting them one by one." He pursed his lips. "There was, if you can believe it, a pattern to it all."

"Was there?"

Ruith suppressed the urge to roll his eyes. If anything surprised Miach of Neroche, it would be death sneaking up on him unexpectedly. "Aye, there was. The spells are seemingly being called. Either that or someone has arranged them in a way that is causing us to follow them."

"Where?"

"North."

Miach looked at him evenly. "Not much in the north that's pleasant, is there?"

"I don't know," Ruith said shortly. "I've confined myself to the hell that is the south. Perhaps you can add to my knowledge."

Miach shrugged. "I wouldn't recommend a journey there, but I don't think you'll have a choice." He paused. "I would be careful."

"And you came all this way to tell me that?"

"Nay," Miach said slowly, "I came to tell you who I think has made himself a comfortable nest in the north, in a place where none but those with a great tolerance for Olc dare tread."

Ruith looked at him in silence.

And then he knew.

He pushed himself away from the wall, then shook his head. "Impossible."

"You know it isn't."

Ruith almost had to look for a place to sit down. It had never occurred—

Nay, that was a lie. He had often wondered over the years if others besides himself had escaped the ravages of the well. Mhorghain had, obviously, and Keir, and Rùnach.

But his father?

He leaned back against the wall and set his jaw, because it was either that or sit down and weep.

"It is," he said distinctly, "impossible. I saw him fall at the well."

"Did you?"

"Very well," Ruith snarled, "I didn't see precisely that, but I saw the wave crash down on him. No one could have survived it. My mother didn't, nor did three of my brothers—and they were protected by her spells. My father had nothing standing between him and that evil but bluster."

Miach held up his hands helplessly. "I have no proof," he said. "Just a feeling."

"A feeling that was apparently strong enough that you felt the need to fly hundreds of leagues to come tell me about it."

Miach shrugged. "I can't help you with this task, Ruith, but I couldn't not at least tell you what I thought."

"Meddler."

"Guilty," Miach agreed.

Ruith considered a bit longer. "I am very tempted to send Sarah with you back to your hovel."

"She won't come, I don't imagine."

"I may not give her any choice."

Miach reached out and put his hand on Ruith's shoulder briefly. "If I could offer one piece of advice, brother, it would be never to be less than forthcoming with your lady, and do *not* leave her behind. It won't go well for you."

"Or for the Sword of Angesand, apparently."

Miach smiled. "Soilléir told you, did he?"

"After I fair beat it from him," Ruith said, dragging his hand through his hair. He looked at Miach. "Don't say aught to Mhorghain. Not until I'm certain we'll survive this."

Miach shook his head. "Ruith, my friend, there is nothing in this world or the next that would make me give her those tidings. She did enough at the well."

Ruith considered. "When do you wed?"

"In a fortnight's time."

"I'm not sure I'll be finished with this by then."

"You can be my wedding present to her, then," Miach said with a faint smile. "After the fact."

Ruith nodded, though that cost him a surprising bit to manage. He didn't want to believe that he might not survive the task before him, but—

He turned away from the thought. He would survive, he would keep Sarah safe, then he would set out on a lifetime of bliss in that beautiful spot on Lake Cladach that Sgath was reserving for him— or Sarah, rather. With any luck, she would allow him to come along and build her a house on it.

He nodded to Miach, who he was certain would understand just what he was thinking, then walked with his sister's fiancé back to where his grandfather sat, chatting amicably with Sarah. He set aside the heaviness in his heart.

He was sure it would return soon enough.

. . .

It was very late, or very early depending on one's perspective, when he finally stretched out in front of the fire with Sarah lying with her head toward his, much as they'd done in Sgath's folly when he'd first thought he loved her truly. She propped her chin up on her folded hands and looked at him.

"Well?"

"I've stopped weeping," he said quietly. "Promising, don't you think?"

She smiled at him. "You have cause."

"I'm only happy Rùnach wasn't here to witness it. He would have never let me live it down."

"I think you might be right."

He leaned up on his elbows, then looked at her purposefully. She shook her head.

"Absolutely not."

"My grandfather is snoring, and Miach won't care."

She pursed her lips. "Your tally is not full, my prince. I told your grandfather about it, and he agreed that it would be useful in at least keeping your mind on your task."

He inched his way toward her. "I'm surprised he didn't suggest a dozen princes for you to examine."

"He did."

Ruith shut his mouth with a snap. "And what did you say?"

"I told him I didn't care for royalty." She smiled faintly. "I think he's still digesting that."

"He's digesting, and I'm postponing," he said with a snort.

"Postponing what?"

"The rest of that bloody list you're holding me to."

"You kissed the barmaid," she reminded him. "And you said she was a princess."

"I lied. But I wanted to kiss Miach. Briefly. As far as I'm concerned, that counts. If you insist, I'll take up my errand again tomorrow."

She frowned. "Tomorrow?"

He leaned over and kissed her softly. "Tomorrow," he said firmly.

"You autocratic . . . elf," she spluttered.

"Only three-quarters."

She laughed a little, then reached out and put her arm around his neck, holding onto him tightly. "I'll take the quarter, then, for a bit. You be Ruith and I'll be Sarah, and we'll forget the rest."

"If it means I can jettison into the ether that bloody tally of women I've no interest in, I'm all for it."

She looked at him seriously. "I don't want you to regret your choice."

He kissed her again, rather thoroughly, because he just didn't have any words left. Then he rested his cheek against hers in silence for another moment or two before he thought he could speak with any success.

"I want you to go with Sìle."

"I know."

He sighed. "Miach has suspicions about things, things that will make for a very unpleasant journey's end, if they're true. I don't want you anywhere near where I'll need to go."

"I can see the spells, Ruith. You can't."

"Nothing, and I mean nothing, my lady, has ever caused me more regret than that fact." He looked at her bleakly. "I am very much afraid, Sarah of Cothromaiche, that whilst I may survive many things, I may not survive that because it means I will have taken you places no man would ever think to take the woman he loves."

She kissed him softly, then stretched back out with her chin on her hands, wincing when she touched the back of her right hand. She put it aside, then simply rested her cheek on her left hand and looked at him.

"We'll do what we must, Ruith, because we must. Then we'll spend the rest of our lives looking at other things. More beautiful things."

He covered her right hand very gently with his own, then lay down with his head turned just so, so he could look at her. He sincerely hoped she was right. Unfortunately, he feared that the trials they would pass through first would be more than either of them would forget easily.

He waited until she'd closed her eyes before he set spells of ward about the entire chamber that no one could break through. Once that was done, he simply watched her and the future both.

They would sleep whilst they could, then, on the morrow, take up the heritages they couldn't escape and the tasks that still lay before them. And then he would do his damndest to keep her safe and accomplish what he had to, because if Gair was alive, the only way for him to make the world safe for Sarah for more than a single night was to make a choice.

His father, or the world.

And if those were the alternatives facing him, the choice was simple.

He could only hope he lived long enough to make it.